EVENT HORIZONS

EVENT HORIZONS

BLOOD AND DIAMONDS ON THE BAYOU

Preston D. Gill Jr.

Palmetto Publishing Group
Charleston, SC

Event Horizons: Blood and Diamonds on the Bayou
Copyright © 2018 by Preston D. Gill Jr.
All rights reserved

First Edition

Printed in the United States

ISBN-13: 978-1641111010
ISBN-10: 1641111011

ACKNOWLEDGEMENTS

Event Horizons was conceived to tell the real story of a dozen murders through the eyes of a fictional character. But I would not have begun this journey were it not for fellow journalist, Roger Emile Stouff, telling me that he had self-published several books. Roger gave me the nudge to try my hand. I thank Roger for his encouragement, suggestions, and the wonderful conversations we always have.

The candid opinion of another friend and journalist, Diane Fears, disabused me of the notion that my project, as envisioned, would succeed. I thank Diane for graciously taking the time to read that first, partial manuscript and making suggestions on what worked and did not.

Months later, I had a completed manuscript. My editor, William "Bill" Greenleaf, laboriously made a page-by-page critique. Over the next several months, Bill helped me polish my story. He coached me on how to become a better fiction writer and how to make this story come alive. He patiently helped me overcome my inclination to write as a journalist as I began to rewrite my manuscript several times. Bill became not just an editor, but also a mentor and friend.

I made a few changes after Bill's extensive editing and I was also concerned about the Spanish idiom. My friend and Spanish editor, Marimar Martínez Sánchez, agreed to copy edit the revised edition and tweak the Spanish. I am grateful for her keen eye and suggestions.

I sat across the newsroom from an outstanding reporter, Jean McCorkle, who agreed to a final look-over and edit of the manuscript. Thank you, Jean.

I would be remiss in not mentioning the sacrifices of my wife, Angela, as I often wrote until daybreak as she slept alone. I also thank my son, Joel, for letting me write with minimal disturbances.

Julie Boyne, who hired me as news director for KQKI, brought me to St. Mary Parish and became more than a boss to me—she became my friend—even before I left my brief stint in radio and went to work with the Morgan City Daily Review.

My sister, Deborah McCalip, has probably read more versions of this story than either of us would care to admit. She was a wonderful sounding board. Thank you, Deb. I love ya.

I would like to thank Michael Shannon II and his helpful, patient team at Palmetto Publishing Group.

I offer a comprehensive thanks to friends and relatives who supported, encouraged and facilitated my efforts in writing this story.

I want to offer a final "thank-you" to everyone who reads *Event Horizons*. I hope you enjoyed reading the story and are looking forward to the next installment in the series. I welcome your comments and feedback at PrestonGill2@aol.com or like "Event Horizons by Preston D. Gill Jr." on Facebook where you can find details of the real-life crimes that inspired the novel.

PART I

CHAPTER 1
JANUARY 26-27, 2008

Three years—and the police ain't done squat to catch Pigenstein.

Darius LeBeaux fingered a loaded Smith and Wesson lying on the torn seat beside him as he sat in his beat-up Impala in the Tarpon Bowling Alley parking lot. A pumpkin-orange, full moon rose from behind the Morgan City Police Department to his right, three blocks away. He drummed the fingers of his left hand on the cracked, worn leather wrapping the steering wheel.

"If I find the bastard, I'll have justice in three seconds," he said through clinched teeth as his breath fogged the air. Approaching his twenty-first birthday, he was consumed by an anger and hatred that had cannibalized his soul for years. The future? What's a future? His only goal was satiating his desire to kill that worthless Pigenstein who'd made him an orphan at seventeen.

He shivered—the car's heater was broken. A cold front was approaching, and Morgan City might get its first freeze of the winter. Flashing blue lights and wailing sirens heralded a pair of St. Mary Parish Sheriff's units speeding by from left to right to investigate lawlessness; probably in Amelia, where drugs flow copiously on Saturday nights.

Darius grasped the gun and slowly turned it over in his hand—the grip was warm; the barrel was cold. He leaned forward and shoved it under the torn seat. His cheek rested on the steering wheel as he stared to his right. The sirens' shrill cry faded as the sheriff's vehicles navigated the hairpin turns of the pothole-infested highway to Amelia. He leaned back, shut his eyes, and shook his head. He grabbed a can of beer from the seat beside him, popped the top and took two swallows. Then he pushed his shoulder hard against the crumpled door until it sprung open and his long, lanky frame tumbled out. Over the top of the Impala, he saw more flashing lights. These left the MCPD station, crossed the four-lane highway and headed toward the railroad tracks behind the bowling alley.

"To hell with all of you," Darius yelled toward the cops.

After a final swallow of beer, he dropped the can and squashed it under his heel; splattering beer on the pavement and on the legs of his jeans. He wiped his lips and then rubbed his hands together to warm them up. A cold north wind slapped his face and blew litter helter-skelter across the cracked asphalt. The night was turning colder than he'd expected. Darius turned and spat on the concrete and then kicked a rock that bounced off his worn-out rear tire; he needed to replace those "may-pops" soon. After checking to make sure his door had closed completely, Darius jerked the hood of his tattered, denim jacket over his head. He hunched his shoulders, lowered his head, and jogged toward the bowling alley; its entrance partially illuminated by a neon sign missing half of its lights.

Balls rumbling down the lanes and pins crashing to the polished floor along with the cacophony of adolescents yelling, laughing, and flirting almost drowned out the country music blaring through speakers recessed in the water-stained ceiling.

"It's crowded in here tonight," Darius said to the pimpled, teenage clerk talking on a cell phone appendage attached to the side of his skull. "Do you have an open lane?"

"All we got is lane one-three," the clerk said, pausing from his phone conversation.

"I'll take it." Unlucky number? Darius's entire life had been unlucky.

He asked for size eleven shoes. The clerk, reengaged in his cell phone conversation, plunked a pair of size twelve shoes on the sticky, cola-stained counter. Darius looked at the scuffed shoes, shook his head and sighed as the clerk blew a pink bubble that popped on his prominent nose. After leaving the counter, Darius selected a lime-green ball—the pickings were slim. The holes were tight for his big fingers, but it would have to do; it'd be a tight ball and loose shoes on lane thirteen.

Freshly-popped popcorn and hamburgers sizzling on the grill subliminally begged for Darius's money as he passed the concession stand. He settled into his lane beside two teenage girls who appeared to have attempted an outfit coordination with forest-green blouses tucked into tight-fitting jeans. Darius could hear most of the girls' giggled conversation. Obviously, the bespectacled redhead—her blonde friend called her Evelyn—wasn't from the bayou. She had impeccable grammar and no hint of a Southern or Cajun accent.

"You need to get over that crush on Mitch," the blonde told Evelyn. Both girls stole furtive glances to their right and past Darius. "What do you see in him? You're literally a genius and he can't beat a Neanderthal in checkers."

Darius observed a group of guys to his right wearing black Berwick High School lettermen jackets with their names scripted in Vegas gold letters on the back. The boys ogled the girls like the last fried chicken leg on the last Sunday of the month.

"He might not be bright, but he sure is a hunk," Evelyn said as she sneaked another peek at the object of their conversation walking toward the concession stand. "He has potential."

Darius sat down to tie his shoe laces tighter. He sized up this Mitch guy—he saw the name on the back of the letterman jacket—as the jock returned with a Snickers bar.

He isn't the God's-gift-to-women-Adonis he seems to think he is.

"I bet twenty bucks that I can get the redheaded brain chick to give it up to me tonight," Darius heard Mitch predict as he palmed his crotch to the merry delight of his buddies.

Taking the bet, the other boys laughed—sounding like bleating goats, to Darius who wondered how the girls failed to hear what those jerks were saying. Mitch sauntered over to the girls, crossing in front of Darius.

The guy is a preening peacock trying to impress a peahen.

Peacock strutted up to Evelyn and tugged on her blouse. "Hey, sweetie. It's Evelyn, right?"

Evelyn smiled and nodded her head as she adjusted her gold-rimmed glasses. She bit at a fingernail and glanced in the direction of the blonde who had stepped toward the lane.

"I'm sort of struggling in a couple of classes." Mitch rubbed his chin and took a bite of his candy. "But I heard that you're, like, kind of smart."

"I just work hard." Evelyn bowed her head and twirled the long pigtails hanging over the front of her blouse. She looked up as the pins crashed and the blonde screamed after bowling a strike.

"I was wondering if maybe you could help tutor me," Mitch said with a mouthful of candy.

Darius felt his jaw twitch; he squinted his eyes and clinched his fists. He knew she failed to discern Mitch's unholy intentions as she apparently wrote her telephone number on a scoresheet. His visualization of Mitch changed from a peacock to a hyena. A visceral rage roiled in his chest. There was something about someone—especially a woman—taken advantage of, that stoked his anger. After Peacock-hyena left, Darius saw Evelyn reach into her pink purse—personalized

with her name scripted across the front—and hand Debra a small wallet. The purse elicited a whisper of déjà vu for Darius. He stepped
toward Evelyn as the blonde walked to the refreshment stand.

"Miss, it's probably none of my business," Darius said, attempting
to be discreet, "but you should know that dude is trying to bed you. He
bet his buddies he could do it tonight."

"Jiminy Crickets! You are right, sir. It is none of your business.
I would appreciate the cessation of your unsolicited and equally
unwanted intrusion into my affairs and leave me alone!" Evelyn held
up her hand, apparently indicating the conversation was concluded.
Her pigtails flew over her shoulders and her shoes squeaked on the
floor as she whirled away.

"Try to help the girl and she goes postal," Darius muttered under
his breath. He decided to finish out his frame and leave. He wanted to
get something to eat before going home.

Fog crept over the twenty-foot Atchafalaya River levee as Darius
turned onto the Waffle House parking lot. He parked and sprinted
toward the building where warm air and hot food beckoned. A tall
black man, perhaps in his fifties or sixties, wearing a warm-up suit and
rolled-up ski mask, adjusted the plastic lid on his coffee as he coughed
and limped toward the exit. Darius—holding the door open—noticed
a small-caliber pistol slipping from his pocket.

"You might wanna tuck that piece in," Darius whispered loudly.

The coughing man briefly looked up. The bright sodium light
revealed a mirthless face lined with deep furrows; his countenance
appeared troubled and his eyes were hollow and dull. He'd undoubtedly seen better days. With a grunt, the man pushed the gun deeper
into his pocket and hacked a rattling cough. Darius thought the man

looked sicker than the cough sounded. He paused long enough to watch Cougher get into an old Buick and leave.

Inside the almost-empty restaurant, Darius inhaled deeply to fully absorb the aroma of fried bacon and freshly-brewed coffee mixing with the distinct seafood odor wafting off the river. He removed his jacket and sat at the counter. Danetta, who'd served him before, took his order of a fried pork chop and a ham omelet with a glass of milk and a separate glass of ice. As he savored the first bite of his pork chop, cold air nipped at Darius's back—the glass door behind him opened. He heard the familiar voice of Ricardo "Thirty-eight" Ortiz. Looking over his shoulder, he saw his twenty-three-year-old former friend favoring his left leg and massaging his right hand.

Thirty-eight—short, dark-haired and wiry with a cauliflower left ear—had lived most of his life with his Nicaraguan uncle, who'd become an American citizen. A veteran of the streets—where he'd spent much of his time since dropping out of high school—Ricardo's nickname matched the caliber of pistol he carried.

His trailing sidekicks half-heartedly tried to keep their jeans above their waists. Those two white boys were as useless as tits on a boar hog in Darius's estimation. Darius knew them by their street names— Striker and Bones. They were high school dropouts from Patterson, a small town straddling the east and west ends of the parish. Being with Ricardo gave them something to do. If they found fun along the way, it was a bonus—or as they say in South Louisiana, "lagniappe."

"Hi, Boo." Danetta met Ricardo at the door with a quick kiss. "Is it cold out there, yet?"

"Naw," Ricardo said as he tossed a chewed-up toothpick into a trash can near the door. "But tomorrow night, they say it'll be cold as a witch's tits."

Looking over his shoulder, Darius observed a smile creep over Ricardo's face as their eyes met. Ricardo stepped forward, took off his windbreaker and placed it on a stool beside Darius. He patted Darius's back as he removed a black fedora from his head, placing it on the counter.

"*Hola, amigo*! Where ya been? Ya over here lookin' like a leftover taco." Ricardo reached into his khaki shirt pocket and extracted a toothpick which he slipped into the corner of his mouth. Darius recalled that a toothpick had been Ricardo's ubiquitous companion. The shirt was torn and spotted with what looked like a recent bloodstain on the collar. Striker and Bones slid into a nearby booth.

"I've been around, bro." Darius wiped his mouth with the back of his hand. "Just trying to clean my act up, you know? It's good to see you again, dawg." They bumped fists.

They'd spent much time together in the not-so-distant past. Ricardo had been a good friend. Ricardo helped him survive after his momma's murder and had even hooked him up with a pretty Latina. But after a brief incarceration in the over-crowded parish jail, Darius had quit hanging out with Ricardo; he was trying to change his life's direction.

"Homie, ya get ya black *culo* busted, and now ya ain't got no *cojones* and all scared of The Man." Ricardo smiled, poking Darius in the ribs.

Striker and Bones erupted in laughter, flashing their gold-capped teeth—the status symbol of what some in the parish called "white trash." They were obviously pleased by Darius's portrayal in a negative light. Darius rubbed his chin and rolled his eyes. He'd always tried to conceal his antipathy toward the pair of fools but thought the dimwitted duo was full of more bad shit than good sense.

"I ain't scared of The Man. I made a promise to my momma that I am going to keep. Besides,"—he gave Ricardo a shove with his shoulder— "I intend on outliving you."

Ricardo smirked and shoved back. "I'll bet ya twenty, and ya can pay me in hell, that I outlive ya at least a week. Remember, I'm tougher than a cockroach." Both of them laughed.

Glancing left over Ricardo's shoulder, Darius thought Striker, too, appeared to have been involved in a fracas, with what looked like blood smears on his pants legs.

"Ain't no future in the streets, man," Darius said. "I'm attending the community college; maybe I can get a job down at Conner's Shipyard and work with your uncle."

"Yeah, well, to each his own, the Good Book says. Look, bro, we was in Amelia earlier, and got some weed from off of X-Man. Ya wanna come party?"

"X-Man?" Street names were a dime a dozen, but Darius had never heard this one.

"Homie outta New Orleans. Anyway, me and X-Man kinda had some words, but I scored some good stuff." Ricardo tapped the pocket of his windbreaker.

"Y'all probably had more than words," Darius said, nodding his head in the direction of Ricardo's torn and stained shirt. "But, bro, I'm cool. I quit the weed."

Darius shifted his gaze to the right. A middle-aged black man—well-dressed and wearing a bow tie of all things—with a press ID on a blue lanyard around his neck, sat at a booth near the restrooms. Extending under the table was a gold-handled walking cane. The man was talking through the speaker of his cell phone and scribbling notes. Darius recognized him as the reporter—Robert something—he'd met that horrendous day of his momma's murder.

"I'm going to mosey over by that newspaper guy and see if the brother knows anything about the bastard who killed Momma." Darius slid off his stool and wiped his hands with a napkin.

"Remember what I said 'bout crossin' that line and killin' a man," Ricardo said. "But if ya find him and need some help, I still owe ya."

"Thanks, Thirty-eight, but you don't owe me squat and I ain't dragging you into my shit storm." Darius tossed the crumpled napkin on the counter, grabbed his milk, and poured the rest of the ice into it. He then slid into the booth behind the reporter and while crunching on ice and nursing the last swallow of milk, he waited for the reporter's conversation to end.

"So what's up on this one?" The reporter scratched the back of his head with an ink pen and unbuttoned his shirt under his bow tie. It sounded to Darius like he was gathering information on a pair of drug related shootings. He watched from behind as the reporter nibbled on jelly-covered toast and scribbled notes as the phone conversation droned on and on. The reporter finally hung up and began two-finger pecking at his laptop as he glanced at his notes.

This guy obviously ain't got time for me. Darius walked back to his stool and left money on the counter for his meal and tip.

"I'm calling it a night, bro," Darius said as he patted Ricardo on the back. "Hey, man, one more thing. I just want you to know I appreciate everything you ever done for me."

"See ya on the other side, homie," Ricardo said with a laugh.

Darius slipped his jacket on; after a departing fist-bump with Ricardo and a perfunctory head nod to the other two, he walked out.

The moon peeked from behind a cloud as fog caricatures lazily waltzed across the parking lot. Darius imagined his momma reaching out to him in the shifting fog patterns. He pulled his phone from his pocket and glanced at the time. It was a quarter-past-midnight It seemed a lifetime ago that Ricardo had bought him that phone. A blood-curling shriek jarred Darius from his thoughts. He peered to his right, through the mist, toward a Lincoln Navigator idling close by.

"Get your putrid paws off me, you big, dumb, obtuse simian!" screamed a female emerging from around the vehicle.

Darius didn't need to see the thespian to know it was the redhead, Evelyn. He stepped closer and saw, coming out of the driver's side of the SUV, Peacock-hyena Mitch. Evelyn had apparently foolishly ignored his warning. Now, she struggled and stumbled as she tried to put on a jacket. She'd rebuffed Darius earlier, but he couldn't leave this girl defenseless, despite her foolish choice. Darius shed his jacket, tossed it onto the trunk of his car, and moved toward the girl. Peacock-hyena was grabbing for the girl when Darius caught his eye from a few feet away.

"Stay out of this, bro," Mitch said with more than a hint of threat in his voice.

Apparently, he thought he could intimidate Darius, but talk don't fry catfish. Darius had lived a life rougher than a dry corncob. Unless the dude was packing, Darius figured he could handle him.

"Cracker, I ain't scared of you." Darius pointed back toward the restaurant. "I got a Mexican homie in there with a thirty-eight that's got a slug with your name on it." Zoo-boy needed to realize Darius meant business. "Do yourself a favor and get your ass back in the truck."

Mitch leaned, squinted his eyes and looked over Darius's shoulder into the Waffle House. The white boy looked nervous. He reached his hand to the girl. "I . . . I didn't mean to upset you."

Darius rolled his eyes. *Suddenly the jerk's a pussy.*

"Leave me alone!" the girl yelled as she adjusted her glasses. "You were trying to rape me!"

"No, I wasn't, Red," Mitch said. "I was trying to keep a mosquito off of you, and my hand got caught in your blouse when you pulled away."

Yeah, right! Darius thought. *And I have a submarine in the bayou for sale.*

"Do not call me Red. My name is Evelyn." She narrowed her eyes and reached into her purse and pulled out something. She held up the object and ran at Mitch, apparently intending to inflict as much damage on him as her short, plump frame could muster.

Darius zeroed in on the weapon. *Is that an inhaler?* He stepped between them, facing Mitch. "Get out of here before you get your ass wasted!"

"Dude," Mitch said, "it ain't what it looks like. We're just—"

Darius despised anyone who would hurt a woman. He jabbed his finger in the air and pointed toward the road as he stepped closer to the jock. "Get the hell out of here, now."

Mitch climbed into his SUV and spun its wheels leaving out of the parking lot. Darius wrapped his arm around Evelyn—her shoulders trembled like leaves fluttering in a breeze. He wondered if she was more angry or scared. Her unflinching eyes and set jaw led him to believe the adrenaline rush she must be experiencing was more from the former than the latter.

"Not sure how that was going to help," he said, pointing to the inhaler.

"I thought it was my Mace," she said as she clumsily returned the thing to her purse.

Darius shepherded her toward the passenger side of his Impala. He reached across her and retrieved his jacket from the top of his trunk.

"Where do you live, little girl?" he asked. "Do you want me to take you somewhere?"

"Can you take me home, please? I live in Berwick, at The Kingdom. By the way, I am eighteen. I am a woman, not a little girl."

The Kingdom? Holy Mother of Jesus. No way!

Neither spoke during the drive through the fog and across the Grizzaffi Bridge. Darius snuck an occasional glance at his passenger. She'd shown more spunk than a cat in a dog show. Like his momma, she appeared to be fearless; but unlike his momma, she was obviously not one to take abuse from somebody. As she nibbled at the corners of her fingernails, Darius thought the pigtails made her look younger than she claimed.

Darius turned the Impala onto the dark Spanish Trail Road, traveling west as the road followed Bayou Teche. She drew her jacket tighter.

Darius dismissed the impulse to put his arm around her to warm her. After a long silence, his passenger cleared her throat and spoke softly.

"I am Evelyn Kingsley. Thank you for rescuing me from that fiend back there."

"I know your name. Mine is Darius. Darius LeBeaux." Darius smiled. He'd already realized he and this girl had crossed paths before, several years ago.

"Oh, you heard me remind Mitch of my name." Evelyn palm-struck her forehead.

The fog dissipated as they drove away from the river to The Kingdom. Darius could see through the window, past his passenger, and illuminated by the full moon now high in the sky, peach trees over-hanging five-foot sandstone walls along The Kingdom's perimeter. He stopped in front of the closed gate and remembered her as a little pig-tailed girl picking peaches atop that stone wall.

Evelyn pulled a remote from her purse and opened the wrought iron gates. Motion-activated faux gas lanterns guided Darius along the broad, quarter-mile-long driveway. He stopped the car in the circle of the driveway in front of the mansion. Just ahead, almost as wide as the lane Darius lived on, the pavement forked to the left. He assumed it led to these rich white folks' gazillion-car garage.

Darius felt a gentle touch on his forearm as Evelyn spoke again. "Please, I am indebted to you for your unselfish and heroic actions. You must allow me to do something for you."

He put his hand over Evelyn's and leaned slightly toward her. "You don't owe me anything. We're squared. But how about you let me take you to dinner next weekend?" Darius surprised himself at the sugges-tion. No way was this rich girl going to have dinner with him.

"Done deal," she said sliding off the seat and getting out of the car. "But I insist you let me pay. What is your number? I will call you tomorrow."

Darius ran around the car, but before closing her door, he reached across her, leaned in and pounded on the glove box until it opened. He snatched a cracked pen from the glove box and wrote his number on the palm of Evelyn's hand. She looked at her palm and then into his eyes and smiled. He wondered if she'd felt a moment of physical attraction.

She agreed to let him walk her to the door. As they approached the broad front porch, she reached into her purse. He now remembered the purse from a few years ago. After briefly fumbling for her keys, Evelyn unlocked the massive front door and slowly pushed it open. She gracefully stepped from the brightly lit porch into the soft amber light of the foyer.

She's right. She ain't a little girl.

Darius wished her a good night as she disabled the alarm on the inside. He turned to walk away but she stopped him with a loud whisper. She stepped toward him, put her arms around his neck and tiptoed to place a quick kiss on his cheek. "Do not get the wrong idea about me. I do not usually kiss boys who I do not know, but I wish to express my appreciation for your timely intercession and subsequent kindness." She stepped back, smiled and began biting at her nails.

Darius wondered if she was about to kiss him again, but she abruptly turned and disappeared behind the massive doors. He didn't know what the wrong idea was, but the idea he got was that this was a beautiful girl—a beautiful woman—he hoped to see again soon. He slowly walked to the Impala—for the first time he noticed his heart was fluttering like it did sometimes—and tarried in the driveway until he saw the second-story lights turned on.

He looked up and whispered, "Momma, what do you think about me having a date with this Kingdom girl?" He wished his momma could answer, but Pigenstein had sent her to heaven. Darius had always known that evil creature was bad news; he'd tried to warn his momma many years ago.

CHAPTER 2
SPRING 2000

"Bitch, you better stay in your place."

It was unmistakably the croaking voice of the miscreant living with thirteen-year-old Darius and his twenty-eight-year-old mother, Sarah, in their cramped Patterson house. Darius imagined this evil monster as Godzilla with a long nose protruding like a vulture's beak or pig snout. The long blond hair protruding from under a purple and gold LSU cap made him look like Einstein. The Brothers Grimm, raised from the dead, couldn't conjure an uglier, more diabolical creature. *Godzilla, buzzard, pig, Einstein.* Darius hated, and almost equally feared, Godzillard Pigenstein.

Darius raced toward the plaintive cry of his momma. In a single bound, jumping over the rickety wooden steps, he was atop the sagging porch. Through the torn screen door, he saw his momma's "friend" hulking over her as she struggled to rise from the floor. Flinging open the door, Darius rushed toward her. The monster bumped him hard—Darius thought intentionally—as they passed each other. Reaching his mother, Darius glanced back toward the porch. Pigenstein's frame cast a shadow of the devil halfway across the room. The ogre she called Marcus Holmes searched his pockets, apparently for the keys to his precious red Mustang GT.

Sarah wiped a trickle of blood from her bottom lip and pushed back the hair splayed across her face like pine straw scattered by a hurricane. Darius noticed abrasions on her face and contusions on her light-skinned shoulder under her disheveled blouse. He scowled at this man-beast, exponentially worse than any other of his momma's "friends" who had traversed through their lives. Some of these "friends" would hit her, but she'd neither hit back nor make them leave. Darius was angry at the men for hitting her and angry at her for letting them stay. But this one was especially deplorable. Godzillard Pigenstein was far too old for his momma—and too damn mean.

"How was school today, little man?" Sarah asked as if nothing untoward had just occurred.

Darius heard footsteps clumping across the creaking boards of the front porch. He craned his neck to better see the injuries his momma was apparently trying to keep from his view.

"Momma, you need to make him leave," Darius said pointing his thumb in the direction of Pigenstein as the Mustang roared to life. Gravel crunched as the demon rode off. He hoped a someone would hit the Mustang, sending Pigenstein's evil soul to hell where it belonged.

"I'm fine, little man. Here, come eat a sandwich." Sarah hugged Darius, tussled his hair and kissed him on the forehead in an after-school ritual that had been going on for as long as he could remember—at least when she wasn't on a drug or alcohol binge.

Darius followed into the kitchen. Even hurt and bruised, she walked with grace. If pretty was an acre, his momma would be Texas. On his fingertips, Darius spun a basketball he'd been given for his birthday as he watched her spread a layer of commodity peanut butter—they couldn't afford jelly—over two stale slices of bread. She turned and handed Darius his usual afternoon snack.

Was that a grimace of pain as she turned?

Sarah unlatched the knobless back door and pushed against it. The door creaked on its rusty hinges. Darius, sandwich in hand, walked behind her and leaned on the rotting door jamb. He saw small black ants marching each way across the threshold at his feet. He shifted his gaze and watched his momma gingerly walk across the yard to the clothesline strung between pine trees. The clothes danced in the stiff breeze blowing off the Atchafalaya Bay, several miles to the southwest.

Darius turned into the kitchen to see if there was milk in the aging refrigerator. There seldom was—but it didn't hurt to look. Instead, he saw some Thunderbird wine, the cheap rotgut of the hood that got anybody piss-drunk for pennies. There were also some leftover white beans, a slice of cornbread, a bottle of ketchup, and half a pickle—but no milk. He ate his sandwich with a glass of tap water at the wobbly kitchen table covered with an old, dingy, stained tablecloth. He spun the ball, occasionally looking out the door to see Sarah reach as high as her short arms would allow and slowly pull clothes off the line.

Sarah paused sporadically to rub her shoulder. Darius shook his head, knowing she trying to hide her pain; he was frustrated that he couldn't protect her. When he was older and bigger, he'd make sure none of this stuff happened. He considered taking his Louisville Slugger to GP while he slept if he could get away with it. To this point, all he'd done was spit in Pigenstein's soda a couple times and once he'd dropped a squashed fly in the scumbag's black-eyed peas. In due time, he planned to escalate measures; he'd make GP's stay as unpleasant as hugging a riled porcupine.

Darius retrieved an unframed photograph, his favorite, from the top of the refrigerator. On the back, he saw the familiar inscription: *Sarah LeBeaux, May 22, 1986, 14 yoa.* He'd heard that at fourteen, a year before he was born, his momma was turning heads in Patterson with beauty, brains, and personality. Her smile, wide as the bayou, shone even on the old, scratched Polaroid photograph. He wished she smiled more often. He gently rubbed the faded picture, as if feeling her soft skin and the texture of her silky hair that reached halfway down her back. He raised the photograph to catch the sunlight through the window for a better view. He remembered enough of his grandparents to see that Sarah inherited the beauty and complexion of her Creole mother and the high cheeks and chiseled features of her Chitimacha Indian father.

He looked outside and saw Sarah wince as she reached for a red cotton shirt with the Chicago Bulls emblem on the front that she bought for him a few weeks ago at the thrift store. She placed it in the gray plastic basket she used to gather the clothes and then slowly stooped to pick up the basket. She slowly climbed the steps and walked inside with the basket of clothes on her hip. He smiled at her as she sat down and began folding and placing the clothes on the table. Darius kissed the top of her head and went outside to dribble.

Angry rap music blared from a boom box across the narrow street as dusk slowly dimmed the light on the horizon. Kids played in and out the shadows in the street—most of the streetlights were shot out. When Darius came back inside, Sarah was sitting on the tattered green living room couch that doubled as his bed. She swatted at a mosquito on her leg as she read a book under the dim light of a shadeless lamp with only one of its two light bulbs working. He allowed himself to entertain the notion that maybe Godzillard Pigenstein would never return.

"What are you reading?" Darius plopped beside her on the couch.

"Reading poetry, Deke." It was the pet name she'd given him as a toddler. "Sometimes it helps soothe my soul." She leaned her head against his shoulder.

Her soul would be much soother if Pigenstein oinked somewhere else. Darius worried that they'd be sucked into the loutish brute's cesspool unless he left—or was persuaded to leave.

He remembered long before Pigenstein, when life was pleasant, that they lived with his grandparents on the other side of town. The house looked like a castle, with a porch wrapping all the way around. His momma, when she was sober, was always reading one of the books from Gramp's library. Even back then, she'd read to him. The books, and the rest of life, were much better in that upper-middle-class white section of Patterson. Darius asked if his grandparents were rich.

Sarah turned the book, soiled and torn from years of use, over in her lap and put her arm around him. "They were comfortable, but not rich," she said.

He lifted the book from her lap and leafed through it. He never understood what people saw in poetry, especially the kind his momma read. It didn't always rhyme, and it seldom made sense. He preferred a good adventure book. Darius remembered how Granny's kitchen was a cornucopia of good food and always smelled of fresh-baked cakes and pies. The refrigerator was never out of milk, the fruit basket was never empty, and there was always jelly to go with the peanut butter. But one thing clouded those sunny memories.

"I remember you and Grandma used to argue," Darius said. "That always upset me."

"She didn't like when Daddy let me move back in when you were a baby because I was wild and using drugs and stuff. She always said I was crazy and a bad person."

"Well, at least I never saw her hit you like some of your friends do."

Since leaving that house when he was four, all Darius knew was a life of uncertainty, deprivation, and poverty. They lived in littered neighborhoods, where the sounds of the night were the shrieks of fighting couples, where adults yelled and cursed children, and where gunshots raised few eyebrows. A couch was furniture during the day and a bed at night. In the existential battle between humans and pests, the primates appeared to be on the losing end.

Darius pulled a dog-eared copy of *White Fang*—his favorite story—from under the couch. It had been bought—like almost everything he had—from the thrift store. He still loved the rare times when they cuddled together on the couch and she read to him in her soft, sweet voice. Darius wished he had the fierce mettle of White Fang.

After half an hour, Sarah slowly closed the book, grinned as she gave Darius an ominous stare, and then, fast as a cat, grabbed him and began tickling him. He giggled and screamed, begging her to stop, but when she stopped, he pleaded for her to resume. When their play was over—much too soon, in Darius's opinion—she pulled the sheet from under the end table. After converting the couch into a lumpy bed, she gently tucked him in. Then Darius became quiet, almost sullen.

"What's wrong, Deke?" Sarah sat beside him again, gingerly reaching over to pinch his cheeks. She smiled, but as she rubbed her shoulder he glimpsed a bruise on her neck.

"Is beak man staying here much longer?" Darius asked. White Fang would've guarded his momma from danger; he wished he could. As much as he hated to admit it, he feared the beast could crush him with a single blow.

"I hope so," she answered slowly and softly. "He's a friend and understands me. He's helping Momma out with bills and helps her get her medicine."

She wasn't referring to prescription medication, Darius knew.

"Then why does he hit you?"

"Your momma's okay. You're really smart, but you think too much." She tickled Darius's belly button and then kissed him good night.

As usual, Darius tried to force good dreams into his sleep by creating the picture of his father living with them. He imagined what his father looked like and where he might be. He fantasized that someday his father would return—come to find his son—and protect them.

Sarah recently told Darius that her life spiraled out of control when she was fourteen; when she crossed what she called an "event horizon," the point an object can't cross without being swallowed into a black hole. That was all she said about the summer of 1986. Darius wondered what it meant to fall into a black hole. As Darius surrendered to sleep, he'd have nightmares of her sucked into a black whirlpool. Pigenstein and other monsters intruded into his dreams, dragging Sarah into a black cave. He'd chase them, slogging through mud with million-pound weights around his ankles.

Sarah saw the photograph Darius had taken from the refrigerator. She held it in her left hand and rubbed her sore neck with her right as she peeked into room to make sure Darius was sleeping. She hoped he wouldn't have to grow up too soon as she had. That's why she tried to conceal her pain and bruises and the troubles she was having with her friend.

"Why are you worried 'bout that little bastard seeing some dope?" Marcus had yelled that morning when she complained about a stash of cocaine lying on the table. "He ain't blind. He knows you're a dopehead."

"Marcus, please don't call my son that," Sarah said as she turned to walk away, ashamed of being called the dopehead she knew she was. Marcus grabbed her from behind and spun her like a top. He squeezed her throat until she almost passed out and then flung her into the wall. Dazed from hitting her head, she fell like a broken plate crumbling to the floor.

"Don't walk away," Marcus said as he stood over her. "And don't tell me what to do."

"I'm sorry for making you upset, Marcus," she said. She rubbed her head as she got up. Looking at her hand, she saw a smudge of blood. "I wasn't telling you what to do. I was just asking that you not to leave the stuff where Darius can get into it."

"The nosey bastard better not get in my stuff no matter where it is," Marcus said as he jammed his finger into her chest. It was only a few hours later that Marcus became angry over something else and pushed her to the floor. He always said shoves were his warning to keep things from escalating. She hated that Darius had seen the confrontation.

With Marcus gone for the night, the house was peaceful as a grave-yard. She tiptoed over the creaking floor, sneaking past Darius and into the bathroom. She drew a bath of hot water past the brown ring half-way up the tub. She gingerly stepped into the tub and lowered her five-foot, ninety-pound frame. She groaned as the hot bath eased the pain in her shoulder. She wept softly, not from physical pain but because of the failure she felt as a person and a mother.

A few days later, Sarah sat at the kitchen table and poured herself a glass of Thunderbird. Her mood was hijacked to a dark wasteland of depression. The only ransom was time, but she used intoxication as a down payment. With enough alcohol or drugs, the voices in her head would go silent and the demons would release their grip from her soul, at least for a few hours.

"Deke doesn't know all I've been through," she said as she swished down a glass of the wine. "Ma'Dear never understood, either." She poured another glass and spoke in a shrill voice, derisively mimicking her mother. "You sinned against God, yourself, your family, and brought disgrace upon us all!" Changing to her own voice, she said, "You never understood what happened during or after that summer." Sarah threw her head back, finished off the glass of wine, and then poured herself a third. "You thought going to church every Sunday made you so holy and sanctified."

Events she couldn't purge from her memories, despite her best efforts, replayed themselves like a horror movie in her mind. Thoughts, she could not throttle, raced wildly through her head. She poured another glass of wine, dropping the empty bottle to the floor where it spun a moment.

"One day, I'll get clean when I get over all this." Sarah whimpered as she swallowed the last drop of the wine. "One day, I'll know peace."

CHAPTER 3
FALL 2000 – SPRING 2001

"Can I have a pet alligator? Pleeeaase?"

Evelyn, almost ten-years-old but going-on-twenty, was squealing like an overheated teapot after learning they were moving to the bayou country, near where Pawpaw and Maw-Maw raised her mother, Martha. She was jumping up and down, her pigtails writhing like inebriated red snakes.

"Gators are not pets, *cher*. Dey are dangerous. And you'll stay offa dat bayou. *Mais*, I done told you dat four or t'ree times dis week." Thirty-eight-year-old Martha's Cajun accent, thick as a gumbo roux, hadn't changed over the years she had lived up north.

"Momma, I must get by the bayou to catch catfish." Evelyn stomped her foot.

"Don't you t'row no temper tantrum wit' me, little girl," Martha wagged her finger at Evelyn. "I ain't your poppa. I'll tan your fanny."

Just then, Peter, Evelyn's fifty-four-year-old father, walked into the room. His long strides took him around stacked boxes filled with items the Kingsleys were sending to the Salvation Army. His full crop of close-cut black hair and a closely trimmed beard contrasted with his bushy, unruly eyebrows. Tall and lean, Evelyn thought he resembled Abraham Lincoln.

Peter scooped his little girl up with his big hands, threw her into the stratosphere, and caught her as she shrieked in pantomimed fright. When Peter put her down, she ran behind her mother, stuck her tongue out, and made a face as she put her hand to her ears and wiggled her fingers, taunting her poppa. Peter turned toward the boxes stacked two, sometimes three, high and walked away.

Evelyn left the sanctuary of her mother's apron and crept closer to her father, tempting him into grabbing her. She saw him watching her with poorly concealed glances. She screeched loud enough to crack walnuts when his long arms grabbed her, quick as greased lightning, and tossed her as high as Mount Everest. At Martha's pleading, the pair discontinued their toss-and-scream game.

"Tell Momma that I can play on the bayou, Poppa," Evelyn said as Peter put her down.

Peter glanced over at Martha, holding her hands on her hips. Her frown defied the suggestion of a veto. "Do not make me any trouble with that redhead mother of yours over that bayou," Peter said as he hugged and kissed Evelyn.

Martha's Cajun Catholic kin, the Heberts, had lived for four generations on the bounties of the Louisiana wetlands near Houma. Evelyn knew her mother's thirteen-year-old twin brother, Matthew, had drowned in Terrebonne Bay when he fell overboard and became entangled in the nets during a five-day shrimping trip out of Cocodrie.

"Dere is more water in dat bayou dan you can swallow. Dis conversation is ova, little girl, and we have a doctor's 'pointment. Den you and your poppa are goin' to de airport." Martha looked at her husband and smiled. "Not'in' seems to scare dat girl."

"Throw me in the air again, Poppa." Evelyn accepted that the bayou would remain unexplored—at least until she could renegotiate this issue with her poppa in private.

After her father bought the eighty-two-acre Delahousier Plantation on Bayou Tech, Evelyn took several flights with him during the renovations of the two-story, six-bedroom antebellum home. The estate was outside the small, upscale town of Berwick, across the Atchafalaya River proper from blue-collar Morgan City. The meandering driveway was lined by two-hundred-year-old live oak trees draped in grey moss with gnarly, bottom limbs nearly crawling along the ground. To the rear of the estate, near the bayou, there was a stand of massive, bald cypress trees. Evelyn enjoyed playing in the trees and walking along the top of the stone fence. But right now, her bayou playland was still hours away; Evelyn wanted the entertainment of one of her favorite stories.

"Tell me how you met Momma when you went to Louisiana."

Peter laid his head back in his seat, stroked the beard on his chin, and grinned. "Ah, Mardi Gras, 1990." He roared a hearty belly laugh. Evelyn often wondered if Abe laughed as much, or as hard and loud, as her poppa. "Your mother stole my heart the first day I met her. She was so sweet that I was smitten with love before the day had passed."

"As sweet as the beignets?" Evelyn asked on cue.

"Ten times sweeter than beignets in a pot of honey," Peter said as his daughter giggled at the answer he'd given dozens of times.

"And she made you the happiest man on Earth?"

"One hundred times the happiest man on Earth and Mercury and …"

"And Mars, Saturn, Jupiter, Uranus, Neptune, and Pluto," Evelyn chimed in.

"Even the whole Milky Way," Peter said as he leaned over and kissed her rosy cheeks. "If I believed in God, I would say it was a miracle that we met and had you."

Evelyn frowned. "Poppa, there is a God."

"Like mother, like daughter," Peter said. "And there is a Santa Claus, too."

"You are the one in a Santa Claus suit!" Evelyn was proud of figuring out the adult ruse of a jolly, obese man traveling across the sky in a sleigh pulled by reindeer and sliding down every chimney in a single night. She'd noticed three years ago that there were never hoof prints in the snow on the ground or the roof on Christmas morning. But the clincher came two years ago.

"I knew it was all a farce when I saw Santa kissing Momma under the mistletoe," she said with a triumphant tone.

"A farce, huh? Well, Miss Priss, you were not supposed to still be up," Peter chastised in obviously mock anger.

"Yes, a farce. And you are not supposed to lie to little kids," Evelyn said, putting a hand on her hip, just as she'd seen her mother doing.

Peter laughed. "You are one smart cookie, but you better not tell your mother that I confirmed your suspicions."

"I won't, Poppa. I promise." Evelyn bit at her fingernail, a habit she'd recently picked up when she was bored or nervous.

"I *will not*," he corrected her. "Not 'I won't.' Speak properly and enunciate all your words. And quit biting those nails. Your mother does not like that."

They were near where the Atchafalaya River empties into the Gulf of Mexico in the southwest part of St. Mary Parish. Below the plane was a vast expanse of moss-draped cypress trees, reaching for the sun in a labyrinth of waterways, some clogged by hyacinths with violet-blue and purple blooms.

"Poppa, can we name our place 'The Kingdom'?" Evelyn asked.

"I see no reason not to call where a princess lives The Kingdom."

The family moved to The Kingdom before completing all the renovations. Thus, with carpenters working on the four-car garage in back,

Peter parked in front of the mansion one wet, spring afternoon. He wiped his feet at the doorway under the twenty-foot-wide porch that ran the length of the front of mansion. As he opened the heavy, oak front door, Peter heard Martha playing on the Steinway grand piano he'd gotten her as a Christmas gift.

He slipped his umbrella into a tall cherry-colored ceramic vase with a scene painted of a Cajun boy in a straw hat floating along a cypress-lined bayou in his narrow pirogue. Peter saw Martha's head swaying side to side and her fingers gliding over the keys of the piano in the paneled parlor. He hummed as he walked across the room, where silver chandeliers with glistening crystal hung from the vaulted ten-foot-high ceilings.

Martha turned slightly, leaning her head and shoulders back to greet Peter with a smile. He gently kissed the crown of her head and sat beside her on the velvet stool which was a few feet from the winding staircase trimmed in Peruvian mahogany. He put his arm around her and looked at her image in the wide mirror hanging on the wall behind the piano. Peter thought she was as beautiful as the day he'd first seen her.

"You are so talented, Marty." Peter closed his eyes and swayed his head with hers.

"T'ank you, Petey." Martha leaned over for a kiss. "Can you check on Evelyn? She darted like a banty rooster outside when she finished her lessons."

"You are not going to like what I am seeing." Peter had walked to the kitchen window and bellowed in laughter. Martha rose from the piano and joined him there. He was mildly surprised she didn't blow a gasket over Evelyn playing in the mud.

"I told you dem nort'ern winters were makin' our daughter sick," Martha said. "Here in Louisiana, she made it all winter wit'out goin' to de doctor. De Blessed Virgin Mary has made her well."

"Well, which one is it?" Peter asked. "The Lord or Louisiana that made her well? Maybe she is outgrowing her illnesses."

"Oh, ye of little fait'. What am I gonna do in heaven wit'out you, Petey?" Martha kissed him on the cheek.

"The same thing I am going to do in hell without you, I guess." He gently slapped her derriere as she passed by to check on some cookies she was baking.

Just then, Evelyn burst into the house through the back double-French doors; mud covered every freckle on her face. She was wearing the short white rubber boots that South Louisiana natives call Cajun Reeboks. The boots were caked with thick black bayou mud. Her denim shorts and her knees were almost as muddy as her boots. Pinched between her first two fingers and thumb was a four-inch-long red-and-black crustacean which was menacingly flailing its tiny claws. She was proudly displaying it slightly above her head as if it were some sort of trophy.

"I caught a crawfish with my bare hands! Can we bring him to Pawpaw's for the Easter crawfish boil?"

"Evelyn Mart'a Kingsley! Look at you trackin' mud all in my clean kitchen!" Martha complained. Everybody knew that Cajun Reeboks, especially muddy ones, in her kitchen were a no-no. "I'm tired of tellin' you to take dose boots off 'fore you come in dis house! Look at dat face. I can't see it, *mais lais*, for all de mud."

"Look at my crawfish, Momma. Can I keep him until Easter?" Evelyn shoved the crawfish higher and near Martha's face.

"We're a couple weeks from Easter," Martha said, gently shoving the crawfish away.

"I can keep him in the bathtub in one of the extra bathrooms!" She headed toward the stairs, undoubtedly to run water in the tub for her trophy.

"That is a wonderful idea, Princess," Peter said from behind Martha.

"Peter Kingsley, behave yourself!" Martha said, turning to swat him with a dish towel.

"Please, Momma, can I keep him until Pawpaw can boil him?" Evelyn pleaded from the foot of the stairs.

"No, you can't keep dat crawfish! Peter, when in tarnation are you goin' to let dat girl use some 'tractions?"

"Let her keep him in the tub," Peter said as he maneuvered to a safer distance. "And she can use contractions when she is eighteen." Peter impishly smiled and winked at his daughter.

"You're not helpin', *mais lais*," Martha said, throwing an oven mitten across the room at Peter. Then, turning back to face her daughter, she commanded, "Don't you go up dem stairs wit' dat crawfish!" Martha stomped her foot on the marble kitchen floor. "Get dat crawfish out of dis house den you take off dem boots and march your little red head into your bat'room and clean up. It's almost suppertime. And don't you dare sit on none of my furniture wit' dem filt'y clothes!"

Evelyn turned from the stairs, frowning as she slowly walked out the door to turn the crawfish loose.

"Petey, you spoil dat girl," Martha said as Evelyn pouted on her way out the back door to give the lucky crustacean its freedom. "She has you wrapped around her pinky."

"Maybe," Peter said with a smile, but he knew she was correct.

One night during a dinner of chicken and sausage gumbo, Evelyn asked Peter to retell the love story of his first meeting with Martha. Evelyn never tired of that story.

"Was she as sweet as beignets?"

"Ten times as sweet as beignets in a pirogue of honey."

Evelyn squealed in laughter at Peter's variation in the story.

"What caught your eye first?" Evelyn wasn't content with the simple abridged version she'd heard so many times. She wanted more information, more details.

Peter smiled and glanced at Martha, who appeared focused on removing the meat from a chicken leg in her gumbo. It was the kind of smile Evelyn knew meant he was up to mischief.

"Well, if you must know," Peter said chuckling, "it was your mother's boobs."

Martha gasped and dropped her spoon into her bowl of gumbo; her head bobbed up, her eyes steaming with disapproval. "Peter Kingsley, I know you didn't just tell my ten-year-old daughter dat, *mais lais*!"

"Did you want me to lie?" he asked as if there were no other option.

"Momma, I know what boobs are." She put her little hand on her left hip under the table and shook her head at her mother for thinking she was uninformed.

"I didn't say you don't. But dat ain't what your poppa should be talkin' 'bout. If you gonna tell dis story, Peter Kingsley, keep it age 'propriate!" She wagged her finger in Peter's direction across the oak table and then retrieved her spoon from the gumbo and heaved a sigh.

"Okay, Princess, let me tell you this story in a way that will pass your mother's censorship."

"Poppa, I am old enough for all the details."

"No, you're not, Evelyn Mart'a Kingsley, and your poppa better watch what he says, or it'll be a cold night for him tonight!" Martha shot Peter another look.

"Well, like I was saying," Peter began again. He paused long enough to savor a spicy piece of Manda's pork sausage he'd put in his mouth. He coughed, wiped his mouth on a napkin and continued. "I had seen enough, umm, raised shirts, and I was about to leave the parades when I heard the most beautiful voice I ever heard say, 'Throw me something, mister.'"

"Is that when the ladies show their ta-tas to get good throws?"

"That is right, Princess."

Martha double tapped her spoon on her bowl and shot her daughter a sharp look, which Evelyn acted as if she didn't see.

"Did Momma show her ta-tas?"

"Evelyn, stop dat talk dis very minute." Martha glared at Evelyn a moment and then wagged her finger at her husband, again. "Peter Kingsley, we can skip dis part." She stirred the contents of her bowl, apparently looking for more chicken. She got a cracker from her saucer and pointed it at Peter. "Your poppa saw me reachin' for a red silk rose somebody t'rew me. But a crippled colored man got it 'fore I did."

"He gave it to his daughter," Peter said before he paused for a swallow of his iced lemon tea. "Pretty little Creole girl. They agreed to sell it to me for twenty dollars, and I brought it to your mother."

"So that is how you saw her ta-tas?"

"Evelyn Kingsley, if you mention dat again, I'm gonna wash your mout' wit' soap and send you up to your room! See what you started, Peter?" Martha frowned and shook her head. She stood up and reached toward the middle of the table to pull the pot of gumbo toward her and scooped out a chicken thigh with a ladle.

"By that time, your mother's Saints jersey was down." Peter winked at his giggling daughter as he made a curving motion at his chest. "When she introduced herself to me, I was not accustomed to that Cajun accent, and I did not know whether to call her Martha or Marta!"

"Oh, Petey, quit pickin' at me for how I talk!" Martha said with a grin. "When your poppa talked 'bout his car, he was sayin' 'caw,' and I t'ought he wanted me to ride his cow out de French Quarter, *cher*."

Evelyn made a mooing sound in her poppa's direction, and they all laughed.

"After we got in my 'caw,' we had dinner, and by the evening's end, I was in love with a Cajun girl. A few weeks later, I proposed to her, and she left Houma and moved to DC. Then, in November, you were born." Peter looked into the pot, grabbed the ladle and pilfered the pot of three more pieces of sausage.

"How long was it before you had your first argument?"

"Well, you know your mother and I seldom argue, and I always say, 'Never go to bed angry,' but we did have our first disagreement fairly quickly."

"Your poppa wanted to raise you a heat'ern, like he is, but I told him I wasn't havin' none of dat! My baby was gonna be a good Cat'olic girl like her momma."

"That was not exactly how it happened. I said I was Jewish and my mother was Quaker, but I did not believe in God. I agreed to your God indoctrination until our child turned thirteen."

"Your poppa insisted you was gonna be a boy, and he said dat was when Jewish boys have dere bar mitzvah. I said you might be a girl, and den he says dat girls have dere bat mitzvah at twelve."

"I think your mother was as scared of me raising you to be a Jew as she was of me raising you as an atheist."

"Dat's not true, Peter. I don't mind you worshippin' God in whatever way he moves you. I just wish you would worship him." Martha nibbled on a cracker.

"That is right, Poppa. You should worship God, because he is our creator and savior." Evelyn made the sign of the cross over her face and chest.

"Your poppa said his people t'ink dat is when you are old 'nough for contracts and to get married. When he said dat, I came unglued, *mais*. I wasn't lettin' my daughter get married at no twelve-years-old!"

Peter laughed and told Evelyn that the argument blew over quickly. He said he and Martha agreed they would never go to bed angry with each other.

"We never broke dat promise in all dese years," Martha said.

Evelyn finished her gumbo and then leaned forward with her chin resting on the edge of the table as she watched her parents still eating. She started to bite at her nails but put her hands down when she glimpsed her mother's disapproving look. Then she recalled a comment she'd heard on the television earlier.

"What is a liberal, Poppa?" She twirled her fingers in her pony tail.

"They are people like me who want to help the disadvantaged . . ."

"You mean give handouts to welfare queens," Martha said.

"And a living wage for workers under safe and less-than-oppressive conditions," Peter added.

"Leadin' to six-dollar Big Macs." Martha choked on a cracker.

"Are you all right, Momma?" Evelyn asked.

"I just don't want de government in my business. Soon dey gonna say dey need to know what books we readin'."

Peter and Evelyn laughed, but Martha did not.

CHAPTER 4
SUMMER–WINTER 2001

"Boy, this is a dog-eat-dog world, and I'll be damned in hell if I'm gonna be eaten."

Darius sat in the dirt and gravel playing with a four-inch-long lizard he'd captured as Pigenstein pontificated from the top porch-step. He only half-listened to his momma's boyfriend.

Who does he think he is? My daddy? I don't think so!

Darius was sick of looking at the vile cretin. He couldn't understand why his momma had tolerated Pigenstein for so long. He'd recently escalated his covert subversion. Twice he placed nails under Marcus's tires. Last month, he tried to shatter the windshield of that precious Mustang with a rock, but the rock merely bounced off and scratched the hood. Still, it was funny to watch Pigenstein squeal like a titty-baby over the scratch when he discovered it.

If Pigenstein doesn't get his ugly ass out of this house, I'll club him with my bat. I wish I wasn't scared of him.

Darius scowled at the scumbag sitting there wiping sweat from his ugly-ass brow. Darius stroked the upside-down lizard's belly with his index finger. The tiny reptile changed from green to brown, closed its eyes and became motionless.

"You gotta take what's yours," Marcus said. "Don't take shit from nobody or anybody else."

"You know that's redundant." Darius was pleased with the opportunity to use a word he'd recently learned.

"Yeah, and you're a bastard," Marcus spat back.

"I've never seen a dog eat another dog," Darius replied. "They all seem to get along just fine." If Godzillard Pigenstein was trying to offer fatherly advice, Darius wasn't interested. The sooner he left with his pearls of wisdom, the better.

"Always carry a gun, and don't worry about fighting fair. Life is hard and it ain't easy. You gotta be hard if you gonna survive. That's the name of the game, boy—survival."

"More redundancy, Webster." Darius always tried to avoid saying Marcus's name or he'd intentionally mispronounce it. "How about I stay out of trouble and have friends who don't fight?"

"Look, I been through hell and seen screw ups you can't imagine. Sometimes shit comes to you, and you just gotta step in it and deal with what it brings."

"Does it come to you or you go to it?" Darius tapped the lizard's nose, and it opened its mouth with the same spunk Darius was showing toward his own antagonist; he was pushing the limits and was as contumelious as he dared.

"Go to hell, boy. I'm here cuz Imma survivor who survives. Don't go judging a man 'til you walk in his shoes. I'm trying to teach you how to be a man and you being a smartass."

The lizard turned green again. Darius brought it to his ear and let the creature latch on like an earring. Then he pulled the lizard off and set it in the grass, where it paused a moment and then scurried away. Darius wished Pigenstein would scurry away. He saw a leprosy of evil painted all over that ugly face. Maybe something gave this monster a short fuse, but that has nothing to do with surviving or being a man.

Whatever sewer he'd crawled from or whatever ghastly sights he'd seen, didn't make him anybody Darius cared to be. He was sure his daddy, wherever he was, could open a jumbo can of whoop-ass and kick him to the bowels of Hades.

The dude has a point about one thing, though. A gun is the great equalizer.

"Didn't mean to piss you off, Marquis." Darius grabbed his basketball lying near the side of the house and began dribbling it back and forth between his legs in the gravel.

"It's Marcus, dammit. You can be such a dumb retard at times."

Darius grinned, knowing he'd gotten under the creature's skin.

I'm not dumb; I'm smarter than you, even if I can't get Momma to run you off—yet.

Darius spotted a yellow plastic antifreeze container. Some neighborhood kids had once used antifreeze to poison dogs. He contemplated finding an insidious manner to slip some into one of Marcus's drinks. As he pondered such a dastardly deed, he glanced up and saw Sarah walking with two bags of groceries near Iberia Street nearly three blocks away. Dribbling the ball between his legs, imagining he was Michael Jordan, he sprinted past yards littered with beer cans and junked cars.

"Why don't you ever ask what's-his-name to let you use his car instead of walking to the store?" Darius asked as he took a bag from Sarah. He continued to dribble with his right hand.

"I don't wanna wreck his car," Sarah said. "Besides, he may get a call for a business meeting and need to leave."

"He's a damn dope dealer. Any call he gets is someone wanting to buy his dope."

"Deke, watch your mouth. You're too young to use that kind of language."

"And you're too good for that hellion!" Darius said, nodding toward their house.

"I wish you could get along with Marcus. You never gave any man a chance."

"Why should I give him a chance?"

"You don't understand, but in some ways, he's like me. He has no family, and he had a bad childhood when he was coming up in Baton Rouge. He was abused and neglected. Still, he made his way out of the projects and now he's a successful businessman."

"He's a dope dealer. That's not the same thing. How do you know all this bull about his childhood in Baton Rouge and escaping the projects is true?" Darius thought his momma was naïve and trusted Pigenstein too much.

"He's been there when I needed him. Like when he gives me money, so we can eat."

Darius peered into the bag and saw some peaches, his favorite fruit. "Peaches! Thank you, Momma."

"Don't thank me. Thank Marcus. It was his money that bought them."

"Mario can have his damned peaches." He pushed the peaches back into the bag.

"Stop it, Darius! You have to learn that not everything will be what you want. Sometimes you have to make sacrifices."

Darius thought any bargains with Pigenstein were Faustian, at best. He had read about Mephistopheles in a school library book. Now, the fiendish Mephistopheles sitting his sorry ass on their front porch appeared to have seduced the good sense out of his momma. It was frustrating to see her try to make this pernicious man into some sort of saint. All of this complicated Darius's mission to rid his family of this ogre.

Darius reached to touch a fresh bruise on her neck. "That's not the kind of sacrifice we should make."

Sarah brushed his hand away and stopped walking. "Don't cross him, Deke, and everything will be fine. He thinks you pissed in his Nikes one morning. Did you?"

"No. Maybe a tomcat pissed in them nasty-ass shoes."

Darius knew there was no cat. He figured his momma knew, too.

Pigenstein can take his shoes off elsewhere if he doesn't want them pissed in.

"Why don't you get a gun?" Darius said angrily. "Then he won't hit you!"

"Guns ain't the answer to your momma's problems, or to any other problem, Deke. They only make matters worse, and maybe get the wrong people hurt. I can handle myself."

"Guns don't kill innocent people." Anybody who watches television knows the good guy always has a gun and shoots the bad guy, and then everybody is safe. If she'd just get a gun, he wouldn't have to research that Prestone option.

"Just don't ever use a gun, little man. Momma will be okay."

By this time, the two of them reached their house. Darius rolled the ball beside the steps as he stepped onto the porch and opened the door for his momma. Godzillard Pigenstein was walking out. He'd gotten a business call, he said, and didn't know when he'd be back.

"Tell that brat of yours to watch that smartass mouth before I jack him up."

Darius thought he needed to hurry and figure out a way to get rid of this monster before it killed him or his momma.

Marcus hadn't exactly been in a kissing relationship with law enforcement. He was arrested several times on drug charges but managed to escape conviction each time. Eventually the New Orleans Housing Authority put him on its "not welcome" list and he left The Crescent City and arrived here where he could do business in peace.

He was listening to Eminem on his Walkman; thinking that except for having to put up with that snot-nosed kid, things were rocking along smoothly. He didn't trust Darius. The sneaky brat always looked like he was scheming something with poorly concealed contempt. Ever since Marcus tasted something odd in his peas while he ate in the dark and watched television, he'd taken to inspecting his food whenever the kid was in the house.

Sarah, on the other hand, was a keeper. She was good in bed and usually knew how to stay in her place, unlike that last woman in New Orleans. He gave that bitch dope, money, and jewelry, and then she put him in jail for a month. That was messed up.

Marcus slowly navigated his Mustang around the potholes, some as big as moon craters, in the parking lot of a little strip mall where he was to meet his new customer. He was on time, but his customer was not. Something didn't feel right. He was about to leave when a newer-model blue Lexus RX 300 drove up.

A tall, lanky guy in his mid-twenties strolled over toward Marcus, who still sat in his car. Marcus finished off his shake and noticed someone else was also in the Lexus. Marcus wasn't comfortable with this situation. He pulled his gun from his backside and set it on the seat next to him. In this line of work, getting your gun late could mean never getting it at all. He lowered the window of the Mustang when the customer got beside the door.

"You Dewitt?" Marcus asked.

"That's me. You Marcus?"

Marcus's street instincts insisted something was amiss. He possessed a fairly acute and accurate sixth sense that warned when trouble was about to sprout. Out of the corner of his eye, he saw the other guy getting out of the Lexus.

"Butch Cassidy and the Sun Dancing Kid?" Marcus asked Dewitt as he pointed with his thumb toward the passenger, who was getting closer to the Mustang.

"That's my friend, Francis."

"I don't do business like that. You want your shit or what?"

"Yeah, and I want your money, too." Dewitt raised a pistol above the car door, inches from Marcus's face. "I guess you can call me Butch, after all. Meet my buddy, Sundance."

Marcus put his right hand on his own pistol and his left hand on the door. He pulled the door handle and swung the door outward into Dewitt, whose gun discharged. The bullet grazed Marcus, drawing a trickle of blood under his right eye.

Marcus whipped his gun around and pointed it at his assailant. Dewitt turned and ran as Marcus's gun jammed.

"Ya lucky illegitimate bastard!" Marcus yelled. He tossed the jammed pistol onto the backseat, reached under his seat to grab a spare gun, and jumped out of the car. A good businessman always formulates a Plan B. He began to fire at the Lexus that was burning rubber and bouncing through potholes on the way out of the parking lot. Then he saw the flashing blue police lights and heard the siren.

"These sons of bitches have done got the cops up my ass and my butt," he mumbled. "I ain't going to jail tonight."

He turned his attention to the cop, who he shot and wounded. Quicker than the tail shake of a cat more police units were in the parking lot, surrounding Marcus. He'd come prepared to sell drugs and fend off a crazy dopehead or two, but not half of the Patterson PD. Out of ammunition, and out of luck, Marcus surrendered.

"I got set up by a cop," Marcus told Sarah when he called her from jail. "The damn pig tried to put a cap in me. I had to shoot him, or he was gonna kill me. Some other cops showed up, and of course they arrest me and say I started it."

At the bail hearing the next morning, wearing his orange jail-issued uniform with *SMSO* plastered in bold black letters across the back, Marcus stood in front of the judge. He peered at his handcuffs, knowing they could be picked with a hairpin. He listened in disgust as the prosecutor told the judge that Marcus was a dope dealer who'd tried to kill a cop and who had rap sheets from Baton Rouge and New Orleans that were as long as the bayou. He said Marcus had served time as a juvenile for an assault with a knife, and that he'd recently been convicted of domestic abuse.

"Mr. Holmes sent a woman to New Orleans Charity Hospital with cuts, a broken arm, and a concussion," the prosecutor said.

Marcus was trying mightily to subjugate his truculent disposition; attempting to remain quiet and respectful. But he'd had his fill with the uppity prosecutor in his blue pinstriped suit and alligator boots. They never gave the whole story when they were talking to a judge.

"The bitch fell down the stairs when she tried to hit me," Marcus blurted out with a petulant toss of his head.

"The incident occurred in a one-story apartment, Your Honor," the prosecutor said.

"I was railroaded." Marcus was percolating with disgust for the system and rage toward those who prospered by making his life miserable.

"Mr. Holmes," the judge said sharply, "be quiet, or I'll cite you for contempt." He looked down at him over his horn-rimmed glasses and banged his gavel.

"Just thought you might wanna know all the facts, Your Honorific," Marcus said.

Sarah told Darius that Marcus was set up by the cops and in jail. She wasn't sure when he'd get out. There was no way for her to raise bail before his jury trial in late-December.

"Maybe that'll give you time to let some of those bruises fade before he puts fresh ones on you," Darius said.

"Don't be like that, Deke," Sarah said. "Marcus is going through a hard time right now."

Darius rolled his eyes. "I don't give a rat's ass about him."

"Okay, that's enough, son!" Sarah turned away and went to the kitchen. *Darius doesn't understand how much a woman can care about her man,* she thought.

She went to the parish jail in Centerville and brought Marcus a turkey sandwich and some banana pudding for Thanksgiving. Marcus insisted that he'd be getting out after his trial. Sarah believed him, but it remained to be seen if a jury would.

For his trial, she bought him a suit from the thrift store. The pants were a little short, and the jacket's shoulders were a little big. He got a prison trim on his hair, and by the day of his trial, she had groomed him into looking like a typical Joe from the neighborhood.

Two hours after a half-day of testimony, Sarah heard the polled jury unanimously return a guilty verdict against her man for assault with a deadly weapon and attempted drug distribution. They acquitted him on the attempted murder charge.

"This is a missed carriage of justice and a fart of a trial," Marcus shouted to the jury. "Y'all convicted me the minute y'all got in that box. Y'all sending an innocent man to jail."

The judge sentenced him to six years in the state pen at Angola, with half of the sentence suspended. Sarah tried to kiss Marcus as he passed by, but he turned away from her and toward the judge, flipping him the middle finger. She cried as Marcus was led from the courtroom. *He wasn't perfect, but he'd been a good man to her,* she thought.

Darius was happy, even if his momma wasn't.

"This isn't all piss and vinegar. Maybe one day my daddy will come here." Darius said. He couldn't understand what she'd seen in that foul monster and how she couldn't see that things would be better now. For one, he could cease nefarious schemes to disguise antifreeze.

"I doubt it, little man," Sarah said. "Don't get your hopes up. He wasn't a good person."

That wasn't what Darius wanted to hear; when he got older, he'd find his daddy.

They moved fifteen miles west into a four-room house on Hawk Street in Franklin. Unpainted cypress siding covered uninsulated walls. The kitchen linoleum had more holes than Swiss cheese. Rugs covered cracks in the wooden floors, nailed-down plywood covered holes a momma raccoon could pass through. The large brown stains on the ceilings where the water dripped from the holes in the rusty tin roof looked like Rorschach inkblots.

Darius set traps for the mice who apparently were under the impression they owned the place. The worst pests were the big brown roaches as big as a man's thumb. He'd squash as many as he could with a stick or a shoe. They would fly off the walls and ceilings when the lights were turned on. Sometimes, Darius woke up feeling something crawling on his face. He'd bolt from the couch and embark on a search-and-destroy mission. God, how he hated those roaches.

Yet, Darius thought they were better off now that Godzillard Pigenstein was gone.

Maybe someday my daddy will come. He couldn't have been all bad.

Darius focused on the basketball spinning on his finger as he walked along Iberia Street on a cold Friday afternoon. He heard a shriek and looked away from the basketball in time to see and dodge a speeding

Cadillac. He also saw, just ahead of him, the source of the warning: a bent-over white woman pushing a shopping cart filled with aluminum cans. An old black man walked beside her. He had seen the couple a few times but had never spoken to them.

"What's your name, son? Where do you live? Where's your momma?" The man pointed his crooked, cracked tan cane toward Darius as he politely interrogated him. He was missing a top and a bottom front tooth and wore two wool caps over his head.

"My name is Darius LeBeaux, and I live down that street. But Momma's not home today." Darius pointed in the direction he lived as he wiped his runny nose on the sleeve of his torn sweater.

"When she comin' home?" Cradling his cane, the man pulled one of the wool caps off and clumsily put it on Darius's head.

"I don't know. Maybe tomorrow or the day after." Darius tugged downward on the skullcap. He liked the warmth, but it smelled like mothballs.

"You got somebody to take care of you when she's gone?" He turned and pointed his cane behind him, down the street Darius said he lived on.

"No. I take good care of myself." Darius wiped his nose on his sweater again.

"Ain't no little boy supposed to take care of theyself. Quit blowin' your nose on your shirt." The old man rummaged through a coat pocket and extracted a rumpled, navy blue hanky which he handed to Darius. "I'm Mr. Lawrence, and this is my wife, Miss Emily." He tugged softly at Darius's thin sweater. "You should have on more than this out here in this cold."

"I'm not a little boy. I'm almost fifteen." Darius took the handkerchief and blew his nose. He handed the soiled hanky back to Lawrence, who told him to keep it.

Darius had watched the old lady slowly bend over to pick up a yellow knitted shawl that fell from her shoulders. She draped the shawl back over her brown coat. A tear in the coat revealed a red sweater underneath. She had a green wool scarf around her neck. Like her husband, she was wearing a pair of wool hats on her head. She also wore a set of mittens as big as jackrabbits. She was a walking Walmart clearance rack.

"You ate supper yet, boy?" Emily spoke for the first time since screaming her warning.

"Nuh-uh." Darius could see her hands shaking, and he thought she looked like Rudolph with her red nose.

"It's 'no, ma'am', " Emily said.

"You come home with us and let me feed you some red beans. Maybe, I got a piece of apple pie left." Emily placed her frail hands on Darius's shoulders and gently turned him in the direction she and her man were heading.

When he got to their house, Darius observed that it wasn't much different from his. All the houses in this area were carbon copies of dilapidation. The gray, wooden, tin-roofed house may've been a little bigger, but not by much. The poor families Darius knew had bigger fish to fry in the worry pan than to complain much about how their houses looked. Inside, a space heater was on full blast, battling the cold air. Aluminum cans spilling out of a dozen stuffed plastic bags gave the house a claustrophobic feel.

Darius sat on a couch and thumbed through a large Bible placed in the middle of the pressboard coffee table. The couch, like the Bible, had obviously been around for a long time. In the low light, Darius squinted to see the front pages of the Bible. He noticed that it served also as a family tree that recorded dates of birth, marriages, and deaths.

"Be careful with that, boy," Emily said over her shoulder as she made her way into the kitchen. "That's been in Mr. L's family since 'fore the Great Depression. The King James is the real Bible, not like all them new versions made by men."

The console television must have been as old as rocks. To change the channel or adjust the volume, you had to turn knobs half as big as your hand. Above the television, dominating the living room wall, was a picture of *The Last Supper*. Across the room, was a portrait of the Reverend Martin Luther King, Jr., and beside it, one of President John F. Kennedy.

Emily called Darius into the kitchen. She was humming *Amazing Grace* as she sliced some corn bread and served it with a heaping helping of warmed-over red beans seasoned with fatback, Manda's hot sausage, onions, garlic, and Tabasco sauce. The beans were piled over rice, a staple of the diet in Louisiana. Darius had eaten tons of beans—white beans, red beans, green beans, pinto beans, butter beans—but none tasted as good as Miss Emily's red beans.

After his meal, he ate two small slices of pie with a tall glass of milk that Emily served him. He didn't understand why but she kissed him gently on top of his head as he devoured the apple and cinnamon treat. He thought it odd that Emily put ice in his glass, but the nearly frozen milk seemed to taste better that way.

It was approaching dark when Emily invited him to stay overnight. Knowing he would return to an empty house, Darius readily accepted the invitation. Emily announced it was time to go to sleep much earlier than Darius was accustomed. She removed several bags of aluminum cans from the bed which cleared the way for Darius to get under a warm quilt with that same hint of mothballs of the wool hat. Something about that house, this couple, seemed to give Darius the best sleep of his life.

Darius rubbed his eyes when he woke on Saturday morning to the smell of fried Spam—the gourmet potted meat of the poor—and percolating coffee penetrating the quilt over his head. Despite the lingering odor of mothballs, the Spam sizzling in a black cast-iron pan was enough to get Darius's mouth to watering.

Darius came into the kitchen, yawned and sat at the tiny square table. Lawrence was already there, sipping a cup of coffee and reading his Bible aloud. Emily was humming *Amazing Grace* again. Darius listened respectfully to the words from the Sermon on the Mount that Mr. L recited scarcely looking at the Bible.

"Blessed are they which do hunger and thirst after righteousness: for they shall be filled," Mr. L had read or recited. Darius wasn't sure what it meant to hunger after righteousness, but he sure was hungering for that Spam and ready to be filled as Emily set the plates on the table. He was about to start eating but was stopped by Lawrence's raised hand and sharp voice.

"Nobody eats without sayin' grace and thankin' the Lord."

They all held hands. Darius watched as the couple closed their eyes, bowed their heads, and Lawrence offered a prayer.

"This is my Saturday mornin' treat," Lawrence said, savoring a bite of Spam. "Durin' the week, I just gets biscuits and oatmeal."

Darius wiped his hands on his pants and finished off his second glass of iced milk. Then he let go with a loud belch of satisfaction.

"Boy, you don't belch at no table," Emily gently, but firmly, scolded him. "That's plain rude. And if you do, then you say 'scuse me'."

After finishing the best breakfast Darius could ever remember, he fidgeted in his chair while Emily cleaned the table and put the dishes in the sink. As she washed the dishes, she told Darius he could stay there until his momma came home.

"Are you cold, Miss E? Your hands are shaking." Darius had watched her hands tremble through breakfast and while she tidied up.

"No, honey. I have a condition called Parkington, and it makes me shake."

Darius apologized for not knowing and went into the front room where Lawrence retired to, feeling ashamed at perhaps embarrassing her. Lawrence mumbled something about the cold and then ambled into a room in the back. He returned with an old coat that he gave to Darius.

The morning warmed up quickly. Darius followed Lawrence outside where they picked nuts from under the pecan tree in the front yard. Darius cracked his pecans with his teeth while Lawrence used his shoe. Darius's pockets were about empty of pecans when they were joined by a boy who was introduced as the Browns' grandson, Walter. Darius learned that Walter—a couple inches taller, and about twenty pounds heavier—was also a few months older than Darius.

Darius quickly discovered they shared a passion for basketball after Lawrence suggested the boys could go inside and watch a basketball game. At halftime, the pair went to the kitchen for some hot cocoa, which Emily had just made and left in a pot on the stove.

Darius had never had hot cocoa, and he burned his lips as he took the first sip from a cup. He went to the refrigerator to get a cube of ice and almost dropped his cup when he noticed Walter stealing cash from Emily's purse. He rushed toward Walter, yanking the purse away. How could he take money from a nice, old lady with Parkington?

"Mind your own business, bro," Walter hissed, but he released the purse into Darius's hand as Lawrence walked in the kitchen, a few feet behind Darius.

"We . . . we're just getting some hot chocolate, Mr. L," Darius said, hoping the old man hadn't seen him dropping the purse like a hot potato on the cabinet. "I think I should be getting home. Momma oughta be home soon." He was too scared by the incriminating close call to finish his cocoa, although it was the best thing he'd ever drunk.

"Be careful crossin' that street, boy." Lawrence poured a cup of coffee and gave no indication that he noticed the boys pilfering the purse.

Walter left the house with Darius. "They's so easy to steal from. Like takin' candy from a baby." Walter was still laughing as the boys parted ways.

Darius began spending time at the couple's house. They had a lot of rules about being polite and having manners, but they were never harsh in word or action. He hoped Miss E's Parkington wasn't going to kill her. Darius considered ratting on Walter, but he didn't.

CHAPTER 5
SUMMER-FALL 2002

Desperately, but in vain, Darius searched for his momma in the crowd of the hot, dilapidated Franklin High School gymnasium on the Friday before summer break.

At least he saw Lawrence and Emily waving at him as he stood on the stage to receive a certificate for being on the honor roll for the entire year. The couple seemed to view him as an adopted grandson, and that was cool with Darius. He saw them struggle to their feet to give him a standing ovation when his name was called.

When the ceremony concluded, Lawrence placed his hand on Darius's broad and muscular shoulders. "I woulda been proud to have you as my son. You doin' good and stayin' out of trouble."

Darius appreciated Mr. L's kind words, but he would've preferred them from his momma, or perhaps from his daddy.

When Sarah finally got home Monday evening, she said she was proud of Darius and his awards. She hugged him and apologized for not being present to show her support.

"I tell you what, little man," she said. "Me and you are going to take that clunker to Bayou Vista tomorrow, and I'm going to sign up for drug counseling.

Darius slept fitfully through a sweat-filled, restless night, kicking the sheet off the couch. It wasn't yet summer, but a heat wave brought in hot, humid air from the Gulf. The two window fans failed to cool the house through the muggy night. He scratched at mosquito bites on his face and legs as he walked into the kitchen to fix a bowl of cornflakes.

"Good morning, Momma," he said when Sarah walked into the kitchen. "I hope you slept better than me."

Sarah yawned and stretched while Darius fixed her a bowl of cereal.

"I'm happy you're trying to get clean, Momma."

"Little man, you have no idea how hard it is."

After eating, they got in the old Ford that ran when it felt like it. With smoke belching from the tailpipe like a parish mosquito sprayer, they went to the St. Mary Parish Mental Health and Drug Counseling Agency in Bayou Vista, a small community between Patterson and Berwick.

"If you don't have a court order to come here," a bored-looking receptionist said to Sarah through a sliding glass window, "or if you're not thinking about harming yourself or someone else, we can't see you today."

Darius sat quietly beside his momma, reading *Sports Illustrated*.

"I ain't considered suicide in a long time." Sarah squirmed in her seat. She cleared her throat and added, "I only want to kill my uncle who raped me, but I ain't got plans to do that."

Whoa! Rape? Is that what Momma just said?

Darius stopped reading but didn't look up. His eyes were fixed on a page his brain refused to read. He'd assumed something about that summer had been traumatic. But rape? And her uncle?

"Would you like to set up an appointment?" the receptionist asked as she kept her eyes glued to her computer screen, chewing on gum like a cow chewing the cud.

"Yeah, set me something up," Sarah said. "I'll come back."

"How about Tuesday, October 31?"

"That's months from now!" Sarah exclaimed.

"We're booked until then unless you get convicted for drugs and sent here."

Her uncle raped her? Could he be . . . ? No! Ain't no way!

"You can see me if I get arrested for drugs, but not if I come here to keep from using drugs? That's messed up." Sarah crossed her arms and sat back in her rigid orange plastic chair.

"That's the earliest we can see you. Would you like to make an appointment?"

"Come on, Deke," Sarah said as she rose from the chair and turned to her son. "These people ain't worried about helping me."

As they turned to leave, Darius heard the receptionist mutter, "Crackheads. They say they want help, but you try to help them, and they walk away."

Darius spun like a startled cat and stormed to the window to face the woman. He'd always seemed able to keep his cool under the most stressful of circumstances. But this comment was rude, insulting, and cruel to his momma.

"Bitch, don't talk about my momma like she can't hear you. She's been through more shit than the Patterson sewer plant, and she still holds her head high. You need to cap your mouth or somebody's going to cap your ass!"

"Security!" the woman screamed as she slammed the window shut and ran to the back.

"Deke, we need to leave before the police get here," Sarah said as she grabbed his hand and began a fast retreat out the door.

"I only want to kill my uncle who raped me."

Those words kept ringing like Quasimodo's bells in Darius's ears. The thought was as disgusting as a mouth full of cockroaches. He knew his momma was fighting demons, but Jesus, he'd never suspected it was *that* traumatic. After a few days, Darius could no longer keep quiet. Sarah walked into the kitchen from the living room wearing a royal blue hat, trimmed with white lace and little silver stars and tiny lavender feathers. Darius sat at the table, eating some crackers.

"What happened that summer, Momma? Your uncle who raped you—is he my daddy?"

"No, Deke. I told you there was a boy named Henry that I liked. We had sex and he's your daddy. He moved away, and I don't know where he's at. Do you like the way this hat looks on me? I got it at the thrift store for two dollars." She adjusted the hat up and down, back and forth as she turned her head right, then left, for Darius to pass judgment.

"Everything looks good on you, Momma. How could my daddy be a bad person if it was a boy you liked?" Darius drank some water to wash down the last cracker he ate.

"I said your daddy wasn't a good person because he moved away and won't be coming back. You don't like my new hat?"

"Yes, Momma. I like anything you have on." Sarah's explanation of his conception relieved Darius. Maybe his daddy would come back someday. "Tell me what happened in New Orleans. You said it sent you into a black hole, but you never said what happened."

Sarah paused and then heaved a sigh. "Maybe I can tell you some." She pulled the hat off, set it on the table and began brushing her hair with a cracked-handle bush missing several bristles.

"Your granny, she didn't want me to go to the Iberville projects. 'Sodom and Gomorrah,' she called the projects." Sarah walked to the sink and stared out the window as she brushed.

"Isn't that where Marlin said he's from?" Darius walked behind her and took the brush from her and began gently pulling it through her long hair, starting from the bottom and working his way up, as she'd taught him. Her hair was soft as a kitten's fur. He was letting his hair grow long, like his grandfather used to wear his. But her hair was much easier to comb and brush.

"Marcus? I think so. I never saw him if he was there."

Darius looked over her shoulder, through the cracked window and saw dark clouds gathering as the wind flung pine straw at the cracked window. Lightning flashed nearby, and a clap of thunder made Sarah jump. She walked back to the table and Darius followed her. He continued to brush her hair as she sat down.

"Ma'Dear and the rest of the family didn't like Auntie Bren marrying a black man and having Sheila Ann by him. Most of Ma'Dear's family passed themselves as white."

"What are you, Momma? Are you black or white?" Darius asked as he put his darker forearm against hers. Darius had never considered bringing up his momma's race or color.

"I'm Creole and Indian. I ain't no certain color. Anyway, none of that matters. When Auntie Bren divorced Sheila Ann's daddy, she started living with Albert. Auntie thought he was tall and fine even though he never worked."

"Why didn't he work?" Darius paused from hair-brushing long enough to take a couple steps to squash under his shoe a roach ambling across the floor. Darius removed a piece of paper from the trash can to pick up the roach and discard it in the trash.

"Ma'Dear said Albert hurt his hip when he was a teenager running from the cops, but Auntie told everybody he got hurt in a job accident. The year before I got to New Orleans, he sued McDonald's when he said he slipped in their restroom. That's how he bought that big Buick he was always so proud of."

Darius walked to the sink to wash his hands. From there, he admired his momma's beauty. She was prettier without a hat hiding her eyes.

"Albert and Auntie had children your granny called 'little black bastards'." Sarah picked the hat back up and turned it over and around in her hands. She tried to get the feathers to stick straight up, but they refused.

Darius looked at the brown skin on the back of his hand, again. Lightning cracked violently, thunder followed, and the wind intensified, beginning to whistle through the cracks in the walls.

"Ma'Dear thought it was shameful that they were born out of wedlock." Sarah made a final examination of the hat and then set it back down, evidently convinced it was worth the two dollars. "Sheila Ann had a baby boy that she put for adoption. I heard he had problems with his hips and had a heart condition when he was born. Then one of the twins miscarried a baby. When she finally decided to let me go, she says, 'You're white as a lamb, and you better come back that way'."

"What did Gramps say about all that?"

"Daddy tried to help. He even tried to get me counseling for a while, but there wasn't anything he could do. I blacked things out for a long time and couldn't remember them."

Sarah got up from the table and walked to where Darius was leaning against the cabinet. Standing beside him, she stared out the window again. Buckets of rain began to splash against the window. Darius leaned into her and kissed her on the cheek. After a few moments of silence, she returned to the table. Darius followed and sat beside her on a wobbly chair.

"The next day was Independence Day. Everybody was having a good time, except for Sheila Ann. She always got depressed on July Fourth. That's when her baby was born. Albert lit a joint as I passed by." Sarah looked down, shaking her head. She sighed, looked up, and continued. "He gave me a puff of his joint. That was the first time I used drugs. I hope you never get started on the stuff."

Darius waved his hands. "Momma, I don't ever want none of that." He looked at his momma and saw tears, big as water drops on the ceiling, sitting in the corners of her eyes.

"He was drunk and snuck into the room where me and my twin cousins AlaTina and AliTanya were sleeping," she said as tears slowly crept down her high cheekbones and dripped off her round, dimpled chin. "I was on the floor at the foot of their bed. When he touched my lips, I wanted to bite him and scream, but I couldn't." Her soft voice faltered as she spoke. "Oh, God, I was so scared, Deke."

Darius's heart was breaking. He wondered why her cousins hadn't come to her aid. He could see unspeakable sadness etched on Sarah's face. She'd always been so strong. Even when some "friend" hit her, she wouldn't cry. It was apparent that she'd held back her pain for far too long. Rain angrily beat against the window as she took a deep breath, let it out, and tried to resume the narrative. Her words tumbled incoherently, like a deck of cards tossed into the air. She buried her face into Darius's chest and moaned.

"Baby, it hurts so bad. That summer was terrible, it destroyed me. I should've never gone."

She was gasping like a catfish on the ground and her pint-sized shoulders shook like a cube of Jell-O. Darius felt demons fighting some great battle inside her and she was the sacrificial fodder they offered to Satan. He held her tightly, and they cried together.

How could anybody have hurt Momma this much?

After a couple of minutes, Sarah's sobs ceased. The rain had subsided, and it was now a soft pitter-patter on the tin roof as Sarah resumed the tale of that awful summer.

"I prayed, but God wasn't listening. I begged Ma'Dear to come get me. By the time she did get me it was too late."

Darius buried his face in her hair.

If any man ever touches a hair of your head again, I'll kill him. Darius knew a man had to do what a man had to do.

"Deke, I'm ashamed. Please forgive me for not being a good mother and doing bad things. I'm so proud that you keep doing right, even when Momma's doing wrong."

The wind picked back up. Sarah sniffled and got up. She paced for a few moments before stopping in front of the sink. Hail began dancing on the roof. *Clack, clack, clickety, clickety, clack, clack* — the pea-size hail bounced on the tin roof. She ripped a paper towel from the roll sitting on the countertop and used it to blow her nose. "I should've resisted more. But I didn't. I couldn't."

Darius walked to her side at the window and put his arms around her thin waist. She leaned her head on Darius's shoulder.

"Momma, you were scared and didn't know what to do," Darius said as they both looked out the window.

"Ma'Dear was ashamed of me when I was pregnant." Sarah sighed and leaned against the cabinet as if it were supporting her weight.

Darius scratched the back of his head and asked how she knew which one his father was.

"Albert used a rubber when he raped me."

Darius just wanted to make sure.

"I started acting up and flunking school, drinking and using drugs. Ma'Dear said I went to the dog's vomit. She eventually made Daddy put me out of the house." Sarah sniffled and blew her nose again. Then a scowl crossed her face.

"I fell into my black hole." Sarah turned from the window, obviously angry with life. She walked toward the living room but paused at the opening between the two rooms and turned toward Darius. "I've been messed up in so many ways ever since and trying to do better, but I keep slipping back. In physics, they say once you cross the event horizon, you can never come out. Marcus said the same thing happened to him."

Darius didn't know where the Marcus comment came from or what it had to do with his momma. He sure as hell knew nothing of event horizons. Darius ignored the mention of the despised name. "One day you'll come out, Momma. I know it."

"Thanks for being here for me, Deke. I'm going to lie down with a book for a while."

Darius looked out the window. The thunderstorm appeared to have ended. He saw a rainbow in the east and wondered if this was a sign of better things to come. Suddenly there was a loud thunderclap behind him. Perhaps, the rainbow was premature, he thought.

"I'm going to buy you a fancy house someday, Momma," Darius said to his momma.

"Maybe when you get to the NBA, you can buy me one of these Berwick houses."

They'd just left from picnicking at Lake End Park on Lake Palourde. Sarah had taken the route home along Spanish Trail Road, so they could admire the mansions behind stone walls. Her hair danced across her face as the car windows were down because the air conditioning didn't work. Darius played wind games with his right hand outside his window. She slowed down and then parked across from an estate where peaches lay on the ground outside a stone fence.

"I'm going to grab a few peaches from the ground," Sarah said, "but you stay in the car."

There was a loud combustion pop as Sarah turned the motor off.

"These sounds of the hood are brought to the fine folks of Berwick by the engineers of Ford Motor Company," Darius said as if he were introducing a commercial.

"Deke, you're something else!" Sarah grinned at her son's theatrics.

There's that beautiful smile, Darius thought.

Sarah walked around fire-ant beds to the perfectly manicured grass on the other side of the road. She'd half-filled a plastic shopping bag with peaches when a silver Mercedes-Benz SUV drove up to the gate. Darius clearly heard the voices.

"Ma'am, can I help you?" the man said as he partially lowered his tinted window. To Darius, it seemed the translation was, "What are you doing here?"

"I'm just getting some peaches from the ground for my boy," Sarah said.

"Well, you are on private property."

"That is not accurate, Poppa," chimed a voice from behind the tinted windows. "The lady is on the public right-of-way and is within her rights to be there."

The passenger door flew opened, and out tumbled a little girl with pigtails of red hair.

"Hello, I am Evelyn Kingsley." The precocious little girl reached her hand out to shake Sarah's hand. After a quick shake, she laughed and then, seeming to bounce with each step, practically forced Sarah to run with her to the stone wall. She inspected a few peaches, tossed them, and then scaled to the top of the wall like a squirrel.

Somebody had too much sugar this morning, Darius thought.

"Princess, get off that wall before you hurt yourself, and your mother kills me," the voice said from inside the Mercedes.

Evelyn tiptoed on the wall and reached out to pick three big ripe peaches off the tree, all her little hands could hold. Without hesitation, she jumped from the wall. She'd made it look as easy as shooting free throws. She ran to Sarah and put the fruit in her bag. "Handpicked from the tree is always better than from the ground," the girl said with a smile. "Tell your son I picked these for him. He can repay my generosity by helping somebody in need someday. Then we will be squared." The little girl looked Darius's way, but he didn't think she saw him.

"Thank you very much," Sarah said.

"Princess, get back in this vehicle, now." The grumpy man tooted the horn.

"Have a blessed day, ma'am." Evelyn turned, waved and smiled at Sarah as she hopped back into the Mercedes which slowly passed to the other side of the stone walls. Evelyn waved her hand out the window as the gates closed behind the car.

That girl is unusual, Darius thought. *She seems really nice—especially for a rich girl.*

"Let's go to the Shrimp and Petroleum Festival," Sarah told Darius a few weeks later, on the Friday before Labor Day. "I want to celebrate two months of no drugs with my baby."

"I'm not a baby, Momma. I'm a man." Darius, now sixteen, stretched out his six-foot frame and towered over his dainty momma. He didn't argue what he knew was an inaccurate assertion. She'd used drugs a couple of times in recent weeks, but there had been no overnight binges. Her demons remained unconquered, but he was glad she hadn't given up fighting.

Sarah tousled Darius's hair. "Can you hang four days with your momma?"

"If you think you can hang with the Dekester, let's roll." They took the thirty-minute drive to Morgan City, where Sarah parked the Ford under the highway overpass.

"I hope the pigeon shit doesn't mess up the paint job," Darius said.

"Watch your language, silly." Sarah laughed as she patted him on the backside of his loose-fitting jeans. "You ain't too old for me to spank even if you have those big muscles ripping out of your Michael Jordan jersey." The remarks on his physique pleased Darius.

Sarah wore a mauve pullover shirt, airbrushed in candy apple red were the words: *World's Greatest Mom*. Darius had saved up money from cutting grass and bought her the shirt for Mother's Day. She was wearing that hat she bought from the thrift store that she claimed made her look like a rich woman.

She strutted down the sidewalk in snuggly-fit jeans hugging her shapely hips that swung from side to side as she walked. He was walking with the most beautiful woman at the festival—even more beautiful than she looked in that photograph, more bootylicious than even Beyoncé. They walked hand-in-hand, laughing and joking and singing with each other. She appeared to ignore the whistles and turned heads, but Darius knew she noticed.

Sweat beaded on their faces by the time they reached free concert's makeshift outdoor stage. Despite the late afternoon heat and humidity, there were twenty or more couples dancing in the barricaded street that ran parallel to the river. Darius and Sarah joined them.

As they shared their first-ever dance together, the world seemed perfect. Darius twirled his momma around, and she spun on her toes with magical grace. When the song ended, he dipped her. She grabbed her hat to keep it from falling off, and then he pulled her up and bowed.

"Deke, you're really a great dancer," Sarah said. "That was wonderful. Let's get some cotton candy and see what other surprises you have in store for me."

Darius left to buy two cotton candies while Sarah went to use one of the blue portable toilets. With a sticky treat in each hand, Darius turned to walk back to where he'd left his momma. A little red-haired girl crossed his path, walking with a gentleman—perhaps her grandfather. She carried a green bejeweled backpack from which a pink purse fell to the ground.

Darius walked a few steps out of his way and picked it up. The name Evelyn Kingsley was imprinted on it. For a moment, he considered keeping it. Obviously, this girl wouldn't be hurt if she lost whatever money the purse might contain. But Lawrence's voice started to echo through his head: "Your character is what you do when no one sees you doin' the right thing."

Darius called out to the man and handed him the purse.

"Thank you, son. I am sure your parents are proud of you. It would be a pleasure to meet them."

"I'm looking for my momma. She went to go pee."

"You could have lost this for good, if it were not for this fine young man," the man said as he handed the purse back to the girl.

"Thank you," the little girl said to Darius. She appeared to be in a hurry to get to the Ferris wheel. Darius recognized her as the little red-head who'd come to his momma's defense and had walked that stone fence to handpick him some peaches. He was glad that he hadn't kept the purse. But they weren't squared just yet. He hadn't come to the aid of someone in need.

The man reached into his pocket to offer Darius a reward from a wad of bills in a gold clip. Darius recognized that voice—this was the grumpy geezer who tried to keep his momma from gathering peaches on the side of the road.

Now he wants to rub his money in my face and toss me a few dollars.

"No, thanks. I gotta go." Darius turned and left to find his momma, so they could eat their treats and then share some more dancing. He didn't tell her that he'd crossed paths with the rich peaches family.

As they left the festival on Sunday night, Sarah ran into an old friend who had had a crush on her in the eighth grade. She encouraged him to come see her sometime. He didn't wait long. He was at her door Monday morning and persuaded her to spend the afternoon with him. Sarah and her friend went to the park where Darius was shooting hoops.

"I'm going to Bayou Vista with my friend for a while," she told Darius. "I'll be back in time for us to go to the festival tonight."

She didn't return that evening. She came home Thursday for a few hours and then she was gone for the weekend. After a week-long drug binge, there was no question that Sarah had fallen off the wagon.

CHAPTER 6
SPRING 2003

"Why do you steal from Mr. L and Miss E?" Darius asked Walter. "They'd probably give you money if you asked."

It was a clear spring afternoon. The temperature approached eighty degrees, with robins forming a slow-moving orange carpet over the playground. The pair was shooting hoops when Darius asked about the thievery he'd been observing during the past year.

"Why ask for what I can take? It's better to steal than to beg." Walter tossed the basketball to Darius to check the ball into play.

"That's messed up, bro. That's your gramps." Darius tossed the ball back to Walter. "And Miss E has Parkington. She's dying, and you stealing her money."

"That don't kill nobody, dummy. It just makes 'em shake. Them old people be happy just to collect cans, eat, shit, and watch TV." Walter dribbled between his legs, pulled up, and canned a twenty-footer over Darius's extended arms. The ball swished through the net, never touching the rim. "That's my ticket out the hood, nigga!"

"It's whack to steal from your own blood, man." Darius tossed the ball to Walter.

"This is the four-one-one ya don't know." Walter set the ball down and sat on it. "Snaggletooth has thousands of dollars. He got two kids, Momma and Auntie. We strugglin' and ain't seen no money. They got a stash somewhere in that house, and one day, Imma find it."

"Why won't he give y'all any money?"

"He say Momma and Auntie disgraced 'em twenty years ago or some-thin'. He is the disgrace, leavin' his wife and kids for that white trash. I take what I can, when I can. That's life, bro. Welcome to the hood."

Walter stood up and tossed the basketball to Darius. "Check ball. Do or die. Game-point, nigga." Darius bounced the ball back to Walter, who dribbled to his left, spun to his right, then blew past Darius for a layup. "Game over, homeboy. No charge for the schoolin'. I gotta jet. I got people to see and places to go. Latah."

Darius dribbled the ball and shook his head at Walter's selfishness. Besides his momma, the Browns were the only ones who genuinely cared about him. Darius sensed he was nearing a fork in the road, when loyalty to his peer would have to yield to his affection for his elderly friends.

A few weeks later, on a late-May afternoon, Darius was sitting on the Browns' front porch, his long legs occasionally scuffing the ground as they swung back and forth. Behind him, Lawrence was rocking slowly in the handmade cypress rocking chair Emily bought him years ago. He'd gathered sticks from under the pecan tree that dominated his front yard and piled them under his chair. He began idly whittling the twigs with his four-inch Pioneer Old Timer.

A light southerly breeze blew; the kind of breeze that did little to minimize the heat but was enough to pick up the distinct seafood scent of the marsh. Residents knew it as the comforting smell of home. Visitors sometimes thought it smelled of something dead.

Miss E was baking another of those apple pies that Darius loved. The aroma of apples, cinnamon, and fresh-baked pie crust drifted out the front door. He leaned back on a post and tossed small rocks at a 7-Up can in the yard. His imagination floated on the stream of stories Mr. L told; his tummy rumbled in anticipation of Miss E's apple pie and a glass of iced milk.

Darius saw Walter coming up the road, throwing rocks at any dog foolish enough not to hide. When Walter strolled into the yard, he kicked the 7-Up can into the ditch and Darius playfully tossed a rock in his direction. Walter wasted no time in getting to the point.

"Momma be needin' a grand to get another ride, but she won't ask ya. Will ya loan her the dough if she promise to pay ya back?" He explained that someone stole her car.

"You know me and your momma ain't on no speakin' terms," the old man curtly replied. "Even if I had the money, it's not likely I'd give it to her."

"Whatever. Ya just too tight." Then, looking at Darius, he spat out, "So much for askin'. Latah, Darius. I got some biz to tend to." Walter walked away, mumbling and raising his right hand with his middle finger extended. Lawrence never stopped whittling as he changed the conversation to a stray dog that had been barking last night.

"Mr. L, can I ask you what happened between you and Walter's momma and auntie?" Darius felt bad for asking, but he wanted to know the entire story.

"Well, boy, that was a long time ago. I got me a job down at the shipyard to operate one of them forklifts. About that time, I was sweet on this girl named Rosa Mae and we got hitched."

Darius used his hand to shield his eyes from the sun as he watched honeybees drift from flower to flower in the rosebushes on the side of the porch. Nearby, mockingbirds sorted through their whistles. A brown shorthaired dog meandered along the street, sniffing for a morsel to scavenge. The scrawny stray wagged his tail in an open solicitation of fellowship.

Lawrence said he steered his forklift in front of a rack of five-hundred-pound pipes breaking loose from their constraints, redirecting tons of steel away from two dozen workers ten feet below. He was injured when his forklift was pushed from the second floor. The company gave him a small settlement.

"What does that have to do with Walter's momma and auntie not speaking with you?"

"Be patient, boy. Let me tell the story." Lawrence paused from rocking in his chair and patted Darius's knee with fingers gnarled from arthritis. He squinted and stared for a moment at the porch ceiling with its cracking paint, as if channeling distant memories from above his head. He picked up another stick to whittle and resumed his story.

"My wife, Rosa Mae, she gets this harebrained idea to go to Vegas without me and blows half the money. That changed the whole picture." Lawrence grabbed the end of his barely-whittled stick and threw it at the hungry dog making his way across the yard next door. "Get outta here, mutt, and take all that yelpin' with you." The stray trotted away from the yard.

"I told her I be wantin' a divorce. I just couldn't forgive her. I shoulda, but I didn't. So we gets a divorce, and she gets half of what's left and custody of them girls."

"Wow, that sucks!" Darius picked up one of the longer twigs and began scrawling doodles in the dirt.

"Emily came along and starts to take care of me and we falls in love and gets married. When my money ran out, all we gots is a gummint check and each other."

"Why are you mad at your daughters?" Darius asked as he swatted the stick back and forth, sending a bee to another flower.

"Well, Rosa Mae, she be tellin' them that I kept all the money and divorced her, so I could shack up with a white woman." Lawrence laughed derisively.

"The bitch was wrong for that!"

Lawrence reached as far as he could with his cane and gently tapped Darius on the shoulder three times in obvious disapproval. "Yeah, she was, but don't call no woman a bitch, boy. Your momma oughta taught you better than that."

"Okay, I'm sorry."

"Them girls came here when they in high school and spray-paint *white whore* on the house; again and again. Finally, I gots me a 'strainin' order. I told 'em 'till they 'pologize to Emily, I never wanna speak to 'em again. I ain't never heard that 'pology, and I ain't spoke to 'em since."

"Now stuff makes sense. I should let you know Walter's been stealing from Miss E's purse. I know I should've told you a long time ago."

"We know, boy. I saw you that first day takin' my woman's purse from Walter. I knew then, that you gonna make a fine man."

"I would never steal from you and Miss E. Maybe from those rich people on the other end of town, but not from y'all." Darius grinned.

"You make sure you do what's right, even when ain't nobody lookin' at you. And that 'cludes leavin' them white folks' stuff alone, too."

Darius thought about telling how he'd given that white girl her purse back, but figured that bragging about doing the right thing wouldn't impress Mr. L.

"Which one of you two fine men want a piece of this old lady's apple pie?" Emily had come to the front door with a tray in her trembling hands. The tray held two saucers with hot pie on them and a glass of milk with ice in it for Darius.

"Whatcha think, boy? You think that pie will be any good?"

"It's the best I ever had," Darius said as he quickly reached for his slice and the glass of milk. "Thank you, Miss E. Can I have a second slice, too?"

"Finish that first piece, son," she said. "And then we'll see. But you should save some for tomorrow, cuz I ain't got 'nough 'gredients to make another one."

Darius was dribbling his basketball around his back and between his legs as he headed home. He crossed paths with Walter and asked if he wanted to shoot the rock.

"Naw, bro. I'm headed over to my cousin Ronald's house. We gotta talk 'bout some family stuff. I gotta hustle some money for my momma to get her a car." Walter was twirling a baseball bat in one hand and flicking a flashlight off and on in the other.

Darius offered condolences for Walter's family.

"We wouldn't be like this if the old fart wouldn't be so selfish with his money."

"You really need to back off your gramps. He's cool, and so is Miss E . . ."

"That bitch ain't nothin' but a whore home-wrecker," Walter said. "And Grandpa ain't nothin' but an Uncle Tom."

"Bro, you ought not talk about them like that." Darius saw his friendship with this little hood-rat was about over. If Walter kept talking like this, it might end with fisticuffs.

Walter was in no mood for the bullshit Darius was trying to feed him. He walked to Ronald's house to plan a robbery of the Browns. He was determined to locate the hidden cash and ensure there would be no surviving witnesses.

Ronald was seventeen, short and rippling with muscles toned from daily workouts on weights. He lived with his mother who worked two part-time jobs and was seldom home. He'd quit school, where he'd been labeled as retarded; no one turned him in for truancy. Walter was the alpha between the two; when Walter proposed robbing their grandparents, Ronald agreed.

Sometime after midnight, the two boys crept toward the Browns' house. Walter had his bat. Ronald had an iron pipe. Each carried a flashlight. As they neared the Browns' yard, they startled the stray dog scavenging through a knocked-over garbage can. Barking, the dog tucked his tail and ran. The malevolent duo waited a few minutes to make sure no one had woken.

Walter sent Ronald to the back of the house to yank the main breaker from the service box, turning off the electricity to the house; everything inside went black. Using a swiped key, Walter open the door and walked straight to where Emily slept in her arm chair. He shoved her with his bat.

She woke up, staring into the flashlight. "What's going on? Who's there? Larry!" Walter swung his bat, striking her head. Her dentures flew from her mouth; Walter felt her blood spatter on his shirt. He looked to his right and saw his cousin making short work with ending the life of their grandfather.

Ronald brought the pipe down from above his head, smashing into the top of Lawrence's skull. Lawrence's head fell forward, but his body stayed in his chair. Ronald brought a second blow down to the back of Lawrence's skull. The old man fell flat on his face in front of his chair.

Walter shined his light on Emily's face. Emily's right hand slowly rose in front of her face as Walter brought the bat back from the other side. Emily partially raised herself with her left hand before the second swing of the bat sent her falling backward into her chair.

"Ol' woman is a tough cooter," Walter said.

"Bro, ya really a friggin' animal," Ronald said in admiration.

"It's time for the treasure hunt now, Ronnie. Go outside and turn the lights back on."

"Oh man, ya ain't gonna like this." Ronald grinned. "I threw the breaker thing over the back fence!"

"Stupid ass! Why did ya do that?"

"I didn't want nobody turnin' the lights back on while we was in here," Ronald said.

"Dammit, Ronald! How we gonna search for the money? Get ya flashlight and look around and see what ya can find. Grandpa always be keepin' money in his pockets. Imma get that, at least."

Sirens were beginning to wail in the distance.

"Somebody musta called the cops," Walter said. They fled with no cash.

The next morning, after he finished off a dry bowl of Fruit Loops—they were out of milk again—Darius grabbed his basketball, tucked it under his arm, and jumped off the porch of the empty house. As he dribbled down the street, he saw new beer cans added to the litter collection along the road and in the open ditch, as was usual for Friday and Saturday nights.

He was going by the Browns' to grab a slice of Miss E's pie and maybe listen to a quick Mr. L story before hitting the court. When he got on the Browns' lane, he saw police tape around their house.

Who would've robbed them? Everybody knows they ain't got no money!

There was only one person who could think the Browns had money, Darius realized. He quickened his pace to a trot. The police were going in and out of the house with gloves on. Darius saw the scrawny mutt lying quietly under the pecan tree in the front yard. A few people gathered on the edges of the yellow tape. The dog stared, tail barely moving.

"Dog, you better get out of here before Mr. L sees you. He won't be in a good mood." Darius stopped at the edge of the tape. He thought the lady nearby might give him some details.

"Somebody killed him and his wife last night," the woman said.

"What? No! Why would someone do that?"

"They was robbed," the lady said. "Somebody called the cops when they heard a dog barking and looked out their window. They saw two people in front of the house and a couple minutes later, poof, all the lights went out."

"It was Walter, wasn't it?" Darius mouthed the words to the dog, which got up and walked around to the back of the house. *You did your job, old boy.*

Darius's seething anger percolated into a hatred. Walter was no better than GP; maybe he was worse. Within days, Walter and Ronald were arrested by Franklin police. Darius thought they should get the death penalty for killing the Browns, who were his only friends. *Life is just too cheap in the hood*, he thought.

"Momma, I thought you said there was not as much crime down here as in DC," Evelyn, now twelve, said at supper. She had just read about the Browns' murder.

"Did it happen on de West End?" Martha asked, nodding in the direction of the newspaper. The headline read, *Brutal double slaying brings parish homicide total to 11.*

"Yes, ma'am," Evelyn said as she walked across the kitchen to get the dessert, the first pecan pie she'd ever made.

Peter savored his last bite of the tender veal. "I will take a slice of that pecan pie, Princess." He pushed his plate away and pointed at a pie on the other end of the table.

"Dat's why we stay on dis end of de parish, *cher*, away from all dat trouble on de West End." Martha took a sip of her Chardonnay.

"There is killing over here, too, Momma." Evelyn set a slice of pie in a saucer for her father. "A few months ago, that man shot his wife in front of their kids and then killed himself. And another guy killed his roommate with a guitar during an argument. Those were over here."

"Well, it ain't as bad as dem West End people," Martha said. She declined a slice of pie, saying she was sticking to her diet.

Peter let out a howl. "Yummy to the tummy, Princess. This pecan pie is superlative."

Evelyn suspected she could bake rocks and he would say they were cooked to perfection. She returned to what Martha said about West End criminal activity. She thought such generalization was prejudicial and found its acceptance unpalatable.

"Remember the school teacher who stole sixty-thousand dollars from the children's field trip fund and blamed it on a gambling problem? She lives here in Berwick. The same thing with that judge's clerk who was arrested in her Mercedes after embezzling thirty-five thousand dollars. Rich East End people are breaking the law, too."

"True," Peter said. "The difference is that these people have money to get a good attorney and stay out of jail and get their records expunged."

Martha shook her head as she rose from the table and made her way toward the piano. There on top of the piano, she opened a fancy box that arrived by delivery earlier in the afternoon. She took out a royal red hat with violet plumes and a golden headband. She gently placed the hat on her head and gazed into the eight-foot wall mirror behind the piano.

"What you t'ink of my hat dat I ordered from Macy's, Petey? I got it on sale for only two hundred dollars. I want to wear it Sunday for Mass wit' my new dress."

"It looks good, Marty, but did you not just get a new hat for Easter?"

"Yeah, but I want anot'er one to celebrate de fifteen pounds I lost. I got you one, too, Evelyn. Let's go upstairs and see how well we match."

CHAPTER 7
SEPTEMBER 9-11, 2004

Even after the passing of a year, Darius still felt an emptiness from the loss of the Browns. They were the first positive thing he'd had in his life. Now the greatest negative thing had returned.

Darius was piqued over Marcus moving back in after his early release from the state pen in Angola. He wondered how the dope dealer could get out after serving so little time. He also wondered if his momma had been waiting for Marcus's return all this time. Now seventeen, Darius had had enough of his momma's bad choices. He rebelled by refusing to go to school in his senior year.

One muggy afternoon after he finished mowing the grass, Darius was sitting on the steps when his momma joined him and handed him a plastic glass of lemonade. He brought up Marcus's presence.

"You won't get clean with him around," Darius insisted.

"Deke, I'm going to get clean, I promise," Sarah said as she put her arm around him. "Angola is hard on a man. He just needs a place to stay for the time being."

"He's going hurt you, and then I'll kill him. And it's going to be your fault!" Darius was uncomfortable upbraiding his momma, but some things had to be said.

They sat in silence on the porch for a minute as he gulped down his lemonade. It was one of those hot days when you could fry an egg on the hood of a car. Sarah handed him a clean shirt as she refilled his glass. She chased away horseflies intent on landing on Darius's shoulders. He brushed grass from his shoulders as he put his clean shirt on.

"I can take care of myself, son. You need to start going back to school."

Sarah was pleading, not demanding. She'd often said that a lack of education contributed to her being unable to get a good job. Darius thought it was more likely alcohol and drugs.

"I'm emancipated, remember?" Darius said. "I can quit school and leave home. And I'll do that if you let him stay here." Sarah had gone with him the previous year to get a notarized statement of emancipation in case something happened to her.

"How does a man get out of prison and find another red Mustang GT, but not find a place to lay his head? Evidently drug dealers have a different system of finances. I'm not going back to school until he finds a different place to stay."

"I don't want you to be like me, baby. Please, promise your momma you'll finish school. Promise me you'll make something of your life and your children will be proud of you." Sarah gently brushed away some grass out of his braided hair. She swatted at the horseflies again, and they seemed to finally give up.

"Okay, Momma. I'll make something of my life and make my kids proud. I'll go back to school, but you have to put him out. I'll start tomorrow if you tell him to leave this weekend."

"Marcus went to New Orleans for business. I'll tell him to find a new place when he gets back." Sarah hugged her son, got up slowly—perhaps sadly—and walked back into the house.

Darius knew what kind of business Marcus had in New Orleans. It wasn't likely going to earn him "Businessman of the Year" from the chamber of commerce.

The horseflies began to circle Darius again before finally land-ing on him. He slapped the back of his neck. Looking at the smashed insects in the palm of his hand, he pondered how quickly life can end. He wondered if he could do the same to Marcus if he had to.

He looked up the street, about a half block down, to a vacant house with a *For Rent* sign in the window. He spotted the brown masked mutt from the Browns' sitting on the corner of the house. The dog had been there since the Browns' killing as if it was watching over him.

"Now there's a survivor for you, Godzillard Pigenstein!" Darius said. He whistled for the dog, but as usual it just got up and crawled under the vacant house. Darius got up to shower. Sarah gave him a quick kiss as he walked past her and told him she was going to the store.

Marcus spent two days in New Orleans tending to business—renewing old and making new contacts and rebuilding his street cred—with new players and apparently new rules. Street-level drug dealing had changed. It was now populated by cutthroat hoodlums who couldn't find honor in a dictionary, even if you opened it up to the definition's page for them.

Everything was cool with his old supply of Columbian powder packaged in a shipment of coffee and routed through Jamaica. Marcus knew some low-paid customs agents who could be induced into look-ing away and expediting certain containers.

His former weed supplier was serving a life sentence after a third conviction for distribution. Someone suggested Marcus meet a fellow in the housing projects he'd lived in a decade ago. He went there and was introduced to a small man with a Jheri curl who came to the Big Easy from Miami back in the '90s and called himself Keelo. He wore ostrich-skin boots and had more bling in his teeth than Mr. T wore around his neck.

They met on the isolated backside of a ten-building cluster. It was a good place to conduct illicit business. After the deal, Keelo left in a Hummer while Marcus got into the GT. As he approached the front of the projects, a group of bandana-wearing thugs flagged him down. Something told him not to stop, but he did. Not heeding his sixth sense seldom worked out well.

"What's up, white boy?" a man with a Jamaican accent asked.

Marcus scanned this dude to surmise what sort of predicament he might be in. The Jamaican's appearance suggested he hadn't been handed anything on a silver platter. There was a scar running from just under his right eye, across his cheek, and into his lip. There were tattoos on his neck and his arms. He was missing parts of two fingers on his right hand. Marcus knew these guys weren't inviting him for tea and crumpets.

"It's all cool in hell, bro," Marcus said. "Just passing through on business."

A pair of the guys stepped in front of his car; in the rearview mirror, he saw two more on the backside and a final man alongside his passenger door. The shit was in the toilet and it was just a matter of where it was going after the flushing.

"I been in Angola, and I'm just getting back into business." Marcus hoped that letting these guys know he'd done hard time, they would realize they weren't messing with a punk. "My boy Keelo sold me some—"

"Get outta the car, cwacker, and shut ya damn mouf up," Scarface demanded with a lisp.

So much for exchanging Christmas cards next year.

He'd passed through the Gates of Hell and the Devil was demanding his due. Getting out alive was going to be a crapshoot. He believed these guys planned to rob and kill him right there. His gun wasn't within reach—a tactical blunder. He knew better than to make those kinds of blunders when survival had a zero tolerance for slip-ups. In this business, you never planned for *if*; you always planned for *when*.

"Your Momma," Marcus shouted as he spat at Scarface and rammed the shift into gear. He floored the accelerator hoping he could dodge the bullets until reaching North Villere Street, from where he'd entered this loop of buildings. If he could get there and then onto Conti Street and out to North Claiborne Avenue, he would survive— but that was a huge *if*.

Driving with his head ducked just below the dashboard, he felt the Mustang's wheels roll over the unlucky hoodlums in front. He heard the *pop-pop-pop* as bullets ripped into the metal of the car and the sound of glass shattering. Then the GT bounced up. He lifted his head in time to see he was headed into one of the buildings. He swerved back onto the pavement, ducked again and headed away from trouble. In less than a minute, he was driving in relative safety on Claiborne.

How dumb could these bastards be to try to rob him in a car before he got out? They didn't even have a car to chase him! Marcus was convinced this bushwhacking wasn't coincidental. Had he been set up by Keelo? Or was he just a white boy in the wrong place at the wrong time? Could anyone be trusted? What were the rules?

Marcus was pissed. He had bullet holes in his car, and the back windshield was blasted out, but knew he was lucky to still be sucking oxygen. He had no idea how seriously he'd injured the hapless fools he ran over, but he didn't care. They brought it on themselves.

This was still a dog-eat-dog world, but he'd survive. You have to figure out if you were messing with pit bulls, Dobermans, or wolves. One thing was obvious: these New Orleans biscuit-eaters weren't poodles. Then again, neither was he.

Sarah hadn't returned home Thursday. Still, Darius returned to school on Friday. He hoped his momma would live up to her end of the bargain. As he got off the bus after his first day back at school, he noticed the old clunker was gone.

The car hadn't cranked Thursday when Sarah left. It was odd that she'd come home during the day and then left in the car. He walked inside and fixed himself a peanut butter sandwich. There was neither milk nor Thunderbird in the refrigerator. He walked to the sink and filled a glass with water. Passing the fridge again, he reached up and pulled down that old Polaroid he'd looked at hundreds of times. He gingerly fingered the photograph and went to the table with it in his hand.

He stared through the kitchen window, thinking that after finishing high school he'd go to the trade school in Morgan City and then get a job welding in one of the shipyards. He'd move them out of this rat-hole neighborhood, perhaps to a nice subdivision in Morgan City.

"We have to get rid of that New Orleans trash before he messes your life up worse than it already is," he said to the photograph. He set the photograph back on top of the refrigerator. To his right he saw a stack of papers on the countertop.

A knock startled Darius. He stepped to the front of the house and opened the door for a young, tall, and slender priest with blond hair and soft blue eyes, and a warm, friendly smile. Without the collar, he would've looked more like a preppy college student than a priest. His soft, boyish face and fair skin made him look out of place in this neighborhood.

"I'm Father Brian Sorenson. Is Miss Sarah LeBeaux in?"

What is a white priest doing on our porch asking for Momma?

"I met your mother last night at the church," the priest said after Darius told him Sarah wasn't home. "I gave her some forms. She told me to come by today and pick them up."

A priest meeting his momma on a Thursday night—Ladies Night at Whiskey Hollow? That was about as likely as a black man getting elected president, Darius thought. "Umm, she didn't mention it," Darius said, scratching his head. "Why would you give her paperwork? I know she wasn't joining your church."

"It wasn't about church," the priest answered. "I'm involved in an organization that offers counseling and helps locate social programs."

Darius remembered the papers on the counter and invited the priest to follow him to the kitchen. He saw they were for admittance into a drug treatment facility and a GED program.

"This is it," the young priest said. "And it's completed. May I take these? These other ones are her copies."

"Yeah, I guess so," Darius said. "Tell me again, how did you meet Momma?"

The priest paused, perhaps pondering how much he should tell Darius. "It's not like she was in confession where I have to keep her confidence, but I do want to respect her privacy."

"Momma's not Catholic, and we share everything. I know everything about her."

"Your mother said she was on her way to the store last night," the priest explained. "She said she'd passed the church hundreds of times. This time, she told me, she remembered her mother used to say, 'God is bigger than any problem you'll ever face,' and she decided to put that to the test."

"Momma's not very big on God because he failed to protect her. But she's been trying to get help to stop making bad choices."

"I told your mother to pray to God, and he would carry her cross."

"Father, I think the Lord forgot to pick up that cross. She never came home last night. My guess would be that she's drunk or high somewhere and will be high until the weekend's over."

"I can't tell you where your mother is right now," the priest said, putting his hand on Darius's shoulder. "But when I arrived early this morning, she was rising from prayer."

"All night in church? My momma? Father, have you been drinking?" Darius led the priest back to the front door.

"No, my son, I haven't. Your mother was there all night."

"That might explain her coming home and getting the car. But I'm not so confident she isn't high as we speak, despite spending the night with Jesus."

"She took these forms for programs to turn her life around. I believe that's her intention."

Despite what the priest said, Darius knew his momma's history. He didn't want to spend the weekend alone, so he thought about Ricardo Ortiz, whom he'd met last weekend at the festival. Ricardo had told Darius to call him if he ever wanted to hang out in Morgan City. He even said he'd hook Darius up with a fine *señorita*.

Ricardo didn't brag about it, but neither did he hide that he and a couple of "*gringo hombres*" supported themselves by walking on the other side of the law. Darius found him to be confident, but not arrogant, with a magnetic personality. He was quick with a friendly slap on the back and always smiling, always ready to crack a joke. He was undocumented, but it didn't matter to Darius, who figured that where a man was born didn't make him a good or bad person. In his view, a friendly Mexican was better than an abusive American any day.

Darius called the number he'd written on a small piece of paper he stuffed into his wallet. An hour later, Ricardo was honking the horn of his Suburban in Darius's driveway, smiling like a Cheshire cat and in the company of two knockout Latinas—one in the front and another in the back seat. Ricardo got out of the Suburban wearing a black fedora with a red feather in the purple band. He removed his top piece and bowed his head slightly.

"Did you call a taxi, *amigo?*" he asked in exaggerated subservience. He opened the back door for Darius to get inside. "Please notice the fine *señorita*, compliments of the chauffeur."

"Bro, you missed your calling to the clownhood," Darius said as he playfully shoved Ricardo.

"Be careful ya don't knock my style off my head, homie," Ricardo said with a grin, "or I'll hafta put a cap in ya *culo*."

Darius sat beside a dark-haired, dark-eyed woman in the backseat. As the Suburban backed out of the driveway, Darius glanced through his window and saw the droopy-eyed mutt lying on the corner of the vacant house. The dog raised his head, and his eyes followed the Suburban.

"Juanita is for me, but Nina can be your date tonight," Ricardo said, looking in the rearview mirror as Nina placed her hand in Darius's hand.

Darius looked at his date and wondered if he'd won the lottery. Her olive skin and long black hair streaked with brown highlights along with her smooth, perfect complexion was much like his momma's. Darius learned that both girls were twenty, also illegally in the States—but again, why should that matter?

"There is a sense of intrigue in your hazel eyes and good looks," Nina said. She grinned and put Darius's arm around her as she leaned into his shoulder. "Me and Juanita live in a little trailer not far from Ricardo. Maybe you can come visit sometime." If Nina's flirtation was meant to make Darius desire her, it was succeeding.

The foursome watched *The Day After Tomorrow* at the theater in Morgan City, and then had a late meal at Shoney's a couple of blocks from the theater. Ricardo paid everybody's way into the movie and for their food.

Nina ambulated with a limp and leaned heavily on Darius as they walked together. It wasn't just for the physical closeness but also because as Nina explained it, she'd had her ankle shattered in her childhood. She didn't say much more about the experience, and Darius didn't ask.

Darius stayed at Ricardo's uncle's house that night. His uncle told him that if he wanted to be a welder, he'd help him get a job at Conner's Shipyard, where he was a supervisor. Then on Saturday morning, the foursome went to Cypermort Point State Park for fun in the sun on the beach of the bay where the Atchafalaya River emptied into the Gulf. With Nina in his arms, a beer in his hand, and friends to party with, Darius put Marcus and all the other hellish troubles of his life out of mind.

Marcus decided he needed to set up business in St. Mary Parish and not the Big Easy. While there was an unending market for drugs in the big city, it wasn't worth the drama. He'd resume where he'd left off before that episode with the Patterson cops sent him to prison. He was physically and mentally exhausted by the time he drove his shot-up Mustang back to Franklin.

Sarah claimed to have waited for him to get out of prison, but he doubted she was being truthful. In any case, he was glad she'd let him come back to stay with her after his stretch in the pen. He'd paid his debt to society and was ready to get on with the rest of his life. As he pulled into the Hawk Street driveway, he noticed that her Ford was gone.

Crazy *bitch probably gone for her weekend drug binge.*

CHAPTER 8
SEPTEMBER 11, 2004

Yellow police tape fluttered in the breeze at the end of Hawk Street.

Darius saw a crowd milling around near the end of his four-block street. The old clunker was parked in his yard, but so were two police units, with two more units parked on the street. His eyes confirmed what his heart didn't want to believe—something terrible had happened at his house. He felt his chest tighten and his heart seemed ready to explode as it raced faster than Usain Bolt. He bailed out of the Suburban before it rolled to a stop behind one of the police units.

"I'm gonna kill the bastard!" Darius screamed shaking his clinched fists. His beeline to the house was aborted by a Franklin Police sergeant. The policeman established who Darius was and from where he was coming. Then he walked Darius back toward a parked police unit. Ricardo and his friends were already gone.

"It was Marcus, wasn't it?" Darius used his nemesis's real name. "Where is he? Where's Momma? Is she at the hospital? Did he kill her?" Darius was firing questions without pausing.

"Take it easy, young man," the sergeant said. "I'm going to get Chief Detective Julie Richmond, and she can talk to you and let you know what's going on."

"Is my momma dead or alive? That's a simple question."

"I can't answer that, son. The detective will answer your questions."

"Is she dead?" Darius yelled as the sergeant walked away.

He looked at the gaggle of spectators. The scene was eerily similar to the one at the Browns'. His eyes pleaded for an answer from a lady who lived across the street. She barely nodded, and then lowered her head. Distraught, Darius wailed in anger and pain as he staggered toward the house. He saw a woman walking toward him, taking off latex gloves. She introduced herself as Detective Richmond as she reached out her right hand and gently pulled Darius toward her. Ensconced in the detective's embrace, he sobbed on her shoulder. After a few moments, she slowly stooped until they were on the ground.

"You're going to be okay, son," she said, rubbing his heaving shoulders. "We're here."

"Is Momma in the house?" Darius started to get up. "I want to see her."

"This is a crime scene, and we're still investigating and gathering evidence." The detective's voice was firm, but gentle, as she walked Darius back to the street.

"Do y'all have Marcus in jail?"

"Who is Marcus? Why do you think he has something to do with this? The only thing your neighbors seem to remember seeing is some Jehovah's Witnesses on the street."

"Ain't no Jehovah Witness killed my momma." Darius scoffed at even the suggestion that it could've been anyone besides Marcus, much less those Watchtower people. "It was that damn Marcus Holmes— that's his name. Y'all don't have him?"

"We haven't arrested anybody, yet," the detective said. "Tell me about this guy and why you think he would harm your mother."

Darius told Detective Richmond how Marcus beat his momma and dealt drugs.

"I warned her that he was going to kill her if she let him stay," Darius kicked at the ground. If only she'd listened. Now, as promised, it was his mission to kill the worthless piece of shit.

"Do you know where he might be?" Detective Richmond asked.

"If I did, I'd be after him myself," Darius said, raising his head and looking over the detective's shoulder to see what was happening in his yard. "He's probably back with his dopeheads in New Orleans."

"I promise that we'll find your momma's killer, whoever he might be, and he'll face justice," she said emphatically. She clicked her pen and put it, along with her small notebook, into the front pocket of her starched blue uniform.

"I swear to God that if I catch him before you find him, I'll kill him." Darius made a gesture with his hands to indicate strangulation.

"I understand how you feel, Darius. But you can't do that. Promise me that I'm not going to have to arrest you for killing somebody."

"I can't make you any promise," Darius said through clenched teeth. Why were they so concerned about this asshole's well-being? Darius was going to do them all a favor and save the taxpayers some money, to boot.

"I'm sorry about what happened," the detective told Darius. "I have two sons and a daughter. One of my sons is your age, so I know you're hurting. Just know that I'm on your side. I don't want to see you hurt any more than you are already."

Darius took a deep breath. He recalled how she'd bought ten bicycles at Christmas to give to underprivileged kids at his school. He believed she meant what she said.

"Is that your dog?" the detective asked.

Darius looked in the direction the detective nodded, and he saw Droopy Eyes. "No. It's just a stray. Why?"

"One of the neighbors said the dog was barking over here around noon." Detective Richmond's radio crackled to life in a call to her from an officer inside the house.

"The dog stays by that vacant house," Darius said, pointing up the street.

The detective handed Darius her card. "Call me if you need anything, or if I can help you with anything," she said before walking back into the house.

Robert Gaines didn't see any other reporters around. He tapped his walking cane on the ground as he worked the perimeter of the crime scene, looking for anybody who would talk. He used the cane to support a weak left hip injured during his breached delivery when he was born. He wrote down a name he heard from a lookout alert on his police scanner. He glanced up and saw Detective Richmond sigh when she noticed him. If looks could hurt, Robert would've been hospitalized.

"Don't walk on my crime scene, Mr. Gaines," Detective Richmond ordered as she passed by. "We don't have anything to release. When we do, I'm sure the chief will see that you're notified."

"Can you confirm that the victim is dead and she's a thirty-year-old female named Sarah LeBeaux?" Robert asked. He loosened his bow-tie as sweat ran down his neck.

"We're not releasing her name until the next of kin is notified," the detective said without turning around as she climbed the steps of the porch.

"You're confirming that it was a woman and she's dead? Was she shot?" Robert was yelling his questions across the yard, attempting to keep the detective engaged and possibly give him some morsel of information. "I heard a BOLO for a Marvin Holmes in a red Mustang GT on the scanner. Is he your suspect?"

"No comment, Mr. Gaines. I'm not confirming anything." Detective Richmond looked back over her shoulder. "Remember, don't cross my tape, or I'll have you arrested!"

Robert knew she wasn't bluffing. He knew this was a murder story, but he didn't have anything solid he could report just yet.

"Who's the crying kid?" Robert asked a woman with whom he'd spoken earlier.

"That's Miss Sarah's boy, Daryl," she said as she took a long drag on her cigarette and then slowly shook her head in the cloud of smoke she exhaled. "No . . . Darius. That's his name."

Robert jotted the name down. Early information often is partial, but nothing gets ignored—or left unconfirmed. The kid was standing beside a police unit in the shade of an old oak tree. Squirrels were barking in the upper limbs of the tree and battling over acorns, which fell with a pitter-patter on the hood of the police unit. Robert walked over to see if the boy would talk.

"I heard something happened to that lady in there." Robert eased up beside Darius, trying to be as considerate as he could. "Have you heard anything?"

"Yeah, bro. That was my momma." Darius was sniffling and drawing circles in the gravel with his feet. "I just got back from Cypermort and the cops were here. They told me she was shot. The coroner's in there, like the cops can't see she's dead." He looked up, and his voice changed from sorrow to anger. "I know who done it. If I catch him, I'll kill him."

"I'm sorry, man," Robert said softly. "I hope they catch the guy before you find him. I don't want to see you ruin your life, too."

"Naw, man. My life can't get no worse."

"I lost my mother two years ago. It was rough. I know it's nothing like you're going through right now. By the way, my name is Robert Gaines." Robert stuck his right hand out.

The two shook hands as Darius gave his name.

"I work for the newspaper," Robert said. "I know this is a hard time for you. Can I ask you a couple questions to help me get the story correct?"

"I don't know, man. What do you want to know?" Darius didn't pull away when Robert produced a pen and small blue-and-white reporter's notepad.

The coroner pronounced Sarah dead from two gunshots to the head. With the body released, Detective Richmond walked outside to locate Darius.

"Mr. Gaines, I told you not to interfere with my investigation," she said as she approached the car where Robert and Darius were talking.

"No, ma'am. You said not to cross your tape and enter your crime scene, as I recall. I'm out here on the highway." Robert raised his hands in a show of innocence.

"Leave the victim's son alone, Mr. Gaines."

"Are you confirming this is her son? Which I believe may be the next of kin you're probably looking to notify. Can you release any further information?"

"I'm confirming nothing, Mr. Gaines—and remember, don't cross my tape. Darius, can you come with me? We're about to bring your mother out. We need you to identify her, but this is going to be tough."

Robert snapped pictures of the detective leading Darius toward the house with a droopy-eyed dog sitting in the shade in the background.

Darius wasn't prepared for the grisly sight, or the overwhelming emotions, when Detective Richmond pulled back the sheet covering his momma's face. He gasped. It felt as if his heart stopped beating as it all hit him like a ton of angry bricks. His soul and spirit seemed for a moment to have escaped him as he froze in a breath of pure hell.

Sarah's beautiful face was disfigured, caked now with a crimson paste that covered her head. Darius's rancor was enough to split his spleen. He'd sell his soul to the devil if he thought it would bring her back. He leaned forward to kiss her bloody face. She didn't kiss him back as she was supposed to, as she'd done hundreds of times. Despite what his eyes told him, his heart refused to accept that she was dead. He blinked away tears and turned back to look at the detective. He hoped she'd tell him it was just another nightmare, that his momma was in a black cave and he needed to fight the evil forces and go inside to rescue her, even with his million-pound ankle weights.

The detective's lips pursed, her eyes squinted. Her expression said, "I'm sorry."

Darius turned to the gurney and fell forward. He felt the detective's grip momentarily tighten as if to hold him back, but then it relaxed. His frame collapsed like a spilled sack of potatoes onto Sarah's cold, stiff body that had always been so warm and soft. He hoped she'd put her arms around his neck, but they remained cold and still at her side on the stretcher.

"Oh, Momma," Darius moaned. His tears softened the dried blood on Sarah's face. Her blood and his tears mixed, rolled down her face, and left a pinkish trail over her battered cheeks. He gently ran his fingers through her soft hair, now matted and tangled with blood. He kissed her on the forehead, as she used to do to him when she tucked him in. Her eyes were closed, but he was certain he saw the faint outline of a smile. He imagined she died smiling, knowing death freed her of all her troubles. He pulled himself together and stood up. Turning slowly to his right, he looked at the detective. She was wiping away a solitary tear with the back of her hand.

"Yeah, that's Momma," Darius said softly to the detective.

She pulled him close to her again as he buried his head on her shoulder and wept. What would he do now, and where would he go in life without his momma?

Robert raised his camera to take the shot a photojournalist always knew he must take—the shot that showed tragedy, pain, and grief. Words can't describe the emotions a lens captures. The image was framed perfectly: dead mother, grieving son, compassionate detective. Ignoring training and professional expectations, Robert lowered the camera and refused to photograph the heartbreak fifty feet away.

Everyone left. Darius sat alone on the front step, where he and Sarah sat together so many times. He still couldn't accept that she wouldn't be back. His fingers fumbled with a handful of rocks he'd picked up from the driveway. He rubbed his knees as he slowly swung his legs back and forth. His soul was empty of joy, and his heart full of hate.

Would things have been different if I'd been here when she came home for the car?

A south wind blew in swarms of hungry mosquitoes from the marsh, supplementing the bloodthirsty hordes already there. They began their pre-dusk invasion early, looking for a quick meal. Darius swatted the pesky insects from his arm as he braced himself to walk into the house. He dropped the few rocks still in his hand, then clapped his hands together in front of his face to kill more mosquitoes. He rose and slowly walked across the porch, each step filled with dread.

Two steps into the house, Darius noticed that the teal rug—he'd hated the color of that rug—was missing. Evidently the police took it as evidence. An inch-wide crack in the wooden floor that the rug had covered lay exposed. He could see the outline of the rug's edge because the floor was stained with his momma's blood. There in the center of it all was the white chalk outline made by the police. He'd overheard one of the policemen say they'd found a knife near her body; the knife was gone—taken as evidence, too, he assumed. The detective said she was shot twice, but they hadn't found the murder weapon.

Two shots in the middle of the day, and all my neighbors remember is two Jehovahs preaching? They are too damn scared to say what they heard or saw.

He walked into the kitchen. A small ham sat on the counter with four thin slices lying on a plate. Maybe she'd been making sandwiches? *For whom? Marcus didn't like ham.*

There were small stains on the kitchen floor. Darius got on his knees and looked closer. They looked like bloodstains, and there was a hole in the wall near the floor. Maybe a bullet hole? He stuck his finger in the hole but felt nothing. *Did the police see this?*

Darius grasped a fresh bag of peaches from the table. Odd that his momma would've bought peaches after partying all night. There was a fresh gallon of milk in the refrigerator and the Thunderbird hadn't been replaced. That was odd, too. A movie ticket stub seemed out of place because neither Sarah nor Marcus went to the movies. *How could the police have missed this clue?*

He reached above the refrigerator, found that old photograph, and carefully placed it in his pocket. He left the kitchen, passed back through the front room and went to the bedroom. He stuck his head inside the small room and looked around without entering it. The usually tidy room was in a disarray. Most of Marcus's clothes were still there. Marcus had probably hurriedly thrown stuff around to get his stuff and then ran like a coward. That stupid guitar of his was gone. Darius chided himself for not throwing it in the Atchafalaya River when he had the chance.

He grabbed a few of his clothes from the small dresser in the hall between his momma's room and the bathroom and stuffed them into his green school gym bag. He took his basketball from off the top of the dresser. He didn't know if he could ever bear to walk into this house again.

When Darius stepped off the porch, the ball slipped from his grasp and slowly rolled to a stop next to the clunker. He grabbed the ball and tossed it into the backseat as he hopped behind the wheel and turned the key; not surprising, it wouldn't crank.

With the gym bag in his right hand, he got out of the car and began aimlessly walking and dribbling his basketball up the street. As he neared Iberia Street, still not knowing his destination, he glanced back over his shoulder. He saw that dog from the Browns' creeping in the shadows. He and the mutt had a few things in common, the biggest being that they were on their own.

CHAPTER 9
SEPTEMBER 11-18, 2004

This was a shitty day, Marcus thought as he drove over the Grizzaffi Bridge.

He'd killed the closest thing to a decent woman he'd ever met. Now, he was fleeing Franklin with a few belongings, his gun, and the drug stash stuffed into his father's ancient, olive-green army duffel bag. He wished he'd grabbed that knife on his way out— surely it had his DNA on it. It didn't matter. The damn, crooked pigs would probably plant evidence to frame him anyway. He looked to his right, over his guitar propped up in the seat, at the shrimp boats moored along the Morgan City seawall. Customers were walking over the levee, buying jumbo twelve-count white shrimp off the boats. He hadn't eaten since last night and was hungry as a horse.

Marcus's mind was running through vignettes of the morning. When he got back to Franklin, he'd pulled that nappy-headed brat's blanket off the couch and started to watch a ball game. An hour later, Sarah was ruining his weekend. He'd told Sarah he wanted something to eat and a beer, not that Thunderbird cow piss. She offered to fix him ham sandwiches, which irritated him since she knew he didn't care for ham. All she said she had to drink was milk. Since he was hungry, he told her to go ahead and fix him two sandwiches, which he never got to eat.

Before she fixed the sandwiches, she'd said, "Marcus, we need to talk. You need to leave by tonight."

What the hell was that all about, out of the blue?

He'd shoved her, his usual warning to end foolishness before it got out of hand. Then two Jehovah preachers knocked at the slightly ajar door. He'd heard their utopian crock before—a message about "a new world to come," where people peacefully worshipped God in a world where lions lay with lambs. He and Sarah ignored the knock and the uninvited visitors left.

Sarah pointed him to the door with that stupid knife, and then had the nerve to push him in that direction. This was the wrong day for her to start stuff. Marcus punched her in the face and knocked her down. Then she got right back up and was in his face again with that damned knife.

His temper erupted like a volcano. His fist came crashing through Sarah's small raised arms. He remembered the sting of the knife blade as it cut through the meat of his arm and how Sarah's nose spewed blood down her lips, into her mouth, and all over him.

Marcus's attention darted back to his driving as he jammed his brakes when a deer ran across the highway. Bayou Black was just off to his right, through a small thicket of woods and marsh. His arm was throbbing, and the bleeding hadn't stopped. That knife cut him more seriously than he initially realized.

Why didn't she just stop? Then none of this woulda happened. You kick a dog enough times, and he's gonna bite your ass.

Sarah had spat blood on him, told him to get out, and threatened to call the police. He yanked the phone from her hand and brought it square on the left side of her head. He heard the bones in her face crack as she crumpled like a wet towel to the floor, her eyes rolled back, blood pouring from her face and head.

He'd never meant for it to come to this. Blinded by an anger that had stewed a poisonous brew in his soul since childhood, he'd lashed out. Although he'd thought she was already dead, he retrieved his gun and shot her twice in the head anyway, to ensure she wouldn't suffer.

"Now things are messed up," Marcus mumbled as he crossed over Bayou Lafourche. He pulled on the shoulder of the highway just before the elevated bridge over Bayou Des Allemands. He yanked a kiwi-colored Polo shirt out of the duffel bag and tied it around his elbow to try to stop the bleeding. That would have to do until he got to Charity Hospital in New Orleans.

Why did she hafta get all up in my face and make me kill her, too?

Marcus knew he needed to ditch the bloody clothes. He stopped at a service station and went to a restroom and changed. It had been over two hours since he and Sarah had fought. In a few more hours, it would be dark and easier to safely ditch the bloody clothes.

"We gave you two liters of blood," the doctor explained to Marcus. "You were in stage three hemorrhage; any longer and you probably would've died."

"It'll take five or six damn stages to kill me," Marcus said.

"There are only four stages of hemorrhaging," the resident doctor dryly explained, "and the fourth stage is usually fatal. We stitched a serious cut to your forearm; speaking candidly, I suspect it wasn't falling on a knife that did this. Do you need to tell me anything?"

"No, Doc," Marcus said. "You done all I need. Like I told the nurse, I just fell on my hunting knife." He realized how implausible his story was.

"Since this isn't a gunshot wound, I'm not required to report it. Please be careful." The doctor sighed. "The nurse will explain what you need to do over the next few days and when to have the stitches removed."

Marcus left the hospital and decided to drive to Baton Rouge to spend time communing with his little brother. Along the way, he could discard the clothes.

Midway of crossing the Bonnet Carre Spillway, Marcus edged over to the shoulder of the interstate outside of New Orleans, where Interstate 10 crossed miles of swamps abundant in nutria, deer, raccoons, rabbits, and other critters like fish, turtles, and alligators. An occasional uninterested motorist sped by on the dark, ten-mile bridge as he tossed the bloodstained clothes into the brackish water below him. He thought for a moment about tossing the gun over, too, but decided to keep it.

He got back into his car, carefully driving the speed limit for an hour so that he wouldn't give a cop an excuse to stop him. That was all the cops ever wanted to do: fund their forays into donut shops by harassing law-abiding citizens going a few miles over the speed limit.

It had been a rough day—getting stabbed while killing Sarah, driving for hours before passing out in a charity ER, and then driving a couple of more hours late at night. It had taken an immense toll on Marcus. He was exhausted when he pulled into the Flying J Truck Stop in Gonzales, about twenty miles southeast of Baton Rouge. He reclined his seat and crashed into a fitful sleep.

Marcus awoke at daybreak; a trucker blew his air horn as he bid his female company farewell. She looked underage, but that wasn't for Marcus to worry about. He was up Shit Creek without a paddle, hip deep in alligators, and in no position to worry about what corn was in the shit floating in another man's toilet.

His arm hurt like hell on fire. Looking in his glove box, he couldn't find a single damn aspirin. He was in a foul mood. Hunger, pain, and killing your girlfriend will do that to a man.

Two deluxe breakfasts at McDonald's quieted the hunger pangs in his belly. A headline on a coffee-stained page in the B-section of *The Advocate*, a Baton Rouge newspaper lying on one of the tables, caught his eye: *Police looking for ex-con in murder of single mother.* There was a small, one-column-wide, unflattering picture of him; his mugshot from his Patterson arrest. They had flashed the camera before he was ready.

He skimmed through the article, noticing that police considered him a "person of interest" and not a suspect. It pissed him off that the writer said he was in Angola for six years for trying to kill a Patterson cop.

"My sentence was six, but I was only there for less than three," he muttered. "And it was for assault and not attempted murder. They fail to mention I was defending myself from some dopeheads who tried to rob me. They don't say nothing 'bout Sarah being a dopehead. People always judging me wrong. Damn reporters are almost bad as the cops."

Marcus looked around, wondering if anybody had seen the picture. He ripped the page from the newspaper and threw it in the garbage, along with the breakfast detritus and the tray itself. He walked next door to a Circle K and bought a small bottle of Tylenol. He thought the store was making an obscene profit on the analgesics. Apparently, he was selling the wrong drugs.

It was midmorning when Marcus parked in front of the now-deteriorating Longfellow Drive house in which he was raised in North Baton Rouge. The acrid stench of petrochemicals from the massive Exxon plant a few blocks away assaulted his nostrils. He recalled that on mornings when the air was warm and still, the odor was especially strong. He looked at the peeling paint, cracked bricks, and the blue tarp covering a roof whose composition shingles had exceeded their lifespan. The single-car carport had been enclosed, and the brown

Masonite siding was rotting along the bottom where it touched the driveway. The rosebushes that his mother, Laura, used to fret over in the front yard were gone. A tire hung from a frayed yellow rope attached to one of the big limbs of an oak tree, much like the one he and his brother Timmy had in the same tree.

Marcus was only six and Timmy was almost two when their father, Malcolm, returned as a shattered man after fighting in Vietnam. As children, they were close but different. Marcus was their alcoholic father's "little tiger," while Timmy was their depressed mother's "good son."

"We'd go to our bedroom with the walls Momma painted that ugly purple color," Marcus said, leaning his head back, closing his eyes and talking to his invisible brother. "We played that 'Sorry' board game and you never did catch me cheating when I took my extra moves." Marcus chuckled. "We acted like we didn't hear what was going on with Momma and Daddy. But I heard every word. We lived through some shit, didn't we, Timmy?"

He cranked the GT and drove away from his childhood home. "I tried to be your protector, little brother."

***

Marcus slowly drove down the west side of Southern Memorial Gardens, twenty miles north of Baton Rouge—his parents had bought a family plot here between two live oak trees. Years ago, Doodie and Julie had pledged their undying love for each other with their names inside of a heart carved into the majestic tree on the left. With Spanish moss draping its limbs, the tree was still casting a late-morning shadow over the family's plot. He thought his family's final resting place was the most peaceful plot in the cemetery. It was an irony not lost on him.

Timmy's grave was at the feet of their parents, who both had followed their youngest son into the ground within a few years of his death. There was an empty space beside Timmy, reserved for Marcus, whenever his time came.

Marcus sat silently beside the granite headstone for half an hour, staring at the inscription: *Timothy M. Holmes, Born May 13, 1966 – Died May 12, 1978. God needed an angel.*

Sitting beside his brother's grave on this sunny Sunday afternoon briefly insulated Marcus from his dark, miserable existence. A murder of crows gathered in a loud convention in the upper branches while a mutation of thrushes quietly chattered in the grass below. A kit of pigeons flew from across the cemetery to shamelessly beg him for a crumb he didn't have.

Marcus inhaled deeply. A gentle breeze held the odiferous Baton Rouge air at bay and something more pleasant filled the air.

Is that jasmine? Smells like heaven today.

He lay prone in the area set aside for his own burial. He wondered when he would join the rest of his family to have his flesh eaten by the worms. Maybe that was the only real way to peace. He'd thought yesterday was going to be peaceful, but it surely didn't work out that way.

He rolled over, leaned on his elbow, and stared at his brother's headstone. "I was gonna hide my dope in a cabinet, and this freaking huge monster rat jumps out at me. Timmy, I swear that thing was a foot long. Big as any rat I ever seen." Marcus formed a pistol with his fingers and aimed it at one of the pigeons. "Bam, bam. I killed it dead as a doornail on the second shot."

He sat up and pulled strands of moss from his long, uncombed hair and sighed as he remembered Sarah arriving at the house around noon the day before.

"She comes in with those groceries and tells me I hafta go so she can get clean and to protect that punk-ass kid of hers. Hell no, little brother. I told her I ain't going nowhere."

Marcus paused as a couple slowly walked to a grave further back.

"She says something 'bout me leaving or she'd murderate me. What the hell does that mean? That's when I lost it, little brother. I mean, it ain't like I wanted to do it. I always had a problem controlling my temper, and I lost it after she provoked me. She knew not to push my buttons, and I came unglued."

Talking things out with his brother always helped. He missed his brother. No one else understood him. Marcus remembered the things they endured in their childhood.

"Daddy's drinking got bad, and he got mean. Then Momma fell all the way down her rabbit hole." He paused and watched a jet passing overhead, having just taken off from the airport. As the jet climbed and became a small speck, he continued. "They never really believed what I told 'em when you died. They blamed me—especially Momma—but she never really liked me anyway. I don't even wanna talk about all that other stuff with the preacher. Daddy blamed me for Momma going off the deep end, but he didn't exactly rescue her."

Marcus sat up. He'd become agitated thinking about things he'd struggled to put out of his head. He walked a circle around the plot and ended up in front of his mother's headstone, still talking to his brother.

"Then Momma decides to blame me when Daddy died. Like I forced him to put the damn gun in his mouth and blow his damn brains out. Who found that? Me, dammit. You know what that does to a dude who's already screwed up to see his daddy's brains all over the back of the shitter? It fucks you up really bad, man, and you can't come back. Sarah used to call it a black hole."

Marcus stood up and looked at his arm. The bandages were still clean. It was quiet, except for a jet coming in to land at Ryan Field.

"I'm sorry, little brother. I was supposed to protect you." Marcus stooped to kiss the headstone. "I lost my temper yesterday with that bitch and now she's dead, too." Marcus walked over to his parents' headstones. He kissed two fingers and placed them against the stones. "Rest in peace, guys. I wish we could've been a normal family."

He turned and walked to his car. There were too many bad memories for him to stay in Baton Rouge. He wasn't interested in setting up in New Orleans, and St. Mary Parish was off-limits right now. He wondered how business might be in Lafourche or Terrebonne Parish.

With a heart burdened by grief and loss, Darius walked between the two rows of pews in the Church of the Assumption. This was the first time he'd been inside a church. He made his way slowly to the front, where his momma, killed a week ago, lay in a closed casket. On the ceiling above the altar, he saw a mural of a bleeding pelican, the state bird—an emblem, he learned, that Franklin parishioners thought to symbolize the pierced heart of Jesus nurturing the sacramental life of the Church.

Father Sorenson had asked Darius for permission to arrange a Christian funeral for Sarah. Darius appreciated the modest casket the church had donated, but he believed a church funeral was a waste of time. There were no family nor friends who would attend.

The priest had put an obituary in the newspaper asking parishioners to come show respect for a woman killed after giving her life to Jesus. Darius was moved by the dozens of strangers who came. They assured him they'd pray for him and for the soul of his momma.

The priest received Darius's permission to mention some of the things Sarah had told him. Darius expected a few short "ashes to ashes, dust to dust" words, but what he and about fifty other people heard was an emotional tribute to a woman who had found redemption.

"Sarah LeBeaux discovered strength to do the seemingly impossible through the greatest power in the universe, the Holy Spirit," the young priest said. He raised his palms up and glanced heavenward. Then, after a pause, he looked directly into Darius's eyes, rimmed with tears. "The next greatest power she found was the love of her son, Darius."

Darius closed his eyes, thinking of how much he loved his momma. He felt someone sit beside him, but he didn't open his eyes to see who it was.

The priest recounted meeting and talking with Sarah. "God reached out to draw her to him before she died. God sent a parishioner, leaving his hour of adoration, as a messenger to invite her into the church. She told me that as she walked down those aisles, she felt as if she was walking into the outstretched arms of God."

Darius, eyes still closed, was slowly nodding his head.

"Sarah was awed by the beauty of the stained glass that depicted Mary's story," the priest continued. "It's something you and I see so often that we take it for granted. Not Sarah. She was humbled. She knelt behind the pew right behind where her son sits today." Darius opened his eyes and saw the priest point to the pew where he said she'd knelt. "How many of us offer an apology for something and then say 'but'? Not Sarah. She made no excuses for years of wrong choices. She simply asked for the strength to quit making them."

The priest paused, smiled faintly and looked directly at Darius.

"Your mother told me she prayed for the strength to forgive herself for, as she called it, ruining your life," the priest continued. "When she told me of how kind and caring you are, when she told me how you are the one who gives her hope every day, when she told me of your loyalty, when she told me how you befriend even the elderly among us, when she told me how you protect her . . ." The priest stopped and closed his eyes, turning his face heavenward.

Darius felt an arm go around him. For the first time, he turned to notice the person sitting beside him—it was Detective Richmond. Darius was surprised to see her, and he noticed that her eyes were misty.

"I told her she had not failed you," the priest said. "Oh, if we could all know such love as your mother had for you."

The detective produced some tissue, which she gave to Darius.

"Last Thursday night and Friday morning, Sarah LeBeaux found a way to face her past and move on." The priest was looking down at the pine casket in front of him. "She asked God for his help. She determined to channel her energy into her son and making her life, and his, a better one."

Darius knew then that wherever his momma had been Friday, it was somewhere good and not with any of her old friends.

"When I saw her on Friday morning, we spoke as sunlight filtered through that stained glass." The priest pointed to the windows. "She said she was changed."

"We would've made it, Momma," Darius whispered.

"I walked her out that front door," the priest said, pointing to the entrance of the church. "She said the sun seemed the brightest it had ever been in her life. She sensed a freedom. She said God was showing her a better way."

Someone uttered an "amen."

The priest caught Darius's eye again. "When your momma headed home, she had a smile on her face. She was happy and free from the machinations of the devil's world."

Darius knew her smile was as beautiful as every sunset, sunrise, and rainbow that had ever existed, but it had been much too rare.

"The Lord has welcomed her into her new home with him. Today she's in his secure embrace, smiling on all of us who are gathered here to tell her good-bye."

Darius nodded his head. His momma was right. She had escaped her black hole and broke back through her event horizon. He knew she had had found her tranquility and had been happy for the last hours of her life. How he wished he could've shared those happy hours with her.

PART II

CHAPTER 10
JANUARY 26, 2008

"I ain't gettin' stiffed out of what I paid for," Ricardo said. "These *grin-gos* will rip you off if you let them."

X-Man hadn't given him his full weight the last time Ricardo bought a bag of weed. Before picking up his new girlfriend from work on this Saturday night, he and his two pals had a piece of business to attend to. He'd give X-Man a good ass-kicking, and then expropriate a reasonable amount of weed to compensate himself for all his troubles. This wasn't a robbery. It was street justice. But he had his .38 in case things went south. He drove with his crew into Amelia, down Friendship Drive, and spotted X-Man in a vacant parking lot. To his surprise, X-Man wasn't alone.

Ricardo drove a couple of blocks to Taco Bell, where he ordered tacos for the three of them at the drive thru. He parked near the drive thru and they began eating the food from a position where he could see X-Man and the other guy under the streetlight.

11:13 p.m.

X-Man had heard that the old guard drug dealers frowned on newcomers cutting into their business. So he was edgy about this new location he'd recently begun to work. Drug dealers weren't exactly the kinds of people you piss off, especially over their business and money. All things considered, he wondered if he was pushing his luck.

He thought his solution lie in James Keller, an old acquaintance who pimped in New Iberia, a small city across the western border of the parish. X-Man trusted James as much as anybody could be trusted on the streets. So he decided to introduce James to his customers, take a cut of the business and turn his attention back to pushing dope elsewhere.

X-Man's cell phone rang.

"You got my stuff?" a voice half-whispered on the other end of the line.

"Yep."

"You on Friendship at that parking lot?"

"Yep."

"I'll be there on a Ninja before one."

"Latah."

James also got a call on his cell at about the same time. He said one of his girls told him business was slow and suggested James come take her and another girl partying in New Orleans.

"These Puerto Rican mommas will rock your world," James said to X-Man. "What you say we blow this place and have a good time?"

"Business first, then we can do whatever."

"How 'bout I go get the girls and bring 'em here? That way, we don't waste no time."

"Sure. Go get your girls."

X-Man got an old lawn chair from near the back of an abandoned building that had once been a convenience store. He hid the powder behind the building and kept a small bag of weed that might supply a couple of customers. He'd tell other customers that he was closed.

11:21 p.m.

Ricardo saw a car leave, but he couldn't tell much else. Throwing his soft drink cup out the window, he cranked his vehicle and slowly drove down Friendship Drive. X-Man sat alone in a chair under the streetlights. His hoodie was over his cap, and he was jawing on something in his mouth. His head was bobbing rhythmically, evidently to the beat of the headset over his ears.

Ricardo parked before he was noticed. He tossed off his windbreaker as he and Striker got out and put on ski masks. Bones got behind the steering wheel. Ricardo put his fedora back on his head, on top of his mask, then donned a set of brass knuckles. He and Striker worked their way to the rear of the building like cats stalking a jaybird.

Ricardo tapped X-Man on his shoulder. X-Man turned, but before he could reach for his gun, Ricardo punched him. X-Man's headset flew off his head, and the Walkman skidded across the cracked pavement of the parking lot. A stick of jerky flew out of X-Man's mouth and landed a few feet away.

Ricardo felt X-Man grab at him trying to rip off his mask; his fedora fell off as he stumbled to the ground with X-Man. He got up quickly and picked up his fedora. The brass knuckles had slipped on his hand before he threw the punch, and he was shaking his hand in pain and complaining about twisting his ankle.

"Dammit, mashed up my fed," Ricardo said as he attempted to work his hat back into shape.

X-Man was trying to get up, cursing, and swearing he'd kill this bushwhacker when Striker kicked him twice in the head. The second kick knocked X-Man out, and then Striker placed a third kick to the ribs. Ricardo stopped Striker from kicking the unconscious dope pusher any more. He put his hat back on his head, and then riffled through X-Man's pockets. He found two baggies of marijuana and X-Man's pistol.

"Let's take the gun and his cash, too," Striker suggested as he took a bite of the jerky, which he'd appropriated from the pavement.

"This ain't no robbery," Ricardo reminded him. Striker and Bones were loyal, but their opprobrious tendencies were irksome. As for Striker, this wasn't the first time Ricardo wondered if he was a psycho-path. "I came for the dope the *hombre* owed me and to rough him up. It ain't but two baggies, but we even. Ya ain't got much morals. And bro, that's just plain nasty to eat the man's stuff he's been chewin' on."

Striker put the last piece of the jerky in his mouth, winked and grinned.

Ricardo tossed the dealer's gun in the grass several yards away as X-Man started to stir.

"I don't want ya gettin' no ideas about cappin' my *culo*," he told his victim. "I don't wanna hafta kill nobody if I ain't gotta. Next time you best give a homie what he pays for."

Striker and Ricardo sprinted to the Suburban, which Bones had pulled into the parking lot. Ricardo jumped behind the wheel, stuck a toothpick in his mouth, and sped away.

11:27 p.m.

X-Man groaned and rose slowly on wobbly knees as his two attack-ers left. The bumper sticker on their vehicle said *Latinos Make Better Lovers. Ask Ya Momma!* X-Man observed people from down the street cautiously making their way toward him as he staggered to his gun.

The sound of an approaching vehicle caught his attention. He looked over his shoulder to his left and saw a car, with one headlight out, slowly headed toward him. Perhaps a customer? He thought he'd seen the old, big, beat-up car before. The door opened, and a masked black man came out hollering profanities and God knew what else as he limped forward. X-Man saw a gun flash and heard several pops. It happened so fast that he didn't know how many times he'd been hit. He felt warm blood oozing down his leg; this asswipe, whoever he was, was trying to kill him.

What was going on? This was turning out to be a bad night. He'd just gotten the bejesus beaten out of him by a Mexican Jean-Claude Van Damme and a damn kangaroo. Now, Wesley Snipes tried to cap his ass for some reason. He was just minding his business and trying to make a living. Was some dealer sending him a message to get out of Amelia?

The shots hadn't carried much punch. The brass knuckles had hurt more than the gunshots. It must've been a small-caliber weapon. If the bullets didn't hit anything to bounce around inside him, he'd be all right. Apparently, Wesley Snipes didn't know what he was doing. If he was a paid assassin, then somebody needed to get their money back, because they had gotten Inspector Jacques Clouseau from the old Pink Panther movies instead.

X-Man fired three rounds from his gun, but he was too beat-up to have any hope of hitting the broad side of a barn. The old car was already leaving the parking lot and headed toward Morgan City. X-Man tried to commit to memory what that car looked like and its license plate, *BREN4EVA*. Jesus, now he has to remember two bumper stickers, a truck and a car, Van Damme, a kangaroo whose pants were about to fall off and Snipes/Clouseau.

X-Man knew the police would arrive shortly, and his difficult night would turn complicated. He patted his pockets and discovered his weed was missing. That was actually a good thing. He was surprised that his wallet and five hundred dollars were still there—strange, but good. The cocaine was in a safe spot. Even if the cops found it, it couldn't be traced to him. He was the victim, not the assailant; he could afford to be uncooperative. He had to buy time until James got back.

The police would be more likely to believe he was just an innocent victim of random violence if he didn't have his gun. He really didn't want to part with it, but tonight he had to—at least temporarily. He was running out of options, and none of them were appealing.

He reached into his pocket and fingered his cash. Among the bystanders that wandered over, he saw someone who he'd sold weed to before. He knew him by his street name, Weasel. It wasn't exactly a name that elicited trust, but in the distance, X-Man heard the sirens, so trust wasn't a luxury he could afford.

"I'm in a pinch here. I don't know what the hell just happened, but I can't let the police find this gun. But I don't wanna lose it. I'll give you five hundred bucks to hold it for me, and I'll come back and get it next week."

Weasel agreed to the arrangement.

"Don't use it or tell nobody 'bout it," X-Man said as he forked over the gun and the money. "Give me you cell number, and then you need to leave before the cops get here."

11:30 p.m.

When the police arrived X-Man honestly professed ignorance of what happened. But his account deviated a bit from the truth so that he could keep it simple. He told them he was just chilling when two guys drove up, beat him up and then robbed him. He said that as he was getting up one of them shot at him a couple of times, but somehow missed. Then the other one shot him. Then they hopped into an old car and left. Just your typical case of random violence. He was peeved that the deputies appeared not to believe his story even though it was almost all true.

While X-Man's creative story managed to explain the two differ-ent caliber bullet casings that police located, it didn't credibly explain how someone at close range with a .38 could've missed him. X-Man noticed the crowd had disappeared, obviously having little interest in an interview by the police. Without other witnesses, X-Man's version was uncontested.

Acadian Ambulance arrived, and the paramedics said it appeared he had a concussion, and had also been shot three times, but the bullets passed through him. When he refused transport to the hospital, he heard the detective tell the paramedics, "It's late. No witnesses. He wants to go home. You want to go home. I want to go home. It's not against the law to get shot. Let's all go home. Happy New Year."

Minutes later James called and said he was on his way without the girls because a couple of wealthy oil execs had flown into Lafayette and were looking for dates.

"It's been a night from hell, man," X-Man said with a groan as he stood in the grass on the edge of the roadway ditch and checking the bloody bandages the medics had applied. "A deranged Mexican and his kangaroo jumped me. Then some crippled nigger shot my ass in a drive-by. The cops are all around here. I had to run off the damn medics."

"You okay, man?"

"I hurt like hell, man, but it is what it is. The fog is moving in, so if the cops don't detain me, it'll be a piece of cake to slip away. I'll call my customer and tell him the deal's off. The weed is gone, and the coke is hidden, I'll get it later."

CHAPTER 11
OCTOBER-DECEMBER 2004

I'm an acorn under a pecan tree.

Darius, always a bit of a loner, was now completely alone. He left the Hawk Street house, unable to bear living there even if he could afford the rent. Now he was staying in an abandoned house on March Lane, a couple of blocks south of where the Browns had lived.

Darius's new home was little more than a shack without electricity. He shared it with an assortment of rodents and insects, but at least it was free. He noticed an old acquaintance seemed to be cautiously offering fellowship. The hungry stray was near the yard.

"Well, Droopy Eyes, I think we're meant to be together." Darius whistled, and the dog tentatively approached wagging its tail.

"Might as well join me," Darius muttered as he invited the dog into his world. "Hope you like peanut butter, Jack. Momma always said the protein is good for you." The new name for the dog had occurred to him when he thought of a commercial for Hungry Jack biscuits.

A couple of days later, he returned to Hawk Street and found remnants of police tape still lying in the yard. He couldn't bring himself to even peek inside the windows. He located the old lawn mower under the backside of the house. He pulled it the few blocks to where he was squatting and began soliciting more customers to cut their grass.

The old Ford vanished not long afterward. Darius scoffed at the stupid fool who stole that piece of junk. Then, a couple of weeks later, the tiny Hawk Street house burned down. Darius thought it was probably the landlord collecting insurance.

"I don't know what I'm going to do without Momma, Jack." He put his arm around the dog sitting at his feet in the dark, empty house they shared. He buried his head in the nape of Jack's neck and groaned. "But I'm happy she found freedom and left her black hole."

Jack whimpered and then licked his new master's arm.

"I'm glad you're here, buddy. The hood has taken everything. I hope it doesn't take you, too, right?" Darius stroked the dog's head. Jack wagged his tail, seeming to like the attention and affection. It reminded Darius of White Fang. "I know she's happy in heaven now, but this hurts."

Jack sat silently beside him, occasionally licking him.

"I hope the cops shoot Pigenstein's ass," Darius said in grief mixed with anger.

Darius became obsessed with reading the newspaper to see if there was any progress toward the capture of Marcus. There was nothing. He spoke to Detective Richmond almost every week. She assured him they had seen the blood in the kitchen, but she wouldn't say who it belonged to, or if she even knew.

The police either have no answers or they aren't sharing them with me.

Besides the haunting questions, there was an emptiness overwhelming Darius. Anger, hatred, and depression began to sneak into the vacuum in his soul. He'd been alone many times before, but he always knew his momma would be home eventually. Now she was never returning, except in his thoughts and dreams. Pigenstein had to be found and killed.

"Looks like I'll have to find him myself." Darius told Ricardo the cops' lack of progress frustrated him. Darius was beginning to view Ricardo as a friend. They'd drink beer or smoke an occasional joint together. Ricardo would even bring Jack a treat whenever he came to see Darius.

"Ya need a piece if ya serious 'bout this *mierda*," Ricardo said. "Things go south with these kinds of *hombres muy rápido*."

"Yeah, I know. I tried to get Momma to get one. Can you get me something? And how much would it cost?"

" 'Bout two bills. I can have one in a couple days."

Ricardo brought him a gun the weekend after Thanksgiving. It was a Smith and Wesson Bodyguard 380, much like Ricardo's own gun. Weeks after the street took the life of his momma, Darius was setting a course in the same streets—using pot and now getting a gun. The irony wasn't lost on him, but he just didn't care.

"Homie, never pull a gun unless ya intend to use it," Ricardo told him. He reached to his side and patted his own gun. "I ain't ever pulled this. But if I do, ya can bet I'm pullin' the trigger."

"I just want to kill piece-of-shit instead of waiting on those slow-as-molasses cops."

"That's a line, *amigo*. If ya cross it, it'll change ya. There ain't no second chances once ya kill a man." Ricardo was shaking his head and crossing his hands in front of Darius's face.

"I don't care, Thirty-eight. All I got in this life is a Mexican and a mutt." Darius put up his fists and shadowboxed Ricardo for a moment.

"I ain't no Mexican. I keep tellin' ya I'm Nicaraguan and proud, and I'm almost legal. Well, my uncle is legal, so that's close enough."

Ricardo adjusted his fedora, and then feigned a shadow punch to Darius's head.

"I'm messing with you, dude, you know that." Darius bobbed, shuffled his feet, and threw a shadow punch to Ricardo's lithe midsection, and then one to his head.

"*Amigo*, I'd spank ya *culo*. Ya ain't seen no hood like where I was born. Ya might have *cojones*, but ya ain't got what it takes to lay a hand on me!" Ricardo weaved, ducked his head, and threw a succession of rapid jabs.

"A'ight, dude. You bad, but don't fool yourself. I got more than big nuts!"

They both laughed.

Ricardo tossed a doggy treat to Jack. "Ya got yaself a decent mutt."

"Yeah, me and Jack against the world." Darius smiled, stroking his dog's head.

Ricardo said Darius's living arrangement reminded him of shanties back home. He said he knew somebody who might let Darius move in as a roommate.

"His name is George Washington, but everybody calls him Prez. He's *loco* as a loon when he starts smokin' that meth, but otherwise the *gringo* is cool. By the way, ya girl Nina might wanna come see ya."

"Really? Does Nina like me, you think?" Darius hadn't seen Nina since his momma died, but he wanted to see her again.

"She mentioned ya a couple times, but she ain't bringin' her fine *culo* to see ya in this rat nest! She and Juanita stayin' at the Hilton compared to *tu casa*!"

A week later, Darius loaded his few belongings, his lawn mower, and Jack into the back of Ricardo's Suburban. He settled into his new home on Bayou Teche at the end of Byron Street in Bayou Vista. The place was quiet, with only a few other trailers on the street. It was far from perfect, but still an improvement; now he could invite Nina to come visit him.

Prez was as volatile as Ricardo had warned. The other occupant, Randy Engels, a fugitive from Texas law enforcement, operated a mobile meth lab. People called him "Doc" because of the drugs he concocted. He had no family or friends, so Prez offered to let him stay there as long as the cops didn't become a problem. They both seemed several flights short of mental stability and were prone to resolving differences with measures other than reason, going off at the slightest provocation.

"It would be crazy to live here with these numbskulls without a gun," he told Ricardo one afternoon, shortly after another of the room-mates' arguments. "Oh, and do you know when Nina would be free?"

"I got ya that piece, *amigo*, but I ain't no pimp. Ya gonna hafta work ya datin' issues out on ya own, homie."

"Aw, come on, Thirty-eight. Help a brother out here. You know I got a jones for the girl!"

"I'll see what I can do, *amigo*. But jones or not, ya need to get some *dinero*, cuz *Mamacita* got bills, and she sendin' money back home, too. If ya gonna be a man, ya gotta take care of ya woman and any babies ya make. That's just some free advice, *amigo*."

Darius leaned in and said in a somewhat embarrassed way, "Tell me something Mexican I can say to her that she might like."

"First, we not Mexican. We Nicaraguan. I already told ya that." Ricardo shook his finger in Darius's face. "Don't call her no Mexican or she'll be pissed. Number two, we speak Spanish, not Mexican."

"Okay, no problemo."

"A'ight here's an easy one for ya, homie: '*Mamacita, qué buena estás.*' That's 'Baby, ya look fine'."

"Got it. That's easy. Anything else?" Darius turned his palms up to show his openness to suggestions.

Ricardo shook his head. He gave Darius a final set of suggestions. "They like that *culo* spanked and hair pulled. They like their *Papi* in control, and ya gotta call her a hot iguana."

"Iguana?"

"Oh yeah, man. In our culture, the iguana is the symbol of good sex. That's the highest compliment ya can give ya woman is to say she has sex like an iguana."

"What the hell, dude? Y'all got some mixed-up ways!"

Ricardo laughed as he gave Darius a cell number for Nina. "Call *Mamacita*."

Prez and Doc were arguing like juveniles while they watched football during the final week of the season. A substantial amount of consumed alcohol had escalated their confrontation.

Maybe this is just how ghetto white people act, Darius thought.

Darius shook his head as he walked out the door wondering if they were this stupid before the drugs fried their brains. Darius thought they were only an argument away from one of them killing the other.

Darius whistled. Jack ran from under the trailer, following closely on Darius's heels as he strolled slowly toward the bayou a few hundred yards away. It was chilly, and the temperature was dropping with dusk not long away. Darius turned the collar of his denim jacket up and looked overhead as ducks flew to their evening roost. He stooped to pick up some flat rocks on the shoulder of the lane. As he neared the edge of the bayou, Darius watched a five-foot alligator gar swimming inches below the surface; it slowly broke the water.

Darius reached in his pocket. Jack's ears pointed up as if he expected a treat. Darius pulled out a small rawhide chew-toy Ricardo had bought and tossed it to his canine companion. As Jack chewed away, Darius reached into his other pocket and pulled out a rock that he threw at the gar, which slowly swam away. Despite the chill of the season, crickets and frogs still tuned up for their nightly symphony.

"Life's hard without you, Momma," Darius saw the stars were just beginning to appear. "I don't know why God didn't save you." Jack was lying a few feet away. "I want to make him suffer," he told Jack, who stopped chewing at the sound of his master's voice directed toward him. "I want to make Pigenstein beg for his life, and then spit in his ugly face and put a bullet between his beady eyes and send his worthless soul straight to hell where it belongs." Darius had worked himself into a fervor to the point of tears.

Jack resumed working on his rawhide. Darius swatted away a couple of mosquitoes humming near his ear. He sniffled and ran his arm across his nose and then threw a flat rock across the water. The throw had too much pitch, and the rock sank as it hit the water.

Just like Momma, he thought. *Never had a chance.*

Darius pulled the other rocks from his pocket and emptied them into the still, shallow water at the bayou's edge. His nose ran in the cold air. *I know, Mr. L. Don't wipe my nose on my sleeve*. Darius wondered why God let bad things happen to good people like Momma and the Browns.

"Rot in hell, Walter, with your cousin burning beside you!" He swiped away the mosquitoes swarming around him. Jack, with the chew-toy in his jaw, trotted beside his master as he made his way back to the trailer. The loneliness of the bayou and cold air had exacerbated Darius's sadness.

CHAPTER 12
FEBRUARY 2005

"That's all I gotta do?" Darius asked cautiously. "Just watch? Because I ain't hurting nobody."

Ricardo had invited Darius into his small ring of thieves by being the lookout in the theft of some copper from Tournament Copperworks.

"Yep. Easy hundred bucks. Interested?" Ricardo put his arm around Darius and pulled him in close as if they were on the verge of becoming bosom friends.

"But I ain't got a cell phone." His momma had insisted that he use proper English and not street talk. With her gone, Darius worried less about grammar and usage.

"I'll get ya a cell and ya can keep it, ya cheap-ass," Ricardo said, laughing and pushing him away.

"A'ight, count me in. Have you heard anything on the streets about Marcus? There's been nothing in the paper about Momma's murder in months, and the cops ain't telling me squat."

"I'll keep my ears to the ground for ya, homie," Ricardo said as he sucked on the toothpick in his mouth. "But I'm tellin' ya to think closely about crossin' that line. The police will get him eventually and fry his ass."

Darius thought he was more likely to find the winning lottery ticket on the sidewalk. He was less concerned about crossing some line by killing Marcus than he was about crossing the line by stealing from somebody. Marcus deserved to die. Stealing from people was another thing. Mr. L had taught him better than that.

"Hey, *Mamacita*. What's up? This is the Dekester."

"*¿Qué?*"

"This is Darius."

 "I'm Juanita. Nina left about an hour ago with her *novio*. She left her phone here."

"*Novio?*"

"Her boyfriend."

Darius cleared his throat. "Well, um, can you tell her I called?"

Darius was disappointed that Nina was with some other man. He figured the *"novio"* probably had plenty of money. Maybe he needed to do more of these lookout jobs with Ricardo because grass-cutting wasn't putting much money in his pocket and nobody seemed to want to hire him without his high school diploma even though he had put in dozens of applications.

 "*Sí*, I can do that. Maybe *Papi* can do somethin' for Juanita? Maybe show *señorita* what you workin' with?"

"Huh?"

"Juanita *muy caliente* and all alone." She giggled.

"I'm sorry. I don't understand." Darius removed the phone from his ear and looked at it as if it would have an explanation of what he'd just heard.

"Juanita is so horny."

"Yeah, well, um, I . . . You see . . ."

"I hear black guys have *gran polla*—how you say, big dick? Juanita would love to find out."

"Um, yeah, um, well, you see, I don't . . . I don't think I should." Darius was caught off guard by Juanita's forwardness. "And, um, Thir-Thirty-eight is my friend, and he'd kill me if he knew I was with you."

"Are you tellin' him? Not me."

"Um, no I-I'm not telling him. I mean, there ain't nothing to tell cuz I ain't doing this. Just tell Nina I called, please. 'Bye."

Darius hung up the phone. He thought he heard her laugh and say, "Somebody has taught your *amigo* somethin' about loyalty."

Darius set up a date with Nina on the evening before the heist. His roommates were out of town and Prez left his truck telling Darius he could use it if he filled it up with gas. Darius picked up Nina, and they went to the Bayou Vista Theater to watch *The Chronicles of Riddick.* After that, they ate Chinese food, and Darius asked Nina if she'd like to spend the rest of the evening at his place.

They settled down in the dark living room of the mobile home, Darius with his arms around Nina. She was soft and beautiful and smelled sweeter than a flower. As they sat on the couch, Darius shared with Nina the pain of losing his momma, but not his desire to kill Marcus. He also told her about the Browns and said they had been the only true friends he'd ever had.

"Well, I'm here for you, *novio.*"

Darius glanced away, nervously looking at the floor. He asked about the *novio* Juanita had mentioned.

"She likes to be messy. She was just talking. I just met him a few weeks ago. He takes me to lunch sometimes, but that's all. He doesn't want a poor, cripple like me."

Darius thought Nina's half-laugh revealed that her self-deprecation might hurt more than she'd let on.

"Don't say that, *Mamacita*." Darius's gaze jerked from the floor, and he looked intently into her big, brown eyes. "You're beautiful. Don't put yourself down!"

"*Gracias*. You're a *caballero*, Darius." Juanita rubbed his face with her soft hands.

"*Caballero?*"

"How you say? A gentleman, you're a gentleman. Anyway, my friend, he won't get past first base with me. Just not my type."

"Well, I hope I can get past first base," Darius said. He took her hand from his face and gently kissed it.

"Who knows, *novio?* Keep swinging and you might hit a home run." Nina leaned over and briefly kissed Darius on the lips.

Darius asked Nina to tell him more about herself. She said she was raised in poverty as the oldest child in a family of seven children. Two of her siblings died in infancy. She was five-years-old and helping deliver fruit to the market when an oxcart crushed her foot. There was no doctor and even if there had been one, her family had no money, so the ankle healed on its own.

Ten years ago, drug lords were terrorizing peasants into working for them. Her father who worked sunup to sundown to support her family had refused and he was shot in front of her.

"*Papá* died in my arms," Nina said. "He knew *mis hermanos* would be taken and he made me promise to do whatever I had to do to take care of *mi madre* and *mis hermanas*."

"*Hermanos* is brothers and *hermanas* is sisters?"

"*Sí.*"

"What happened to your brothers?"

"One is dead. We were sent his headless body. My baby brother is missing, but probably dead. *Mamá* took us to another village to find a better life. That's where I became friends with Juanita. *Mamá* found a man who took us in, but he was mean."

"I understand. My momma always made the wrong choice in men. I don't remember any I ever liked." Darius noticed Nina's eyes were swimming in tears that refused to roll; he sensed those eyes had seen way too much pain and suffering.

"I swore to *Dios* that I'd do all in my power to help *Mamá*. That's when me and Juanita decided to come to America, despite the danger and hardship. I did things I'm not proud of to get here, *novio*. I pray *Dios* will forgive me. Now I send almost all my money back home."

She's lived through more crap than I have!

Darius softly rubbed her hands then he reached over to hug her. Nina put her head on his shoulder and kissed his neck. Darius brushed back her long, straight, black hair with his fingertips. He put a hand on each side of her face and gently stroked her smooth cheeks.

Nina kissed him again, and this time the kiss was longer and more intimate. "Do you want to take me to your bedroom?" she asked.

It appeared Darius wouldn't be a virgin by the end of the night. Darius fumbled with the buttons on her blouse as they undressed each other. Her breathing, like his, was rapid.

"*Mamacita, qué buena estás,*" Darius said, remembering the words Ricardo had suggested.

"*Muchas gracias, novio.*" Nina moaned as she wrapped her arms around Darius's neck and nibbled on his ears, then kissed his lips. As she kissed his face, her nails drifted sensually down his spine, digging a line into his strong, muscular back. She grabbed her wrist and squeezed the circle formed by her slender arms to press Darius's chest harder into her breasts. Her legs intertwined with Darius's legs. "*Hazme el amor, Papi,*" she moaned softly.

Darius wasn't sure, but he guessed she had just asked to be made love to. Then he remembered the other advice Ricardo had given him. "Roll over, *Mamacita,*" Darius said.

"¿*Qué?*"

"Roll over for *Papi.*" Darius preferred that Spanish pet name over his corny inventions.

"Oh okay. If that's what you want. I mean, I like . . ."

Ricardo said Nicaraguan women like men in control, like it rough, but Nina appeared reluctant. Maybe that's part of the game, Darius thought. He worked his way behind her, pulled her hair, and slapped her ass.

"*Eh, eso duele,*" Nina said.

Darius thought she was asking for more. He loved when she spoke Spanish like that! It was so sexy! He reached forward, gripped her long hair, and pulled it toward him.

"*¡Ay, eso duele!* Darius, you're hurting me," Nina said much louder as she pushed his hand away from her hair.

Maybe she wasn't asking for more. Maybe he was too rough. He would make it up to her by letting her know how hot she made him feel.

"*Mamacita*, you're one hot iguana!" Nina rolled over and pulled away; fiery anger darted from her squinted eyes as she scowled at him.

"*¡Qué demonios*, Darius! Calling me a nasty lizard and yanking on my hair and slapping my *culo*. You got a lot to learn, *niño*. You were *romántico* earlier, but you are way out of line." Nina got out of the bed and gathered her clothes.

Darius was shocked. He'd done everything Ricardo had said. Then it dawned on Darius what had happened, but he was too embarrassed to tell Nina that he'd asked Ricardo for advice on how to satisfy her and was played the fool. By this time, Nina was dressed.

"Please, Nina. I'm sorry. I messed up."

"*Sí, niño.* Just take me home—*en este momento.*"

Darius knew he had screwed up big time. All he could do was apologize and respect her wishes to leave. Driving her home to her trailer,

Darius repeatedly expressed his contrition to Nina who remained mute as a knot on a log. He was still too proud to admit Ricardo had caused all of this. When he arrived at her little trailer, Darius was going to open the door for her.

"*Vete al infierno.* Don't act like a *caballero* after hurting me and calling me a lizard. Just stay in the car. *Vete a casa ahora.*"

Darius understood only a little Spanish. He understood *infierno* as hell and *casa* as house, so he deduced he'd been told to go to hell and go home. Not exactly the way he'd hoped the night would end.

"Can I call you tomorrow?" Darius was sad that she thought he'd ever intentionally hurt her. He'd never hurt a woman, like men had done his momma.

The taciturn Nina turned her back to him and walked into her trailer. Darius was saddened because he was sure she was crying, and he knew he was the cause of her pain.

Darius got no answer when he tried to call Nina on Sunday morning. He hoped the damage was reparable, and that she'd give him a second chance. He'd felt a connection as they shared their troubles and heartaches. Darius was as steamed as cooked cabbage at Ricardo for the practical joke that put him into hot water with Nina.

"I took your advice with Nina last night," Darius told Ricardo when he picked him up Sunday evening.

"Oh, so homie got him some good Latina *coño* last night?"

"Hellafrigging no. She blew up when I called her an iguana and made me take her home."

"Oh, *Mamacita* didn't like being called a lizard? Homie, use ya head and don't believe everything nobody tells ya! See, I gave ya a lesson ya can use for the rest of ya life!"

"That's cold, bro. Now Nina won't talk to me."

"She'll talk to ya, *amigo*. She knows ya cool. Now let's go make some *dinero*. Ya need it to buy some flowers." Ricardo laughed.

After introducing Darius to Striker and Bones, Ricardo carefully explained the operation. "We should be in and out in under an hour. Any questions?"

"Naw, Thirty-eight," Bones said. "We ready to roll."

Darius's heart was pounding like a jackhammer as he was about to take part in his first felony. His chest was so tight, he could scarcely breathe. Arriving at the target, Darius ran into the thicket of woods that lined the boulevard and kept watch. He shuffled and stomped his feet on the ground and rubbed his hands together to keep his extremities warm. Maybe he should've worn some gloves, he thought. He took a few steps deeper into the thicket, wondering if the vapor from each breath could be seen outside of the woods where he was hiding.

Forty minutes after ducking into the woods and becoming an accessory to the theft of several thousand dollars' worth of copper, he saw headlights speeding toward him on the boulevard. Immensely relieved, Darius jumped into the Suburban as it stopped beside him with a trailer loaded full of purloined copper. Shortly before arriving back at the Byron Street trailer, Ricardo tossed five twenty-dollar bills to Darius in the backseat.

"Sorry 'bout Nina, homie," Ricardo said to Darius and then he tossed him another pair of twenty-dollar bills. "Here, the forgive-me flowers are on me. Call *mamacita* tomorrow. Makeup *coño* is the best anyway!"

Darius sent flowers to where Nina worked. He also sent a teddy bear and a note pleading for a second chance. She called and thanked him for the gift. She didn't rule out getting back together

CHAPTER 13
MAY 2005

Granted, some of what Darius was doing was illegal, but he'd become his own man in the months since Sarah's murder.

Maybe Marcus was right on something besides the gun issue.

A man had to learn to be a survivor in this world. Darius had a decent grass-cutting business in Bayou Vista. He learned you can't trust anybody all the time, how to pick the low-hanging fruit, and that crime does pay. He was beginning to learn how to treat a woman, too. For starters, he didn't call them lizards.

He was glad Nina had forgiven him for his iguana gaffe. Darius was impressed with everything she'd done to try to help her family. She loved her momma as much as he'd loved his.

Yet he was restless and unhappy, largely because Marcus had disappeared without a trace and until his momma's killer was taken care of, Darius believed happiness was impossible. He also wondered if he'd ever meet his daddy now that his momma had died. The lack of a car limited what he could do in locating Pigenstein or his daddy. That situation changed with a major job Ricardo asked him to help pull off.

"A New Orleans *gringo* has a legit business," Ricardo told Darius. "But he makes big money as a fence. He's lookin' for a bay boat with a two hundred on it. I know the place to get it. It's a two-man snatch-and-grab. Ya up for it?"

"That sounds kinda risky," Darius said cautiously. "Are you sure we can do that without getting busted?"

"*Sí*, and there's seven grand in it. Three grand for ya and four for me."

"Three thousand bucks?" Darius whistled. "I can buy a car with that."

"And in case ya wonderin', it's all tax-free money." Ricardo rubbed his fingers together.

"You mean the government don't get none of our hard-earned money?"

"I ain't reportin' it. Wait a minute. I'm illegal, and all my money is tax-free."

They both laughed.

It was shortly after midnight when the duo made it to the house on a quiet street where the boat was parked. It was a Skeeter twenty-two-foot bay boat with a 250-horsepower Yamaha and all the boating accessories one could imagine.

"Thirty-eight, we stand out in this Saltine Cracker subdivision like clowns at a funeral, so we better be quick and quiet." In his lexicon, a Saltine Cracker subdivision was an all-white neighborhood where blacks and Latinos were neither expected, nor welcome.

"What *estúpido gringo* goes on vacation and leaves his boat like this for me to steal. An open door will tempt a saint, and I ain't no friggin' saint." Ricardo laughed.

"Come on, bro," Darius looked around. "Let's get this done and get out of here before somebody calls the cops." Felonies still made him nervous. A barking dog began to worry him. He remembered how Jack's barking had busted Walter in the Browns' murder. Darius looked around again, expecting cops at any moment.

Ricardo opened his door, tossing his toothpick on the ground. He grabbed a bolt cutter under his seat and walked straight to where the boat was parked. There was a lock on the trailer hitch. *Snip*, *clank*, and it was off. Two of its wheels were locked to the trailer with chains. *Snip, clank, snip, clank,* and the wheels were unfettered. The trailer was secured to an iron post cemented in the ground. *Snip, clank,* it was free.

In fifteen minutes, they had circumvented the entire antitheft system and hooked the boat and trailer to Ricardo's vehicle. Minutes later, they headed out of Saltineville. Biting on a fresh toothpick, Ricardo turned the radio on.

"It's ten minutes after midnight and fifty degrees in St. Mary," the KQKI nighttime deejay said. "We hope you had a great weekend and your New Year is going well for you."

"The American way of wealth redistribution! Latinos robbin' *gringos* with the help of Negroes!" Ricardo looked at his partner and bumped fists.

"You're a character, bro—a real frigging character." Darius laughed until his side hurt.

"That sign says Iberville Housing Projects!" Darius strained his neck out the window to look behind them as they drove into New Orleans. "Pigenstein used to stay in the Iberville projects." Darius also wondered if Henry still lived in those projects, but he kept that to himself.

"Paul knows everybody in the projects that pimps, sells, or steals," Ricardo said. He tossed the toothpick he had been chewing and offered to ask the fence if he knew anything about Marcus. He located a new toothpick in his console and stuck it in his mouth.

"Ya gonna recognize this gringo as soon as we get there," Ricardo said changing the subject. "His lily-white ass and BMW is gonna stick out like a fly in milk."

They found Paul lighting a cigar and waiting for them. The short fence—Darius thought he looked like Danny DeVito—directed Ricardo to pull the boat behind an eight-foot-tall wooden fence that ran around the rear. They unhitched the boat, and Paul gave Ricardo an envelope stuffed with cash with "a couple of extra bills to help the new guy with his butterflies."

"*Muchas gracias, amigo.* By the way, he wants to know if you ever heard of a Marcus Holmes who lived here about ten years ago. He was a dope pusher."

"Marcus Holmes, Marcus Holmes." Paul sounded out the name as he scratched his goateed chin and puffed on his cigar. "Yeah, the white boy who beat up his woman and left. He shot a cop or something and they sent him up the river."

"He got out of jail, and *mi hombre* is lookin' for him. Do ya know where he is?"

"I heard he went back to his woman over your way when he got out of the can," Paul said as he pointed with his cigar across the Mississippi River.

"We know that, but he moved. Ya heard somethin' more recent?"

"Somebody told me he changed his name and is dealing out in Houma or somewhere out there, but I don't know that for sure. Why you wanna know all that? Are you looking to get into the business now?" Paul smiled and pointed his cigar toward Ricardo's chest.

"No, *amigo.* I'm not goin' down that road. I just buy me enough to use and don't want no more. I'll just stick to stealin' ya some boats." They both laughed.

Paul told Ricardo that the pair could go to his guesthouse to clean up and get some rest. Then he pulled out his cell phone and set up tabs for them in the French Quarter, along with a room for Tuesday night.

"*Muchas gracias, amigo. Usted es el número uno.* Always good doin' business with ya." Ricardo tipped his fedora and walked back to the Suburban. He turned back and called for Paul. "Ya need to quit them nasty cigars before they kill ya! Then who's gonna be my fence?"

"I'll hook you up with my cousin before I die," Paul said as he took a deep drag on his cigar.

Ricardo laughed, and again tipped his fedora as he reached for the door to the Suburban. Darius was keen on finding out if Paul had any information on Marcus.

"I have good news. *Uno*, we got paid, and Paul said to give ya a couple extra bills for ya work tonight. So I guess that means ya buyin' breakfast."

"And?"

"*Dos*, we rest up at his *casa* and then party on his dime in the French Quarter tonight."

"And?"

"*Tres*, Paul says your man Marcus might be in Houma. But the bad news is that he might be operatin' under a different name."

"Did you get the name?"

"No. He wasn't even sure Marcus is in Houma. At least it's a lead, right?"

"That's right. Thanks for helping."

Ricardo counted out $3,200, which he gave to Darius.

"Not bad for a night's work. All of this is still tax-free, right?" Darius grinned.

"I'm not reportin' it, homie—not me. Now we headed to the *gringo's* guesthouse."

Darius had never slept on sheets smelling so fresh or eaten food tasting so good. Whoever said crime doesn't pay never saw the house Paul owns.

"So how ya gonna spend ya *dinero*, Darius?"

"I gotta get me a ride, so that will take most of it. But I think I might get *Mamacita* something, too. This is the life, my friend. This is the life!" Darius reached over and bumped his fist into Ricardo's.

The day after they got back from the boat heist, Darius called Ricardo and asked for a ride to Morgan City to buy a car. By the afternoon,

Darius was in a 1988 Impala, dented doors and all. He wished his momma could see him now. Darius drove the car to Franklin, where he asked to see Detective Richmond.

She said she was busy, but she made a few minutes to speak with him. She encouraged Darius to finish his schooling, or at least get a GED. "It's important so you can get a decent job and not get pulled into the street life," she said. "So how can I help you today?"

"I have a friend who knows somebody who lived in the projects where Marcus Holmes lived before he moved in with me and my momma the first time. He told me Marcus is living in Houma now, and may be using a different name."

The detective reached for a notebook lying by her computer. She thumbed her way to somewhere in the middle and started writing. "Okay, what name is he using?"

"I don't know, Miss Richmond."

"Any idea where he's supposedly staying in Houma?"

"Naw."

"Does he have a job somewhere? Would your friend know more? Would he talk to me?"

"My friend said that's all he knows. I don't think he wants to talk to the police. I'd think Marcus is still selling his dope and ain't got no regular job."

"Okay, Darius. I'll keep this in mind." She closed her notebook and set it down on her cluttered desk. "You must understand, I can't do much with this little bit of information. But every little bit helps."

"Can't you call Houma police and ask if they got any new drug dealers in town and have them pick him up?"

"I'll do what I can. We're still working to find Mr. Holmes. We have a DNA match of his blood on that knife and in the living room. So we can place him there at the time of the killing. He's definitely a person of interest."

"Person of interest? He's the damn murderer!"

"Darius, we're looking as hard as we can. We still have an alert out to have him detained for questioning. Just because his blood was there, that doesn't give us enough evidence for a murder warrant yet. After all, he lived there. But we are making progress."

"He killed my momma! He's not a person of interest! And you still ain't told me whose blood that was in the kitchen." Darius's face and voice were filled with anger and frustration.

"We're doing all we can, and we'll get your momma's killer. I promise. Just let us do our job. I have to get to an appointment. Can I help you with anything else?"

"No. Just call Houma and see if they got any new drug dealers in town."

"I'll do what I can," the detective said as she walked Darius to the door.

Darius left the police department angry. Maybe that reporter at the newspaper could do a story on how sloppy the police were handling this. He called *The Daily Review*, but Robert Gaines wasn't in. He didn't leave a message.

Darius drove to the RV park, so he could show off his new ride to Nina. Maybe if he could visit with her, she could help put his mind in a better place. He drove up and saw only one bicycle. He knocked, and Juanita came to the door.

"Sorry, Nina's at work. Do you wanna come in?"

"No, thank you." Darius turned quickly and went back toward his car. He didn't want to be in the trailer alone with that nymphomaniac. "Tell her I came by in my new ride to see her," he said from the safety of the Impala.

On the way home, he stopped at Burger King and sat down to eat his Whopper with no onion and heavy mayonnaise. Two female cooks were going at each other like a pair of banty roosters about some man they were fighting over. His attention drifted from the females to a group of Patterson white guys he used to see occasionally in Franklin.

The alpha of the group had his back to him but was looking outside. Darius saw a silver Trans Am parked near the door which he'd seen before and was told it belonged to Tommie Johnson, the leader of a small group of thieves. He'd heard Tommie did some drug-dealing and had a reputation for being violent with those whom he disagreed. There was word on the street that he had an ongoing feud with a family of hoodlums over on the West End.

Darius was concerned when he thought he heard Tommie say something about Thirty-eight. Maybe he wasn't talking about his friend but was talking about a gun. Just to be safe, he called Ricardo and got his voice mail.

"Hey, Thirty-eight," Darius said once he heard the beep. "Call me, bro. Got some crackers over here in Bayou Vista dissing you. They sound like they up to no good. Latah."

Darius finished his meal and passed close to the group on his way out. "One of these days, that spick is gonna get shot," Darius heard Tommie say.

CHAPTER 14
DECEMBER 2005–JANUARY 2006

Sometimes it was like Marcus warned: You need to be ready for shit-slides coming at you.

One night while Prez was working and Doc was out selling drugs, Jack started barking. That didn't strike Darius as worthy of notice because Jack seemed predisposed to barking mode. But when the doorknob started jiggling, Darius bolted from the couch to retrieve his gun. He had the gun raised when the front door burst open and Doc tumbled in, shutting it behind him.

"Mother of Jesus, that was close," Doc said, flopping on the couch beside the door and taking off his wet tennis shoes.

"Yeah. I was a split-second from shooting you, Doc," Darius said as he lowered his pistol.

"The cops almost caught my ass. Some narc saw me, and I had to run here through ditches and over fences to shake him from my tail. Your friggin' dog wanted to bite me!"

"He was just barking," Darius said. "You the frigging fool knocking down doors in the middle of the night."

"I didn't knock it down. I knocked it open when I couldn't find my key. I think I left it on my dresser." Doc seemed unconcerned over his brush with a lethal case of lead poisoning. "I saw the cop turn on our street, so I had to bust in."

It didn't surprise Darius that Prez went ballistic over the damaged door the next morning and told Doc he had to start looking for another place.

"It's all cool, man. That won't happen again. Just give me some time to get my feet under me and find where I can go. Ain't no rush."

Prez was placated somewhat by Doc giving him the money from the drug sales he had made the previous night.

"Ya got a rock?" Prez changed the subject, wanting a quick morning high.

"Ya wanna smoke some?" Doc asked Darius, who had been sitting on the couch saying nothing while he ate a peanut butter and jelly sandwich. Darius never used Doc's stuff, but his roommates were usually polite enough to invite him to join. He declined, finished off his glass of iced milk, and walked to his room. Darius may've smoked a little weed every now and then, but a life revolving around drugs was something he never wanted. He saw what it had done to his momma, and these two boneheads reinforced his aversion to jumping in that pit of vipers.

Darius went to his room and fell into bed. Rolling over on his back, he dialed the digits to his woman. Nina answered and said she'd love to talk, but she was tired. She'd just worked a sixteen-hour shift and was worn out. Darius said he understood and hung up. He was disappointed because he wanted to talk to her about all the drama he was going through.

Ricardo called Darius the day after New Year's with a job promising a bigger than usual payday. BT Bergeron Cadillac in Morgan City had ordered a Gallardo Lamborghini for some rich dude in Berwick. Ricardo spoke with Paul who said they could make $30,000 by boosted the car and delivering it to him.

"That's twelve G for you, fifteen for me, and three for my inside man." Ricardo flashed his wide smile. "But don't expect a two-hundred-dollar bonus this time."

"It can't be easy to jack a quarter-million-dollar car and sell it on the streets," Darius said.

"Sellin' it on the street is *hombre's* problem. Jackin' it is mine, and I got it covered." Ricardo showed his confidence with a thumbs-up on each hand.

"Man, you got more connections than a Greyhound bus. A'ight, Thirty-eight, you the man. Count me in." Darius bumped fists with him to seal the deal. "We can watch the playoff game Sunday and then go do this."

Jack was pulling on the other end of a discarded orange life jacket when Ricardo drove up. Darius let go of the life jacket, and Jack shook it while he lay between Darius and Ricardo. Darius told Ricardo that he'd seen Striker and Bones and invited them to watch the game, but they declined.

"They woulda wanted in on the Lambo action!" Ricardo said with a frown. He leaned in closer to Darius, shaking his head and tapping his finger into Darius's chest. "Don't go thinkin' those *hombres* are ya *amigos*, cuz they ain't. They'll steal from ya as fast as steal with ya!"

Jack edged closer to Darius and gave a low growl. Darius rubbed his dog's neck.

"Whoa there, Jackie boy. Don't go growlin' at the ol' Three-eight or I won't get ya no more rawhides!" Ricardo reached down and offered the dog the back of his hand.

Jack sniffed his hand and wagged his tail.

"It's cool, bro," Darius said. "They not here, and I'll remember what you said."

"Let's go watch the game with ya psycho roommate."

"News alert," Darius said with an exaggerated whisper. "They're both psychos."

He led the way into the trailer, where the acrid odor of burnt weed greeted them. Jack stood at the foot of the steps and barked.

"Get under the trailer," Darius commanded with a wave of his hand. Jack whimpered, but obediently trotted under the trailer.

Prez was leaning back in a recliner more stained than a politician's reputation. Doc was spraying deodorizer in the air; the room smelled like strawberry marijuana. There were some chips in a bowl on the table in front of the couch where Darius and Ricardo sat. To the far side of the couch was a 150-quart ice chest with a few twelve-packs of iced beer. Darius had heard Doc say he'd stolen eight cases of beer the other day. He didn't ask how he'd accomplished the feat.

"The game is startin' in a couple minutes," Prez said politely. "Grab a beer."

Doc returned from a bathroom visit and reached into the bowl to grab a handful of chips.

"Did ya wipe the piss off the seat and wash ya nasty hands 'fore you stuck 'em in the bowl?"

Thus, began the first argument of the afternoon. Darius shrugged and glanced at Ricardo, who rolled his eyes. "Get the popcorn and let's watch the show," Darius said, referring to his roommates' shenanigans.

"We ain't got no popcorn," Prez said as he briefly paused in his argument with Doc to apologize to his guest. "Have some chips on the coffee table."

Prez and Doc traded insults throughout the game. It was obvious this relationship had passed the strained stage and was about to conclude, probably violently. After the game concluded, Prez and Doc attacked each other's intellect and understanding of football. Ricardo grabbed his fedora from the coffee table, looking ready to leave before a fight broke out.

Darius went to his room and retrieved his pistol which he stuck in his waist band. He walked back to the front and motioned for Ricardo to follow as he walked toward the front door.

"I'll be gone a couple days," Darius said as he stood in the doorway and looked back over his shoulder. "I hope they don't kill each other," Darius said as he and Ricardo stepped into the yard.

Jack ran from under the trailer with an old yellow tennis ball, which he dropped at Darius's feet. Darius picked it up and threw it across the yard. Jack bounded after the ball which he retrieved, dropping it at Darius's feet.

"He'll do this 'till the skeeters run us off. Let's go to Subway and eat," Darius said.

After leisurely eating their meal, they left Bayou Vista and headed across the river to Morgan City to relieve a dealership of the most expensive car in the parish.

The boosting of the Lamborghini proved even easier than the theft of the boat. Of course, stealing some millionaire's special-ordered toy from a prominent business might bring some heat, but Ricardo assured Darius that he had all the bases covered. The showroom door was unlocked, the keys were in the ignition, and all security cameras were off. Darius didn't know how Ricardo could've done all that, but Ricardo insisted his man on the inside knew what he was doing.

Within minutes of arriving at the dealership, Darius was behind the wheel of Ricardo's Suburban, and his partner was driving the

Lambo on US 90. Thirty miles east of Morgan City, in a ten-mile stretch of swampland, Darius was horrified to see the Lambo blast out of sight.

As Darius passed State Highway 317, he saw a state trooper turn on to the highway with his lights and siren on. Darius had gotten way over the speed limit to catch up. He pulled into the right lane, expecting to see the trooper pull in behind him, but he didn't.

Whew, that means he's after somebody else. That could only mean one other person. Shit Creek is out of its banks.

Would Thirty-eight outrun the Louisiana State Police in the stolen Lambo? What happens if he gets caught? Darius reached into his pocket and got out his cell phone. His throat was so tight with anxiety that he could scarcely breathe. Ricardo didn't answer. He called again. The line opened, and Darius heard sirens in the background.

"What's up, *amigo?*"

"Where are you? The cops are after your Mexican ass."

"There's a bad accident over here," Ricardo said. Darius heard Thirty-eight laughing. "Traffic was stopped. I'm pulled over on the side of the road, but they lettin' traffic roll now."

Darius caught up with his partner-in-crime. He pulled behind Ricardo, who was waiting for him with the wing doors raised. Darius lit into him as he glanced up the road at the accident scene, which was crawling with cops.

"You damned Mexican." Darius was so worked up that he was spitting. He'd never called Ricardo a name except in jest until now.

"It's a V-ten, *amigo*. Two hundred miles an hour. Ten miles in three minutes. Who can resist that temptation?"

"Ya asking to get us busted and thrown in jail forever. A Mexican and a nigger ain't got a chance in Hades if they get caught in some white man's Lamborghini. Are you a fool or just have a frigging death wish? Whatever it is, I don't want no part of it."

"Bro, you stay on edge too much. Any little thing sets ya off," Ricardo said.

Darius stepped to the front of the stolen car, looking north at the squadron of trigger-happy cops waiting for them. The traffic was moving slowly past several vehicles with emergency lights on. He almost expected to see the flashing lights start toward them.

"There's a hundred cops up there." Darius kept jabbing his finger in the air, pointing to the cops. "You know how many guns would be aimed at us? You know how long they'd pause before they started shooting if either of us sneezed, dammit? You take your damn truck; I'll walk home." Darius threw Ricardo's keys at his feet. He wiped saliva from his lips with the back of his hand.

Ricardo picked up the keys. "I'm sorry, homie," Ricardo said as he stood up. He moved his toothpick from the right side of his mouth to the left and smiled in contrition. "I was wrong. I won't do it again. Come on, let's go get our paycheck. I'll split it fifty-fifty witcha. We cool?" He held the Suburban keys out to Darius.

Darius looked north again. First one trooper and then another pulled away and went north, not south. Darius calmed down.

"A'ight, we cool," he said. He snatched the keys from Ricardo. "But don't ever freaking do something like that again when we're on a job. *Comprende*, you *loco* Mexican?"

"You two should consider doing this full time." Paul appeared impressed as he chewed on his cigar.

"Hell no," Darius answered quickly. "My partner is loco. The money's good, but I ain't down for getting caught."

"They got dudes at the port that for a couple grand will let you roll anything off a shipment and give you some stolen VINs," Paul told them. "Boosters over here make half a mil a year jacking a few cars a month. If they didn't waste their money on women, booze, and dope, they could retire in two years."

Paul rubbed his fingers together and began counting out the cash he owed the pair. "Oh, by the way, I got a name for you," he told Ricardo as he put an envelope in his hands.

"Naw, bro," Ricardo said. "I already got me a street name. I'm cool."

"No, man. I mean I have a name for your dope dealer you are looking for. I'm told he's using the fake ID of a Samuel Rider."

Before setting up business along Bayou Lafourche, Marcus had met with Keelo about his New Orleans mugging. They walked among the Saint Louis Cemetery's 200-year-old, aboveground tombs so they could talk in private.

"You're assuring me this can't be traced back to you?" Marcus asked Keelo, who had insisted the mugging was purely coincidental. "If I find out otherly, it won't be pretty. We understood, right?"

They agreed to continue their business relationship and sealed their trust with a fist bumping.

While in New Orleans, Marcus contacted a counterfeiter who provided him documents that could help insulate him from the problems he'd face if his true identity was discovered by law enforcement. The name on the documents was Samuel Rider.

With a revised business plan and fabricated identity, Marcus made his way to Houma to begin his life anew for what felt like the fifteenth time. Using his fake ID to register himself, he began living at the C'est Bon Motel a couple miles northwest of Houma, along Bayou Croix.

The bayou wasn't much more than a muddy slough populated by white egrets who stood almost motionless in ankle-deep water as they dined on small fish, frogs, snakes, and crawfish. The hotel was a rendezvous spot for cheap trysts and twenty-dollar hookers.

Marcus knew street dealers at the bottom of the food chain seldom lived in mansions, especially if cops were looking to hook a needle to their arm. This was a cheap place to sleep during the day after doing business all night. He could tend to his drug business and other issues without anybody messing with him.

CHAPTER 15
FEBRUARY 2006

"Have you heard from the Houma police about Marcellus?"

Darius was standing in Detective Richmond's office for the thousandth time, trying to get the wheels of justice unstuck. He suspected his last visit there was a waste of time, and the cops had done nothing since he last spoke with them. Maybe this new information would get them off their asses.

"You mean Marcus Holmes? We've been in touch with them," the detective said, "but maybe your friend could be helpful and come in and talk to us."

"Like I said, Miss Richmond, he ain't going to do that. But he gave me a name Marcus is using. He has a fake ID and uses the name Samuel Rider."

"How did he get a fake ID, and why is he using that name?" The detective reached for her notebook and scribbled the name.

"I don't know. It is what it is. But I remember seeing that ID one time on my momma's dresser just before she was killed."

"It would be helpful if your friend came here so we can tie up loose ends and find out how solid this is."

"This is solid, Miss Richmond. But my friend ain't gonna talk with no cops. That has nothing to do with where Marcus is. I have his face burned right here," he said, pointing at his eyes. "Maybe I can find him." Darius was telling her that he'd do their job for them if they refused to act on the information. If he did the job, there'd be no jail—only a funeral.

"We can handle it. But I have something you might like to know. We developed enough evidence to issue a murder warrant for Mr. Holmes. If he's stopped for anything, we'll get him."

"Cool. So now all Houma has to do is pick him up."

"I hope you're being careful about who you hang out with and who your friends are, son. Don't let them get you in trouble."

Darius knew she suspected his police-averse source was involved in criminal activity. He wasn't fond of the unsolicited advice. His friends were good people. She should quit worrying about his friends and worry about the bad guys like the murderer who was still running free.

Darius stopped at the Franklin Winn Dixie store to get a Valentine's Day cake he'd ordered for Nina. He walked to the bakery and asked if the cake was ready.

"It's ready," the bakery manager said. "If you have a few minutes, I'd like to talk."

Darius gave the woman a look-over. She was stout with short hair, and her complexion suggested an adolescence spent battling the teen-age scourge of acne. The extra makeup indicated to Darius that she wasn't comfortable with her natural looks.

Why is this white woman hitting on me? Darius thought. *She's old enough to be my momma.*

She wiped her hands on her black apron, splotched with flour. Then she offered the tips of her fingers in a limp handshake. "I'm Meghan Theriot. I was at your momma's funeral. Me and your momma went to school together. She was my bestie in grade school."

Darius's knees weakened as he grasped the woman's fingers. This was someone who had known his momma before she crossed her event horizon. He felt bad for having thought she was hitting on him.

"I'm happy to meet you. I don't know nobody from Momma's past. I'd love to talk."

Meghan took him to the employee break room. In the center of the room were two long beige tables; tops splattered with brown coffee and red jelly stains. On one side of the room was a Coke machine, a snack machine, and a tall green refrigerator. The other side had a sink big enough to wash the *Titanic* in and a cabinet with a coffeemaker set on top. Mugs—some plain and some with graphics—lined the length of the cabinet top.

Darius's heart was racing. He sat across the table from Meghan, put his chin in his hand and leaned forward to savor every word. He hoped he'd learn things about his momma from before he was born. He didn't really have anything from her past except for that fading picture.

"We were BFFs before anybody knew what a BFF was," Meghan said, laughing. "Your mom was the most beautiful, sweetest, and most considerate person I knew. She had angel eyes. All the boys wanted to be her boyfriend, but she told them they should be after me instead. Yeah, right." She motioned in front of her face as if to invite him to imagine what she'd looked like. "Your momma could've had any boy she wanted, but she always said she wasn't going to kiss a boy unless he loved her. Of course, they all claimed to love her." She chuckled and nodded. "I was an ugly duckling really, but she always said I was beautiful. She gave me confidence and helped me be the woman I eventually became."

"How did y'all get to be friends?" Darius asked.

"We were eight when a bully—he was about two years older than us—took my doll from me. Sarah, she was always a tiny thing. But she ran up to this boy, kicked him in the family jewels, and grabbed my doll. She told him that if he ever bothered me again, she'd murderate him. I've no idea where she came up with that word. She said she just made it up on the spot, but we used it all the time between us when we talked about somebody that was a bully. She'd say they needed to be murderated, and I'd die laughing."

"I never knew my momma to stand up to nobody." Darius leaned back in his chair and smiled his approval at his momma's actions.

"Your momma was a saint, Darius, to everybody she was around. When she got to high school, the light went out of her eyes. She seemed to pull away from everything, like she thought she didn't deserve any-thing good. But there was no one in this world who deserved love, happiness, and success more than your momma."

Darius nodded his head as he continued to smile, pleased to get to know his momma as he'd never known her.

Meghan pushed her chair back, rose from the table and walked to the other side where she sat beside Darius. She clasped his hands and patted them lightly. "The last time I saw your momma back then, she had you in her arms, just a tiny, little baby. She'd look in your eyes, and you'd giggle and make her smile. We were sixteen, and some guy who had to be at least twenty or twenty-one came over and said they had to go. She held you in one hand and reached over and hugged me and said she missed me. We were just kids. None of that meant anything. I told her I missed her, too."

"I always sort of thought she felt guilty about having me and that was part of the reason she went wild and stuff."

"I don't know what happened to your momma. But when I saw how she looked at you, I knew she loved you, and you were the most important thing in her world. She was showing you off and bragging about how cute her baby was."

"I had no idea she was glad to have me." Darius looked up at the suspended ceiling, trying to imagine his momma being proud as she held him as an infant.

"I wanted to talk to you at the funeral, to tell you something else, but I didn't get a chance. I'm glad I have a chance to tell you now. I saw your momma the day before she died. Well, it was that Friday night."

Darius gasped. He turned his chair to the side and leaned toward Meghan. Every word she'd spoken was as delicious as Miss E's pies.

"She seemed happy. She said she was turning her life around and moving you out of the hood. I had no real idea what she was talking about until I heard Father Sorenson speaking."

"Where did you see her?" Darius was on the edge of his chair, his legs tapping the floor.

"We'd watched *Malibu's Most Wanted* at the Bayou Vista theater, and we bumped into each other, literally. She laughed about the movie's portrayal of life in the hood. Then she said that if the movie showed it like it really was, we'd be crying and not laughing."

The movie ticket!

"Momma was a good person. You knew it from her childhood, and I know it from her adulthood. She fought terrible demons, most of 'em having to do with either men or drugs."

"Father Sorenson was right. Your momma found a way to overcome her problems. She told me she'd spent all day looking for work. I told her I was the bakery manager here, and if she came to see me, I'd give her a full-time job with benefits. I believe that's what she was planning. She said she wanted to do it for herself and for you."

"That would explain why she was gone in the car when I got home Friday."

"She was going to buy a ham and fix you a special supper Saturday night."

The ham and the peaches!

"Your momma performed a final act of kindness for me that I will always be in debt to her for. She told my daughter that she looked like me, and that I was the most beautiful girl in school. Ever since then, my little girl has been telling people that her momma was the prettiest girl in school!" Meghan was smiling. "I was the ugly duckling," she repeated. "Your momma was the most beautiful girl in school, and was still beautiful, inside and out, when she died."

"Thank you, Miss Meghan. This explains some stuff and makes me confident that Momma found her way back. You have no idea how happy you made me."

"I hope they find whoever killed your mom. I'd like to murderate him."

"Me, too, Miss Meghan. Me, too!"

"I have to get back to the bakery," Meghan said as she slowly stood up from the table. "Don't forget your cake. I'll comp it out, no charge. Come give me a hug."

Darius was a little embarrassed about the hug, but after all Meghan had shared, it seemed natural to hug her. He held on to her a little longer than he'd intended.

"Take care, Darius. I wish you the very best. I'm sure you'll make your momma proud."

CHAPTER 16
FEBRUARY-MARCH 2006

"You don't live far from here. Let's take a romantic walk back to the trailer and tend to this tomorrow."

Darius knew Nina's offer to walk home wasn't about romance as much as it was about Nina trying to make him feel less embarrassed. After a pleasant Valentine's Day dinner of Mexican food at Tampico's, Darius couldn't get the Impala cranked, and then the battery died. Darius profusely apologized for the inconvenience, but Nina assured him everything was okay. Why did disaster seem to strike every time Darius thought he might get to make love to Nina?

"Let's put on some soft music and forget about this little bump in the road," Nina said when they got in the trailer. She began unbuttoning his long-sleeved shirt.

Darius knew Prez was spending the night with his momma in Thibodaux, and Doc would be gone all night selling dope. So maybe the night would end up blissfully after all. He turned off all the lights as he led Nina to his bedroom.

Nina told Darius how wonderful this Valentine's Day had been to her.

"*Quiero hacerte el amor*," she whispered in his ear.

Darius loved when she spoke Spanish even though he only understood half of what she was saying. But he knew enough to know that
she wanted to make love. He fumbled with the buttons on her blouse
until she placed his hands on her breasts as she finished unbuttoning
the blouse herself. She fell backwards into Darius's double bed and put
her arms around his neck as he kissed her.

Darius ignored Jack's barking as he kissed Nina's breasts. The
barking changed into a deeper, more aggressive tone. It was the gut-
tural sound Darius used to imagine White Fang would make before an
attack.

There was a pop of a small-caliber handgun and a yelp. Darius
jumped from the bed and looked out the window where he saw two
silhouettes on the porch. Jack was biting the leg of the fat one on
the porch. The other intruder raised a pistol and shot a second time.
Darius grabbed his gun and threw on the lights as he ran to the front
door. The intruders were fleeing when he got to the door. They were
wearing hoodies, shielding their identities. They jumped into a Trans
Am parked under the streetlight. Darius fired six rounds from his gun.

Nina had come to the door, wrapped in a sheet. "*Papi*, Jack is hurt."

Darius stepped off the porch and onto the ground where Jack lay
bleeding and struggling to breathe. The temperature was falling, but
Darius, half naked, didn't notice it as he cradled his canine companion
in his arms. Darius brought him inside to the warmth of the trailer, a
sanctuary he'd never been allowed to enter. Blood trailed across the
porch and threshold of the trailer. Darius's underwear became red with
Jack's blood.

"I'm sorry for bringing you here and letting you get killed," Darius
moaned as he hugged the glassy-eyed dog.

"He's going to be okay, *Papi*," Nina said, trying to comfort her lover.

There was a long pause between each of Jack's breaths, as if it had
been his last.

"No, he's not, *Mamacita*."

Jack's eyes focused, looking directly into Darius's eyes for a few seconds, as if he was saying good-bye. He whimpered and then convulsed and became still. Jack's body, no longer thin and emaciated, shuddered as he exhaled his final breath.

"Good-bye, my friend. The hood has taken you, too. You watched over the Browns, and Momma and me. You were a survivor and a true friend."

Darius was beginning to wonder if he had some kind of voodoo Midas touch, where everybody or everything he cared about would have some sort of death curse. He secretly began to fear something bad would happen to Nina or Thirty-eight.

"I've never taken a day off," Nina said. "But I'm going to call in sick to be with you when you bury Jack." Darius knew Nina was making a sacrifice. He would make it up to her on the next job with Thirty-eight.

Prez and Doc had made it home, and they helped him dig through the sticky black mud to make a grave for Jack along Bayou Teche. His two roommates and Nina were at his side as he put his companion in the shallow grave.

Darius was convinced it was Tommie Johnson's Trans Am he'd seen in the dark. Prez believed that Tommie and his crew had been staking the place out to rob Doc. They'd probably seen no vehicles in the yard and decided to seize the opportunity for a burglary.

"Bro, that mutt saved ya life," he told Darius. "Whoever was tryin' to break in was packin' heat and wasn't expectin' ya to be in there. They'd a shot ya ass when they saw ya."

"I'll find his cracker ass and cap it for him." Darius's anger was simmering like slow-cooked beans.

"Make sure ya check his pockets 'fore ya leave," Prez said, "cuz he's sure to have some Benjamins on him."

After Jack's burial, Prez helped Darius retrieve his car. He told Darius that the ignition coil had gone out, so they drove to the Auto Zone in Berwick and picked up the part. By noon, Darius had his car running again. He and Nina spent the rest of the day together. But his mood, dark as the barrel of his Smith and Wesson, refused to brighten. He spent much of the day talking of revenge.

"*Papi*, I'm sorry you lost your dog," Nina said as she kissed Darius good night at her trailer. "You're a special person. Please be careful with this hatred you have in your heart. Ricardo is right about crossing a line in killing a man, *Papi*. That's a bad line."

"I hear you," Darius replied softly. He knew he wasn't going to kill Tommie over the dog, although killing Marcus remained an option. "Thank you for everything, *Mamacita*, and for staying with me today. You and Thirty-eight are my only friends, although you're hotter and sweeter than he is." Darius laughed and kissed her. As he stepped on to the steps outside of her trailer, Darius turned and added, "I'm glad you're in my life."

"*Me haces feliz*," she said.

"Huh?" Darius had no idea what that meant.

"You make me happy, *Papi*."

When Darius got back home, his two roommates had locked horns over some misunderstanding about the terms of Doc's living at the trailer.

"The Constitution says a verbal contract is the same as a written one. So I have the right to stay here. That's the law, dude."

"Well, I changed my mind," Prez said. "I don't want ya here. Ya bringin' too much attention from the cops. They 'bout to bust ya ass, and I don't wanna be caught up in it. Au revoir, adios, ciao, aloha, hasta la vista, arrivederci."

It amused Darius that Prez had thought that learning how to say good-bye in several languages allowed him to claim he was multilingual. But right now, Darius was in no mood for all this bickering. He walked to his room, grabbed his Beretta, and stuck it in his waistband. One of these days his path would cross with Pigenstein and he'd finally get to use his gun. He eased by his squabbling roommates and walked out the front door to battle the mosquitoes in the bayou solitude.

"That *gringo*, Tommie Johnson, ya heard at Burger King talkin' 'bout me is trouble, bro," Ricardo said to Darius a couple of days after Jack was killed. "His guys are stealin' *mierda* everywhere, on the west and east ends. On top of that, they gettin' into big-time dope sellin', and I hear they tryin' to start a gang."

Tommie lived east of the Calumet Cut, the unofficial east-west boundary of the parish. But he and his guys had, until this time, kept most of their criminal activities on the West End.

"Prez thinks he was trying to hit Doc for his drugs when they tried to break into the trailer," Darius said.

"Nina told me 'bout ya dog, *amigo*. I'm sorry."

"Thanks, bro. The hood is taking everything from me. All I got now is you and Nina."

"Well, I'm tougher than a cockroach, and they been around a million years. I ain't goin' nowhere, homie."

"Why don't you go to the police and tell 'em what Tommie plans?"

"Ya never rat out somebody to the cops. I mean ya momma's killer, that's different. But besides that, no way. Ya never, ever do that. Ya hear me, homie?"

"We can't run around scared like punks, letting 'em steal our stuff and kill our dogs."

Ricardo agreed, saying that Tommie needed to keep his shit in his own toilet and not bring it into the East End. A home invasion and a roughing up, maybe even a robbery of Tommie and his wife Bianca, would send that message. It would make Tommie—and by extension, his wife and unborn child—realize he was vulnerable.

"Me and some *hombres* are 'bout to take matters in our own hands. I think he may've gotten wind of it, and that might be what ya overheard him talkin' 'bout at Burger King."

"Marcus is the only man I'm willing to kill and go to Angola for. But, bro, killing my dog. That's messed up. I wanna hurt this asshole."

"Let me handle Tommie, and if I hear anything on ya boy Marcus, I'll let ya know. Might even help ya out."

Ricardo told Darius that he hadn't implemented his plan because he was considering all contingencies. Patterson chief of police Jimmy Langston wouldn't take this too kindly. Everybody, the good guys and the bad, knew that Langston had brought peace to the Wild West that once existed in Patterson.

CHAPTER 17
APRIL 2006

Ricardo was out of town. So Bones and Striker, along with Striker's cousin Michael, were looking for mischief on their own. A casual acquaintance, twenty-three-year-old Jerry, still living with his parents, rode along with them in a Toyota Sienna minivan driven by his nephew from Houma, eighteen-year-old Jamal. The bored, ragtag group ended up in Franklin at the house of a duo known as the Thug Brothers.

Lil Thug, at six-foot-four, two-hundred-sixty pounds, with a dozen tattoos, shaved his head but not his face. He was called Lil Thug to differentiate him from Big Thug, his father, who had a rap sheet as long as a roll of unused toilet paper. Lil Thug's seventeen-year-old brother was called T3, short for "Thug Three."

This impromptu confederacy concluded that a robbery of Tommie could net them several thousand dollars. They left Lil Thug's house with a light rain falling. They hadn't gone far in their fifteen-mile trip when the minivan sputtered.

"Sweet baby Jesus, I forgot to get gas," Jamal said. They were three miles from the nearest gas station.

"Let's call Darius and tell him to bring us some gas," Striker suggested. "We can tell him Thirty-eight sent us to rough up Tommie for killin' that dog of his."

When Darius arrived with a five-gallon can of gasoline for the van, he insisted on joining. He left his Impala in a parking lot and hopped into the crowded van. Most of the occupants appeared giddy with excitement but he saw a mask of trepidation covering Jamal's face.

Saying he didn't know anything about Patterson, Jamal suggested somebody else assume the driving. Michael volunteered. After running off the road twice, Michael claimed he wasn't used to driving a minivan. Then he said the steering was getting difficult, so he pulled over.

Jamal got out in the rain, walked to the front, and saw the front passenger tire was almost flat. "Michael musta hit somethin' when he ran off the road," he said, sticking his head in the van.

"Why the hell it's gotta be my fault? Ya the one with the bald tires?"

"These are brand new tires," Jamal said.

"Oh, Jesus H. Christ," Lil Thug grunted. "Whose Wheaties did I piss in to deserve these jackasses?"

"Um, hey guys, the spare is flat, too." Jamal had just inspected the spare tire.

"Damn, Jamal," Lil Thug yelled. "You are a worthless motherfucker, ain't ya?"

"It's cool, man. Calm down. Don't worry 'bout it. Momma keeps a can of Fix-A-Flat in the back."

Darius stepped out to help as Jamal screwed the can of emergency repair aerosol into the valve stem. Jamal wiped away a trickle of water that had dripped from the bib of his cap down his face. He could tell Jamal's nerves were as frazzled as old Christmas lights.

"What have I gotten myself into? I shoulda gone to the movies like I told Momma," Jamal grumbled.

"Don't worry so much, dude. Let's just get back on the road," Darius said as he put a hand on Jamal's shoulder.

"Well, at least we got all the bad luck out of the way, and it can't get no worse," Striker said once they were on the road again.

"So what's the plan?" Darius asked. "How are we roughing up this asshole?"

"Ya the lookout," Lil Thug snapped back as he reached for the joint from his brother.

"It was my dog. I want to get in my licks."

"We already got plans," Striker said. "We can't change 'em."

Darius reluctantly agreed to stand guard as he took a toke from the reefer that had finally made it to him.

"A'ight, the party's 'bout to begin," Lil Thug said as the minivan rolled to a stop. "Everybody get their masks on. Jamal, ya the getaway driver."

"I'm fuckin' jacked, man," Jerry said with a psycho, Jack Nicholson grin. "Let's do this." He let out a wolf-like howl.

"Shut up, ya stupid fool," Striker hissed. "Sweet Mother of Jesus. Ya wanna get us shot?"

"Bring it on, baby! Bring it on!"

Jerry, Lil Thug, and T3 each had a handgun. Striker and Bones each carried a knife. Jamal, Michael, and Darius were unarmed. The burglars got out of the van carrying backpacks to bring out whatever loot they could expropriate. Lil Thug had a rope and duct tape in his pack.

"Imma bust the door and go first," Lil Thug said. "Little brother, ya cover me. Jerry, ya come in last."

"Why I gotta bring up the rear like a horse's ass?"

"Cuz I said so. No more time for talkin'. Shut up and let's do this."

How is Lil Thug in charge of a Thirty-eight-sanctioned operation? Darius wondered. *This plan-as-you-go gig was a joke about as funny as a pissed off skunk.*

The drizzle had stopped as the six intruders lined up in the mud at the front door like grade-schoolers going to lunch. Darius hid by a tree, just a few feet from the door. He had a good view of the street, and he'd also be able to observe what was going on in the trailer. A loud noise announced that the trailer door was crashed open as Lil Thug hurled his bulky frame into it—obviously not his first breaking and entering.

Jerry, in a hurry to get inside, ran over Bones, who had paused to try to pull up his pants. Both Jerry and Bones tumbled from the steps. Jerry bounced back up but slipped in the mud and his gun discharged. Darius, concerned by Michael's loud pronouncement that he'd been shot, ran to help Michael, but he was shoved away.

"Dammit, Jerry," Michael yelled while rubbing his right thigh. "Ya shot me in the ass, man. It hurts like hell!"

Darius couldn't see any blood from Michael's injury.

"Quit bein' such a pussy and get outta my way." Jerry picked himself up and looked down the barrel of his gun as he wiped away mud from the trigger.

"Ya supposed to be bringin' up the back, not shootin' me in the ass, ya stupid ass." Michael was now in Jerry's face, almost nose-to-nose.

"Outta my way, I said. It's time to rock and roll."

"Rock and roll with this, asshole," Michael said as he swatted the side of Jerry's head.

The blow sent Jerry reeling backward, tumbling into Bones again. Bones had just gotten up out of the mud. Now the two fell on the ground together. Jerry's gun fired a second time.

"Dammit, I shot myself. Right in the damn foot. It's ya fault, Michael. I can't feel my big toe. I think ya made me blow off my damn big toe." Jerry raised his gun and waved it at Michael, but he was mostly focused on his bloody foot. "I'm tryin' to wiggle my toe, but I can't feel it."

"Get that gun outta my face, ya clumsy fool," Michael said.

He pushed Jerry backward with one hand and swiped the gun away from him with the other hand. Jerry fell backward into Bones, who tripped over his sagging pants. Down went Bones a third time. Fortunately for the three of them, Jerry's gun fell out of his hand into the mud without further collateral damage.

"If somebody knocks me in this mud again," Bones said, "I'm quittin' and callin' the cops myself!"

Michael, Jerry, and Bones began lashing out in a gumbo of arms and legs, wildly throwing punches in the front yard of their intended victim. Striker stepped into the fray, trying to separate the three belligerents. Darius thought they looked like pigs wallowing in the mud.

"Guys, guys!" Darius yelled. "Get your incompetent asses inside!"

"Who's callin' who incompetent? Our dogs are alive." Bones was wiping mud from his hands and face, mad as a wet hen and obviously in no mood for Darius's comments.

Darius looked back inside the trailer. Apparently, Tommie and Bianca were interrupted in the middle of sex on the living room floor. Bianca wore only a cowboy hat and held a riding crop while a porno played on the television; evidently, she'd been knocked off of Tommie who at the moment was pinned down by a muddy Nike in his chest and staring at the barrel of two guns. Bianca screamed as she bolted from the floor and ran toward the back of the trailer.

Lil Thug fired his gun; the bullet put a hole big enough for Darius to see in the wall over her shoulder. "Tell ya bitch to shut up and get her pregnant ass back here," Lil Thug irritably growled. "The next bullet is in her head." Darius saw him shake his head and shrug his shoulders when he looked behind him; apparently noticing that part of the crew hadn't made it into the trailer yet.

Bianca returned, covering her privates with the cowboy hat and putting her free hand across her breasts. "Please, you can have anything you want, just don't hurt my baby."

Darius was anxious. Mad or not, he wasn't prepared to kill anybody over Jack's killing.

"Cowgirl, I ain't gonna hurt nobody if ya shut up and everybody does like they told," Lil Thug said, his gun moving back and forth between his two victims. "Little brother, get the duct tape. Tie 'em up and tape their mouth."

"Hot-damn," Jerry said when he finally entered through the door, limping. There appeared to be blood and mud tracked on the floor from Jerry's shoe. "I knew this was gonna be fun, but I didn't know we was gonna get kinky." Jerry maniacally laughed as he continued wiping mud off his gun.

Michael passed by Darius and entered next, calling for fire and brimstone to fall upon Jerry. Then, slipping on the muddy linoleum, he collided with Jerry, who at that moment was looking down the barrel of his gun again. The gun discharged, and Jerry stepped back in seeming surprise and relief that he hadn't been shot.

"Ya almost made me shoot myself again," Jerry said.

"What idiot looks down the barrel of a loaded gun?" Michael replied as Striker and Bones finally straggled in. "Jesus, man, you a motherlode of stupid."

"What the hell? Where's the masks, ya retards?" Lil Thug exclaimed as he looked at the four unmasked intruders entering the room. Striker and Bones pulled their muddy shirts up over their faces as Michael ducked back out to find his mask. Darius thudded his head on the door jamb as he thought of how this operation was unfolding. Half a barrel of monkeys would have more brains than this group.

Stupid fools better be glad Tommie and Bianca are facedown and can't see them.

"Man, this ain't goin' too good," Michael said as he looked at Darius on his way back into the trailer.

Jerry sat down in a love seat and put his gun on the floor as he inspected his foot under a lamp. He'd done nothing about retrieving his mask.

"Jerry, cover ya face," Bones shouted.

"Why the hell ya wanna call my name?" Jerry shouted, looking up from his bloody, tattered shoe and glaring at Bones. "Now Imma have to kill these two. Damn, my foot hurts. I think my toe got blown off. I should be lookin' for the thing." He was trying to take his shoe off for a better look at his toe, but Lil Thug stopped him and told him it would leave too much DNA. "Messed up my Air Flights, man," Jerry said of his new shoes.

Yep, half a barrel of monkeys.

Darius was thinking about how Ricardo's operations were well-planned, efficient in-and-out jobs—not this Laurel-and-Hardy stupidity. Seeing and hearing what was going on inside the trailer convinced Darius that the bill of goods he'd been sold regarding the purpose of this misadventure was bogus as a three-dollar bill.

Striker and Bones sat on the couch, holding a knife to the back of the necks of the victims as Lil Thug had instructed. Together they managed to talk Jerry out of killing Tommie and Bianca.

Michael, finally back inside with his mask on his face, was holding the back of his leg and saying that he needed to get to the doctor.

"Hey, T3, throw that blanket over here so I can cover up these two," Bones said. "It ain't right to keep them naked."

"I'm busy," T3 said. "Just don't look at that ass if ya can't handle it."

The Thug Brothers and Michael ransacked the house; Jerry walked in circles like a yard chicken with its head cut off, whining about his toe and saying something about putting it on ice in case it could be reattached. Striker and Bones argued over whether a microphone boom was showing in one of the scenes of the porno, so Striker grabbed the remote from the coffee table and rewound the movie.

Darius was vexed by the realization that he'd been deceived and that this had never been about Jack's killing. It was an armed robbery, pure and simple.

Thirty-eight probably knew nothing about this. He's gonna be pissed.

The bandits found a little cash, some jewelry, and a small amount of marijuana. Lil Thug rolled Tommie off his belly with his foot and then ripped the duct tape from Tommie's mouth. "Where's the cash and the dope?" he demanded.

Tommie's cell phone started ringing, then stopped.

"Ain't ya ever heard not to get in no pissin' contest with a skunk?" Tommie said defiantly as he sat up. "Ya ain't thought none of this through very well, nigger. I ain't got jack here, and my boys are on their way since I didn't answer their calls." The phone rang again as he was speaking. "Ya best bet is to leave now while ya can. What ya white boys doin' with these niggers, anyhow?" Tommie asked of Striker and Bones. "Are y'all with Thirty-eight? Tell him if he wants war, he got it. I ain't scared of no—"

Darius jumped, startled by a pair of shots that rang out. He heard Lil Thug say that he'd had enough. Tommie fell backward, apparently shot twice in the chest with his hands still tied behind his back.

Oh, helladammit, no! Darius thought. *These piss-ant fools done went and pinned a murder rap on themselves, and here I am a part of it. All for a couple of Benjamins!*

"Ya talk too much, cracker," Lil Thug said as he stood straddled over the bleeding Tommie. "Ya should know when to shut the hell up."

Darius saw Tommie struggle to rise, but he was apparently injured too badly to do so. Even in the dim light, Darius saw Tommie spit blood on Lil Thug.

That was real ballsy of the white boy. It's surprising Lil Thug didn't end it all right there.

Striker and Bones appeared as nervous as cats in a room full of rocking chairs.

"Let's get outta here, dude," Bones said to anybody who might be listening as he headed to the door. "The cops'll be here soon, if his crew ain't. We never agreed to all this."

Darius had seen enough of this half barrel of monkeys. He'd been duped into stepping into the middle of this mountain of stupid. He was almost hyperventilating from anger and frustration over how the evening had devolved into senseless violence and greed. Galled by his associates, and even concerned about Tommie, he walked to the van and told Jamal he was splitting.

"I had no idea this was gonna happen when I came out here," Jamal said. "My momma is gonna kill me if she finds out. I'm thinkin' about leavin', too."

"They'll kill you if you do. Hang tight long as you can. I'll hitch a ride to my car."

Jamal began honking the horn. A neighbor's light turned on, and then another set of lights. Not far away, a siren began to wail. Darius looked back over his shoulder, and from half a block away he saw the intruders rushing into the van, which started backing up before the last one had shut the door. The van sped by him, out the back end of the neighborhood in the opposite direction of the sirens. He would've refused if the fleeing idiots had bothered to offer him a ride.

Darius was glad he'd kept his involvement in this caper at a minimum. He thought to himself that he had to be more careful that he wasn't carried away in a river of folly by these dumb asses; he needed to try to stay away from Striker and Bones. Hanging out with a decent fellow like Ricardo was one thing. But street thugs, like this pair, were just trouble from the get-go. They had the disposition and inclination to become major menaces to society.

Ricardo was fuming as he ranted, raved, and paced the rocky shore of Lake Palourde in a rendezvous Striker had requested to explain what had happened.

"*Qué chingados!* Ya ain't got the brains God put in a hummin' bird. Y'all sure know how to mess up Easter." Ricardo's toothpick flew from his mouth as he spat at Striker's feet. Sometimes I think ya just *estúpidos gringos* I should leave!"

"We're sorry," Striker said while holding the backside of his pants up with one hand.

"Ya sure Tommie mentioned my name and said there'd be war?" Ricardo asked as he threw a rock out into the lake and searched his shirt pocket for another toothpick.

"Yeah. He said to deliver that message," Striker said.

"He knows it was Lil Thug and T3 doin' all that," Bones said. "So that's who he's goin' to go after. *If* he lives," sounding more hopeful than confident.

"Yeah," Striker said. "He'll probably go after them others, but not us."

"I didn't want somethin' to just fly over. I wanted to send a message. *Pinche idiota!*" Ricardo kicked at rocks on the ground. "This ain't the end of it, *amigo*. Alligators feed in still waters. Ya *putos* need to get out of my face, cuz I'm 'bout to lose it."

Darius had spoken to Ricardo before the two idiots had arrived and explained what had happened. When the two Princes of Dumb departed, he again apologized for his role in the caper, and accepted responsibility for not making sure Ricardo had sanctioned the job. He'd quietly listened as Striker and Bones tried to minimize what was done until they walked away like scolded puppies.

"It looks like they'll need industrial raincoats once the shit starts falling," Darius said.

"These *cabrónes* don't know the *mierda* they're in." He took his toothpick from his mouth and pointed it in the direction that Striker and Bones had taken when they left. "They think Tommie is only goin' after the Thug Brothers. But none of those *putos* are safe."

Eventually Ricardo calmed down, and the two of them discussed a job that involved stealing some diesel fuel from one of the shipyards.

"God says an eye for an eye, so we'll hunt down those bastards and put a cap in their asses." It was five days later when Bianca said this to Tommie as she brought him home from the hospital. She put Tommie's hand on her belly to rub it as she felt her unborn child move. "They could've killed our baby."

Bianca peaked through the window after hearing a knock at the door. She saw Tommie's two brothers and a couple of friends. She let them in and the group talked about who had done this and what they should do about it. Tommie said he knew T-3 and Lil Thug were involved.

"One didn't have a mask on," Bianca said, "they called him Jerry. He wanted to kill us." She'd just poured them all a glass of tea; she wouldn't allow beer in the house since she had gotten pregnant. "He had the bleeding foot and kept saying he had to find his toe somewhere."

Tommie raised his shirt and checked the bandages on his chest. "If I see him again, I'll know him. He's a tall, scrawny dude with a goatee—easy to pick out."

"Wait a minute," Tommie's older brother Riley said. "Let me get this straight. This Jerry clown comes in your trailer lookin' for his friggin' toe?" He was slapping his knees in laughter.

"Yeah, man. I never figured what was up with that. He was Lex Luther crazy." Tommie put his shirt back down. "He never worried about coverin' his face. I'm not sure who the other three were. I think a couple of 'em belonged to Thirty-eight. I think it was those two crazy assholes who always ride with him."

Bianca slowly rubbed her belly. "There was another one that was going through our stuff, limping and rubbing his ass."

"Yeah, he said Jerry shot him in the ass," Tommie said.

"Holy shittin' crawfish," Riley said. "You mean Psycho-Four-Toes shot one of his own crew? What kind of spastic retards came to your house, bro?"

"I know, right?" Tommie said. "Except for the Thug Brothers, this was a group of real amateurs. Moe, Larry, Curly, Shemp, and two sons of the devil!"

They all laughed again.

"I got a gut feelin' Thirty-eight had somethin' to do with this," Riley said. "You sure that new nigger that runs with him wasn't here?"

"Naw, unless he was drivin' the getaway," Tommie said. "The one honkin' the horn out there. That Oreo ain't dumb, from what I heard, so I doubt that was him." By the time the powwow concluded, it was determined that Lil Thug, T3, and Jerry had to be eliminated.

"The Good Book says a man's gotta do what a man's gotta do." Tommie was looking at the hole in the wall from the bullet that had missed Bianca.

"I don't think that's in the Bible, baby," Bianca said, smiling as she gently tapped Tommie's arm.

"It's in Revelations when it talks about the whore of Babylon and the dragon," Tommie said defensively. "It said there was a great battle, and then it said a man's gotta do what a man's gotta do."

"Who won the battle, Tommie?" asked Daniel, one of Tommie's crew. "The whore or the dragon?"

"I don't remember. I think the whore died in Sodom and Gonorrhea and the dragon drowned in a flood."

"Baby, that's Sodom and Gomorrah," Bianca gently tried to correct. "And that was long before the whore was born."

"I don't know," Tommie said. "All them stories get confusin'. All I know is that God said that a man's gotta do what a man's gotta do. Ask the priest. He'll tell ya. It's the American way. Payback is a bitch. I think somethin' like that is in the Bible, too."

"No, that's not in there either," Bianca said. "And the Bible don't use four-letter words."

"*Bitch* ain't a four-letter word," Tommie said after counting the letters on his fingers. "For the record."

CHAPTER 18
MAY 2006

Maybe someone living in the Iberville projects could help him. Somebody might help put him on the trail of either his momma's killer, his daddy or even the uncle that raped his momma.

After delivering the stolen fuel to a barge on the Westbank, Darius got Ricardo to cross the Mississippi River into New Orleans and bring him to the projects where his momma's auntie once lived. Ricardo parked near the intersection of Conti and Treme streets in front of Saint Louis Cemetery No. 1.

Darius walked across the broken sidewalk and pressed his face against the four-foot wrought-iron fence surrounding the Catholic cemetery. He saw the hundreds of aboveground brick and concrete vaults, some as high as twenty feet, topped with crosses and elaborate images of saints. It felt ghoulish being so close to monuments and crypts that had housed dead people for two centuries.

"No need in me slowin' ya down, *amigo*," Ricardo said. He appeared uncomfortable parked next to the cities of the dead. "Imma drive to that po'boy shop and come back here at seven to get ya *culo*. Call me if ya finish ya business sooner."

Darius trotted across the narrow street and walked toward the cookie-cutter brown brick buildings. These drab, dilapidated dwellings under red clay tile roofs housed the city's elderly, disabled, and poor. Several noisy cliques milled around on this late-spring afternoon while tenants sat outside on tiny porches and yelled across narrow streets to neighbors. Boys ran barefoot and shirtless in small yards, girls played hopscotch on the concrete parking areas and in the streets. Bicycles and skateboards bounced across broken sidewalks. Azalea bushes bloomed on the edges of the property but there was scarcely any vegetation growing in the dusty courtyard.

A Jheri-curled guy asked if Darius wanted to buy some dope, and some Jamaican-looking hoodlum appeared to be eyeing him suspiciously. Darius said he was looking for a couple of old friends.

He spoke to a young white woman walking with a diaper-clad toddler on each hip and a cigarette dangling from her lips. She wore tight purple spandex pants and a pink blouse tied at the midsection. The top buttons were unfastened, and she was braless. Darius tried to describe Marcus, but she was unable to help. He asked if she might know Albert Thomas and his common-law wife, Brenda.

"I 'member Albert. He was tall and fine." The woman smiled. "He lived wit' his woman, Brenda Cormier. She was Creole or maybe white. She had cat eyes but not nearly as pretty as dem dat you got, baby. I 'member Albert cuz he was always tellin' me how fine I was. He had a limp but he was fine, too. I ain't seen him since Katrina. If anybody tried to get back in, dey may've called administration over in de K-Building. Go over dere and ask."

On his way to the K-Building, Darius spoke to a woman dressed in a McDonald's' uniform and carrying a college biology book. This was undoubtedly one of the black girls working her way out of the projects that too many white people seemed to think didn't exist.

"Marcus Holmes?" She looked over the rim of her glasses and spat the name out with contempt. "Dat wort'less, woman-beatin' piece-of-shit was run out de projects a long time ago. Always on a pity trip 'bout how bad his life was and how he was abused but he was always beatin' up on women in here."

Apparently, Marcus wasn't short of people who didn't like him, Darius thought as he walked toward the administrative office.

"Marcus Holmes shacked up with a few different women in here," the director's assistant told Darius. "We managed to get him out of here and banned from the premises for five years for selling dope and beating up a tenant. Miss Cormier was a longtime resident. She had five kids. She had a man named Albert who lived with them. They moved out of here when Hurricane Katrina hit last year, but they haven't been back."

"I know this is a stretch," Darius said, "but would you know if there was a Henry living over here in the late '80s?"

"There is a Henry Domangue who lives three buildings over from where Miss Cormier used to live. He's about forty and has lived there since he was a teenager. That's not much, but it's the best I can do with no last name."

What are the odds of two Henrys living there then and of that age?

Darius went to the unit the lady told him about. There, he saw a well-dressed middle-aged man drinking a beer on the porch and trimming his nails. Darius inquired if the man knew where he could find Henry Domangue.

"Depends on who wants to know." The soft-spoken man ended his self-manicure, put the nail clipper in his shirt pocket, and began shuffling a deck of cards. He downed his beer and grabbed another from the blue-and-white Igloo beside him.

"I think Henry Domangue might be my daddy, and I'm hoping to meet him."

"Well, son, you lookin' at Henry Domangue, and I ain't your daddy." The guy never looked up from the cards he had dealt. "I got a bad heart and I ain't into girls, if you know what I mean."

"Oh, okay. Different strokes for different folks. Would you know any other Henrys who have lived around here twenty years ago and might know my momma, Sarah LeBeaux?"

"Don't know any ot'er Henrys and don't recall no LeBeauxs livin' here." The guy moved some cards around, evidently cheating in his game of solitaire.

"Momma didn't live here. She visited in the summer of 1986 with her auntie Brenda Cormier and the man she lived with, Albert Thomas."

"I knew Bren and Albert. I used to hang wit' dere boys, and dey had two sistahs dat were twins." The man shuffled the cards a couple times and then added, "Dey had anot'er sistah, too. She was a real looker, really hot, but complicated, sad girl. Anyway, dey all been gone since Katrina."

"Yeah, that's what I was told. So you don't know a Sarah LeBeaux, or maybe a Henry around here who would've known her in 1986?" Darius wondered if a gay man would refer to a girl as really hot and he seemed to know an awful lot about the family. He wondered if Henry was telling him all he knew, or if he was even telling the truth at all.

"I sure don't. I can't help you." Henry gathered all the cards off the table and began to shuffle them again. It was evident Darius would get nothing more from him.

Neither Prez nor Doc were home when Darius arrived back in Bayou Vista, although Doc's Harley was in the yard. It was dark and quiet, except for a dog on the corner breaking his nighttime boredom by barking at imagined intruders. Darius missed having Jack run out from under the trailer to greet him. Perhaps Prez was at his mother's house, but Doc didn't have relatives or friends. Maybe he was selling dope tonight, Darius thought.

Why would he leave his motorcycle?

The living room was in disarray. It looked as if it had been redecorated by a blind man in a rush. He smelled fresh paint.

What's up with the painting and a used rug simply laid over the old rug? What is that ill-fitting cover draped over the couch? Man, how ghetto is that? New paint on just two walls? I know Picasso ain't just painting two walls and stopping.

He stared at the ceiling and saw dark, blotchy stains as he sat down on the couch. He was sure they hadn't been there before. Something wasn't right. He sniffed. There seemed to be an odd smell in front of the couch. He moved the couch and pulled the top rug back.

Holy Baby Jesus in a blanket! What is that?

Darius gasped at the dark thoughts crossing his mind. The last time he saw Prez and Doc, they were threatening to kill each other as they fought on the floor in this very spot. These were bloodstains on the old carpet—from a lot of blood!

At that moment, Prez unlocked the front door and walked in.

"What happened here, Prez?"

"Me and Doc got in a fight and I told him he had to leave, but he didn't wanna leave. Ya know how crazy he can get. He starts swingin' at me, and before I know it, we're in a big-ass fight."

"Where's Doc?" Darius suspected the worst.

"The last I saw him, he was walkin' down the road. I told him to never come back."

"Why didn't he take his motorcycle?"

"I don't know, bro. He said he'd come back for it later. He was really pissed off."

"That don't make sense," Darius said. "What's all this under the rug?" He pulled back the top rug at the edge of the couch. "That looks like blood to me, Prez."

"Doc pulled a knife on me." Prez showed Darius some cuts and bruises.

"That ain't bad enough to leave no blood like what's on the floor!"

"No, I took the knife from him and cut him on the arm. We had to put a tourniquet on his arm to get it to stop bleedin'."

"Why you covered up all this stuff with a rug?" Darius pointed to the bloodstains on the bottom rug.

"Dude, I tried to get it out but couldn't. I didn't wanna see all that blood every night when I watch TV. So I got a rug to put over it."

Darius was convinced Prez was lying. Nothing made sense to the story. The motorcycle in the yard, the amount of blood he'd seen under the couch, the circumstances of Doc leaving. He was thinking maybe he should call the police, just in case. But he didn't.

Darius wondered why Prez had only painted two walls, but he figured it was best not to ask questions. For a few days, the two of them walked on eggshells around each other. He heard Prez tell his mother that he'd lent her ice chest to a friend. Darius couldn't think of anybody who'd asked for the ice chest. He decided it was none of his business.

"Dey need to keep dose illegals out," Martha said. She took a sip of her Chianti as she leaned back in her recliner and read an article in the newspaper. "And de ones dat are here, ICE needs to get dem out."

"What has gotten your panties all in a wad, Marty?" Peter asked, laughing loudly. He was sitting in his recliner—the newest one in the parlor and slightly bigger than the other three.

"I'm talkin' 'bout all dese Mexicans dat ICE and ADIAND rounded up sellin' drugs and killin' our kids."

"I only remember one Hispanic who was arrested for murder in the last couple of years, Momma," Evelyn corrected. "He killed his brother when he was drunk, not a kid." She was doing Sudoku puzzles and chewing on her nails.

"You are so right, Marty. We cannot let the Mexicans come in here and do what Americans do just as well or even better. Things like selling drugs and killing our kids."

"Oh please, Peter. Your sarcasm gets under my skin sometimes. I wanna see if dis is gonna be on de news. And Miss-No-Nails, quit chewin' on your fingers. Dat's not ladylike." Martha got up and got the television remote from the stool in front of the piano. She lowered the thermostat to the central air conditioning a couple of degrees, then sat back down in her recliner, which was almost identical to Peter's but several months older.

Riding a wave of anti-immigration, the sheriff's office and police from Patterson, Morgan City, Berwick, and Franklin had formed a task force called Arrest and Deport Illegal Alien Narcotic Distributors. ADIAND worked with Immigration and Customs Enforcement in addressing the new hot-button issue of illegal aliens. The two agencies embarked on a one-hundred-day joint campaign to arrest and deport dope-dealing illegal aliens.

"I t'ink dis roundup of de illegals is good," Martha said as she turned on the television. "Dey arrested twenty-six drug pushers in the first sweep, and now dey got anot'er seventeen. It's goin' to make de parish safer."

"So you desire to keep everybody out of this great country and have it all to yourself," Peter said. "I mean, after all, the white man fought the Indians and stole the land fair and square, so it is all ours now, right?"

"Look at you over dere, Mr. Nobody-Sits-in-My-Chair-but-Me. You have room to talk. I just don't want all de crime dat comes wit' dese Mexicans and den havin' to pay taxes to support dem babies."

"Why do they want to blame Hispanics for doing the bad stuff that it is mostly Americans doing?" Evelyn asked. She was starting another page of puzzles. "And, Momma, it is too cold in here!"

"Sixty-six degrees is not too cold in de summer, *cher*. And take dat finger out of your mout'." Martha got up and raised the thermostat to sixty-eight. "Dem dat stay here illegal, dey need to send dem back home, before dey take over America, and we'll all be speakin' Spanish and not English, *mais lais.*"

"Is that what you speak, Marty?" Peter asked with a teasing smile. "English?"

"Don't you go dere, Peter Kingsley." Peter's comment obviously stung Martha. She turned up the volume of the TV and tuned it to Fox News while waiting for the local station, KWBJ, to begin its newscast.

"Your grandfather barely speaks English, Marty, and I do not understand half of what your relatives say at times."

"Why you talkin' 'bout my family and takin' de side of dese illegal Mexicans, Peter Kingsley?"

"Marty, did the Acadians fill out immigration forms to come here?"

"And not all the aliens are Mexicans," Evelyn added. "Nor are they all undocumented, which more accurately describes them." Evelyn loved her mother dearly, but that didn't prevent her from thinking she could be a bit xenophobic, at times.

"De Cajuns was a long time ago, before dis was even a country. And dat was different, Peter. You know dat!"

"I do not know how different that is. If you and Princess were starving or lived in a shack, would you not expect me to do whatever I could to change that?"

"Dat isn't de same t'ing, Peter. Besides, dey takin' away work from Americans!"

"Many of these jobs are jobs Americans do not want," Peter said. "But again, I ask you, would you not do the same thing to get a better life for your family?"

"I would do it de legal way, *mais lais*!"

"What if the legal way was closed?" Evelyn asked. She put her puzzle book down and walked across the room to sit at the piano. She kissed the top of Martha's head as she passed.

"You two can be so stubborn sometimes," Martha said. "*Mais*, if I didn't know better, I'd t'ink you have illegals at Kingco de way you 'fendin' dem, Peter."

"Maybe I do."

"Well, if you do, shame on you, Peter Kingsley, because dat's against de law. What kind of example does dat set for Evelyn? I'm goin' to Houma and go shoppin'. I'm upset."

"Well, since you are leaving, I guess I can turn the television back to real news."

"Go watch one of your liberal stations and bury your head in de sand and t'ink dis country and Christianity ain't under attack." She tossed the remote to Peter who switched the set over to the local news which had just begun.

KWBJ reported that only ten of those arrested were suspected of drug activity, and only three were suspected of dealing drugs. A raid on a Morgan City trailer park led to the detention of several undocumented aliens working in the local hotels, none of them on drug charges. All those detained were expected to be deported.

"That reporter knows her stuff and is holding these people accountable for painting a picture that is not always accurate," Peter mumbled to himself as he switched off the television.

CHAPTER 19
JUNE–JULY 2006

"Poppa, I want to be a reporter."

The Kingsleys had just left Washington, DC, after staying there for several days visiting old friends. Evelyn was in the backseat thumbing through a stack of *The Washington Post* newspapers her new reporter friends had given her.

For Evelyn, the highlight of the trip was her Walter-Mitty experience as a cub reporter—tape recorder and notebook in hand—in one of the premier newsrooms in the nation, a newsroom where her poppa had worked as reporter and editor.

"Have you ever interviewed the president?" Evelyn was playing the role of a reporter and interviewing those in the newsroom as she wrote in her notebook.

"Yes, I have," the reporter replied. He leaned forward, whispering into her pink digital recorder. "In a minute I'll be asking Representative Joe Langley, the Speaker of the House of Representatives, about last month's killing of Abu al-Zarqawi. Would you like to ask him a question? You could be the only high school girl interviewing the third man in line for the presidency."

"Really? OMG! I would love to." Evelyn was more excited than she'd been after finding a diamond the previous year in Arkansas. She nervously paced around the reporter's desk—tapping her pen on her pad, double-checking the battery on her recorder, and chewing her nails—until the call came in. When it did, Langley's assistant refused to let Evelyn speak to the representative. But he said—patronizingly, she thought—that he'd field a question from her.

Evelyn had planned to ask a softball question about the removal of black bears from the endangered species list, but she was offended that she'd been denied her once-in-a-lifetime opportunity by some recently-graduated intern. She wasn't some dumb country bumpkin; she would play hardball if that is how he wanted to be.

"My name is Evelyn Kingsley, daughter of a very famous reporter, and I would like to ask an important question about our liberty."

"What's on your mind?" The voice sounded impatient.

"Six years ago, my momma predicted the government would have the power to snoop around in my library records. I thought she was exaggerating. Then Congress passed the Patriot Act, and Section 215 lets the government monitor my library records. Can you tell me if the government knows the books I am reading?"

"Well, since you know about Section 215," said the obviously miffed assistant, "I'm sure you know it imposes a gag order on any production of those records. I can assure you, Miss Kingsley, the government doesn't know what books you're reading, and talk like that or speculation that someday the government would be collecting data on private phone calls comes from paranoid nuts in tin hats and their friends in the liberal media."

The assistant hung up the phone. Evelyn apologized profusely for having cost the reporter an interview with the Speaker.

"Don't worry your little red head over this," the reporter told her. "I have my story, and he wasn't likely to add anything but a quote or two. Listening to you give that snot-nose a comeuppance made my day."

Evelyn was relieved. Peter patted her on the back, and within a few minutes the entire newsroom was abuzz with what she'd done and was congratulating her.

With the nation's capital behind them, Evelyn closed her eyes and relived the excitement. When she opened her eyes, she saw Peter glance at Martha, then look in the rearview to give her a wink. Evelyn knew her poppa wanted her to be a journalist, but her momma wanted her to be a doctor. She bit her nails as she gazed out the backseat window, seeing a world teaming with possibilities. She couldn't wait to get out there and grab them all.

Martha had voiced her displeasure over how this vacation had gone. She made it plain that she'd thought they were going to visit where her daughter was born, and maybe meet some old friends and catch a few plays and was disappointed her daughter was brainwashed in what she called "some Edward R. Murrow training facility."

"Don't you go rulin' out doctorin' just to interview people who don't mean squat," Martha said as they cruised south on Interstate 81 shortly after leaving Virginia and entering Tennessee. "Dis was a disastrous vacation. I knew we shoulda went to Disney World."

The day after they returned home, Peter saw Evelyn sitting on the wooden deck of the patio and working on a new Sudoku puzzle book. Two hummingbirds, suspended in midair, were feeding from the red sugar-water bottles that hung upside down from a roof beam. A sparrow nervously flitted on the ground under the red and yellow rosebushes that were in bloom in the backyard. Evelyn had just coated herself with a milky layer of sun block.

"Princess, get out of those jeans and wash up," he said. "Put something nice on. We are going to the newspaper. The publisher agreed to give you a tour of their newsroom, just like in DC."

"Jiminy Crickets and ice cream!" Evelyn exclaimed. "Another newspaper and meeting some more reporters!" She bolted from her chair, and the two hummingbirds flew off. She tossed the puzzle book onto the kitchen counter as she rushed through the kitchen and into the parlor and then bound up the stairs like a jackrabbit two at a time.

"Really, Peter? Don't you t'ink you're puttin' too much pressure on our daughter to be a reporter?" Martha obviously wasn't pleased with this father-daughter outing. "When you get back down here, young lady, you put your book up where it belongs. Dis ain't no barn, and I ain't your maid."

"Where did she pick up that god-awful expression?" Peter asked, wrinkling his nose and lips. He ran his fingers randomly across the keys of the piano as he craned his neck and looked up the stairs.

"What? Jiminy Crickets and ice cream? Just be glad my daughter don't use no profanity!"

Twenty-five minutes later, Evelyn skipped down the stairs with a fresh application of makeup and mascara, dressed to kill and smelling sweet as honey. She had her digital recorder in one hand, a notebook in the other, and three ink pens secured in her pink purse strapped over her shoulder. She was even wearing high heels, which she seldom wore, even to church.

"Princess, are you going to audition for beauty queen or take a tour of a newsroom?" Peter asked as he bellowed out one of his deep, hearty laughs.

"I want to make a good first impression, Poppa!"

"You make a good first impression wherever you go."

"You always exaggerate about me!" Evelyn was smiling as she sat beside him and kissed his cheek. "Can we go now?" Patience had never been her strong suit.

"Don't keep her in dat musty newsroom too long, Petey," Martha said as the pair walked out the door, arm in arm. "We're goin' shoppin' in Houma dis afternoon."

"Can we go to Office Depot and try to find a reporter's notebook?" Evelyn asked as she looked back over her shoulder.

"Please, Blessed Mary, help me rescue dis girl," Martha muttered.

Peter crossed the river on the old bridge that ran beside the Grizzaffi Bridge. They came off the bridge and circuitously drove toward where the newspaper was located on the riverfront, across the street from one of the concrete gates of the levee. Suddenly, Peter slammed on his brakes to keep from colliding with an old Impala that ran a red light. Evelyn threw her hands up over her face; her notebook and recorder flew onto the floorboard.

"It is okay, Princess. Nothing but a close call." Peter reached over, trying to calm his hysterical daughter.

"That man could have killed us without the protection of the Blessed Virgin!" Evelyn made the sign of the cross on her chest and forehead. "My life flashed before my eyes, Poppa. I will never forget that old, ugly car."

"Well, we are alive, no worse for the wear than whatever your Diet Coke can did to the dashboard." Peter pulled over to the side of the road. After he'd gotten the Mercedes cleaned, his daughter calmed, and she'd fixed her makeup they continued to *The Daily Review*, where the publisher, Malcolm Scott, greeted them.

"Welcome to *The Daily Review*, young lady. I heard many impressive things about you from your father."

"Poppa, you embarrass me, bragging so much about me everywhere you go." Evelyn was being modest, as was her custom, but she basked in her poppa's approval.

Malcolm gave a tour of the cavernous room where a long, towering printer was hungrily devouring a huge roll of paper, almost twice as tall as Evelyn and spitting out a finished newspaper that was being bound in knee-high stacks. After that tour, that didn't end fast enough for Evelyn, Malcolm paged for Theodore Bentley, the paper's editor.

Theodore poked his head around the corner of an opening and quickly flashed a toothy smile toward the pair. He took a sip from a cup of tea, the tea bag strings dangled over the edge of the cup, and then shook hands with Peter and Evelyn.

Peter explained that Evelyn was contemplating a journalism career, which he was encouraging. "Her momma thinks it is more noble, or maybe more financially wise, to become a doctor or lawyer," he said with his typical guffaw.

The pair followed Theodore into the newsroom like puppies. Evelyn was a smidgen disappointed in the atmosphere and décor of the small, drab newsroom. This was a far cry from the enchantment she'd experienced when she entered the bustling newsroom where her poppa had worked. Perhaps she'd overdressed.

"I'd like you to meet my reporters," Theodore said after taking another sip from his tea and then placing it on his desk that was littered with newspapers. He pointed to the far corner of the room at a reporter typing on his computer. "Robert Gaines is our most experienced reporter, with dozens of awards from when he worked in Atlanta and a few more here."

"Hello, Mr. Gaines. My poppa used to be an editor at *The Washington Post*. He was a famous reporter with a plethora of awards."

"It's a pleasure to meet you, sir," Robert said as he looked up from his computer screen. Evelyn thought he had the look of a man who had just returned from a funeral as he appeared to struggle in his attempt to offer a smile. "And Miss Evelyn, we're glad to have you both visit us." Robert winked at Evelyn and grabbed his cane to lift himself from his chair.

Sarah thought he might be friendlier than his countenance suggested. She looked him over as he shook Peter's hand and then reached for hers. She liked his bow tie and thought his hazel eyes made him look all the more distinguished.

"Robert is our investigative reporter," Theodore said. "He also covers crime and the courts. He tends to be a bit on the cynical side, at times."

"Any man not a cynic has either not lived or has his head buried in the sand," Robert said.

"God can help take that edge off, if you let him, Mr. Gaines." Evelyn tried to improve his disposition with a warm smile.

"Perhaps one day I'll let him, Miss Evelyn. Maybe he'll heal my bad heart and bum hip. But right now, the god of money calls me to write copy."

Evelyn wondered if the reporter carried the heavy cross of pessimism every day.

"Next, please meet Virginia Simon, our ace education reporter." Theodore led the pair across the room.

"I know a little bit about you already." Virginia was apparently researching something in a red soft-bound book from the Associated Press. Evelyn remembered Virginia's name as the person who'd written several articles about Evelyn's scholastic exploits. "Congratulations on all of your accomplishments and awards."

Virginia was slim and well-dressed, her hair and nails done perfectly. She had a picture on her desk of her husband and two sons. It looked like she kept a library of books on a rolling table by her desk. A quick glance at the books, and Evelyn surmised they were in alphabetical order. *Type-A personality, undoubtedly.*

"Next," Theodore said, moving along, "I'd like you to meet our newest reporter, Michael Daniels. He covers the city government meetings of Morgan City, Berwick, and Patterson."

"Welcome to *The Daily Review*," Michael said as he accidentally knocked over a baseball trophy on his desk when he rose to shake Peter's hand. "I never made it to the majors because my glove wasn't as good as my bat," he said, grinning. "So I put my Manship communication degree to use. If you ever want to meet any of the mayors, just let me know and I can arrange that."

"Listen to Mike fuckin' pimp out the mayors," Virginia said, laughing. "Pardon my French."

"That is not French, Miss Virginia," Evelyn said with a finger wag. "My momma speaks French, and she never says that word." *Can Type-A's have potty mouths?* "Thank you for the offer, Mr. Daniels, but Poppa frequently has the mayors over to The Kingdom for supper, and I find them all a bit boring."

"Well, we do, too," Michael said. That got a loud laugh from the entire newsroom. Evelyn wondered what was so funny.

"Betty Dualle covers health, religion, and lifestyles," Theodore continued. "She's been with the paper for longer than anybody in this newsroom. There's not a mouse squeak in Morgan City that she doesn't know about."

"I got tired of chasing stories and making enemies," Betty said. "I figured I'd finish my career working on the kind of stories we all need—stories that make us feel good. Now the only one I piss off is Teddy when I want to have a little fun."

Neither Theodore nor Betty laughed.

"Bryan Kemper covers sports for us," Theodore said. "He's out doing an interview. He's forgotten more statistics than I'll know in my lifetime. He even covered Michael during his baseball career at LSU. Oh, and Sally Rochelle is our photographer, but she's out on assignment, too." Theodore was leading the visitors out of the newsroom. "It's always a pleasure to see new people wanting to be a part of the Fourth Estate."

Evelyn looked at her poppa and smiled.

Darius had gone to a Morgan City jewelry shop not far from the newspaper and pilfered a gold necklace and pendant. He'd wanted to give Nina something elegant for her birthday, something he couldn't afford to acquire legally. In the hurry of his flight, he barreled through a red traffic light. He heard a horn blowing and tires screeching, and felt bad about inconveniencing those people, but he needed to put distance between himself and the jewelry shop as quickly as he could. He drove a few miles to the Waffle House to wait for Nina to rest up from her night shift.

His server introduced herself as Danetta. He ordered an omelet and tarried as long as he could without the manager reminding him of their "no loitering" policy. Businesses seemed to think black men who stayed at a table too long were up to no good.

Leaving the restaurant, Darius drove to Nina's trailer. A group of teenage boys were setting off firecrackers a few trailers down.

"I had a rough night last night, *Papi*," Nina said as she yawned and let Darius in. She jumped when some firecrackers loudly exploded. "Those *gringos* at work can be so demanding. They know we can't complain or they'll fire us or call ICE on us."

Darius kissed and hugged her, and then they sat together on the couch. She laid her head on his shoulder, and he put his arm around her.

"I'm sorry to hear that. Bet I can make you feel better." Darius kissed her neck.

She giggled and drew closer. She put her soft hand inside his shirt and began rubbing the smooth skin of his chest. He reveled in her soft touch. "Do you want me and Thirty-eight to burn the place down?" He was only half-joking.

Nina laughed. "Then where's *Mamacita* going to work?" Then, gazing into his eyes, she became serious. "I wish you and Ricardo would quit that illegal stuff. It's not right and I fear for both of you. Plus, I can't get caught in something like that and get deported. They already took Juanita away. I miss *Mamá* and home, but I need to make this money for her."

Darius knew she was homesick. She couldn't go home because she might not make it back, and there was no way to bring her family here. She was as much without a family as he was. He understood what she was going through, and he wanted to comfort her.

"I can never replace your momma, but I'm here for you."

"*Papi*, you're so kind and sweet to me," she said as she wrapped both arms around his neck. "You make me feel special. I hope you can get your life together."

After kissing and necking for several minutes on the couch, Nina suggested they go to where they could be more comfortable. Entering the bedroom, she kissed Darius again and then flung herself on her bed. Lying on her back, she shed her pajama bottoms and unbuttoned her top, exposing her firm, supple breasts.

"*Hazme el amor*, *Papi*." She smiled and beckoned him with her index finger.

As aroused as Darius was, he paused at the side of her bed. Instead of dropping his pants, he reached into his pocket and pulled out the gold necklace and angel pendant he'd stolen earlier.

"I might have something else *Mamacita* wants." Darius handed her the unwrapped, still-boxed jewelry. "Happy birthday, *Mamacita*."

There was a knock on the door. Nina ignored it until the knock became a pounding and the police identified their presence. When she opened the door, there was an officer on each side. The male officer with a crew cut asked if she knew whose vehicle was parked in front of her trailer.

Darius could tell that she sensed he was in trouble and was about to lie to protect him. He also knew if she were caught lying about this, the police would have ICE or ADIAND there in minutes, and she'd be in custody and taken out of the country. He couldn't let her risk that.

"Officer, that's my car," he said, stepping to the door. "Is there a problem?"

"Step out of the trailer with your hands over your head," the officer said loudly as he reached for his gun.

"Whoa, officer. I'm unarmed. I'll do whatever you say." Immediately after Darius stepped out of the trailer, the officer with the crew cut slammed him to the ground, facedown.

"Hands behind your back," the officer ordered as he fumbled for his handcuffs.

"What's going on, Darius?" Nina asked from the doorway.

"Lady, stay out of this and don't interfere," the other officer, a female, barked. The male officer pulled Darius up by the handcuffs and read him his rights as he led him to the patrol car; he was arrested for felony theft.

Darius looked back over his shoulder before the officer pushed him into the back of the police cruiser. He saw the female officer walked to the steps of the trailer. Nina was crying and had her hands over her face. Darius could hear the cop warning his beautiful girlfriend, "Miss, you need to be careful who you let in your trailer, especially if you don't have papers. I'm sure you understand what I'm trying to tell you."

Ricardo bailed Darius out of jail two days after his arrest. Humiliated, Darius went to visit Nina, wish her a belated happy birthday, and explain what had happened. He told her why he was arrested and insisted she keep the jewelry. He'd pay the price for his crime, whatever it was, but he wanted her to have the gift. He told Nina that she had opened a new world to him, one that allowed him to see something good and kind in people. She had brought bliss into his life.

"We're the right people at the wrong time and in the wrong place, *Papi*," Nina said with tears in her eyes. "I can't afford to have the police here. *Mamá* is the most important thing to me. I must not hurt her, even if it means losing you."

Darius kissed Nina and told her he understood. He agreed that circumstances were working against them. That in no way affected how much he cared about her, but he didn't want to jeopardize her safety or freedom.

"*Papi*, you need to do what's best for your future and quit living just to kill some man who you may never see. Remember the promise you told me you made to your *madre*. We both have our entire lives ahead of us. The things we do now will affect our future."

Midnight approached, and Darius could see Nina was exhausted. He asked her to see him to the door. They had a long kiss before he stepped into the warm summer night. They both knew it was a kiss good-bye. He turned to look at Nina before she shut the door. She had a crooked smile, the kind that looks out of place on a sad face. Even in the dimly lit doorway, Darius saw tears trickling down her cheeks.

With a heavy heart, Darius drove away from Nina's little trailer on that muggy July night. Somewhere along the way, he'd wandered afar from his moral compass. He remembered how his conscience had panged him when he'd stood watch during the Copperworks theft. He remembered how Mr. L's voice used to guide him in doing the right thing whenever he considered doing what was easy.

He was cognizant of the fact that Nina had helped reset that compass and veer him from the wayward path he had embarked upon. She had pushed him into making better choices. He remembered making a promise to his momma that he'd make something of himself. He was determined to make the changes necessary to live up to his promise.

CHAPTER 20
SEPTEMBER 2006–MARCH 2007

Despondency, at times, was almost suffocating.

Darius walked aimlessly around during the Shrimp and Petroleum Festival. He recalled his first festival, and how happy and beautiful his momma was as they danced together. Now the two-year anniversary of Sarah's death was approaching. He usually didn't visit her grave because it brought back sad memories, but this week he'd been several times. Depression began to tighten its tentacles and slowly squeeze from Darius his desire to live. The vultures of despair circled his soul.

Darius swatted mosquitoes from his face and neck as he knelt at Sarah's grave near dusk. A jukebox of sounds was playing as the cicadas—better known in these parts as locusts—crickets, tree frogs, bullfrogs, and even a lonely whippoorwill were all performing.

I don't know who or where my daddy is, and you're gone. I wish we could be together as a family.

He left the grave after telling his momma good-bye. He wondered if the only way to be together as a family was for the three of them to be dead.

Arriving in Bayou Vista, he drove to the end of Byron Street. He parked with both hands tightly fixed on the steering wheel. He breathed deeply—it seemed he couldn't extract enough oxygen from his lungs—and stared straight ahead. It was too dark to see the other side of the bayou. His mind was blank of any thought but that of joining his momma. He reached under his seat and felt the leather of the holster holding the piece he kept with him for the inevitable day he crossed paths with Pigenstein and killed him. He pulled on the holster, and it hung up on something under his seat. He broke his gaze across the bayou to look down. He pulled the gun from the holster. The grip was soon warm in his hands.

I wonder if I'll feel pain when the bullet goes in my head . . .

Raising the gun to his temple, he knew he wouldn't feel anything that his momma hadn't already felt when Pigenstein murdered her.

Pigenstein has to be brought to justice!

He was saved that night by the same thing destroying his soul: his visceral animus for Pigenstein. He refused to take his own life before making sure that vile monster was punished or preferably dead. He put the gun back in its holster and drove back to the trailer.

Prez was sitting on the couch watching television. Darius walked straight to his room. Neither man spoke a word to the other. Darius was suspicious of what Prez had done to make Doc disappear and wasn't sure what he should do about it. He was in no mood to give it much thought. Doc's disappearance became less of a mystery later that month when a tractor-driving cane worker noticed an ice chest in the middle of a cane field. He got off his tractor and saw large blow-flies swarming around the container. The worker removed the bungee cords strapping the lid down and was overwhelmed by the stench.

Within a few days, the carved-up body in the cooler was identified as belonging to Doc. Prez couldn't explain why Doc's Harley was still parked in the yard. The bloodstains on the carpet and ceiling and burning through the two partially painted walls were enough to have Prez arrested for first-degree murder. Darius was questioned and agreed to take a lie detector test. Police quickly cleared him as a suspect in the killing and disposal of the body.

Darius had heard that the Thug Brothers made it known they'd be shooting basketball late one night at the Broussard-Harris gym in Franklin and challenged Tommie to show up with his crew. He heard it because they also sent word of the showdown to Ricardo and his crew.

Ricardo said that he didn't consider West End grudge matches any of his business, and it was no surprise that Striker and Bones preferred knife fights over gunfights. Ricardo told Michael to stay out of the dispute. But Michael, full of piss and vinegar, appeared determined to ignore the advice. Darius couldn't understand Ricardo's reluctance to let the police know what was looming.

"I told ya before, homie," Ricardo told Darius. "Ya don't rat out nobody on the streets."

Darius was faced with another dilemma: be loyal to his friend or tell the police about an impending street battle. He chose loyalty to his friend. The newspaper reported on the subsequent melee and called it a blood-bath. After a four-minute firefight, both Thug Brothers were dead, along with Jerry and Michael. Tommie was killed, leaving Bianca a widow to raise her son alone. Also killed were Tommie's brothers, Riley and Willie, along with his friend Daniel. Also, a stray bullet killed a twelve-year-old girl trying to protect her six-year-old brother during the fray.

Ricardo and Darius were discussing the carnage as they drank beer on the wharf along the river, where the shrimp boats parked to sell their catch. After a while, Striker and Bones joined them. Ricardo flew into a rage and threw his fedora at Striker. A gust of wind almost blew the hat into the river.

"Nine people dead, includin' a little girl," Ricardo said, retrieving his hat at the edge of the wharf. Then, poking his toothpick into Striker's chest, he drove his point home further. "Ya *estúpido* cousin is dead and ya probably would be, too, if I hadn't told ya not to go there. All because ya two friggin' *putos* decided to go rob Tommie!"

Darius wondered how his friend could have such rage over the bloodshed when he'd done nothing to inform the police to keep it from happening. Darius was convinced more than ever that he needed to turn his life around and heed the promise he'd made his momma before it was too late.

"Me and you are tight, Thirty-eight; I love you like a brother. But this life is stupid. It ain't nothing but a dead-end road to the cemetery. It's killed my momma, and it's taken everything from me that I care about."

"If ya can't take the heat, maybe ya need to get out the kitchen," Striker said.

Darius scowled back at him. Between the two misfits that parasitically clung to Ricardo like leeches, Striker was the one he least liked and the one Darius thought might even be a psychopath. Mentally unbalanced or not, Striker was right. Darius needed to get out of this hellhole of a kitchen which only cooked up trouble and heartache. "I know I ain't got clean hands, and I'm about to go to jail, probably. All of this took Nina from me, too."

"Bro, don't go blamin' yaself over that," Ricardo insisted. "She made a choice."

"And she made the right choice. She broke my heart, but maybe saved my life."

"*Mamacita* got married over in Texas to some Mexican-American and has her citizenship now. She chose that over you, *amigo.*"

"Maybe homeboy wasn't puttin' nothin' good on his woman," Striker said.

Darius didn't even bother to glare at Strike; instead he chose to ignore the insult from the Supreme Leader of the Land of Dumb Miscreants and told Ricardo that he'd known ahead of time of Nina's nuptial plans. "She told me that she had to do the right thing for herself and her family. I understood and wished her well."

"Ya a fool, dawg, is all I gotta say," Bones said, shaking his head.

"A real fool, dude," Striker added, nodding in agreement.

"Naw, life in the street has made me a fool. I only have one bad choice to make. That'll be to kill Marcus or Samuel or Pigenstein or whatever name he has."

"Bro, just remember, if ya cross that line, there ain't no turnin' back!"

"I'll find a way back. But a man's gotta do what a man's gotta do."

"*Sí, amigo*. On that we agree," Ricardo said. Then he put his arm around Darius. "I wish I could follow ya, *hombre*. My uncle is always on me to get a real job and I've tried. But no one hires an undoc with no skill or diploma."

"Dude, you're stupid," Striker said. "This is the life. We do our own thing and ain't nobody tells us what to do."

"You think I chose this *mierda?*" Ricardo tossed his toothpick at Striker. "I had nothing but the shirt on my back and no family when I got to the States. There is nothing back home for me and there isn't much here that I can ever have legally."

"Quit bitchin', Thirty-eight," Bones said. "We're young, free and havin' a blast."

"Whatever," was Ricardo's only word as he put a new toothpick in his mouth. He threw a shadow punch at Darius and then they bumped fists.

Darius suspected this was good-bye. He wondered if Ricardo thought the same. The voodoo Midas touch appeared to have struck again. His momma, two friends, and dog had died, and now two other friends had exited his life.

Charlie Towns, the assistant district attorney, sat across the table from Darius and his public defender, Julio Mendez. Darius impatiently listened as the well-dressed, well-manicured prosecutor and Mendez discussed a way out for Darius.

"We believe Ricardo Ortiz is running a theft ring," Towns told Mendez. "Ortiz's fingerprints were at the car dealership where that Lambo was stolen. We have other evidence, as well, that puts Mr. Ortiz there. I'm certain Mr. LeBeaux has information on the theft and maybe participated." He looked directly at Darius.

Darius was uncomfortable with the prosecutor's stare that was unequivocally accusing him of participation. The prosecutor smiled and spoke in a friendly tone, but Darius knew this man was not his friend. He wondered what other evidence the authorities could possibly possess. Perhaps, the prosecutor was bluffing. Darius started to fabricate alibis for himself and Ricardo, but his attorney firmly put a hand on his arm and urged him to remain mute.

"I'll allow your client to plead to misdemeanor theft on this felony shoplifting charge and I will suggest probation to the judge, if he cooperates and gives us information that puts Mr. Ortiz away. He'll also have to turn in the jewelry he stole."

Towns rose to excuse himself from the small room to allow Darius an opportunity to discuss the offer with his public defender. Before opening the door, the prosecutor turned around and walked slowly to the table. He placed both of his hands on the table and leaned in toward Darius; the smile had disappeared, and the tone was sharper.

"I suspect you know about a missing boat, too." The ADA lowered his voice; barely over a whisper. "I can make all of that go away. All you have to do is tell me what we both know is the truth."

As soon as the door closed behind the prosecutor, Darius balked at the offer. "I don't wanna go to jail, but I ain't throwing my friend under the bus."

Mendez tried to reason with Darius. "The prosecutor is being fair and generous. Why go to jail for somebody you don't associate with anymore?"

"Because it's not right to stab a friend in the back. If he goes to jail, it won't be because I'm trying to save my own ass."

Despite his refusal to cooperated with the prosecutor, Darius was allowed to plead guilty to a misdemeanor. He was handcuffed and taken from an almost empty courtroom after the judge gave him a six-month sentence with all, but thirty days, suspended. In jail, Darius experienced an epiphany. He didn't want to return behind bars, except maybe in exchange for killing Marcus.

A week into his confinement, the inmates got a laugh at the expense of their jailers. While the guards watched the Super Bowl, two inmates crawled into the ceiling and knocked out a section of a cylinder block wall. Before escaping, they returned with concrete blocks and put them in their beds under the blankets, so the guards would think they were in bed.

No one discovered the inmates missing until breakfast. They went through the two fences around the facility and hopped a train about a quarter mile behind the prison. They were found stowed away on a bus three days later in Lafayette, about seventy miles away.

"Hey, guard," the prisoners would say for days afterward. "Can you come check my bed? It feels like concrete." Others mocked with, "Can I go check on my stuff in the attic?"

Finally, the guards had enough and cut off the television sets and cut off the heat. The inmates rioted, and twenty-five of them seized control of a training room. They held five prisoners hostage, including Darius. The guards threatened to tear gas the room, but Darius yelled and reminded them that there were innocent prisoners in there who'd suffer the consequences. After a thirteen-hour standoff, the situation was defused, and the prison returned to normal.

A few days later, on the weekend before Darius's release, Sheriff's deputies brought in Harry Benson, a family man with three kids. Harry was treated roughly. Whatever his crime, he'd obviously pissed off the deputies.

"What they got you in here for, Harry?" Darius asked him the next morning.

"I kind of have two problems," Harry said, smiling. "Well, maybe three. One, I like to go fast on my motorcycle. I've gotten four tickets for speeding in the past two years. Two, I've had too many concussions and forget stuff, like my court appearances and paying my fine. So I got two failure-to-appear warrants on me."

"They threw you in here over a couple of tickets?" Darius wasn't buying that version as the complete picture. "Bro, something you not telling, 'cuz the deputies were kicking your ass when they brought you in."

"That's my third problem. I tend to run my mouth when I'm pissed. Yesterday they had a driver's license checkpoint, and my license was expired by two days. When they gave me a ticket, I called this sergeant a fat, frigging doughnut-eater. Me being in here is proof that the First Amendment is dead in St. Mary Parish. I may've called them fascists pigs when they brought me to my cell."

Darius was impressed that this seemingly mild-mannered man had the audacity to taunt his harriers and could laugh at his dire predicament.

Later that evening, Brian DeLee, a repeat violent offender tougher than leather and meaner than a pit bull, bumped Harris in the chow line and Speeding Harry spilled his food.

"Dammit, fool, watch where you're going," Harris said, shoving the convict.

Oh shit, Harry. Wrong man to get mad at and run your mouth!

In an instant, Harry was gasping and gurgling with a metal shiv sticking from his throat. By the time a guard got to Harry, he'd collapsed and was white as a Klansman's sheet. Freedom of speech is costly inside prison unless you're at the top of the food chain.

Three kids just lost their daddy whose only crimes were a heavy foot and loose lips.

After his release, Darius returned to the Byron Street trailer and began getting together his lawn care customers for the grass-cutting season beginning in March. He also applied to get into the trade school in Morgan City to become a welder. He wanted no more of prison.

So far, Marcus's business was running smoothly. He transported his shipments from New Orleans in secret compartments of his Mustang GT. Then he'd return to Houma and sell his stuff out of Shiloh Lounge along Bayou Terrebonne. He hung out in the bar, drinking and flirting with the women and scoring deals there each night. After the bar closed, he'd push dope from a decrepit thirty-five-foot shrimp boat moored on the bayou behind the bar.

Marcus's Houma cronies weren't acquainted with his past. So when he heard two of them mentioning Sarah's murder and the recent bounty put on his capture, he listened but was careful not to reveal his interest too much.

"They say homeboy had just got out of jail when he killed his woman," a young pothead said to another.

"They had a bunch of murders over there, and they can't keep track of the murderers they lookin' for," his pothead buddy said

"Yeah, they are swamped," the first pothead said. "They want to catch that one bad. Just think of all the weed we could buy with a thousand bucks."

That's why he'd continued to lay low and not let potheads like these know who he really was, Marcus thought. But he was as getting restless as a chained dog. Paying the bar's owner, tipping the bouncer, and a monthly stipend to the boat captain; all of this was more than a small bother.

CHAPTER 21
JUNE–AUGUST 2007

"What happened to being open-minded? I cannot believe you are judging my friends."

Evelyn was at the foot of the stairs, facing Peter in one of her first arguments of adolescence. Peter was expressing his disapproval of the boy he'd seen bring her to the door.

"That boy has more earrings than a girl," Peter was saying. "And he had more ass out of his pants than in them."

"So Rickey's grooming means he's a bad person?" Evelyn asked, using a contraction purposely as she headed to the stairs to go to her bedroom and stew.

"Dress alone does not make a man, but it allows insight into his attitude. A boy showing his ass is basically saying f-you to society's established norms."

Three steps up the stairs, Evelyn turned back to face her poppa. "Weren't you the one preaching not to accept anything just because the powers that be establish some capricious rule?" She raised her hands in exasperation and in a mocking gesture to the powers that be. She stepped back down the stairs and defiantly stood beside the piano with both hands on her hips, waiting for a response.

"It is okay to challenge capricious rules that infringe on people's rights," Peter said.

"Arbitrary rules, you mean. A pair of sagging pants shows less buttocks than the bikinis me and Momma wear, and nobody says they make us bad people." Evelyn shook her head and clicked her tongue.

"Princess, I am afraid your friends will lead you to choices you will regret." Peter gestured with both palms opened. "Like this rap music junk. It encourages rebellion for the sake of rebellion, violence for the sake of violence. This is symptomatic of people who make bad choices. It is a way of life from whence the only way out is in a body bag."

"Poppa, do you hear the words coming out of your mouth? Maybe it's symptomatic of a populous tired of police brutality or held down because of the color of their skin or where they are from! Your trite pontifications are contrary to every value you instilled in me." Evelyn was tapping her chest with four fingers of an open hand.

"Bad choices of a lifetime begin early, Princess. Associating with people who make bad choices can influence you into similar bad choices." Peter walked slowly toward her as she leaned against the piano.

"I can have friends as long as they are members of the country club. In other words, as long as they look like we do." Evelyn pointed her finger first at her poppa and then at herself.

"That is not true." Peter shook his head. "You are placing words in my mouth you have never heard me utter. I want what is best for you. Your mother and I are giving you more freedoms now, but it is our responsibility to protect you and guide you in your choices."

"As long as my choices are with rich white kids who wear starched clothes and mouth Puritan values?" She spun on her heels and began to angrily march upstairs.

"Your sarcasm has crossed appropriate boundaries, Evelyn Kingsley, and borders on disrespect." He was speaking louder than usual and was wagging a finger. "I do not want to see that boy at my door again, nor any boy with earrings, nor a boy or girl with jewelry stuck in their lips and nose. That is final. This is not Africa."

Evelyn froze in her steps. She couldn't believe what her poppa had just said. She turned and faced him from the top of the stairs, and for the first time in her life, yelled at her poppa. "Oh my God! Those are the most racist words I have ever heard you articulate!"

She ran through the wide hallway to her room and brooded at her desk in front of her tiny shrine to the Virgin Mary. She'd respect her poppa's wishes and not bring these friends to The Kingdom, but she was becoming a woman and had the right to choose who her friends would be.

The domestic tranquility at The Kingdom had been restored by the time the Kingsleys journeyed to the Hebert's Fourth of July family gathering near Houma. The smoky aroma of barbecued hamburgers floated to the road two hundred yards away as they pulled into the short driveway filled with old cars, pickup trucks and an occasional muddy four-by-four. The first of three forty-pound sacks of live crawfish was boiling in a huge stainless-steel pot heated by a propane burner. A bottle of Zatarain's Cajun Boil, a liquid that looked suspiciously like orange piss, had been emptied into boiling water chocked full of peppers, onion, garlic, lemon, and salt. Also floating in the caldron were mushrooms, corn, potatoes, brussels sprouts, and sausage.

After an instant death in the boiling water, the mudbugs soaked in the seasoned brew a few more minutes before being dumped into a huge, empty ice chest. There, the final ritual involved sprinkling them with an orange-colored, spiced mixture called Tony Chachere's that looked like a powdered version of the Zatarain orange-piss.

"It's a secret 'gredient to put some kick in dem," said one of the Thibodeaux cousins from Destrehan. "It's 'ginst de law to sell it outside Louisiana!"

Everyone laughed. Some laughed more from the beer than the humor.

"It makes it a lot hotter, though!" Peter said.

"Duh," was the cousin's one-word reply.

"Uncle Pierre, do you know de difference between a Yankee and a damned Yankee?" one of the Thibodaux cousins asked. "A Yankee comes to visit at de Mardi Gras and a damned Yankee stays or marries your daughter."

Evelyn began to say something, but Peter stopped her with a raised hand.

"Well, that makes me a double-damned Yankee!" he said.

Evelyn joined the ensuing laughter.

The crawfish were emptied onto a makeshift newspaper-covered plywood table along with several pounds of the other boiled items.

"We put all dese vegetable in here for you Yankees," said a Bonvillion cousin from Lafitte. "Dat way, y'all won't starve since you don't know how to eat de tails fast enough."

All, except Peter, were pinching off the pinky-sized tails and effortlessly pulling out the spiced meat with their teeth. Reach, grab, bite, chew, suck juice out of head, repeat. Peter, on the other hand, was clumsily shelling the tail and picking the meat out with his fingers, eating one crawfish by the time the person at his elbow had eaten the tails and sucked the heads of four.

"*Cher*, when you gonna teach your man how to suck de head of a crawfish," one of Martha's brothers asked, grinning and wiping his hands on his pants.

"There is no way I am going to put my lips around the head of a mudbug," Peter said, raising his hands up after tossing a head into the trash can at his side.

"A Yankee ain't ever seen no family gat'erin' 'till he's been to a coonass crawfish boil," one of Martha's uncles told Peter.

Peter nodded and smiled. "I still will not suck the head of a crayfish," he said.

"Dat's crawfish, Petey," Martha reminded him.

After the clan set off fireworks, they began gathering aluminum-foil-covered leftovers to bring back home. Except for the Thibodeaux cousins from Opelousas and the Bonvillions, the Kingsleys had the longest drive ahead of them. Peter shook his father-in-law's hand, dried and cracked from years of exposure to the brackish waters he worked. The old Cajun shrimper smiled wide as a cucumber.

"I never said dis before," he told Peter as he patted him on the back, "but t'ank you for makin' my Mart'a such a happy woman,"

"And Momma made him the happiest man in the whole solar system," Evelyn said as she left Mawmaw's hug and walked to get a Pawpaw hug. She had the mischievous twinkle in her eye her poppa often had. "You should ask him what caught his eye on Momma."

"Evelyn Mart'a Kingsley!" Martha said. "Your poppa has way too much corruptin' influence on you, *cher*." She was laughing when she softly swatted her daughter on the rear.

"Well, Peter," Pawpaw said, "however it happened, I t'ank you."

Both men shook hands again as Peter told his father-in-law good-bye.

"Petey," Martha said, "how many times I gotta tell you, *cher*, dat we don't say good-bye. Dat's bad luck."

Martha kissed her father on the cheek, and he placed something in her hand. It was an old Saint Christopher pendant, the patron saint of travelers.

"Dis was your brot'er's."

"*Merci, Papere.* I'll cherish dis as a gift from you and from my brot'er in heaven and will always have it wit' me."

Martha stopped Peter before he could back out of the driveway so that she could ride in the back with her daughter. Martha kicked off her flip-flops—a cheap rubber sandal with a thong between the big and second toe—which she'd die if seen wearing anywhere besides a crawfish boil. She fingered her Saint Christopher as she talked with Evelyn and stroked her hair.

"I see you're starting to let your nails grow," Martha said, sitting beside Evelyn without a seatbelt fastened. "Dey are pretty wit' dis polish you have on. And you look so much more ladylike wit' your hair down instead of in pigtails."

"I like my pigtails, Momma," Evelyn said, smiling.

They began talking about Evelyn's approaching senior year in high school. Martha playfully teased Evelyn about a good-looking boy upon whom Evelyn had developed a crush.

Evelyn laughed. "Yeah, well, Mitch goes more for the blond cheerleader type, if you know what I mean. I do not think he knows I exist."

"When you become a famous doctor, dis Mitch boy will be eatin' out of your hands like all de rest of 'em." Martha patted Evelyn's arm and gently moved her long curls from her face as she leaned over to kiss her.

One moment, Evelyn was feeling her mother's gentle kiss, and the next, she felt the seatbelt bite into her chest and her mother's head violently smash her face. Something—maybe it was an elbow or a knee—hit her in the shoulder as Martha was flung forward in the car. Air bags deployed throughout the Mercedes, but nothing kept Martha—who hadn't put on her seatbelt—from flying out of the backseat and hurtling forward.

The moments of the collision played out in slow motion. She reached out to grab her mother, but it was like trying to squeeze water. Evelyn forced open her door and stumbled out of the vehicle. Pain shot through her ankle and she collapsed to the ground. She pulled herself partway up and looked inside the vehicle where she saw Peter struggling but unable to get out of his seatbelt. Evelyn couldn't see her mother very well; her poppa had her view blocked. He was alternately yelling at Martha and at her.

"Marty, Marty, dear God! Baby, talk to me. Princess, call for help."

Leaning against the crushed door, she pulled out her iPhone from her pocket and called nine-one-one.

Peter turned toward the window, which he'd let down. "Are you hurt, Princess?"

"I'm okay, Poppa. How is Momma?"

Peter didn't answer.

The dispatcher came on the line. Evelyn frantically explained the situation while she struggled to open Peter's door.

"We had a bad wreck. My momma and poppa are hurt and trapped in the car. There is a truck in the bayou. No one came out of it." Evelyn gave the dispatcher their location and then hung up.

She was weeping as she wiped away blood that had trickled into her eye. She turned her attention to opening the car door by her poppa. She saw the steering wheel pressed against his chest; a white dust from the airbags covered his face. The door refused to open, so Evelyn craned to peer through the window, over her poppa's shoulder. She saw her momma clearly for the first time; bloody and apparently just regaining consciousness. Martha opened her mouth; her lips quivered, but no words came out.

"Oh, dear Jesus!" Evelyn screamed. "Poppa, get her out! Blessed Mary, Mother of God, please help Momma!" She began again frantically, and futilely, clawing at the jammed door handle.

"I can't get to her. I can't move," Peter said as he glanced at Evelyn and then reached over to touch Martha's bloody face. "Marty, hang in there."

Using both hands, Evelyn pulled on the door with all of her strength. She lost her grip and stumbled backward, screaming in pain as her ankle refused to support her. She tried to get back up and collapsed again in pain. She knew the door was not going to open and there was no way she could get to her momma. From what she'd seen, she knew a miracle was needed.

Evelyn crawled toward the car and then got on all fours, with the crown of her head leaning against the door of the vehicle, to pray. She choked on her sobs and tears but managed to utter her pleas. "Blessed Mary, full of grace, mother of my Lord Jesus, I beg with all my heart, please intercede, and, in your infinite mercies, do not take Momma from us."

She reached above her head and clasped the door from inside open window. She struggled to stand again, hoping to maybe reach across her poppa and hold hands with her momma until the ambulance arrived. Her grip slipped, and she fell again. She clasped her hands together and pleaded heavenward with trembling fervor as sweat and tears fell like raindrops on the dry grass at her knees. On the other side of the door, she heard her poppa praying to God.

"Please, God, have mercy," he prayed. "Please, if you are there, do not take this saint from our lives. If you spare her, I will go to the synagogue and worship you. Amen."

Suddenly, Evelyn heard sorrowful howls that could only originate in the deepest regions of Hades under the torments of the cruelest demon. The bellowed shrieks preceded bitter blasphemy.

"Damn God for taking this righteous soul!" Peter shouted with a violent fury. "I was a fool to think for a moment that there is a just God."

Evelyn knew her father's outcries meant that he thought her momma was dead. She knew better; her momma would be alright.

"Blessed Mary, full of grace, please intercede on behalf of Poppa, for he knows not what he has done." Evelyn saw butterflies, as if transporting the supplication, float upward on the gust of a southerly breeze. She could hear sirens approaching as she determined again to get up and reach her mother. Then, out of thin air, a first responder appeared and gently helped her rise.

As the paramedic supported her, Evelyn leaned into the window to reach across her poppa and touch her momma and assure her that all would be okay. But the medic restrained her and pulled her away, even as she saw two other medics open her momma's door. Evelyn flailed and screamed as she was pulled away from the car. They tried to calm her as she sat beside the ambulance and they splinted her ankle.

Soon, they had Martha on a stretcher and were administering CPR as they wheeled her into an ambulance and whisked her away.

Peter, finally extricated from the vehicle, was also strapped on a stretcher and wheeled across the bumpy ground toward an ambulance. The paramedics had secured his legs and hips in an inflatable device. As they loaded him into the ambulance, they helped Evelyn get into the back with him. She overheard a medic say that a doctor had pronounced Martha dead after she'd arrived at the hospital. She and her poppa held hands and wept during the eight-mile ride to Terrebonne General.

PART III

CHAPTER 22
JANUARY 27, 2008

12:10 a.m.

After a fist bumping with Darius, Ricardo walked over to sit with his two pals. Striker got up and joined Bones on the other side of the booth, so Ricardo could have a side to himself.

"Homie's solid as gold," Ricardo said, pointing a toothpick toward Darius, who appeared lost in some sort of daydream in the parking lot. Striker and Bones grunted contemptuously.

Danetta walked up, now off the clock. "Did you miss me today?" she asked playfully as she sat beside Ricardo and kissed him.

"Ya shoulda seen me and ya man roughin' up X-Man," Striker said. "Thirty-eight took him out cold."

"Keep ya voice down, *estúpido puto*," Ricardo said in a harsh whisper as he looked around.

"Baby, you know all this street stuff you do scares me. You gonna get killed."

"I'm not *estúpido* like my homies here," Ricardo said. "We caught X-Man by surprise. He fought a little, but he went down like a sack of rocks in the river."

"I worry about you out there." She put her arm around him and kissed him.

"I always got my thirty-eight," Ricardo said, patting the gun in his waistband.

Danetta said that didn't make her feel any better.

12:13 a.m.

Robert called Bernie again. "You got anything new on either of those alleged drug deals in Amelia that went bad tonight?" He was doodling question marks on a page of his notebook.

"We're kinda shorthanded tonight. People out with the flu, vacation, and whatnot. We need guys out here, but it's just two more shootings in Amelia, right? Neither victim wanted to go to the hospital, but there's something about this one that doesn't feel right."

"Are the two crimes connected?" He began doodling exclamation marks in his notebook.

"I don't know, Bobby. They both had the crap beat out of 'em and got shot. Any drugs they might've had were gone by the time we got there, but the similarities could be a coincidence. Neither of 'em are cooperating."

Bernie added that he was unable to provide any positive identification, yet. Robert complained that he didn't have a gnat's turd of information he could use.

He looked up from his notes and saw the patron who'd just left, standing with his hands in his coat pockets and staring off toward the river. The patron reached into his pocket and retrieved what looked like a phone, but then something seemed to catch his attention on the other side of the parking lot. Robert couldn't tell what it was through the fog.

"I've seen that profile before," Robert whispered to himself. He closed his eyes and then opened them. "That's the kid whose momma was killed in Franklin."

12:20 a.m.

"God was watchin' over us tonight, *amigos*," Ricardo said. He looked up at the sound of a horn blowing and tires squealing. An SUV almost wrecked getting onto Brashear Avenue.

"Yeah, we was blessed," Striker said. He was spreading an extra layer of jelly on his toast. "By the way, how's that hand?"

"It's good," Ricardo said. "But my ankle got hurt when the *puto* fell on me, and I'm pissed he messed up my fed." He picked up his hat and examined it. "I'm glad I didn't hafta use my piece."

"I don't like this kind of talk," Danetta said. "I'm going to go get some ice for that hand."

Striker reached out to examine Ricardo's swollen hand.

"Leave my hand alone with ya sticky jelly fingers," Ricardo said, yanking his hand away.

"Ya better let ya girl put some ice on it," Striker said as he licked the jelly off his fingers.

Ricardo finished off his black, unsweetened coffee as Darius walked by the window with a girl. He remarked that he'd schooled his homie in the ways of love.

Danetta began groping between Ricardo's legs under the table. "I'm off the clock and ready for some cock." She giggled as she felt Ricardo getting a hard-on. She asked Ricardo to drop her off at her apartment and come back after he took his boys home. Her mother had the baby, and she was alone for the weekend.

"Dude, it's supposed to be bros before bitches," Bones whined in protest. "I thought we was gonna party tonight and smoke some of the weed you got off X-Man."

"Change of plans, *hombres*. A man's gotta do what a man's gotta do, and my woman has plans for her man."

"You boys get my man all the time. I hardly see him. Y'all are gonna get him killed before he makes me a baby." Danetta leaned over on Ricardo, kissing his neck and adding in a whisper, "Don't keep Momma waiting."

12:28 a.m.

"I'm getting too old for this shit," X-Man said to himself. "But those ass wipes better hope I never catch 'em." He hurt all over and he didn't know what had just happened or why. He knew he was lucky the cops had accepted his bogus story. He had to get his ass out of Amelia. He knew it had been a bad idea to start coming here, but the money was just too good.

Still, things could've been worse. If his car and partner were there when the police showed up, there would've been too much stuff in the wrong place at the wrong time. All hell would've broken loose.

12:33 a.m.

Robert called Bernie again. He knew he was probably getting to be a bother, but he wanted to get a story posted online before that female anchor from KWBJ-TV. He liked her, and she was a very good reporter, but he never wanted to be scooped by her.

"We found three thirty-eight-caliber casings near where the victim was shot and five twenty-two-caliber casings on the road," Bernie said. "Eight bullet casings, and we still haven't found a gun."

"Nothing you can give me on either guy's identity?" Robert asked. It was looking like the pieces wouldn't come together for a story until tomorrow.

"I'll give you something if you promise not to use it unless you get it from the PIO. The guy over here claims to be Samuel Rider from Little Rock, Arkansas."

"And . . . ?" He stopped drumming his fingers and leaned forward as if he was getting closer to the detective.

"We don't believe that's who he really is. If it isn't, then this guy is lying and hiding something. But we didn't have enough to hold him."

Robert's hair tingled in excitement, but he was frustrated. He suspected he was sitting on a big story, but his hands were tied by his promise to his source and a lack of information. He suspected the two crimes were connected, but it was too risky and unprofessional to report on what may be, rather than what is. Too little information and too much reporting had burned the credibility of more than one journalist. Robert had no intention of joining the ranks.

"I wish we had more people tonight to investigate this before we let this guy walk," Bernie said. "I got a bad feeling that this one's going to come back and bite us in the ass. I better not see that quote in the paper, or you won't get a piss drop in hell from me ever again."

12:40 a.m.

X-Man slipped into the fog out of view of the cops and medics when James called to say he was nearing Bradley Drive. James said he'd gotten a call from a friend in Amelia, who said another "businessman" had gotten himself shot on the job.

"Yeah, I heard a cop complaining 'bout it," X-Man said. "We out here trying to make some money, and they complain about having to protect us. Do you know who got shot?"

"Naw, bro. I ain't heard. Do they suspect anything 'bout the drugs? I'm near the corner, flashing my lights."

"The cops don't know bug shit yet. They ain't got nothing. This fog is thick as peas, but I see you. They ain't paying me no attention and can't see me. I'll hop in and drive. You can go do whatever, but I'm hurting like hell and just wanna go home."

X-Man got in the car, and they headed into Morgan City.

12:51 a.m.

X-Man saw a Suburban stopped ahead as he approached a red light in Morgan City. They were the only vehicles at the intersection. He recognized the vehicle and he read the bumper sticker: *Latinos Make Better Lovers. Ask Ya Momma!*

"That Mexican is one of the illegitimate bastards that just beat the hell outta me," he said.

X-Man pulled alongside the Suburban at the next light. He could clearly see the driver. "I sold that bastard weed before," he said to James as he reached under his seat and grabbed the spare gun he always kept there. He laid on the horn of his GT to get the driver's attention, then lowered his window as he raised his gun. Their eyes met.

"Hey Mexican, now you gonna die and be dead," X-Man yelled.

The driver flipped X-Man the middle finger and then leaned forward apparently to grab a gun. "I ain't no Mexican, ya thievin' *gringo*."

"See you in hell, wetback," X-Man said. "It's time to die, asshole."

X-Man's first shot knocked the driver into his door, his head striking the window and sending his fedora into the backseat.

"Go to hell, *gringo!*" the wounded man yelled. He was raising his right arm, apparently to get off a shot of his own, when X-man's second bullet hit him and knocked him back into the door again. The glass behind his head shattered as the third bullet missed. X-Man knew the Mexican Vann Damme met his maker when the fourth and fifth bullets struck him in the face.

"Why did you do that?" James said. "Ya just threw a murder rap on us both! Let's get the hell outta here."

"Damn Mexican messed with the wrong white boy," X-Man said. He knew the gunshots would bring police within a few minutes. "Now I just gotta figure out who the damn Clouseau hit man is that tried to kill my ass."

CHAPTER 23
JANUARY 27-29, 2008

Evelyn smelled sausage wafting upstairs while she showered. When she came downstairs, Peter greeted her with a smile as he finished cooking.

"Good morning, Poppa." She stretched her arms as wide as she could and yawned. "The breakfast smells delectable, and I am famished." Evelyn kissed her poppa on the forehead. "How is your hip this morning?"

"It is fine. Nothing that complaining will change." The black mahogany cane he used to help him walk since the accident was beside him, propped against the cabinet. "Are you going to tell me about this new friend who brought you home last night?" Peter emptied a pan of sausage and flipped the last pancake in another pan, adding melted butter to the top.

"I am sure he will meet with your approval, as he is a perfect gentleman." Evelyn poured glasses of orange juice and milk and brought them to the table. "I will tell you about him later, but I need to rush through breakfast and then get my pretty on for Mass."

"Princess, your pretty stays on. That is why the boys love you and the girls envy you."

"Hardly, Poppa, hardly." Evelyn laughed. After years of glasses and an excessively sensitive, self-conscious awareness of her weight, Evelyn was far from confident in her looks.

"You are beautiful, just like your mother. That boy you say is such a gentleman is lucky to have had you as a date." Peter brought the pancakes and sausage to the dining room. Evelyn saw him looked to his right, into the parlor, and set his gaze on Martha's portrait sitting atop the quiet piano. While Evelyn and Peter had accepted Martha would never be there again, except in pictures and memories, that stool had silently screamed how empty their souls were since Martha's death.

"I am going to call him later. We are supposed to go on a date next weekend." She wasn't sure if Peter had even heard her as he continued to stare at the picture.

After Mass, Evelyn put on a pair of jeans and an old sweatshirt and walked to the bayou. The sun was high, and the chilly afternoon air suggested a nighttime freeze. She grabbed her Zebco rod and reel and then dug some night crawlers from the compost pile underneath a gnarly cypress tree, to use as bait for the blue cats. She had some Morse code bites, little picks and patters that hardly moved the tip of her rod. The catfish wouldn't start feeding well again until spring, and the rising barometer was no help. No matter. Time spent on the bayou was always time well spent.

She picked the sticky mud off the bottoms of her Cajun Reeboks with a stick from a willow branch. Then she threw the stick as far into the bayou as she could. A brown pelican sitting on a broken piling turned its head to investigate the splash, then dismissed it. Not far away, a white egret stood still as a brick until some hapless crawfish or minnow became part of a day-long meal that wouldn't end until the sun began to set. Evelyn watched as a twelve-foot alligator slowly moved toward the egret, who appeared to decide that fishing would be better in another area. The big bird rose a few feet above the bayou with slow flaps of its broad wings and landed under a giant cypress tree leaning over the bayou.

God, Evelyn realized, was reminding her that life must go on. In death, there was rebirth. Without moving forward, the survivors would die. She reeled in her line and, walking back to the mansion with no fish, reminded herself to count her blessings. She had a beautiful home and any material comfort she requested. She had her health. She'd been raised by parents who loved her and taught her right and wrong. She thought of Darius. She knew she'd oversold him somewhat to her poppa. He was a poor black man with dreadlocks and a car that a Kingsley wouldn't get in except in an emergency. Darius was a gem in the rough, like that diamond she'd found in Arkansas.

She wondered if this would be a good time to call him to talk about their date next week. She pulled out her iPhone and called the number Darius had given her. They spoke several minutes and eventually decided they would meet next Saturday night for a dinner-date at Chili's restaurant in Houma.

"I just saw him last night!" Darius yelled as he read the lead story in the newspaper on Sunday afternoon. He stopped dead in his tracks, looking up and down Byron Street as if the answer to his question might magically come riding up the road. His jaw was set in anger and sadness as he shook his head and let the words sink in:

> *A 23-year-old Morgan City man was killed when his truck was riddled with bullets from a drive-by shooting in the middle of Brashear Avenue early this morning, according to police.*
>
> *Morgan City police identified the dead man as Ricardo Ortiz. Police do not have a suspect or motive in the killing,*

according to Police Chief David Larose. Ortiz was struck in the upper body by at least four bullets and died on the scene . . .

"You, too, Thirty-eight?" Darius asked in shock. "You were supposed to outlive the cockroaches, bro." He walked into the trailer, plopped heavily onto the couch, and continued reading.

The fatal shooting occurred within a couple hours of a pair of late-Saturday-night shootings in Amelia, reported by St. Mary Parish Sheriff's office spokesman Todd Malloy. Those shootings remain under investigation with no suspects named. The victims, whose identities have not been released, in the earlier shootings declined transport to a hospital, according to Malloy. Both departments refuse to say whether the shootings were related.

She must not know.

Danetta was smiling and chipper when she took Darius's breakfast order on Monday morning. She was obviously unaware that her boyfriend was dead. Darius persuaded her to sit by him. He pulled the newspaper out of his back pocket and slid it across the table to her.

"No, oh my frigging God," she said as she pushed the paper away from her as if it was on fire. Her mouth was wide open, and her Waffle House hat fell off her head as she ran her fingers through her hair. She put her hands over her mouth. "I thought he stood me up, but he was dead!"

"Do you have any idea who would've done this?"

"Well, you heard him talking about fighting with that X-Man guy. I bet that had something to do with it. Striker and Bones might know. We should go to the police."

"And do what? We can tell them what we know about X-Man, but that won't do nothing. They'll file it in some notebook and never do anything about finding the killer."

Danetta insisted they should visit the police and tell them about X-Man.

Darius said he was going to try to talk to the reporter who wrote the article first. "He was in here the other night, sitting right over there. I heard him talking to a policeman about a shooting. I'll tell him what we know about Thirty-eight and this connection with that X-Man guy. He might have an idea about what happened that he didn't write in his article." He told her that he'd return afterward and they could go to the police together.

"Have you heard anything lately about the police looking for my momma's killer? They seem to have gone nowhere with that." Darius fidgeted in the beige leather executive chair in the conference room at the newspaper. A long oak table, with nothing on it except two legal pads and three ink pens, virtually filled the room. Awards and plaques won by the newspaper and its journalists lined the drab brown walls.

"I haven't heard anything recently," Robert rolled his chair closer to Darius. He grabbed one of the legal pads and a pen. "That doesn't mean they aren't making progress. I'm sure they're investigating all the leads, and they'll find her killer soon enough."

"It's already too late for soon enough, and I don't share your confidence in the police." Darius drummed his fingers on the table. "That article you wrote about Ricardo Ortiz's murder said they don't have any suspects. Well, they should, because I believe I know who killed him."

"Why do you think you know?" Robert's eyebrows arched as he wrote on his pad.

"I spoke to Ricardo an hour before he was murdered," Darius explained. "He and his two friends had been in a fight with a drug dealer in Amelia. He called the guy 'X-Man.' If I was the police, he'd be my suspect."

Darius thought Robert looked like a police investigator, leaning forward and scribbling furiously in the notepad.

"There were a couple of incidents in Amelia Saturday night," Robert said. "They may or may not have been related. But none of the police indicated that they think this shooting in Morgan City was related to those incidents."

"Like I said, the police can't connect the dots to a numbered stick-man." Darius grunted with disdain. "I told them that Marcus Holmes, the man who killed Momma, is using the name 'Samuel Rider,' and I don't believe they looked into that!"

"Excuse me? What name did you say?" Robert stopped as he fumbled with his pen. His expression changed into a huge question mark.

"Samuel Rider. I told them two years ago that he's using that name and that he's in Houma and they should start looking for him there. Evidently, they never told you about him."

"How did you find out he was using this name?" Robert was scribbling away in his notebook and not looking at Darius.

"I got a friend in New Orleans that ain't exactly kosher with the police, if you know what I mean. He knew Marcus a long time ago. He said Marcus is selling drugs in Houma and calling himself Samuel Rider. Have they told you that name before?"

"I heard it for the first time Saturday night," Robert said. He excused himself, saying he wanted to get something from his desk in the newsroom. When he returned he sat down at the table with a different notebook which he thumbed through for a moment before looking back up at Darius. "I was told that Samuel Rider was involved in one of those incidents in Amelia. They interviewed him, and Acadian medics looked him over. They didn't have anything to hold him on, so they let him go."

"Jesus Christ, man!" Darius bolted from his chair and began pacing around the table, clenching and unclenching his fists. "They had my momma's killer, but they let the doctors patch him up and then let him go?" The veins were bulging from Darius's neck, and saliva flew from his mouth as he spoke. "They couldn't find darkness in a cave!"

"Calm down, Darius. You're upset. I'm sure there's an explanation."

Upset? That's what happens when you eat a stale taco. Darius was livid. People's lives were at stake, and the cops twiddled their thumbs while Rome burned. "Yeah, there's an explanation. It's called in-friggin-competence." Darius hit the table with a closed fist.

"Would your friend know anything more about Samuel Rider, and would he speak to me? What about X-Man? What do you know about him?"

"I doubt my man will talk with you," Darius said. "But I don't know anything about X-Man. Saturday night was the first time I heard about him. Ricardo's friends might know. I only know their street names—Bones and Striker. They live in Patterson somewhere. They might tell you who X-Man is."

Darius left the newsroom even more riled than he'd been earlier. He seemed to be making more headway in finding Marcus than the police. There would've been a helladifferent story in Sunday afternoon's paper if he'd found him Saturday night. Now some Rambo calling himself X-Man had killed his friend, and these were the same bozos that would have to find him. Half a barrel of monkeys could do better.

Darius drove back to Waffle House and picked up Danetta. She was pacing the parking lot; her heavy blue parka protected her from the cold north wind that had ushered the Arctic cold front into south Louisiana.

"It's gotten cold," she said, shivering as she got into Darius's car which was only a few degrees warmer than the outside air. A moment later she shifted the conversation from the weather to Ricardo's death. "I feel so bad that I was mad at him. I thought he chose them over me. I been so mad at him that I ain't even tried to call him."

"Don't blame yourself, Danetta. You had no way of knowing."

"I'd just told him the streets was gonna kill him. When he didn't show back up at my apartment, I was gonna tell him it was the streets or me. I see the streets made that decision for him." She ran her hand through her hair as she rambled on about how unbelievable this all was and how good Ricardo had been to her and her son. Finally, she seemed to refocus her attention. "Did you find out anything at the newspaper?"

"The cops can't find fire in hell. They don't know about X-Man, and I also found out that they interviewed the man who murdered my momma and gave him medical assistance."

"What do you mean?"

"My momma was murdered, and I told them who the murderer was. Then I told them the new name he's using and where to find him. And they ain't done shit in a bucket to pick him up. I ain't got no confidence in these clowns."

Arriving at the MCPD office, the two went inside, where each told an investigator that Ricardo had come to Waffle House with his two friends. They related the same story Darius had told Robert. Neither knew how Bones or Striker could be contacted, and both said they didn't know who X-Man was.

Then Darius asked the question burning inside him. "What about Marcus Holmes? The guy that goes by Samuel Rider—the one y'all had Saturday night in Amelia and let go?" He was trying to control himself and not get worked up like he'd done at the newspaper. "He murdered my momma, and y'all turned him loose."

"We don't work Amelia," the sergeant explained. "That's the sheriff's jurisdiction. But nobody told us anything about a Samuel Rider. We know Franklin PD is looking for Marcus Holmes, and if we stop him, we'll hold him." He handed each of them a card and told them to call if they heard any further information. He said it would be helpful if they find out what X-Man's real name was.

Darius didn't notice the cold. He was angry over the loss of his friend and furious that Marcus was still at large. His momma was gone, his dog was gone, and his girlfriend was gone. He couldn't help but be angry about life.

"Do you want to go to the sheriff's office and tell them about Marcus?" Danetta asked as they pulled out of the police station. "That sergeant said they were the ones who questioned him Saturday night."

"For what? It's a frigging waste of time, just like this visit was a waste of time."

Robert had just walked in for work on Tuesday morning. He had half a notebook of information on the weekend shootings. He knew he was on a major story, but there were still loose ends to tie up.

His editor, sipping on his morning cup of hot tea, sidled up beside him.

"What do you have so far?"

Robert covered his mouth as he coughed. He was fighting a cold.

"An SO source said they questioned a shooting victim Saturday night who used the name Samuel Rider. Then they let him go. I'm trying to get the PIO to confirm that. Darius LeBeaux—he's the son of the murdered LeBeaux woman in Franklin—said Samuel Rider is the name Marcus Holmes, the man he says killed his mother, is using. Franklin police confirmed he shared this information with them two years ago. They also confirm that there is a murder warrant for Holmes. I don't have positive confirmation that Holmes and Rider are the same."

Theodore shook his head slowly. "Not solid enough for a story, yet."

"I'm trying to locate the New Orleans source who said Rider and Holmes are the same person."

"That might be a long shot. Anything else?"

Robert knew his editor was itching for the story. "Ortiz's girlfriend said he'd been in a fight with a drug pusher called X-Man. LeBeaux corroborates her story." Robert gathered up his recorder, camera, and notebook. He leaned on his cane as he slipped into his jacket and grabbed his press ID. He was ready to go chase his story.

"What about your theory that the shootings in Amelia were related? Maybe some type of drug lord or gang connection?"

Robert grunted and shook his head. "That's not looking to be the case. SO is pretty sure the two incidents were unrelated."

"A drug war woulda made a good story," Theodore said.

"I have a gut feeling that this Darius kid and Ortiz's girlfriend are onto something." Robert tapped his cane a couple of times on the floor. "I think whoever X-Man is, he went looking for Ortiz after their fight, found him, and killed him. I'm going to try to talk to street sources in Amelia and see what happened over there and if X-Man was one of those victims. I have a feeling that whenever X-Man is found, the murderer will have been found."

"Will you have something for print by this afternoon?"

"After I ride out to Amelia and see if anybody will talk to me, I'm going to review the arrest reports and try to get more from the SO. I think we'll have your front-page story by tomorrow afternoon."

"I don't want to get scooped. I want something this afternoon." Theodore tapped his desk with his empty teacup.

Robert walked out the door into the cold and wiped his nose on his sleeve. He seemed never to remember to get a handkerchief.

Try as he might, he was unable to get a comment from the sheriff's office on the Amelia shootings, but he got Bernie's permission to use some of the information if it wasn't attributed to him. By early afternoon, he was comfortable that he'd tied up most of his loose ends. The presses were held for an hour, so Robert could get the story in the Tuesday afternoon paper.

Theodore and Robert smiled when they yanked the first copies fresh off the press.

"We'll sell an extra thousand today, and the web hits will soar," Theodore predicted.

Darius slammed the newspaper down on the porch and kicked his basketball across the street. The stench from this crap just kept growing.

> *The man wanted for the 2004 murder of Franklin resident Sarah LeBeaux may be the same person who shot and killed Ricardo Ortiz, 23, Sunday morning, and he may have killed Ortiz after being questioned and released by sheriff's deputies about an hour earlier, Morgan City Police Chief David Larose said today.*

Pigenstein was X-Man! Now besides killing his momma, he'd killed Thirty-eight, and the douchebag was still free. The frigging Mayberry cops had him and let him get away! This reporter oughta be a police detective. He knew his stuff.

> *St. Mary Parish Sheriff's detectives believe Holmes iden-*
> *tified himself to them in Amelia as Samuel Rider, after he*
> *was beaten and robbed by Ortiz and two other masked men*
> *late Saturday night, according to a source close to the inves-*
> *tigation. The source spoke on condition of anonymity. The*
> *alleged muggers fled in an SUV shortly before Holmes was*
> *shot three times by a different and unknown assailant in an*
> *older model car, the source said . . .*

Darius read through the article as he crossed the street to retrieve his ball. How the hell do you have a murderer and then turn him free? The guy doesn't have an ID, and the cops just take his word even though he was shot three times. What moron doesn't see something wrong with that picture? Barney Fife would've done better. Darius looked up into the clear sky, and with his mouth open, he shook his head in disbelief.

"How stupid can these cops be?" he screamed at the top of his voice.

> *MCPD detectives believe Holmes also used the street name*
> *X-Man. They say he left Amelia and shot Ortiz three or*
> *four times in Morgan City shortly before 1:00 a.m., killing*
> *him on the scene. No gun has yet been recovered in the Ortiz*
> *killing.*
>
> *"Caution needs to be exercised in jumping to that con-*
> *clusion," St. Mary Parish Sheriff's spokesman Todd Malloy*
> *said. "Until a gun is found and ballistics are examined, who*
> *killed Mr. Ortiz is speculation."*

Darius angrily slammed the ball against the trailer. It rolled back and lodged near the back of the Impala. He kept reading.

> *Franklin chief of detectives Julie Richmond learned two years ago that Holmes might be using the Rider alias. That information came from Darius LeBeaux, son of the woman killed in 2004. She said LeBeaux got the information from an unidentified source in New Orleans who refused to talk with police, and that she doubted the veracity of the tip. She acknowledged that she had not disseminated the tip because of those doubts.*

This really pissed Darius off. He'd suspected she hadn't done anything with all the information he'd given her.

> *Holmes was one of two victims in unrelated Amelia shootings late Saturday night, according to the source in the sheriff's office.*
>
> *Detectives are still investigating the shooting of Holmes in Amelia but have no suspects. Holmes is thought to be living in Houma and recently began frequenting the Amelia area, possibly selling drugs.*

"He *is* living in Houma," Darius said out loud. "I told Miss Richmond where he lives. This is as disgusting as opossum shit for supper."

X-Man was a nom de guerre Marcus had picked up in Angola, where everyone said that he'd cross out any man standing in his way. He liked the reputation he'd gotten as a tough guy in the pen, and he liked the nickname. Ever since he left his brother's grave in Baton Rouge, he called himself X-Man and had immersed himself in this new identity. The crowd he ran with wasn't known for discretion in good times nor for loyalty in bad times. So his history, including his real name, became on a need-to-know basis—and no one needed to know.

The Samuel Rider alias, along with his fake ID, had saved his white hide Saturday night. As lucky as he'd been to get away from the police, X-Man didn't have much else over which to thank his lucky stars. He was hurting as if he'd been run over by a sugarcane truck. He'd parted ways with his lucky gun that he'd kept all these years—a gun that, if in the wrong hands, would prove that he'd shot Sarah. His business was in a temporary standstill until the heat passed. On top of that, he had some incompetent Clouseau assassin out there somewhere, looking to put a cap in his ass. He was wondering if he should lose himself in the jungle of New Orleans, where it would be easier to stay off the police radar and out of Clouseau's sight.

He needed to recuperate, and it was too cold to work the streets this week. In a few more days, his head would be clear, and he could decide what he'd do.

CHAPTER 24
FEBRUARY 2, 2008

"Please do not think that, because of my age, I am a little girl."

Evelyn nibbled her nails as she and Darius perused a shared menu at Chili's. She felt bad over fudging her age last week. She hoped Darius would accept her apology and not think she was a pathological liar. She was also worried that her new friend would think she was too young.

"I will not be eighteen until November. I am still in high school, but I start college this fall. I thought you should know in case it is a problem."

"Age is only a number," Darius said. "I can tell you're a very mature person."

Their server showed up, and the pair placed their order.

"Since we're setting matters straight and being honest," Darius said when the waitress had gone, "I have something to tell you."

"Please do not tell me I am having dinner with a mass murderer who cannibalizes his victims and I am next on your list!" Evelyn put her hands to her cheeks and feigned fright.

"No, silly. Nothing bad, really. I met you a long time ago. So when you told me last week that you lived at The Kingdom, I recognized who you were."

"Really? Intriguing. What kept you from sweeping me off my feet in our previous meet?" She started to bite a fingernail, but stopped, remembering her mother had said it was unladylike.

"Probably because our paths crossed when you were a little red-headed girl in pigtails."

"Umm, Mr. Darius LeBeaux, I still wear pigtails!" She played the part of indignation, hands on the hips included, rather dramatically. "But that is beside the point. Pray tell me of this meeting."

"We met twice, in fact." Darius held up two fingers and paused a moment, looking at them. "Well, maybe one and a half times. The first time was only half of a meeting."

"You have piqued my curiosity and possess my undivided attention. Please continue." She leaned in closer to him, holding her chin in her hands with her elbows on the edge of the table.

"Do you remember that last weekend I told you that you didn't owe me anything? I said we were squared. Does that term mean anything to you?"

"I sometimes use it to say that a debt is paid off. But I never viewed you as in my debt. I felt like I was in your debt." She wondered where Darius was going with that question.

"Well, I borrowed the term from you. I was in your debt by your own words."

"Darius, you are not making sense." Evelyn furrowed her brows and shook her head.

"Please call me Deke. But let me explain. Do you remember a long time ago, like maybe when you were ten, that a small, beautiful, light-skinned Creole woman was gathering peaches outside your stone fence and your gramps tried to run her off?"

"Oh, you must mean my poppa." People sometimes confused Peter with being her grandfather. "I sort of remember that. I got out and picked some off the tree for her." She remembered her poppa wasn't very kind to that lady.

"I was in the car, and watched you scale that stone fence like a gazelle. I thought you were a cute tomboy." Darius gestured with his fingers as he described Evelyn climbing the fence. "Do you remember what you told the woman?"

"No, not really. Was that your sister?"

"It was my momma who was gathering them for me because it's my favorite fruit. You told her she should give those peaches to me, and that we'd be—quote—squared—unquote—when I helped somebody in need."

"Oh, how sweet of me." Evelyn laughed.

"Yes, it was sweet of you, and it made an impression on me, Miss Peaches."

They both laughed at the nickname.

"So that's why I said we're squared after I helped you and brought you home."

"That is really the sweetest thing I ever heard. You are such a gentleman." Evelyn leaned over, put her arms around Darius, and gave him a kiss on the cheek. She looked into his eyes and smiled.

She'd seen captivating eyes like that before, somewhere; it was somebody else. Then she remembered. It was two years ago; that reporter with a cane who seemed to carry a chip on his shoulder about how bad life can be.

She kissed Darius, again. She'd never kissed a boy twice, like that. She was a little embarrassed by her actions.

"Do not get the wrong idea just because I kissed you," she said.

"Well, you did kiss me twice. That's bound to give a guy some ideas." Darius grinned.

"Now, do not go getting fresh with me, Mr. Deke." Evelyn giggled and reached to hold Darius's hand. "Back to your little narrative. If that was only half of a meeting, where did I have the pleasure of my full meeting with you?"

"It was a few months later, when me and Momma went to the festival. You dropped your purse and I . . ."

"OMG! That was you?" Evelyn dropped her fork and almost knocked off her glasses as she put a hand on each side of her face. "That purse was a gift from my Maw-Maw Hebert. I still use it. I would have expired if I had lost that purse. I cannot believe this, Deke."

The conversation stalled momentarily as their food arrived. Evelyn overcame the surprise of Darius being the boy who had found her purse and tacked the conversation in a different direction, asking Darius about his future plans and if he was going to college.

"I just enrolled in South Central Technical College for welding. A friend's uncle is supposed to get me a job at Conner's when I finish. My friend was the guy murdered Sunday night. The guy who murdered him murdered my momma almost four years ago."

"Oh, my God. I am so sorry." Evelyn stopped eating and put her right arm around Darius and reached with her left hand to hold his hand. "You are such a gentleman to honor your commitment and take me to dinner tonight under these circumstances. I do not want to press, but if you want to talk about it, I will listen."

"That's sweet of you, Evelyn. But if I start talking about it, I'll get angry and it'll ruin our date. You're such a beautiful woman and pleasant company. I just want us to have a good time tonight, if that's okay."

Evelyn blushed slightly, but she was smiling. "I am not beautiful. I am fat. You are too kind, Deke." She ran her hand lightly across Darius's face.

"Why do women think they have to be perfect to be beautiful? First, you ain't fat." Darius took her hand and gently kissed it. "Second, I see a beautiful woman, even if you don't. And third, you look past me being a poor black man from the West End with little education and a beat-up Impala, and now you're here holding my hand and having dinner with me. I don't have to see you to know you're beautiful."

"You are deep and know how to sweep a girl off her feet. I bet you say that to all your dates." Evelyn laughed with just a hint of insecurity and self-consciousness.

"Naw, I usually just call 'em an iguana."

"Huh?"

"Nothing. Inside joke I'm making at my own expense. So since you're going to college in the fall, I guess that means you'll break my heart and leave me in a few months."

Evelyn choked on her Diet Coke laughing. "No, actually I have many scholarship offers, and Poppa would love if I went to Harvard where he and my grandfather went to college. But I want to remain here and go to Nicholls. So, you see, I will still be around my knight in shining armor if he still thinks I am not too fat when I graduate."

"What will you major in? And quit talking about you being fat!" Darius shook his finger at Evelyn.

"I am inclined to pursue journalism for my undergrad, which would please Poppa. Momma wanted me to be a doctor, but that does not interest me as much." Evelyn paused, and a momentary look of sadness fell over her face.

"What's wrong, Peaches?" Darius noticed a change in her expression.

"Nothing, just battling through some sadness of my own. Like you, I do not want to spoil our evening together by talking about it."

After dinner, Darius asked Evelyn if she'd like to go bowling.

"Maybe we can have a do over of our third meeting." Darius was teasing her over their initial meeting from the previous weekend.

"Quit reminding me, Deke. That is mean!" She gently hit him on the shoulder as if she was angry. "Wait! We cannot go to the bowling alley and redo our third meeting." She put her hands up in Darius's face as he opened the door to the Impala for her to get in.

"We don't hafta go there, if you don't wanna."

"No, that is not it. I just realized something. I had this sense of déjà vu when you picked me up this evening, and again just now. Now I know why. This is the vehicle that almost killed me two summers ago. It was flying out of a shopping center by the old bridge and almost collided into us!"

Darius remembered almost hitting a fancy car when he fled from the jewelry store. He feared this was the end of a beautiful date and any chance of another date had irretrievably disappeared.

"You almost gave me a coronary infarct that day, Deke. So we are not squared yet."

She bent over laughing, and Darius knew his fear was unfounded.

"So, you see, when we go to the bowling alley, we will be having a second chance at our fourth meeting! Where were you going in such a hurry?"

"Just get your fine ass in the car and quit messing with me, Peaches," Darius dodged. "I thought you were going to say you didn't wanna see me anymore!" There was no need to run her off with unflattering stories of his past before he could demonstrate that he'd changed.

"Oh, so you like fat booties?" Evelyn teased him as she slapped her own rear.

"Do you want to leave?" Darius asked Evelyn. "That jerk is here." They were renting their shoes from the pimpled, gum-chewing teenager who was still glued to his cell phone. Darius noticed Mitch and two of his buddies were bowling in a lane near the center of the alley.

"Why should I let a barbarian baboon spoil my fun? How about we go bowl in the lane next to him?"

"Are you serious?"

"Yes, I am serious. You can teach the Bohemian to be a gentleman, and he can see what he is missing."

It occurred to Darius that while Evelyn was surprisingly cocky, he was feeling a little apprehensive. This wasn't fear; it was caution. On the streets, a man didn't back down when his pride was challenged. Just a few days ago, he'd threatened this dude with bodily harm and had run him off a parking lot. He'd even threatened him with being shot. Evelyn's world might be different, but in Darius's world, this had the makings of a violent encounter.

"Are you really sure you want to strut there with your fine ass and bowl with him leering at you all night?"

"If he does, we will just tell the management that he is bothering us, or I will call Poppa and he can have the police handle the matter."

What planet does this girl live on? Maybe the question is, what planet have I been living on? Where I come from, you never go to management to resolve a problem. As for calling the police, well that's just plain dumb. Ricardo must be rolling over in his grave.

Since his date was committed to this foolishness, Darius resigned himself to the inevitable. All things considered, Evelyn's idea wasn't very good. Actually, it was terrible. Strategically, it was fraught with danger, but if this was what she wanted, there was no way he was going to appear to be a punk and wuss out of it.

"If things get out of hand, just make sure you get outside. I'll take care of myself. Don't worry about me."

"Nothing is going to get out of hand, Deke." She spoke as if Darius had suggested that the sun might not rise.

The pair put their bowling balls into the ball return as the trio next to them looked over. Evelyn kept her attention ahead, but Darius looked into the eyes of each high school boy and stared them down. Before Evelyn could bowl the first frame, Mitch rose from his chair, obviously intending to cross to their side of the lane.

I knew this was going to be a problem, but I didn't think it would be this fast. Darius positioned himself between Evelyn and Mitch.

Mitch stopped three feet from Darius and reached out his hand. "Hi, I'm Mitch. I think we met last week. No hard feelings, right?"

I threatened to whip this white boy's ass, and now he's shaking my hand and saying no hard feelings?

Darius tentatively offered his hand in return. "I'm Darius. Sure, no hard feelings as long as you respect my woman." Darius was still expecting some sort of altercation.

"No problem, dude. I'm cool, you cool, we all cool." Then, looking over Darius's shoulder, Mitch tried to talk to Evelyn. "I'm sorry about last week. I was out of line, but I wasn't going to hurt you."

Evelyn turned her back and sipped on her Diet Coke.

"She's still pissed at me, I see. It's cool. Like I said, no bad blood, right?"

"No bad blood, bro. Just make sure you leave her alone."

"Since she ain't talking to me, let her know I won't need her tutoring like she wanted to do."

"I'll pass the message," Darius said.

This is a crazy-ass world Evelyn lives in, but I guess it's no crazier than the world I been living in all my life.

Different world or not, there was something about Evelyn that made him comfortable. She ignored the incongruence of her wealth and his poverty. She accepted him as the man he showed himself to be, not the man society judged him as being.

They bowled a single game before Evelyn asked him to take her home. She was tired, she said, and tomorrow she was getting up early. They held hands during the drive back to the mansion, where Darius opened the car door for her to get out. "Will I see you again?"

"Please, yes. I had a wonderfully spectacular evening, Deke. I have not enjoyed myself like this in many months." She looked down and pulled her keys from her purse as they walked across the front porch. She paused, still looking down, and seemed to be searching for words.

"What's the matter, Peaches? Is something wrong?"

"No, I was just wondering . . . Maybe I should not ask." Evelyn looked up and had a weak smile.

"What is it? Ask." Darius couldn't figure out what she had in mind.

"Well, on Sundays, I have sort of a ritual. I do not want to discuss it tonight. But would you pick me up about eleven and share a very important hour with me?"

A ritual? An hour? What did she want him to be part of? He wasn't down for any religious stuff. Yet, she had said it was important to her.

"Sure, Peaches. I'll be here in the morning."

"Thank you, Deke. That would be special for me." She tiptoed and kissed him on the cheek, then hugged him and kissed him on the lips.

"I know. Don't get any ideas from you kissing me, right?" Darius grinned.

"Well, if you are postulating that I like you, that would not be erroneous."

Postulating? Where in the hell did this girl learn to talk? But I do like this postulation.

CHAPTER 25
FEBRUARY 3, 2008

"I'm sorry you lost your momma. I had no idea."

Evelyn smiled her gratitude for Darius's kind words. She was glad he'd met her here after church; his presence filled her with serenity and peace, much like her father, but in a different way.

Darius put an arm around her as they walked through the Morgan City Cemetery near Bayou Shaffer. She held fresh flowers for her mother's grave and wore the sky-blue dress with little white angels on it that she'd worn to Mass. She felt a tear crawl down her cheek as she struggled to force a smile and a choked-out "thank you." Darius gently wiped the tear away.

His hand, holding hers, was strong but gentle—warm and comforting. She peered into his hazel eyes—soft, beautiful, and full of care—and then leaned her head against Darius's chest and began to cry. "Why did God have to take her from us? Deke, I miss Momma so much. I get so lonesome for her."

Darius rocked her gently as he wrapped his long arms around her.

She thought she'd come to grips with her sorrow and pain, and even her anger with God. It had been seven months since the Kingsleys spent their final day together at the Heberts. Evelyn had seen Peter grieving as much as she had. She wondered if his pain exceeded hers. After all, she knew she'd be seeing her mother in heaven one day, while he had no hope of ever seeing her again.

In any case, they'd seemed to come to terms with the tragedy and the echoes of silences in the rooms of The Kingdom. By the time of the Christmas break, Evelyn had determined to get on with her life. She no longer felt she was disrespecting her mother if she allowed herself to have fun.

But when Darius held and consoled her, it was as if all the grief, emptiness, sorrow, and anger swept back over her like an emotional cyclone, and she just melted and broke down.

* * *

The memory of his momma's passing was still fresh after all these years, and the emptiness Darius felt inside was as cold and bitter as it had always been. Unlike Evelyn, he found no peace by going to Sarah's grave. Visits to the grave prompted memories of the day he buried his momma that were too painful to bear. When her casket was lowered into the ground—someone had bought a small plot in the Franklin Cemetery—it struck Darius like a ton of bricks that he'd never see his momma again. He'd fallen to his knees, crying and sobbing, even more than he'd done the afternoon she was killed.

In the weeks and months after Sarah's passing, Darius had found a way to acceptance, but remaining on the road to vengeance precluded finding a way to happiness. He laughed and joked, but the laughter was empty of joy. Even the pleasure he'd found in Nina's arms didn't fill the dark void in his life. So Darius empathized with his new friend and the pain she felt.

He was flattered that she'd asked him to share in her Sunday-morning ritual. There were few people in his life that Darius thought were a blessing to him. In fact, just two or three, and they'd all been taken from him. There were the Browns, Nina, and Ricardo—maybe you could include Jack. It was beginning to look as if Evelyn might be added to the short list. He just hoped she wouldn't be taken prematurely from him, too—that voodoo Midas-touch thing.

"I understand how you feel, Peaches," Darius told her as she led him toward the back corner where her mother was buried. "We can never replace our mommas." Darius stopped walking to gently brush away more tears.

"I bet I look a mess," Evelyn said with a smile and a sniffle.

"You look like a woman that hurts," Darius answered.

Was it only a week ago that she had met this kind, caring young man? Evelyn felt comfortable in his arms, as if she'd known him all her life.

He is so thoughtful and gentle. Darius must have had loving and caring parents who trained him well, who taught him right and wrong and how to care about other people.

It occurred to Evelyn that she'd never talked to anybody about what had happened that afternoon, not even Pawpaw and Maw-Maw. She'd silently listened as her poppa gave sparse details to those family members who needed to know. Other than that, she and Peter hadn't spoken about that terrible day. It was time to unload that burden from her soul. Talking about those painful last moments was the final step she had to take to let go of her mother.

The sun tried to chase away the chill of the morning as the pair reached an oak tree, bare of leaves, near Martha's grave. Evelyn set the flowers down and began to take off her fur-lined jacket, which Darius assisted her in doing. She spread the jacket on the ground to sit upon it so as not to soil her dress. Darius stopped her, insisting they sit on his jacket instead.

He held her hands as she opened her mouth to speak, but no words came out. Even now, she was finding it nearly impossible to talk about. She buried her face in Darius's shoulder and began to weep again as she remembered her poppa's voice shouting, "Oh, my God!"

Darius patted her on the back and gently ran his fingers through the ends of her hair that hung halfway down her back. She stopped crying, and with a deep sigh, began to speak.

"Poppa slammed on the brakes, and in the middle of Momma's kiss, she was flung forward. I think the truck hit us head on as soon as Poppa hit the brakes." Evelyn put her hands over her face. She shuddered as she remembered those tragic moments. "The man was drunk as a skunk. They told us later that he had a blood alcohol content of point-two-one. Sometimes I think I want to be a prosecutor and put away drunk drivers. I may go to law school after my undergrad. Deke, if you drink, you have to promise me you will never drive afterward."

"I don't drink a lot, but I promise I won't drive after I drink." Darius rubbed her shoulder and kissed her on top of her head.

Evelyn took another deep breath and closed her eyes. "Poppa was trying to talk to Momma and was asking me if I was all right. He couldn't move. He had a broken hip and a broken leg and some broken ribs."

"Were you okay?" Darius asked as Evelyn felt the wind ruffling her hair. She pulled the hair from her face and took a couple of rubber bands from her purse.

"Yeah. All I could think of at the time was if Momma was all right. She was not saying anything, but I could hear her moaning." Evelyn had made one pigtail. She sniffled and began working on the other.

"She was still alive?"

"Poppa kept telling me to get out of the car and call nine-one-one, but he was telling me that Momma was okay."

"He didn't want you to worry." It occurred to Darius that he was defending a man he hadn't liked very much.

"Everything was bloody, Deke. Her face, her clothes, the dashboard—everything. I knew it was bad."

Evelyn had finished braiding her hair into pigtails. She put her jacket back on and picked up the flowers as she and Darius slowly walked over to Martha's grave. She set the flowers down, touched the headstone, and then knelt and offered a silent prayer with her eyes closed and lips barely moving. She finished her prayer and opened her eyes but was still on her knees. "I never heard my Poppa pray until that day," Evelyn said, barely above a whisper, as she peered into the sky. "Poppa begged God not to take Momma. He promised to start going to a synagogue if God let Momma live."

Darius placed a hand on Evelyn's shoulder and another on the other side of her neck under a pigtail. Evelyn reached to her shoulder, still looking heavenward, and placed her hand on top of his. "You cannot bargain with God, Deke. But even I was begging God not to take Momma. And I was angry when he did."

"I'm sure you were, Peaches." Darius knelt beside her, to her right, and put his arm around her.

Evelyn bit her quivering bottom lip, bowed her head, and closed her eyes again. "Dear God, please give me the strength to understand and to forgive you," she whispered with her head bowed and hands clasped together. She took a light-blue silk handkerchief embroidered with the burgundy Kingsley family crest of a lion, shield, and pair of scales from her pink purse. It was the purse Darius had rescued a decade earlier. She used the handkerchief to dab at her eyes and nose.

"It's okay to be angry, Peaches."

"Not at God, Deke. That is a sin." Evelyn removed the flowers she'd brought last week and began arranging the fresh ones at the head of her mother's grave. "When Momma died last summer, I realized I was not prepared to accept God's timing on when he takes people."

She was conscious of Darius's arm around her shoulder. She liked the warm feeling that it gave her. She slid her hand across the top of the tombstone and caressed the edges of the headstone. With an open palm, she rubbed the letters of her mother's name as if she were touching her face in the kitchen, where they had shared so many wonderful times. She ached for her kindness, her wisdom, and her guidance. None of that would be in her life anymore.

"The Kingdom seems so empty without her, Deke." She looked at her fingers and found some nails were longer than others. "I even miss her reminding me not to bite my fingernails," she added with a half chuckle. "Every time I walk into the parlor," she continued, "the silence is deafening. I see that piano sitting there, not making beautiful music." She paused, hummed a tune, and played an imaginary piano. "Gosh, she was good on that piano."

"I know the silence takes a lot of getting used to," Darius said in a soft voice.

Evelyn raised her head and looked up at Darius. She sensed that he understood her.

"Poppa told me that before she died, she whispered to him to tell me that she would sit at the foot of my bed at night like she did when I was a little girl. That is so much my mother."

Evelyn stood up and tried to blot away any makeup left on her face as she and Darius walked back to the oak tree. They sat down on Darius's jacket, while Evelyn kept her jacket on.

Evelyn picked up a couple of acorns and rolled them in her hand. "I sit here every week and think about Momma and all the good times we shared and how she helped me build a strong faith. That is what sustains me through all of this." She sighed. "I know Momma was happy to hear Poppa praying. I just hope on the way to heaven, she did not hear his blasphemy. That was the first time I ever saw Poppa cry. The only other time I saw him weep was at the funeral." She tossed the acorns in her hand toward a squirrel several feet away. The squirrel darted one way then the other before scampering up a nearby tree.

"If God heard anything, he'd understand," Darius said.

"God hears and sees everything, Deke." Evelyn paused. She was looking down, folding and unfolding her silk handkerchief. Then she smiled and looked back up at him. "A couple days before we buried her, Poppa was going through her belongings, and he found something she had kept without him knowing." Evelyn began to get up.

Darius hurriedly rose before Evelyn so that he could assist her in getting up from the ground. "What was it?"

They began walking toward the car.

"I should tell you the story someday of how my parents met. But he gave her a silk rose that day. She kept it all those years. Poppa did not know it. We buried that rose with her." Evelyn looked and pointed in the direction of Martha's grave. "Poppa put it in her right hand that was folded on her breasts. He said that is where it belonged." She was too sad to tell Darius what her poppa had thought of those breasts.

Darius squeezed her hand.

"We took a vacation to Mount Rushmore when I was a little girl, probably about the time your momma picked those peaches. On the way there, we spent a Saturday in Arkansas at the Crater of Diamonds State Park, where I dug for diamonds until I got blisters on my fingers."

She and Darius were close to the parking lot as they passed a bench under a tree with vines growing around it. Evelyn sat down on the bench, looked at her dainty fingers, and placed her hand in Darius's hand as he sat down with her. "Can you imagine mud under these nails and blisters all over these hands?" she asked with a laugh. "They had just plowed up the forty-acre field to make it easier to excavate, and it had rained a day earlier, so I was really a hot mess."

Darius had seen her act like a tomboy and stand up to guys twice her size, but Evelyn carried an air of royalty about her. "No," he said. "I can't imagine you with blistered hands and dirty fingernails."

Evelyn grinned and patted his leg. She shivered and buttoned up her jacket. "Anyway, Momma said I should quit digging, but I kept digging and saying that if I found a diamond, I was going to put it in my engagement ring." Evelyn tossed her head back with a dry laugh.

"Did you find one?" Darius asked, putting an arm around her. His touch and his comfort warmed her inside and out.

"Yes, I did." Evelyn stopped. She leaned her head against Darius's shoulder, closed her eyes, and smiled. "I was just a little girl then, but I remember I was jumping up and down with excitement, holding this white diamond. It was round and smooth, with a slightly oily feel to it."

"Was it big?" Darius asked as a blast of wind blew leaves in front of them.

"It was a carat."

"That's a sizable rock!" Darius said.

"Momma got tired of my whooping and hollering over that diamond." She grinned as she talked like Martha. " '*Cher*, you actin' like dat uncut diamond is de centerpiece of de crown jewels,' Momma said."

Darius laughed. He looked closely at her.

Evelyn was a little embarrassed by his gaze; she knew she must have looked rough, cheeks red from exposure to the cold and wind, eyes red from crying, her smiles forced and crooked, and her hair blown all over the place like the leaves at their feet.

"When we got to South Dakota, I panned for some gold from small wooden sluices outside an abandoned mine. I got twenty-six flakes and put them in a small, clear glass tube. When I got home, I told all my friends I had found a diamond and gold. Momma would just laugh at me when I told those stories."

"I bet that was worth a lot of money," Darius said.

Evelyn got up from the bench and started walking toward the car again. "Not really. The diamond was uncut and would have been worth a couple hundred dollars if I had had a jeweler do something with it. And the gold was probably worth a nickel." Evelyn chuckled. "Anyway, I decided to put the diamond and the gold in the casket with her."

"That's touching," Darius said.

Evelyn looked at him in amazement. What guy says anything is touching? She believed Darius had to be special.

"I would like to introduce you to my poppa," she said as Darius opened the passenger door to his car for her.

"How about we have a couple more dates, and then you can bring me to your daddy."

"Done deal," Evelyn said. "This has been special to me. Thank you for being willing to come with me."

As was her nightly custom, Evelyn kissed the picture of her mother which she kept on her desk. Then she knelt in a brief prayer at the tiny shrine with candles on each side which she had in her room. Lying in her bed, she wept quietly before going to sleep. The silence of the night was still painful. God gave her the strength to bear this heavy cross, but not to slumber without tears.

Evelyn closed her eyes, and a smile sneaked across her face. Darius was different from other guys. He was handsome in his own right, although the braids took a little getting used to. Yet, it wasn't a physical attraction that made him appealing to her.

In a way, he's like me, she thought. *He's different and willing to make a stand for what is right. He acted tough that night we met, but I wonder if he has ever had a tough moment in his life. You do not see many tough guys bowling alone on a Saturday night. It does not matter to me. Tough guys usually think the answer to everything is a gun and a fight anyway.*

CHAPTER 26
FEBRUARY 15–17, 2008

Evelyn had been eagerly anticipating another date with Darius and the evening at Chili's hadn't disappointed her. But Darius's mood seemed to turn more serious toward the end of the meal.

"Before you decide to introduce me to your daddy, I should tell you something about myself." Darius slowly set down his cold drink. "I'm telling you this because I like you, and you need to know this now and not later."

"I like you a lot, too, Deke." Evelyn was looking deeply into Darius's eyes, convinced she saw a man made in the mold of her poppa—with a few obvious variations. There was something about a tall, well-built, good-looking, muscular man who would rescue you from danger, take you to dinner, be kind and sweet and considerate, and let you share your pain.

He'd sent a sweet card along with flowers to The Kingdom yesterday, and then gave her a box of chocolates when he picked her up for their date Friday evening. Like I need the calories on these hips, she'd thought, but they were delicious, and the gift was sweet to her soul.

She glanced out the window of Chili's. The sleet and rain had ended. She wondered what deep, dark secret Darius might be about to reveal. She hoped it wasn't too bad because she was liking Darius more than she was letting him know.

Darius reminded Evelyn of his friend Ricardo, who'd been murdered a month ago. He told her that they'd become friends after his momma's murder, and that Ricardo ran a small-time theft ring. Darius admitted he'd been part of that ring until about a year ago when he went to jail behind a shoplifting charge.

"Jail for shoplifting?" Evelyn said. "People are arrested all the time for shoplifting, and they never go to jail. Why did they send you to jail?"

The waitress stopped by their table and asked if they wanted to order dessert or anything else.

"I do not want anything else," Evelyn said with a wave of her hand. "I have already put too many calories on my fat gluteals."

Darius chuckled. "You're not fat, Peaches, and what the hell is a gluteal?"

"It is the three muscles in the buttocks, the maximus, minimus, and medius."

"Okay, Dr. Peaches. But you're still not fat."

They both laughed. Evelyn was glad Darius was comfortable with her few extra pounds.

"Anyway, I went to jail because the DA wanted me to rat on my friend, and I refused to do it, so he squeezed my balls to try to make me squeal. I ain't betraying my friends. Besides that, I stole a pendant and a necklace worth close to a thousand dollars, and I wouldn't give it up."

"What did you do with the necklace? Why wouldn't you give it back?"

"Well, even if I gave the necklace back, they were going to send me to jail if I didn't give Ricardo to them, which I would've never done. I gave the necklace to a girl I was dating for a birthday present."

"Are you telling me this to say those things are in the past or that you still do this stuff? And where is this woman you gave a thousand-dollar stolen necklace to?"

"I assessed my life during my month in jail, and I never want to go back there. I ain't stole nothing since. I even quit smoking weed. Sometimes I get drunk, but that's it. I want to get my life straight and make Momma proud of me. Before I went to jail, me and this girl—her name is Nina—broke up and she left town."

"You gave her a thousand-dollar necklace and then broke up with her?"

"It's a long story. We stayed friends, but I hadn't made my commitment to leave the streets, and she needed a man who could give her a future."

"Well, that makes sense," Evelyn said, nodding. The tinge of jealousy she felt when Darius mentioned another woman embarrassed her. The chocolates didn't seem quite as sweet. "I am pleased you changed the road you were traveling. Poppa says once you start on that road, the only way out is in a body bag. You are proof that sometimes a person can get out without being killed."

"I promise I've changed. But I'll tell you that that man who killed my momma—and now he's killed my friend—needs to be stopped. If the cops don't do it, I will."

"Oh, please do not do something foolish. Let the police handle the situation."

"You mean the same police who had the piece-of-shit in custody and turned him loose? The same police who ain't caught him in almost four years, even though he's been selling his poison right under their noses?"

"If they catch him again, I am sure they will keep him." Evelyn dabbed at the corner of her mouth with her napkin.

"Yeah, and if my aunt had balls, she'd be my uncle. Evelyn, the only way to be sure of justice is to take care of it yourself. My Momma didn't believe in guns, and she's dead, but I always keep a gun with me."

"Yikes! I do not believe in guns, either." Evelyn put her hand across her chest and frowned. "Too many people are murdered by them, and all the school shootings and accidental killings. People shoot and kill to protect material things. I do not subscribe to that belief. Still, I understand how you feel, Darius." She patted his hand. "Remember, I lost my momma, too, but you cannot take justice into your own hands."

"He's guilty of killing my momma and my friend, and the police know it, too."

"I hope the police catch him before you do something and destroy your life, Deke."

"Well, they better start doing their job before I do it for them, is all I can say." He was shaking his head, with his jaw set, obviously frustrated and angry.

"Well, I think when I introduce you to Poppa, we should keep your past our secret for the time being."

"Probably so," Darius said.

"Oh, and about the drinking you mentioned. Remember, you promised me not to drink and drive."

"Yes, I remember."

"A drunk driver killed my momma. So I have a real antipathy toward drunk drivers."

I can understand that you would hate them," Darius said as he caressed her face.

"I cannot hate them. That would be sinful." Evelyn kissed Darius's fingers and smiled at him, appreciating his understanding and empathy.

There's the scumbag. Today is Judgment Day!

Darius was leaving Morgan City over the Grizzaffi Bridge, thinking of what he should say and how he should dress to meet Peter, when on the other side of the bridge he saw a red Mustang GT heading east, the opposite direction. Darius floored the Impala. It was slow to respond, almost stalling. Finally, the engine caught new life and sped to Berwick, across the river, where Darius made a U-turn and took off in pursuit.

Darius reached under his seat and found the Smith and Wesson in its holster. Pulling it from under the seat as the speedometer needle shakily approached a hundred miles per hour, Darius unholstered the gun and flipped the safety off.

Ahead on the straight, flat highway, Darius glimpsed the red car. He was ready to unload all seven bullets when he caught up with Marcus. Adrenaline ran through his veins, and his heart was pounding as hard as the engine in the old Chevy. In a few minutes, he was going to smoke that Godzillard Pigenstein's ass and conclude this journey for justice.

Cypress trees lining the periphery of the swamp beside the highway rolled past him in a blur as he passed several vehicles. He kept his attention laser-focused on the red Mustang as he rapidly closed the distance between he and his nemesis. The three-fifty was pinging, and the out-of-line tires were shaking the front end. The worn-out shocks groaned as he flew over dips in the highway. Darius knew he couldn't get much more out of the Impala, but he was determined to catch up with Pigenstein and kill him. Then he passed a white-and-brown vehicle with emergency lights on the front, but not on top. It threw on its siren and gave chase.

Damn, a cop! Pigenstein is getting away!

With a sheriff's deputy behind Darius, there was nothing he could do but pull over and beg the cop to pursue the killer wanted by at least three different law enforcement agencies.

Darius opened his door to tell the cop that a murderer was escaping, but he was commanded over a loudspeaker to remain in his vehicle. It seemed like an eternity before the deputy got out of his car and slowly walked toward Darius's door, one hand conspicuously placed on top of his holster. Darius wasn't sure if the deputy had seen him slip his own gun back under the seat. He knew there'd be trouble if the cop saw that loaded gun.

"There's a murderer in that red Mustang driving toward Houma," Darius told the deputy.

"Let me see your registration and proof of insurance, please."

"Yes, sir, but you need to call in a red Mustang headed to Houma. It's Marcus Holmes, and he's wanted for two murders." Darius pointed up the highway while reaching into his glove box for the paperwork.

"Let me see your registration and proof of insurance, please."

What is this? Some kind of tape-recorded robot?

"I know I was speeding, officer, but please call in for that car. The man killed my momma and Ricardo Ortiz!" Darius sighed as he drummed his fingers on the steering wheel in frustration.

"Mr. LeBeaux, I clocked you going ninety-eight in a seventy-mile-an-hour zone," the deputy said as he began scribbling on his ticket pad.

"I know. I was trying to catch up to that murderer." At this point, Darius realized he was about to paint himself into a difficult corner. What was he going to do if he caught up with Marcus? Kill him? With the gun under his seat? Not a good position to be in for a recently jailed black man.

"I could arrest you for going twenty-eight miles an hour over the speed limit and for dangerous operation. But I'm just going to give you this speeding ticket." With a gloved hand, he handed the ticket pad for Darius to sign the bottom. "Why do you think this red car you were supposedly chasing is the car of a murderer, and what were you going to do if you caught him?"

"I wanted to make sure it really was Marcus Holmes, and then I was going to follow him and call nine-one-one for the police to arrest him."

"Well, he's gone now, son. I advise you to let the police do their jobs. They're the professionals, and if he comes around here, they'll arrest him. You should slow down before you kill yourself or somebody else."

You probably just killed somebody yourself by letting Pigenstein get away.

Darius had a truckload of butterflies in his stomach ahead of his meeting with Peter. Additionally, his emotions were stewing over his frustration in a system that held a black man down, even as it let a white murderer run free. His momma was white. Or maybe she was black. He'd never really decided what race she was, and she'd never told him how she identified herself. Evelyn was white, too. So this wasn't about white people being bad. Maybe it wasn't even the system. Maybe God was a sadistic comedian having a barrel of laughs at the expense of all the little, confused minions running around on the Earth.

Life is just frigging unfair!

Darius's phone rang. It was Evelyn.

"Poppa and I are going to the grave today. Would you like to come to The Kingdom at one-thirty for a late lunch and meet Poppa then?"

"Okay. What should I wear? I don't have a tie. Should I buy one?"

"No, just be relaxed. Poppa is cool. He is not like that. Just be yourself."

Evelyn was the kindest and smartest person he knew. She was also the richest person he'd ever met, given that Peter Kingsley was one of the richest men in the parish. Darius wondered why Evelyn was even interested in him. She'd never seemed ashamed of him, and she'd never made him feel self-conscious about their differences in education and social standing. That did little to mitigate Darius's worries about meeting her poppa.

"Welcome to my humble abode," Evelyn said as she opened the front door to the mansion. "We have been expecting you." She'd changed out of her church clothes, but even in black denim jeans and a blue pearl-buttoned blouse, she was looking fashionable to Darius.

"Was that 'The Star-Spangled Banner' playing on your doorbell?" Darius asked, pointing his thumb behind him to the door he'd just entered.

"Yes. Poppa's father fled Nazi Germany as a child. He is very proud to be an American and quite patriotic."

"That I am," Peter said with a booming voice as he stepped forward to meet and shake hands with his daughter's new beau.

Darius felt the big man's eyes sizing him up. He was uncomfortable as he thought he was underdressed in his khakis and navy-blue shirt with a collar. *A tie would've been nice*, he thought. In any case, everything seemed to pass inspection, although the old man's eyes did linger on the long dreadlocks.

"The name is Peter Kingsley. I am the father of this beautiful princess with whom you have been spending so much time."

"Pleasure to meet you, sir," Darius said, shifting his feet nervously.

The boy's handshake is firm, Peter thought, *and he looks you in the eye as he speaks. Maybe this kid is not so bad. But that hair . . .*

Peter invited Darius to have a seat in one of the recliners in the parlor. Evelyn excused herself to go fix hot cocoa.

"Not that one, son," Peter said. "That is my seat."

Darius had started to sit down in the closest recliner.

"I'm sorry, sir. Well, umm. My name is Darius LeBeaux. I was raised in Franklin, but I live a few miles away in Bayou Vista now. I'm in trade school to be a welder and hope to move to Morgan City."

"So you are a West End boy," Peter said. Evelyn had omitted that rather significant detail.

Marty must be rolling in her grave.

"Sir, I'm a man, and I don't characterize myself based on where I live. I'll be twenty-one soon, and I've supported myself since I was seventeen and my momma was murdered."

The boy is assertive, maybe a little too much. But at least he is not a coward.

"Evelyn told me about that. Please accept my condolences. So how do you support yourself?"

"I have a lawn-cutting business with nearly a hundred customers."

Peter suspected he was exaggerating.

Evelyn returned with three large mugs of hot cocoa. "I see you chose the right recliner. Poppa forbade me to tell you which recliner was his. He says he uses that as a test to see if my friends respect him enough not to choose his recliner." Evelyn laughed, but neither of the men joined her.

"Well, umm, he sort of had to tell me. I just took the first chair. They all look nice and expensive to me." Darius made a broad sweep of his hands, covering all the furniture in the room. He was stammering and obviously embarrassed at his faux pas.

"Poppa, they really do all look the same," Evelyn said. "How about we drink the cocoa while it is hot."

"Have you ever been in trouble with the law? I mean besides a speeding ticket." Peter casually sipped his cocoa, his eyes peering over the mug. As a reporter for so many years, he'd learned how to spot the little signs that indicated somebody was lying. When Darius choked on his drink, Peter knew he wasn't going to be fond of whatever answer he received.

"Well, sir, I got in trouble for stealing a gift for a girlfriend a couple years ago."

At least the kid had given an honest answer, even if the answer wasn't flattering.

"Well, do not steal this girl any necklace. One, it is illegal. Two, it is morally wrong. And, three, we are wealthy enough to afford whatever we want and do not have to resort to thievery."

"Poppa, he already explained all of that to me. He knows how we feel about stealing." Evelyn stood up from the couch and walked to where Darius was sitting. She sat on the arm of the recliner beside him. "He told me it was a mistake he learned from and has never done anything else like that. He will not do it again."

"I certainly hope not. I will not have my daughter dating a thief."

"You have nothing to worry about there, sir," Darius said.

Darius was looking into his mug as he spoke. Peter wondered if he wasn't looking straight into his eyes because he was lying or because he was ashamed.

Evelyn set her mug on the coffee table and jumped up from the arm of the recliner. Facing Darius, she took the still-full mug out of his hand and set it next to hers. Then she grabbed both his hands and pulled backward to get him out of his seat.

"I am going to take my wonderful boyfriend out to the pier and spend some quiet, romantic time with him," she said. "Poppa, you have grilled him enough."

She let go of one of Darius's hands and dragged him across the room as she kissed her poppa on the forehead, putting her free arm around his neck. "See you later, Poppa Grand Inquisitor!" She smiled, turned her back to him, and walked Darius through the kitchen out to the back of The Kingdom.

Her momma was right, Peter thought as he watched her skip out of the room. She has me wrapped around her pinky.

"Now that did not go so badly, did it?" Evelyn asked as they walked past two Mercedes sandwiching a pickup truck and then a twenty-two-foot bay boat. She grabbed her rod and reel and a bucket that had a few worms in it before they stepped out the side door of the garage. "How about we go catch some catfish for supper."

Darius couldn't understand her optimism as he walked beside her. He looked back, expecting to see Peter looking around the edge of the garage, watching him like a hawk.

Where the hell was she the past half hour? That couldn't have possibly been any worse!

"Huh? Your daddy hated me before he even knew me. He's hated me since my momma picked his damn peaches. He hated me when I walked in that door with no tie. You shouldn't have told me not to worry about getting a tie. Then when he found out I'd been arrested, it was all over. I'm nowhere near good enough for you."

Darius couldn't understand why Evelyn was laughing. This was not funny!

"You worry too much, Deke. I have Poppa covered. All you have to do is make me happy, and he will treat you like a son."

"Right now, I feel like the prodigal son who everyone's hoping will never return."

"Stop that nonsense, Deke. Like I said, you worry too much." She began baiting her two-aught hook with a worm that was wiggling like a geisha girl and squirting out mud on the back end. "This worm is rightfully worried. Poppa ain't put a hook up your derriere and thrown you into the bayou with the alligators!"

"Yeah, that's true. But you better quit saying 'ain't,' cuz I'll be blamed for it!"

They both laughed.

CHAPTER 27
SPRING-SUMMER 2008

"If God wanted me to fly, he would've screwed wings on my back."

"Quit acting like a scaredy-cat. He did not put wheels on your feet, but you get in a car and drive seventy miles an hour and dodge the drunks."

Darius and Evelyn were walking barefoot and hand in hand along the shore of Lake Palourde on a cloudless and warm spring Friday afternoon as kids swam in the still-cool water.

"Touché. But back to your question. No, I've never been in a plane."

"Do you trust me?" She stopped and spun Darius to face her.

"Yeah, but why do you ask?"

"Show me that you trust me and get in an airplane with me this weekend."

"I ain't got money to buy a ticket on a plane," Darius said, laughing. "And what does that have to do with trusting you?"

"I did not say buy a ticket. Get on a plane with me in Houma—one that I will be flying. We can fly over the Atchafalaya swamps and then back to Houma." Evelyn tossed her sandals to the ground and began tugging on Darius to wade into the water.

"Girl, you are messing with me. I'm giving you driving lessons because you haven't learned to drive, but you can fly a plane?" Darius tossed his tennis shoes to the sandy ground.

"I have a sport pilot certification. If you trust me, come fly with me this weekend." Evelyn led the way as they waded into the water. "Please, Deke. You will love it, and I will not let anything happen to you!" She tiptoed and put her arms around his neck, raised her knees, and kissed him.

"Oh okay. But if you crash that thing and kill me, I'll never trust you again."

Trepidation overwhelmed Darius, but Evelyn looked giddy with excitement as she walked around the plane, performing a safety check on the bright orange-and-white plane parked on the tarmac of the Houma-Terrebonne Airport in Houma.

"Poppa bought me flying lessons for my seventeenth birthday instead of a car, since I didn't want to drive after Momma died." Evelyn disconnected the tie-down to the left wing and checked the fuel level. "I have been flying this 'bug-smasher' Cessna 152 every week."

"A Cajun Amelia Earhart?"

"I can only hope to be. Maybe someday Poppa will buy me an airplane."

Rich people! I used to hope that Momma would have money to buy milk.

Evelyn finished the exterior inspection and they climbed into the small plane and buckled in. Darius watched her tick off more of the preflight inspection. Then, she set the fuel mixture to "rich," the carb heat to "cold," and turned on the master switch and strobes.

"Get ready, Deke, for the thrill of your life. Flying is better than sex!"

"How would you know?" Darius said, laughing.

Evelyn taxied out to the runway. With the plane accelerating, Darius clinched his teeth and through half-closed eyes he saw Evelyn pull back on the yoke. The nose of the little plane lifted, and the wheels left the ground.

"Oh, sweet Jesus, help us." Darius closed his eyes, grabbed his chest as he felt his heart fluttering. He remained speechless even after opening his eyes a few moments later. After what seemed an eternity, Evelyn was smiling at him and said the little plane was at two thousand feet.

"Piece of cake," Evelyn said over their shared intercom system. "I just love takeoffs and landings. Now that was not so bad, was it?"

"I'm still alive, so it could've been worse." Darius tried not to show how scared he'd been.

Evelyn told him they were cruising at a hundred-miles-per-hour, yet it felt as if they were barely moving. Cars and houses below looked like miniature toys. Gradually, Darius's anxiety disappeared. The view from a half mile above the ground was breathtaking.

With no clouds anywhere in the sky, Evelyn climbed higher— she said they were a mile high. Darius was awed by the beauty of America's largest swamp, the Atchafalaya River Basin, below him. After crossing over the twenty-five-mile-wide wetland, Evelyn descended again. Darius saw people in bass boats fishing with their families, and others in wide aluminum bateaus harvesting crawfish. He saw something moving along the edge of a bayou. Darius pointed to Evelyn's left.

"There's a bear and a cub out in that opening," Darius said.

Evelyn circled around the bear. The momma bear looked up and then ambled out of the field, with her cub tumbling behind her, into a large stand of cypress trees. As Evelyn guided the plane over the populated areas around the island city of Morgan City, she taught Darius how to read the altimeter—they were at a thousand feet. After giving

Darius an aerial tour of the places he'd lived in Bayou Vista, Patterson, and Franklin, she banked the plane in a wide, slow turn and flew east, back toward Houma.

"This is beautiful, Evelyn," Darius said over the intercom. His smile disappeared as Evelyn descended for the landing in Houma and the ground began rapidly getting closer. "Oh, damn to damn, damn, damn!" There was a sense of impending doom overwhelming him as Evelyn cut back on the power. After the wheels bumped the runway twice, Evelyn lowered the nose.

"I am still sort of working on getting my landings smooth," she said as they taxied back to the hangar. "Sorry about the bumpy landing."

Darius wasn't sure, but he thought he might've pissed in his pants. Of course, he didn't tell her that.

"Flying makes me hungry. Do you want to go to Chili's?" It seemed to Darius that this was becoming a favorite location for Evelyn.

Despite getting the bejesus scared out of him from the takeoff and landing, Darius had enjoyed the two-hour flight. At the moment, though, his greatest pleasure was safely walking on firm ground. Not far behind that pleasure was the thought of another evening spent with this redhead who made him feel special. He realized he was beginning to like this girl a lot.

Weasel had given him his money back, but money wasn't the issue. The cops had his gun—the gun he'd shot Sarah with. He'd made it very plain to the kid that this gun was important to him.

"I'm sorry, X-Man," the kid had told him. "But the heat was heavy over here for a few days after you got shot. I don't know why they had such a hard-on over somebody gettin' mugged. Somebody ratted me out that I had your gun and I had to give it up."

It'd been two months since killing that Mexican at the red light. He still had headaches from the kangaroo asshole kicking his head. He suspected a couple of ribs were cracked, too.

He still didn't know who the black Clouseau assassin was. All he knew was that it was somebody in an old Buick with fancy rims who couldn't hit the broad side of a barn. Who was pissed off so much that they wanted him dead? And why was there no word on the street about any of this?

After a brief recuperation, he'd resumed his dope dealing. After all, a man has got to eat and pay his bills. He couldn't chance going back into St. Mary Parish, so he was back to selling his stuff out of Shiloh Lounge along Bayou Terrebonne, near Houma.

There's that GT again, and I'm a thousand feet in the air.

Darius and Evelyn had just taken off and were flying northeast a few miles from Houma-Terrebonne Airport when he saw the car pull into a supermarket.

He felt that he couldn't let Evelyn know he'd been scanning the landscape looking for that GT during their flights. He kept glancing over his shoulder and then behind him to get a better look at where the car was parked. When they passed over the shopping center on their return to the airport about an hour later, the car was gone. The police may not have been making progress, but he was closing the net. It was just a matter of time before Marcus would be dead.

Maybe he should locate Marcus and then tell police where they could find him, he thought. If only it were that simple or the cops were half competent.

As they drove home, he told Evelyn that he thought he'd seen Marcus's car in Houma. "I want to determine where he operates so

I can turn that murderer in to the police." He wasn't sure how truthful he was being on the last part of that statement—killing Marcus remained the preferred option.

"I am glad you are going to let the law take care of this, Deke. Not only would it be wrong to kill this man without a trial, but I would be devastated if I lost you."

Perhaps Evelyn had known of his intentions after all.

"I understand, Peaches," Darius said. "I'll try to do this your way. But if the cops don't arrest him and put him on trial for killing Momma, I can't say what I'll do."

Darius appreciated Evelyn's offer to help him scan the highways as they flew about Terrebonne, Lafourche, and St. Mary parishes, but that red GT seemed to have disappeared.

"I really think Poppa is starting to accept you, Deke," Evelyn said at the end of one of their driving lessons he'd started giving her in the Impala. They had parked in the parking lot of Rouses Supermarket, and she was going in to buy some fruit. "Maybe I can cook a meal, and you and Poppa can have another visit."

"I believe you're deluding yourself with wishful thinking, Peaches," Darius said, shaking his head as they walked into the supermarket together. "He never comes to the door when I drop you off. I believe he's hoping he can ignore me and eventually you'll grow tired of me and I'll disappear."

"Oh, Deke, please, never disappear."

Darius thought it sounded like a plea. Maybe she liked him as much as he liked her. If only he could be sure of how she felt. He thought he was falling in love with this woman, but he was reluctant to tell her his feelings.

"Well, Peaches, I can promise you I won't disappear, unless you run me off." There! He'd just said it. He'd told her he loved her and wanted to marry her.

"Wonderful! I hope that is a promise because I am never going to run you off." Evelyn smiled and kissed him on the cheek.

She'd just accepted his marriage proposal—or at least so it seemed to Darius.

"You promised me you would give him the benefit of the doubt!"

Evelyn tossed the calculus book she was reading. Peter had just walked into the parlor and told her he was disappointed to discover that he'd not been told that Darius's shoplifting had landed him in jail for a month.

"I did not say I was not going to ask around and investigate," Peter said, setting down his briefcase.

Evelyn saw that look in her father's eye, along with the set jaw. She'd seen that look when they had their argument over the boy with the pierced nose. But she knew something Poppa did not. Darius was a good, decent man who had made one mistake. Of course, there was that issue about him wanting to kill Marcus, but she was working on that. No need mentioning that to Poppa. He would just jump to the wrong conclusion.

"Poppa, Darius paid his debt. He has moved on from his mistake." Evelyn got up from the couch to make a stand for something she believed in—that was how Poppa had raised her. "You claim to be a liberal, but now you are acting like a conservative who thinks people make mistakes and they should be put away forever." Maybe it was still a bit early to have Darius over for another sit-down with Poppa.

"I never said he should be put away forever." Peter leaned forward on his cane. "I am just saying that you are too good for him and you cannot throw your life away just because of a teenage infatuation!"

"I'm a woman, Poppa, and you know it!" She stomped her tiny foot. Poppa always said to never back down when you were right and to stand up when someone took away your rights. "I'm not infatuated. I'm in love!"

"Princess, you cannot be in love. You have known this boy for only . . ."

"He isn't a boy. He's a man. He made his way in life. He wasn't born with a silver spoon in his mouth, like I was and like you were!" Evelyn knew the passive aggression of her contractions had to be getting under her poppa's skin and an argument attacking the privilege of wealth would score with him.

"I was speaking," he said. "It is rude to interrupt."

Evelyn knew her poppa was right about being rude. It was one thing to use contractions and another to be rude. She also noticed he didn't challenge what she'd said. She knew she'd made her point. "I am sorry, Poppa, for interrupting."

"I was saying that you have only known this young man about a month." He'd lowered his voice, and he put his arms around Evelyn.

She was upset with him but didn't pull away from his embrace. She'd already determined what she was going to say at the first break in the conversation. No more being rude.

"You cannot have fallen in love with someone you have only known for a matter of a few weeks," Poppa said. "Especially when he is from a different culture and different background."

Thank you, Poppa, for making this argument so easy to win.

Evelyn was ready to execute her coup de grace. "Poppa, when did you say you fell in love with Momma?"

"The first time I met her."

"Did you know her before that?"

"I see where you are going, Princess, but this is different."

Evelyn pulled back a little from her poppa's chest, but she was still in his embrace. She looked into his eyes. Poppa had always told her that you look somebody in the eyes when you mean business and you know you are right.

"Different cultures? Different religious beliefs? Even different ages?"

"Yes, yes, Princess. But all that was different."

Saying all that is different is the weakest argument that anybody can ever use. It means logic has defeated them. Poppa has said so himself.

Evelyn noticed he'd looked away as he replied.

"I am not being judgmental, but Poppa, I can do the math. We never had this conversation, but I was born three weeks early in November. Mardi Gras was the end of February, and you left after a week. When was I conceived?"

"Evelyn Martha Kingsley, do not even go there!" Peter stepped back from Evelyn in obvious embarrassment. He didn't look directly into her eyes.

"Well, Poppa, we both know the answer. I am not going to have sex until after I am married. I know what I am doing. I am mature. I am a woman. I am in love. Get used to that, Poppa, because if Darius asks me to marry him, I will." She'd crossed her arms but made that final point without contractions or disrespect.

Evelyn and Darius began seeing even more of each other. Peter chose not to broach the issue with her. As long as the boy kept his nose clean and was a productive citizen, Peter realized he could say anything critical without contradicting principles he'd instilled in his daughter.

He was proud that she was graduating valedictorian of Berwick High in a couple of weeks. Martha would've been proud, too. Not only was Evelyn at the top of her class, but she'd also taken almost a full year of college credits and was prepared to enroll in Nicholls State University as a seventeen-year-old prodigy of sorts in the mass communication program.

Peter would've preferred Evelyn had accepted her scholarship offer from Harvard or Columbia, or even from LSU, but he was glad she was pursuing journalism. All the more reason for her to go to Harvard was that it would take her away from this Darius kid, who was determined to train-wreck his daughter's future.

Peter had driven by the house in Morgan City the kid had moved into. It was little more than a shack with a broken-down chain link fence around it, and it was in a dangerous neighborhood. How could Evelyn not see that this kid could never support her?

Peter was determined, as he'd always been, to support Evelyn in whatever she chose regarding the school she attended and the major she pursued. Supporting her in her choice of a boyfriend was an entirely different matter. She was just too young, too naïve, and too inexperienced to know what this choice would mean for the rest of her life.

She'd undoubtedly won that last discussion they'd had on the issue. He had to admit she was brilliant in making her point. Yet, it didn't change the facts. This kid wasn't good enough. She deserved much better.

Darius began working his first real job at Conner's Shipyard. He loved his work, his independence, and the sense of self-worth he was developing. He thought his momma would've been proud that he'd pulled himself from the cesspool of life in which she'd left him.

Additionally, he seemed to have something good to live for if Evelyn was around. For the first time since his momma died, Darius was planning for a future that involved more than killing her murderer. Nina had made him feel special, but Evelyn made him feel alive.

Even when she started pulling up in that red Ferrari Spider convertible sports car that Peter had bought for her high school graduation present, she made Darius feel special. It didn't matter to her where he lived or what kind of ratmobile he drove. She said her poppa had told her not to let anybody drive the Ferrari but her, but anytime she and Darius were together, she was the passenger. He was in love with this girl, despite how impossible that might seem or how the odds might've been stacked against them as a couple.

I gotta find a way to get on the old fart's good side.

He knew what he had to do, but Darius wasn't looking forward to sitting down with Peter. Ever since the day the old man had tried to run off his momma, Peter had seemed like an asshole. But asshole or not, if he was going to marry Evelyn, he must find a way to coexist with the man. Evelyn obviously loved, adored, and admired her daddy. So maybe he wasn't as bad as he appeared.

Darius wished his own daddy was around to give him some advice on how to handle this.

Evelyn just wanted to be alone—no Poppa, no Darius. She wanted to spend July 4 with her momma, just the two of them. She needed to say some blasphemous things she didn't want anyone else to hear.

"Are you sure you do not want me to go to the grave with you," Peter asked as he walked into the parlor.

Evelyn was at the piano, slowly playing "Auld Lang Syne." She was sniffling, eyes moist but not crying.

"Yes, Poppa. Thank you for going early without me and letting me go on my own."

Evelyn slowly rose from the stool. She ran her fingers aimlessly across the ivory. She turned and saw her poppa's reddened misty eyes. He'd probably only stopped crying when he entered the foyer. She ran to him, burying her head in his chest.

"Poppa, I hurt from missing Momma so much. Why could it not have been me instead? Sometimes I just want to die and join her in heaven." Evelyn started crying. "Why? Why? Why?"

"I miss her, too, Princess." Peter kissed the top of her head and stroked her hair.

Evelyn knew her poppa had grieved in silence for months and that grief had aged him. The past year had taken a physical toll on him. He no longer had those long powerful strides but limped along on his cane. His hair was turning gray, his face had developed wrinkles, and even his booming voice had dropped an octave or two. Evelyn felt Peter's arms wrap around her, but she also felt his chest shaking and heard his heart pounding. She knew he was trying hard not to cry, for her sake.

"I loved her as strong as a man can love, and I love you with that same love."

Evelyn stopped crying. She stood in the middle of the floor and rocked back and forth in her poppa's arms as he hummed "Auld Lang Syne."

"We must live on and find a way to be happy," Peter said. "That is what your momma would have wanted. All I want is to spend the rest of my days seeing you happy."

"You make me happy, Poppa; so does Deke. But today I want to be unhappy."

Peter stooped so Evelyn could kiss him on the cheek. She grabbed her purse as she walked through the kitchen toward the garage. She turned and looked at her poppa, who had walked back toward the piano.

Evelyn left the kitchen door open and slid into the Spider that had replaced one of the Mercedes in the garage. She glanced through the open door and saw her poppa bent over the piano, undoubtedly crying. She would've gone back in, but she knew he couldn't grieve with her there.

Evelyn placed fresh flowers at the head of Martha's grave, beside the ones that Peter had brought earlier that morning. She'd progressed through all the stages of grief in the past year, except for allowing herself to be angry.

She knelt and began an angry prayer. "Lord, you can read my thoughts, so you already know how I feel." She closed her eyes and bowed her head. Her hands were clasped over a set of black rosary beads, but she wasn't going to be praying the rosary today. She opened her eyes and stared at the ground. She hoped she could be forgiven for the words she felt in her mouth—too many words to swallow. She closed her eyes again and took a deep breath.

"You were wrong for taking Momma. She was doing your service: tending the sick, taking care of her family, and raising me! It was hard going to Mass the past year because . . . I am scared to say this . . . but you already know. I hate you for taking Momma!"

There! I said it.

Evelyn opened her eyes and looked up, almost surprised that God had not hurled a bolt of lightning her way. She might have welcomed it as it would've reunited her with her mother—unless her words would've sent her straight to hell. Relieved that she'd escaped the Lord's wrath, she stood up and walked over to that oak tree she liked to sit under. She was too restless to stay seated. She began walking slowly around the cemetery, talking to Martha. After a long walk, she returned to the grave and sat beside her mother.

"Momma, if you have any pull up there, please tell God I am not a bad person. Tell him I am only human, and I am trying hard to love him again. You always got your way with Poppa. I am sure you can convince God that I deserve another chance."

It was beginning to get hot and she was sweating. She thought a walk at the beach would be refreshing. Deke probably already had plans, since she'd said she wanted to be alone today.

"Momma, I am in love. I know you understand this better than Poppa." Mothers always understood love better than fathers. "You probably did not like him at first, since he is from the West End, but you have seen how he treats me. I wish Poppa would accept him. If you can help me out on this after you talk to God about what I said earlier, I would appreciate it."

CHAPTER 28
AUGUST 2008

Darius knew Evelyn was going to her mother's grave and he felt bad that he wasn't at her side as he usually was to support her on these trips. But she'd been insistent that she wanted to be alone. He was looking forward to tomorrow when he could see her again.

The next evening, Darius took her to a movie and then to dinner. She appeared to be in a better mood. He was glad; he hated to see her hurting. He loved her too much to be away from her for long, or to know she was in pain and he couldn't help.

"I hafta work the next three weekends, Peaches," Darius told her as he brought her home. "They trying to get all this work done in case there is a strike in October, but the turnaround will be over at the end of the month."

"It is okay, Deke," Evelyn said. "We will still talk on the phone, and when things get back to normal, we will see more of each other again."

They'd been dating for several months when Darius told Evelyn he wanted to do something special together before she started college in the fall. "Let's have a special date in New Orleans," he suggested. "Let's go to the zoo and hang out, and then go to dinner in New Orleans. Bring your camcorder, and we'll record it."

"Done deal, Deke. That will be fun."

"Do you remember I promised to never leave you as long as you didn't run me away?"

Darius and Evelyn were leisurely walking through Audubon Park in New Orleans after spending a couple of hours in the zoo. Not many steps away was a red refreshment stand on wheels that was topped by a huge plastic candy apple the size of a minor planet.

"Yes, I do," Evelyn said. "And I have never given any hint of an intention of running you away." She shook a finger back and forth in front of his face and grinned.

Darius grabbed her finger and pushed it down. He pulled her close and kissed her. He thought she smelled particularly good. "I intend on making sure you never do," he said as he squeezed her tightly. Then he relaxed his hug and reached around her neck, and his hand caught on something in her hair.

"Ow, Darius, you pulled my hair."

"Well, at least I didn't call you an iguana," he said, laughing.

"What is this fascination you have with iguanas?"

"Maybe one day when I'm old, I'll tell you." He got untangled from her hair and stepped back. He'd fastened a gold chain and pendant around her neck.

"What is this, Darius?" Evelyn asked as she fingered the pendant. She could see on the back was inscribed her name and today's date, August 9, 2008.

"First, for the record, let me assure you that it's been bought and paid for. I'm sure your daddy will ask." Darius laughed, and took the pendant out of her hand and placed it in the palm of his. "This is a gold peach to symbolize the first time we met."

"Deke! That is so thoughtful and romantic. This is why I like you a lot." She hugged him and kissed him squarely on the lips with a kiss that made his toes curl. Judging from the kiss, Darius thought her feelings were more than just "like." He walked her to the refreshment stand and ordered two cotton candies.

"Do you know what the significance of this cotton candy is?"

"No, I do not." Evelyn laughed as she pulled off a piece of the purple candy from its paper cone. "But I believe you are about to tell me."

"The second time we met, I had two cotton candies in my hand."

"Jiminy Crickets, Deke. You are crazy, remembering all this stuff. But it is so sweet of you. Now I guess you are going to run me over and say that signifies the third time we met." She ran her hand across his chest and unbuttoned the top button of his shirt. Her hand brushed the bare skin of his chest.

"No. The third time we met, I was leaving a jewelry store." He took Evelyn's camcorder and gave it to an elderly Japanese couple. He addressed the woman. "Ma'am, would you please be so kind as to record this?"

With the tape running, Darius dropped to one knee and produced a ring. "Evelyn Martha Kingsley, I love you with an eternal love that will never die. Will you become my wife and give my love an eternal home?"

"Dear Blessed Mary. Are you serious, Deke?" Evelyn was jumping up and down. She scarcely looked at the ring. "Yes, yes, yes—a thousand times yes! I love you, Deke. Yes, I will be your wife!" She kissed him close to a million times.

Darius stood up, grabbed his fiancée by the waist, and raised her above his head. Then he lowered her and held her with her feet off the ground as they kissed to the applause of people nearby.

"*Omedetou gozaimasu*," the Japanese lady said as she handed the camera back to Darius and wished them many happy years together.

Darius bowed and thanked her.

His radiant fiancée wasn't the same little girl he'd seen climbing a peach tree. This wasn't even same vulnerable lass he'd rescued at the bowling alley. This was a beautiful woman who had agreed to spend the rest of her life with him.

"Deke, you know you will have to ask Poppa's permission to marry me." It was getting late and with the top down in the Spider, they were on their way home to St. Mary Parish. Evelyn leaned over in her bucket seat so that her head was on Deke's shoulder as the wind blew through her let-down hair. "We cannot just elope." She was of age in Louisiana, but that didn't matter. Evelyn desperately wanted her poppa's approval and for him to give her away at the wedding.

"How do you think that is going to go? I still don't think he likes me." Darius looked at Evelyn as the lights on the interstate flashed on her face.

"I told you before, Deke. You worry too much." Evelyn ran her hands along Darius's thigh and wondered what it would be like to make love to him. "He may want us to wait until I turn eighteen, though."

"We don't hafta wait. We can do it next weekend, if you want to."

She was insistent that her poppa put his stamp of approval on all of this. Besides, there were other relatives she wanted to invite. "Maybe you can talk to him tomorrow."

"That's too soon, Peaches. I need more time to figure out how to do this, and maybe you can work it on your end so he kind of sees it coming."

Evelyn turned on an interior light to admire how her ring looked on her finger. It didn't bother her in the least that it wasn't big or expensive. All she cared about was that it symbolized their eternal union. "I am so excited that I want to shout the news, but I cannot do that until we talk with Poppa and get his blessing."

"Okay. Maybe I can just call him and tell him we're getting married?"

"No, you must do this right." Evelyn was disappointed that Darius would have even suggested that. "I only get one chance to get married, and I want it perfect. Poppa will be happy for me. It is going to be okay, Deke."

"Welcome to my humble abode," Evelyn said Sunday afternoon as she invited Darius into the mansion. The huge front door was plastered with Halloween decorations, the holiday only a week away.

"Not for much longer, Miss LeBeaux," Darius whispered.

"Shush! Poppa will hear you!" Evelyn giggled with a finger on her lips.

"Good afternoon, young man," Peter said as he stood stiffly at the end of the broad foyer. "Welcome to The Kingdom. It is good to have you back."

They shook hands and looked each other in the eye. Darius didn't think the welcome sounded genuine. At least he'd called him a young man and not a boy.

"I see you managed to stay out of jail these past months," Peter said as the two sat down.

Was that a joke?

"And I assume you have, as well." Darius grinned, but he saw no humor. Things weren't going well already, and he'd even avoided taking the wrong damn chair this time.

Who gives a rat's ass about what chair you sit in, anyway?

"My daughter starts college soon, and you two will not have so much time for frolicking in leisure. I guess you realize you will not see as much of her for the next few years." Peter sounded a bit condescending.

"We'll find a way." *You the one who won't be seeing so much of her!*

"Just do not interfere with her education, son. That is what it takes to succeed today."

Evelyn walked in from the kitchen, where she had catfish in the deep fryer. "I trust all is going well with the two most important men in my life."

"Lovely," Darius said.

"Splendid," Peter said.

"How would you two like your potatoes? Fried or mashed?"

"Mashed," Peter said.

"Fried," Darius said.

"Do you want peas or corn as a side dish?" she asked.

"Corn," Darius said.

"Peas," Peter said.

"Biscuits or cornbread?" Evelyn asked.

"Biscuits," Darius said.

"Cornbread," Peter said.

"Wonderful," Evelyn said. "I will fix it all. You two just carry on. It makes me happy seeing the two of you getting along so well. This is going to be a wonderful evening."

"Lovely," Darius said.

"Splendid," Peter said.

Evelyn turned back into the kitchen, smiling as if happy her men were having such an obviously grand time together.

The moment she left, they went back to the jugulars.

"It does not bother you having Evelyn drive you around in the Spider for your dates?" Peter asked.

"I'm not so shallow that I let material things bother me, Mr. Kingco." Darius resorted to his childhood habit of intentionally mispronouncing his antagonist's name.

"It is Kingsley, son. Kingco is the name of the multimillion-dollar company I own."

"Yes, and it is Darius. Although, someday it might be appropriate for you to call me son."

Darius knew Kingsley's chuckle was meant as an insult; not that his funny bone was tickled.

"So how did it go?" Evelyn whispered. "What did he say?"

They were almost through with their meal, but Peter had excused himself because of a sudden bowel movement.

"He says I'm an asshole his daughter will never marry," Darius said with a hiss and a frown.

"That is not funny, Deke." Evelyn slapped his arm. "Really, what did he say? How did he take it?"

Darius noticed she'd slipped her engagement ring onto her finger. "I'd move that ring to another finger before he gets back. I ain't asked him, and I don't think I'm going to ask him. Your daddy is being a jerk on steroids."

"Stop that, Deke. When did things change? You two were having such a wonderful time together earlier."

"Not!" Darius said as he looked over his shoulder after hearing the toilet flush upstairs. "He is Attila the Hun, and he's plain rude." He spat those words out as if they were undercooked beans.

"Poppa would not be rude to you. He is just having a hard time letting his little girl go. And he is not Attila the Hun. He is a gentle teddy bear. His bark is worse than his bite."

"Teddy bears don't bark. You mixed your metaphors!"

"Touché, Mr. English Major." Evelyn appeared embarrassed at her bungled metaphor.

"As I recall, you've been insisting that you're no little girl. Maybe you should let him know that." Darius just managed to get the words in before he heard Peter coming down the stairs. He was tired of how this old man was treating him.

"Maybe I will," Evelyn said as Peter limped back to the table.

Darius wasn't sure what she meant.

"I hope you two can excuse my manners, having left the table," Peter said. "It appears I had something that was a pain in the ass I had to get rid of." Peter chuckled at his less-than-subtle pun and ate a bite of mashed potatoes.

Darius started to say something, but Evelyn kicked him under the table and squeezed his hand. Evelyn grinned, and gave Darius a look that said, "Don't worry. I have this under control."

"Poppa, I am going to be missing you a lot when I start school," she said.

Darius wondered where she was going with this conversation.

"Yes, that is all part of growing up," Peter said. "I was just telling your little friend over there that he probably will not see much of you."

Little friend? I can whip your ass right now, old man!

Evelyn squeezed his hand again, obviously meaning for him to chill. "Like you said, I am growing up. I am not your little girl anymore."

That's where she's going with this. The girl is good!

"You will always be my little girl." Peter pushed away his plate. "I am stuffed. The food was delicious, Princess."

"I know you will always view me as your little girl, but I am a woman now, and I have woman's needs and feelings. I told you I love Darius."

"Yeah, you did," Peter said with a bit of a scoff in his voice as he took the napkin from his lap and wiped the corners of his mouth.

"Well, he told me he loves me."

"Good for him." Peter took a sip from his glass of wine.

"And he asked me to marry him. I said yes, and I hope you will accept my decision and make me happy by supporting it."

Peter dropped his wine glass onto the table. "Jesus Christ! Are the two of you crazy?" He stumbled and almost fell as he attempted to jump up from the table and quickly wipe up the spilled wine. "You are a child, and he isn't much more than a kid!"

Hey, old man. I'm in the room over here. Don't talk like I don't exist.

"Remember, you told me that all you want is to spend the rest of your days seeing me happy? Well, Darius makes me happy."

"You were happy before him, and you will be happy after him." Peter was still talking to her as if Darius wasn't in the state, much less at the same table. "You have your whole life left ahead of you. Now is not the time to make a mistake like this."

"Does that mean you won't support a wedding next weekend?" Darius asked.

Evelyn kicked his leg under the table so hard that it hurt.

"Her momma would not have wanted her to get married until she finished college and went to medical school to be a doctor! So, hell no, there will be no wedding anytime soon." Peter's face was flushed; even his mutinous eyebrows seem to quiver with anger. "I am going upstairs to watch football. You know the way out, right? If not, Evelyn can see you out." Peter pushed his chair from the table and stormed to the stairs.

"You do know football season hasn't started yet?" Darius asked.

"Preseason has, Mr. Know-it-all," Peter yelled back over his shoulder from halfway up the stairs.

Evelyn waited for Peter to get upstairs. "Darius, you can be as stubborn as Poppa. You were not helping things!"

He hadn't heard her call him by his true name in months. He supposed this would be how she addressed him whenever she was upset with him.

"A man's gotta do what a man's gotta do, Peaches." *Everybody knows that.*

"Well, you didn't gotta do all that you just did! Anyway, I think that, all things considered, it went over well, don't you?"

"Huh?" Darius said, perplexed. "You're shitting me, right? That was an unmitigated frigging disaster."

"You worry too much, Deke. And you should not use all that profanity."

"Are you going to marry me or not?" Darius asked as he talked by phone with Evelyn on Monday night. "Your daddy has made it plain he won't support our marriage."

"Deke, I love you," Evelyn replied. "Of course, I am going to marry you. Please try again with Poppa. It is important to me that he agrees to this."

"I tried, but your daddy is an Archie Bunker. He's impossible to deal with." Darius kicked at the basketball lying on the floor at the foot of his bed.

"Archie Bunker? Who is Archie Bunker?"

"You've never seen any *All in the Family* reruns?" Darius asked. "Archie was a bigoted, conservative WASP who didn't like blacks, Jews, or any other minorities. He couldn't stand Michael, who married his daughter who he always called 'little girl'."

"You have Poppa all wrong, Deke. He wants to protect me. He fears losing me. He is not a bad man, and he is far from a bigot. Besides, he is a Jew, not an Anglo-Saxon Protestant."

"Well, he certainly could fool me."

"Poppa is the most generous man I know, and he is always trying to help people. You will see when you get to know him."

"Well, it don't make me no never mind, as long as you marry me," Darius said. "I love you, and I want you happy, so I'll keep trying to get on his good side."

CHAPTER 29
OCTOBER-NOVEMBER 2008

Evelyn was now in college, and Darius was off from work due to the strike. He used his free time to go to New Orleans to look for something that might lead him to Pigenstein. Maybe Paul West had heard something recent.

As he faced a beefy, hairy clerk at the counter of one of Paul's stores, he knew the fence was around because he could smell the strong odor of his cigar. Without saying anything, the clerk turned and walked out a side door. A few minutes later, Paul walked through the door, cigar in hand, and greeted Darius like a long-lost friend.

"What's up?" Paul said. "Long time, no see. How's my *hombre* Thirty-eight?"

Darius's eyes shifted downward as he noticed Paul wiping what appeared to be blood off his hands on the side of his pants. He couldn't help but think of Prez and Doc.

"We are killing some chickens out back for a gumbo," Paul said.

Darius chose not to question the explanation, but Paul didn't strike him as a chicken-killing kind of man.

"I got some bad news, Mr. Paul. That dude I been hunting, Marcus Holmes, Samuel Rider; he killed Thirty-eight."

"Jesus, that's a shame. Thirty-eight was a righteous dude." Paul put his arm around Darius and led him to a room behind the counter. There was a load of undoubtedly stolen goods stacked as high as a man could reach. "I don't know what's going down. But this Marcus, he's suddenly become popular. I had another guy, much older than you, come in here the other day looking for him, too."

"Really? That's interesting. Do you know where Marcus is?"

"He's selling dope out of Houma. Off a boat in Bayou Terrebonne, and in the bar in front of that boat. It's called Shiloh Lounge."

"Thanks, Mr. Paul. That really helps me."

"Look, my man. You're an amateur at this stuff. Watch out that you don't get hurt. This other guy, he was old and crippled, and kind of sickly. He looked kind of like an amateur, too, but he's out to kill Marcus. Don't get caught in no crossfire."

"That makes two of us out to kill Marcus," Darius said. "One of us should get him."

"Just be careful is all I'm sayin'. When you mess with a tiger, you can get killed." The fence ominously waved his machete. "You might find yourself in a gumbo. Holla back at me if you got anything you want fenced. Be careful, my man."

Darius left New Orleans feeling a step closer to resolving this situation with Marcus. He wondered who else was trying to kill the bastard. Darius found himself again wishing his father was around for some advice.

"Jesus, Peaches, your daddy is acting like a big, spoiled titty-baby."

Darius was complaining to Evelyn as they fished on the pier behind The Kingdom. They had set the date of the wedding for November 29, two weeks after Evelyn's birthday. Not only had Peter not yet given his blessing and was refusing to speak to Darius, but they weren't even sure if he'd show up for the small church wedding.

Suddenly Darius's pole twitched, and he started reeling.

"No, not so fast," Evelyn said. "Let him take the bait, and then set the hook hard." She pushed Darius's rod tip lower.

Tap, tap, tap, pause, then *boom!* The big blue cat had decided it was supper time.

"Now, Deke, now! Set the hook hard and keep your rod tip up."

Darius chuckled, thinking her instructions sounded sexual. He started reeling when he felt the pull.

"No, Deke," she said. "Set that hook. Pop it to him, baby. Do it hard. There you go! You are doing it good! Now reel him in. Why are you laughing?"

Darius couldn't bring himself to point out how sexual she was sounding to him.

"That's it, baby. That's good. You have a big one, baby. You are working it good. Stop laughing or he is going to get away."

Darius brought the fish to the pier. Evelyn reached down with the net and pulled it up.

"You have yourself a ten-pounder here," Evelyn said as the catfish wiggled, flopped, and grunted its disapproval while Evelyn put it on a stringer.

"I didn't know fishing could be so nasty," Darius said regarding the sexual interpretation of what she'd been saying.

"You must be willing to get nasty to do it right," Evelyn said as she wiped the catfish slime from her hands. "I am going to show you how to fillet this thing, and then I am going to cook him. Poppa cannot resist my eyes and smile, nor my fried catfish."

"You sure are confident. I ain't seen him budge an inch off his stubborn ass."

"Deke, you worry too much. Leave it to your Peaches, and I will show you how to reel a man in tonight, too."

Later, back at the house, Darius caught Peter sneaking a look out the window as Evelyn filleted the catfish. Maybe Evelyn was right, and he'd been worrying too much. They walked back out to the bayou and tossed the carcass in the water.

"The turtles will eat what is left," Evelyn explained. "Then, we set out traps for the turtles and make turtle soup. No waste."

Darius was amazed at how much his fiancée could do. Now it was time to watch her reel in her poppa.

"Poppa," Evelyn said once they were inside, "Darius is staying to eat with us tonight. I am frying the catfish he caught."

Peter was sitting at the piano, hands on the keys but not moving, and looking at a portrait of Martha. The family portrait hung on the wall just above Martha's picture.

"I am not going to be able to make it tonight," Peter said as he pecked a few piano keys. "We are having a problem getting a shipment out down at the dock. I will grab a bite to eat in Morgan City." He rose, kissed Evelyn on the cheek, and walked out the door without acknowledging Darius's presence.

"Big titty-baby, I say," Darius said after Peter had closed the kitchen door and headed to the garage. "Looks like you started reeling in before you set the hook." He tried to smile, but about all he managed was a scowl.

"We still have two weeks, Deke. He will come around. You worry too much."

Darius was itching to get to Houma and see if he could locate Pigenstein. Whatever was to be done, if he was going to get the police involved, it would have to be in Houma. They'd proved their incompetence in St. Mary Parish. He was confident the information Paul had given him was solid. He just needed to decide how to handle it.

With the strike over, they were working long hours trying to catch up at the shipyard. He was in line for a raise and a promotion, possibly before Christmas. He wanted to show his supervisors that he was worthy of the bump up; he needed a momentary pause in the hunt for Pigenstein. Darius figured it would probably be sometime in December before he could spend time in Houma. Yet, he was determined that his nemesis wouldn't see another Christmas without an accounting.

Thanksgiving arrived, and Darius was disappointed to find that Evelyn was spending it with Peter and not with him. He couldn't understand why he was getting penalized just because Peter was being an ass and didn't want to invite him to a family function.

The grumpy old man might as well accept the inevitable because two days after he eats his turkey, his daughter will become Mrs. Darius LeBeaux!

"Deke, he is not coming." It was the morning after Thanksgiving, and Evelyn was crying on the other end of the phone. "I spent all afternoon yesterday, and all of last night, begging him. He just refuses to approve of our marriage and says he will not be there."

Darius realized this wasn't the time to say, "I told you so," or even to say that the old man could just go to hell. "I'm sorry, Peaches. Do you want me to come over and get you?"

"No thank you, Deke. I am not good company right now. I just want to be alone. I cannot believe Poppa is going to ruin my wedding day."

"You worry too much, Peaches," Darius said jokingly. He was disappointed when he didn't hear her laugh.

"I have some final preparations I need to make," Evelyn said, sniffling. "And I want to spend some time alone at the grave this afternoon."

The wedding was set for ten o'clock on Saturday morning.

"I will see you in the morning at the church, Deke."

"Don't worry, Peaches," Darius said. "He'll come around."

"No, Deke. His mind is set. But we are doing the right thing, and I love you. Thanks for doing all that you could."

"I love you, too, Peaches." Darius was angry that Peter's stubbornness was causing Evelyn such sadness.

"Pawpaw, it looks like you will be the one giving me away," Evelyn said on Saturday morning, a half hour before the wedding. "I was hoping Poppa was playing a game of chicken and would see that I wasn't going to blink. I am not changing my mind, if that is what he thought."

"You're de spittin' image of your momma, Mudbug," Pawpaw said, calling her a nickname only he used. He was wearing the same green and beige tuxedo he had worn when he gave Martha away to Peter eighteen years ago. "You're beautiful, and Darius is lucky to have you. Your momma would be proud."

Evelyn knew that since her mother was sitting in heaven, she'd seen how good a man Darius was. She was confident her momma approved this marriage. She spun on her heels, shook her head of bad thoughts, and looked ahead. In a few minutes, she was going to be married to the man she loved, and there was nothing in this world that could stop the wedding or keep her from being happy.

The organ began to play in the church. The church door opened as her cue to walk in. Out of the corner of her eye, she saw a tall, handsome man walking up the sidewalk with a cane. Her heart leaped in surprise and joy.

"Thank you, Jesus, for bringing my poppa," she said, looking up and making a sign of the cross. Then she ran to Peter and put her arms around him.

"Thank you for coming, Poppa. This means everything to me." Evelyn had tears of joy as she raised her veil to kiss him.

"I would not have missed it for the world," Peter said.

"I never doubted you would." It was the first time she'd fudged the truth since she'd met Darius and claimed to be eighteen. That all seemed like a lifetime ago.

"I hear music in the church. Are you not supposed to be getting married in there today?"

"Yes, I am. Will you give me away?"

"Ain't that what a poppa's supposed to do for his little girl when she grows up and makes her own choices?"

Evelyn laughed at how her poppa was saying he was wrong by using contractions and poor grammar. She didn't need an apology or confession of error. His presence was all she desired. She took his hand, smiling wider than a shrimp boat, and walked into the church like a princess meeting her prince. When she got to where her future husband was standing, Peter let go of her arm and reached out and shook Darius's hand.

"Welcome to the family, son. Take good care of my little girl. She is a woman now."

Peter's wedding gift to the couple was a cruise to the Bahamas. He used his connections to get managers at Conner's Shipyard to approve Darius's time off with pay. Evelyn would be able to make up her missed classes without much effort.

When the newlyweds returned home, Peter had a final wedding gift for his daughter: her own Cessna 172, christened *Kingsley Princess E.* Evelyn and the two men in her life took the plane up and flew to New Orleans.

Peter led the way as the trio went to the exact spot where he'd met Martha. Holding her poppa's hand, Evelyn saw her aging father's eyes mist over as he stood silently for several minutes and relived the day he'd retrieved that rose for the sweetest, most beautiful woman in the world. He put one arm around Evelyn and another around Darius.

"You will always be my little princess," he said, hugging his daughter tightly. "I love you for who you are and everything you will be. I love you as a part of your mother and a part of me. Anything I have is yours, but most importantly, my heart and my life are yours forever. Never forget that."

"I will not forget, Poppa."

"Darius, you are now a part of my family and will be treated as my son. I hope we develop the type of relationship that I have with your wife's Pawpaw Hebert."

"Thank you, Mr. Kingsley. I appreciate that."

"Call me 'Dad'."

Darius paused for a moment. "I've never had anyone to call Dad, and it looks like I'll never find my father." He swallowed hard and then placed his hand on Peter's shoulder. "Okay, Dad. Thank you for everything."

Evelyn could've procured the finest living arrangements in the parish, but they both agreed they would live in Darius's little house until they earned enough of their own money to move into a better and safer neighborhood.

"It is bad enough I am going to lose you from The Kingdom," Peter told her when she refused his offer to buy her a house. "Knowing you are in one of those seedy Morgan City neighborhoods is going to keep me up nights."

Still, he said, he was proud of the independent spirit she and Darius were demonstrating.

When Evelyn moved in, she was horrified to discover that Darius kept a gun in the house. Guns scared her. She took the liberal's position: guns were one of America's deadliest scourges, wreaking havoc in the streets, schools, and homes of thousands of people every year. She remembered Darius telling her that he carried a gun, but she thought he'd gotten rid of it.

"You should trust in God, Deke, not in guns." She told Darius that having it in the house scared her. "Two-thirds of American homicides are committed using guns."

"I wouldn't have lost Momma if she'd listened to me and gotten a gun before that douche bag killed her," Darius said. "She could've defended herself, and he would've either left her alone or she might've killed him first."

"Marcus doesn't live here, Deke, and no one is trying to kill us. Guns kill more innocent people than guilty ones. Every time a gun is used in self-defense, they are used eleven times in either an assault, homicide, or an unintentional death or injury, and another eleven times in a suicide attempt. That's twenty-two times that somebody is hurt for every time a gun might help somebody."

"You're the only person I care about, Peaches, and I promise I won't shoot you." Darius apparently was trying to deescalate, with humor, what was obviously an emotional topic for both of them.

Evelyn pleaded with him to get the gun out of the house, but Darius insisted they were safer by having the gun, especially in this neighborhood. She knew Darius had a point about the neighborhood, but she wasn't convinced a gun would protect them. She asked that at least he keep it locked in a box. Darius agreed to do that. She dropped the subject after telling him that she'd be more comfortable if the gun was gone.

CHAPTER 30
DECEMBER 19, 2008

Darius's impatience was increasing, knowing his momma's killer was thumbing his nose at justice, and the police were doing nothing about it.

Paul had told him where to find the bastard. Marcus's fate was in his hands now. Justice and Darius demanded that Pigenstein not see another Christmas. His conscience was rapping him about reneging on letting the police handle the situation. But he'd tried to let the police handle it; their failure was obviously complete.

He remembered Ricardo's warning about crossing the line in killing a man, but he wasn't a murderer. He was God's executioner. After all, God told Adam that it was to be an eye for an eye and a tooth for a tooth. He'd heard those words were somewhere in the Bible.

The week before Christmas, Darius resolved to put Paul's information to use to locate and kill Pigenstein. The night of reckoning had arrived. This would be his Christmas gift to himself and to his momma.

Darius told Evelyn a half-lie as he put on his jacket. "Some of the guys from work want to take me out to celebrate the new contract and me getting married and getting a promotion."

"Please don't drink more than a couple drinks if you are going to be driving," Evelyn said as she hugged and kissed him. She said she wasn't happy with him having a Friday night with the boys when they hadn't yet been married a month. Darius insisted on going.

Her hand snaked into his trousers and found "Louie," beginning to stand at attention. "When you get home, I'll tend to that erection you seem to have developed."

Darius smiled. How had she shown such self-control to remain a virgin until she was married? He was tempted to stay home. But a man's gotta do what a man's gotta do. And it was time to send Pigenstein to hell.

Darius rubbed her ass and kissed her again. He ducked into the dark bedroom and quickly grabbed his gun from the nightstand where he had it hidden in a box. For a moment he thought the gun didn't feel right. Maybe this was a sign that he shouldn't do this. He shook his head, ignored the passing thought, and jammed it inside his coat.

He kissed Evelyn on the way out. He pulled hard to get the door of the Impala opened and then slid in behind the wheel. The engine groaned slowly as he turned on the ignition; it almost didn't crank. In some ways, it reminded him of the old Ford he and his momma used to ride in. He would've taken the Spider, but it was in the body shop after a fender bender Evelyn had been in. She was still working the kinks out of learning to drive.

I need to get a battery for this thing before it puts me down.

There wasn't enough light outside the Shiloh Lounge to fill a five-gallon bucket. Perhaps that was intentional—to make it easier for illicit drug exchanges or sex-for-money with minimal intrusion from prying eyes. Darius chose to park in the darkest corner. This place looked like the hole-in-the-wall juke joints his momma used to visit. He looked around and wondered what attraction this stuff had had to his momma.

For all his talk through the years about killing Marcus, and as much as he hated this abominable creature, he was feeling internal resistance—pangs of conscience. Thirty-eight was right. This was a major line he was about to cross. It wasn't as easy as he'd thought it would be—certainly nothing like he saw on television.

Darius began to realize he'd planned this about as efficiently as the Thug Brothers had planned the Tommie invasion. That hadn't worked very well that night. Thirty-eight would've advised him to plan for all contingencies.

Where did Marcus set up to sell his dope? Would Darius be able to recognize him in this poor-ass lighting? What was he going to say to him before he shot him? And where the hell did you shoot a man to kill him, anyway? The head? The belly? What would he do if he missed, or if Marcus got the jump on him? What would he do to get away and not get caught?

The only thing Darius had brought with him was a gun, a ski mask, and a four-year-old desire to see Marcus dead. Maybe this wasn't such a good idea.

Then, parked not far from the working floodlight, he noticed an old Buick. It looked like the one the crippled old man had entered at Waffle House the night Thirty-eight was murdered. The personalized license tag read *BREN4EVA*. Maybe this was where the crippled guy hung out.

Darius started to worry. With no definitive plans for how to kill or escape, this wasn't going to work—at least not this way, at this place, on this night. Additionally, he couldn't shake the nagging feeling that it had been wrong to lie to his wife. This just wasn't the night or circumstances to do what needed to be done.

It was getting cold in the Impala, and by the time Darius decided to leave, the windshield had fogged up from his breath. He reached for the ignition to crank the Impala. Then the red GT pulled into the parking lot and parked.

Darius watched the man he hated more than anything else walk in front of his car. This was the opportunity he'd been waiting for all these years. All the reasons not to do this tonight flew out the window like a bat out of hell. He pulled the latch to his door. The door had been getting harder to open lately; it was stuck tight as Dick's hatband. Darius hurriedly slid over to the passenger side and opened that door. Pigenstein was nearing the barroom entrance.

Darius quickly got out the car and fumbled the gun as he got it out of his pocket and then to top off the absurdity, he kicked it under the Impala. He pulled the pistol from under the car, near the tire, and stood up. Pigenstein had already entered the bar. Everything was going wrong; worse than a barrel of drunk monkeys.

Damn, this as bad as the Tommie invasion by Bones and Striker.

Evelyn would be proud of his next decision. He would back off, call the cops, and give them another opportunity to handle it. He reached for his cell phone to call the Houma police. Then he realized he'd been so preoccupied with sneaking his gun out of his bedroom that he failed to get his cell phone.

Don't think you're getting away, Godzillard Pigenstein.

It took Darius fifteen minutes to find the police station and a half hour before someone took his report. He wondered if these cops were as inept as the ones in St. Mary Parish. He had to admit that he hadn't been all that efficient, either. At least he'd made a final stab at trying Evelyn's way.

Darius headed home. Although he was tired, he decided to go to the Morgan City Civic Center for a brief stop at the community Christmas party. He would have a couple of drinks and go home. Then the cover story he'd given Evelyn wouldn't have been a complete lie. Tomorrow's newspaper would tell him if his nemesis had been arrested.

Maybe it was time to diversify, Marcus thought. Maybe with the proper investments, he could get respectable. Either that, or he needed to expand his operations and buy some respect. But he had that murder rap to worry about—well, two of them. That complicated evolving into a legitimate business. He knew he was lucky to still be alive at forty-four in this business.

Right now, that was inconsequential. He was loaded with money and had all the women any man could want. He never used the dope and seldom drank the booze. He lived high and large and saw no reason it wouldn't continue that way, as long as the cops didn't bust him.

He pulled his GT into the handicapped parking space where he always parked and was looking forward to the act tonight; two of his girlfriends were performing. They weren't really girlfriends, but as long as he kept them supplied with dope and money, they kept him happy. Perhaps after conducting some business, he could talk the owner into letting them have the rest of the weekend off and they could go hit the French Quarter.

He worked his way toward the back-corner booth he always claimed on the weekends. Marcus sat there so his back would be to the wall and he could see anybody approaching him. It also allowed him to hide his hand in case he needed to subtly move his gun from his pocket to the booth seat. He waved at one of his performing girlfriends, who was filling her G-string with dollar bills from horny middle-age men. At twenty, she was the older of his two girlfriends.

He sat down, but something he couldn't put a finger on triggered his sixth-sense alarm. Even in the smoke-filled, dimly lit bar, he knew something was amiss. Until he found out what it was, he'd keep his other five senses at DefCon-10.

A tall, scantily clad server brought him his usual: a Dr. Pepper and a bowl of nacho chips with spicy thick-and-chunky salsa. He gave her twenty bucks, which he would continue to slip into her skimpy, see-through shirt each time she brought him a drink. She kissed him with more of her tongue in his mouth than hers.

"Keep 'em coming, baby," he said.

She showed a little ass when she turned away. "The kisses or the drinks?" she asked, giggling.

"Both, baby. Both." He'd have an hour of relaxation time. After that, he'd make repeated trips to the men's room to sell his dope until calling it a night.

The sixth-sense was itching his skin like poison ivy. Somebody was walking directly toward him. It wasn't a normal customer, and he didn't have the nervous look of a new customer.

Marcus's fingers twitched as he leaned forward and pulled his gun from behind his back and slowly set it at his side. The man abruptly stopped ten feet away from Marcus and pulled a pistol. At that instant, Marcus remembered the coughing, old, crippled assassin in Amelia.

They still sending the damn Inspector Jacques Clouseau to kill me?

Marcus spun to face the assassin. Clouseau's aim was as errant as a drunk goose flying south in the summer. Three bullets nicked Marcus. By the time JC pulled the trigger a fourth time, Marcus had shot him in the chest. The assailant retreated quickly. Marcus's wasn't sure if his second and third shots hit anything as he stumbled getting out of his booth. Somebody was probably already calling 9-1-1.

Click, click, click. Nothing.

Marcus only had three rounds in his gun. For a murderer and criminal running a dangerous enterprise, he realized he was too cavalier about checking his weapons. "Nigga, if you shoot at me, you damn well better kill me dead," Marcus said, making his way outside, hell-bent on pursuing Clouseau who was getting into a Buick and clutching at his side.

"That illegitimate bastard can't shoot!" he yelled to no one in particular. "I ain't hurt." He had his other gun in the GT and knew he'd catch up with that smoke-belching Buick quickly. He'd end this shit with Clouseau, conclusively, just as he'd done with Van Damme.

When he got to the Mustang, he realized he'd left his coat with his money, drugs and keys inside the bar. He half-sprinted, half-stumbled back inside, grabbed the coat, and felt the pockets. The keys were there, but some asshole had stolen his money and drugs.

Who the hell steals a man's drugs after he gets shot?

"Who stole my stuff without my permission?" Marcus yelled for anyone within a mile to hear. No one spoke up.

Too late, Marcus heard sirens pulling into the parking lot. He doubted the Samuel Rider ruse would work again, and he was holding the gun that had killed Ricardo Ortiz, and they already had the gun that had shot Sarah.

"Darius, you drove home drunk. You could have killed somebody. How could you break your promise to me? How could you disrespect the memory of my momma and drive drunk?" This was the first time Evelyn had yelled at him.

"I'm sorry. I'm not really drunk, but . . ." Darius attempted an explanation, but she cut him off.

"Not drunk? You smell of alcohol, and your speech is slurred! And you don't have to be drunk to be impaired enough to kill somebody!"

Evelyn wasn't interested in an apology, and most certainly not interested in an explanation or justification. He knew her feelings on the subject, and she'd emphasized them before he'd gone out.

"I'm tired and don't wanna fight, Peaches," Darius said as he walked to the bedroom and sat on the bed.

"I didn't want Momma to die, but she did. You could kill some-body's momma driving under the influence!" Eighteen and married, Evelyn had begun to use contractions.

"I'm not drunk, and 'sides, I ain't . . ." Darius fumbled with his shoes to get them off.

"You've been drinking, and you promised me you would never drive after drinking. You know how strongly I feel about this!"

"I'm tired and don't wanna fight, Peaches, and anyway, I didn't . . ."

"Darius, I'm not fighting. But I'm not the one staggering in at midnight."

"If you're not fighting, then quit yelling," Darius said as he swung his feet into the bed and lay back. "I'm just tired, and I don't wanna fight." As he came out of his pants, he waved a hand, apparently indi-cating he was ready to check out. He lay back, still wearing his white No. 26 Deuce McAllister Saints jersey.

"Don't you go to sleep on me! Why did you drive home after drinking too much?"

"I only drank two beers, maybe three. I'm trying to tell you. . ."

"Three? That's too much to drive, and you probably had more than three!"

"I'm tired, and I don't wanna fight, Peaches," Darius repeated. He shut his eyes.

"What would have happened if you had gotten stopped? You would be in jail right now. You know what? I would not come get you out! Wait a min-ute! I know you are not going to sleep on me. Wake up, Darius! LeBeaux" Despite attempting for several minutes to keep her husband involved in the argument he seemed not to want, she realized he was drifting to sleep.

Evelyn tried to rouse him, but the only response she got was a mumble. She went to the front of the house and turned out all the lights, got a drink of milk, and returned to the bedroom, where she put on the negligee she'd worn every night since Darius bought it for her on her birthday the previous month. By this time, Darius was asleep.

She spent the next three sleepless hours alternating between being upset with Darius and remembering the heartbreaking day she'd lost her mother. She was feeling guilty that she was breaking a cardinal rule of her poppa's. "You do not know when you will lose the person you love," he'd often said. "Never go to bed angry with someone you love."

CHAPTER 31
DECEMBER 20, 2008

Maybe Deke wasn't that drunk, but he should not have been driving.

Evelyn decided she'd talk about it in the morning and not let it ruin the weekend, especially so close to Christmas. She tugged on the blankets to pull up to her chin and chase away the chilly air. She giggled as Darius snorted and grunted. She was no longer angry with him; now the hormones of a teenage bride were beginning to percolate. She rose to her elbow, shook her long curls away from her face and smiled as she looked at Darius sleeping and snoring as loudly as ever. She pushed her negligee from her shoulders so that a breast was exposed. The cold night air and her hormones had her nipples erect. She wanted to feel Deke's mouth on her breasts and his hands over her body.

Going to sleep horny is as difficult as going to sleep angry!

She tried kissing that spot on his neck that seemed to always get him aroused. Now he seemed to be waking up as he rolled over and opened his eyes.

"Are you a little horny, Peaches?" he asked.

Evelyn had placed her bare breast against his face. "If Deke is thirsty, he could suck on these nice, luscious titties he likes so much." She slipped off the other strap of her negligee and left both of her breasts available.

"Okay, I'll keep that in mind," Darius said as he rolled over.

He is not going to do this to me! After all he put me through tonight, I ought to make him beg for it, but I'm too sweet for that. I'll give him some, anyway.

Evelyn kissed the back of his neck again. Her nails slid down his muscular back. Putting her hands in his underwear, she found solid evidence that he wanted her. "Momma is hot, Deke. Be a good fireman and put out my fire." She laughed as she stroked him.

"Is there a kitty the fireman needs to rescue?" Darius had rolled back over. If he'd been playing hard to get, it had passed over.

"Meow! What can you do?" She didn't wait for an answer, nor did she take off the jersey that Darius was wearing before she got on top of him and took control. After an hour, they were satiated and falling asleep in each other's arms.

"I love you, Peaches," Darius said as he drifted off to sleep.

"I love you too, Deke," she said, kissing him on the chest, neck, and face. Soon she heard Darius start to snore. "I'm sorry for being mad at you earlier," she whispered before closing her eyes.

Just as she dozed, Evelyn was jolted awake by a noise in the living room. Her mind raced as she realized that in her haste to argue with Darius, she hadn't made sure the door was locked behind him. She hadn't checked the lock when she got up for a glass of milk, either. Had they left the front door unlocked in this neighborhood?

"Deke!" Evelyn whispered as she shook her husband. "Wake up. Somebody is in the house!"

"Go to sleep, Peaches. I need some rest. We can do it again in the morning."

"Somebody is in the front of the house! Wake up!" Evelyn heard voices and noticed a flicker of light under the bedroom door. It appeared that two intruders were in the house with flashlights in the living room.

Darius bolted up in the bed. He put a finger on Evelyn's lips and shushed her. He reached into the nightstand for his gun. He had that feeling again about the gun. After all these years, why was it suddenly feeling wrong in his hands tonight? This wasn't the time to wrestle with his conscience or worry about those details.

"Don't get that, Deke!" Evelyn hissed.

"You want me to go in there unarmed and get shot?" Darius snorted in a whisper. He opened the bedroom door and looked down the hallway. Silhouettes pointed flashlights in his direction, blinding him. Darius raised his gun as he ran toward the intruders. The closest intruder stumbled over furniture, tripped, and fell. Darius pounced on him and easily overpowered the burglar, who was much smaller than Darius. By that time, the other one had fled.

"Who are you?" Darius shouted as the burglar continued to struggle in the dark. "What are you doing in my house?" Darius felt long facial hair on this slightly built burglar.

"Deke, I'm calling Poppa," Evelyn said.

"Call the cops, not your poppa, dammit!"

Darius threatened to shoot the burglar, but he didn't want to pull the trigger. Yet, moments later, as the pair struggled for control of the gun, it discharged while pointed at Darius. It felt like he'd been struck with a bat and stabbed with a searing hot knife. The burglar scrambled to his feet and dashed out of the house. Darius shot at the fleeing intruder; he missed with two shots before the gun ran out of bullets.

Evelyn had already called 9-1-1 when she heard the gunshots. She dropped the landline phone, but didn't hang it up, and ran out of the bedroom into the still-dark living room. "Deke, what's happening?" she yelled.

She turned on a hall light and saw her husband sitting on the floor on the other side of the room, naked except for his shirt, holding his chest and gasping for air. After turning on the living room light on the wall beside him, she shrieked in horror as she saw Darius's shirt had turned a dark crimson from blood seeping through his fingers. A small pool had formed around him.

"Blessed Mary, please help," she moaned, rushing to his side, crying.

"Shut the door, Peaches. I don't know if they'll come back. Make sure you lock it." It appeared to take a major effort for Darius to speak.

Evelyn went to the door and looked out. Darius's Impala was gone. "They took your car, Deke," she said as she shut the door without locking it.

"I didn't drive home. It's at the Civic Center, broken down. Call an ambulance. I need to go to the hospital." Darius paused between each word.

She grabbed the cell phone on the kitchen table and called 9-1-1 again. She said that she needed an ambulance. "My husband has been shot!" she yelled into the receiver. "Please send somebody quickly!" She dropped the phone again as Darius suddenly leaned over, his shoulder touching the floor. The pool of blood around Darius was becoming a lake. "Deke, stay awake. Don't you leave me!"

Darius groaned. Evelyn grabbed his head with both hands and looked into his dazed eyes. "Deke, don't you die on me, dammit. I love you too much for you to die." She kissed his lips and tried not to look at his bloody chest. She ignored the blood she felt soaking into her panties.

Darius smiled faintly. "Dammit? That's the first time I ever heard you cuss." His speech slowed with each word he spoke.

"I did not curse," Evelyn said, doubling her sin by adding a lie to cover it up.

"Yes, you did, but you have tokens saved . . ." Darius spoke barely above a whisper. His lips moved, but no words came from them. His head drooped.

Evelyn was sure he was about to lose consciousness. "Hold on, Deke, and let me worry about my tokens and penance." She put his head in her lap as she sobbed and begged Darius not to die.

There wasn't a spot of white on Darius's shirt now. Evelyn realized that if she didn't slow the bleeding, he would die. She gently laid Darius's head down and stumbled to the bathroom to get a towel. When she opened the cabinet door, she saw her hands were covered with blood. A wave of panic came over her, but she quickly regained control. She ran back to the living room and knelt beside Darius who was struggling to breath.

Darius groaned. "I'm cold, Peaches."

"I'm here, Deke. I will try to slow this bleeding." She raised his shirt and fought off another wave of panic when she saw blood running from the hole in his chest. Each breath Darius took sounded like a gurgle. She put the towel over the wound and applied pressure. She heard the nine-one-one dispatcher trying to get her attention but Evelyn ignored the voice coming from the phone. If her husband died in this wretched house, it would be while she gave him her undivided attention.

"Deke, I'm sorry about arguing earlier over something you didn't do."

His eyes blinked open. Then he heaved a deep sigh and coughed up blood. It was evident he was trying to tell Evelyn something. Finally, the words weakly dribbled from his lips.

"I tried to tell you, but it's okay," Darius said.

"I feel so bad. If you promise to live, I will never fight with you again."

"I promise, Peaches. I'll live . . . Ow! This hurts bad."

Evelyn had never heard him complain of pain. She saw him struggling to breathe. With each breath, there was a cough, and blood dribbled from his mouth. Sirens were wailing close by.

"They're almost here, Deke. You promised you would not die! Hang in there, baby."

Darius's lips trembled. "I still got plenty of fireman duties."

"Deke, quit making jokes. This is not funny!" As her husband closed his eyes, Evelyn refused to let herself contemplate the possibility that she might have heard his last words. She hadn't felt such sadness and fright since her momma died.

It seemed like an eternity, but someone finally pounded on the door and announced that he was a policeman. She yelled for him to enter. Behind him were paramedics. They hooked an IV into Darius's arm and attached a clear plastic bag of saline. They told Evelyn his vital signs were weak, but her efforts had probably kept him alive. They let her in the back of the ambulance as they took the four-mile ride to the hospital.

Doctors worked for six hours on Darius. Evelyn felt a tightness in her chest as she impatiently waited. Peter's arms, not as strong and big as they once were, wrapped tightly around her as they sat for what seemed an eternity in the waiting room. She was barely aware of his kisses to the top of her head. She battled but couldn't restrain the tears that trekked down her cheeks.

"Your faith has always sustained you, Princess," Peter said. "Keep your hopes up."

Evelyn, resting her head in her poppa's lap, bolted up at the sound of Dr. Greeley calling her name. The surgeon—surgical mask hanging around his neck and green gown splattered with blood—appeared grim and exhausted. Her knees buckled at the news and she grabbed Peter's neck and cried. She heard little after the doctor's first six words: "We were able to save him."

Evelyn caught pieces of what the surgeon was saying; bullet fragment … infection … fever … out of the woods … something about his heart. Nothing mattered right now. The man of her dreams, the only man she loved more than her poppa, was alive. Before leaving, Dr. Greeley said

Darius's survival was a miracle aided by Evelyn's actions to stop the bleeding and that something had given Darius a superhuman strength to fight.

"Maybe it was your love, or maybe your prayers," Peter told Evelyn as she dried her eyes and smiled. "I am convinced that one or the other, or maybe both, saved Darius."

"He promised me he would not die," Evelyn said. "My husband is strong and a man of his word." She hugged the doctor and then returned to the secure embrace of her poppa.

Evelyn read a front-page article in *The Daily Review* to Darius while he was still in the ICU the next day.

> *A three-plus-year manhunt appears to have come to a bloody end with the capture of the man Franklin police say killed Sarah LeBeaux with two shots to the head on Sept. 11, 2004.*
>
> *Marcus "X-Man" Holmes, 46, of Houma, was transferred to the custody of the Franklin Police Department this morning following his arrest by Houma police Saturday night. Holmes had been involved in a shootout with Albert Thomas, 55, of New Orleans, Franklin Police Chief Brian Hatch said.*
>
> *A gun fight inside Shiloh Lounge, a Houma bar, between Thomas and Holmes broke out late Saturday night. Thomas, who initiated the exchange, remains hospitalized in serious condition at a Houma hospital, according to Houma Police Chief Pierre Charpentier. He said Holmes sustained non-life-threatening injuries and the reason for the attack remains under investigation.*

"Let me see that," Darius said as he weakly reached his hand out for the newspaper. There were beads of sweat on his forehead from the fever he was fighting. He looked at the mug-shot pictures. "The night we met, I saw that man at Waffle House and he got into an old Buick. Momma said she was raped by Albert Thomas and he had a Buick. That's my damn uncle who raped her." He sighed, closed his eyes and handed the paper back to Evelyn for her to continue reading.

> "A Houma policeman arrived at the scene as Holmes was trying to flee," Charpentier said. "Thomas had left the scene and checked himself into the hospital. He will be booked on attempted murder when he is released from the hospital."
>
> Holmes and LeBeaux, 32, were living together when she died after being shot twice in the head, Hatch said.
>
> Holmes had identified himself to Houma police as Samuel Rider, Charpentier said. That is the bogus name the St. Mary Sheriff's Office said he supplied in January after he was shot in an apparent Amelia drug deal. No suspects have been named in that shooting.
>
> When Houma police discovered his true identity, they arrested Holmes on a first-degree murder warrant issued by Franklin police in 2006.
>
> Morgan City Police Chief David Larose said Holmes is suspected of killing Ricardo Ortiz, 23, in Morgan City on Jan. 27. Ortiz was killed an hour after SMSO allowed Holmes to leave the scene of the Amelia shooting, Larose said.

"I don't know why he shot Marcus, but it's poetic justice to have both bastards caught after they shot each other. I wonder how all this shit is tied together."

Evelyn kissed him and didn't remark on his profanity. She took a damp washcloth and wiped his forehead. "We will get some answers," she said. "In any case, I am glad you are okay, and these people were caught before you did something to get in trouble."

"When I get out of this hospital, would you visit my momma's grave with me?"

"Done deal," she said.

Darius was content. The only page missing from this chapter of his life was finding his father. Maybe Albert Thomas could help him with that endeavor or at least help him dismiss the lingering suspicion that Albert was indeed his father. For now, at least, the black hole of his momma's life had closed, and the risk of crossing his own event horizon lay behind him. He'd broken the chains of his past and had both feet in a world offering a brighter future where he could live past thirty, have kids with his own name, have a home, and make his momma proud. Who could know what lay ahead? But, for the first time in his life, Darius was at peace.

The narcotic administered a few minutes ago was beginning to dull the pain. There were no black holes, crazy roommates, Pigensteins, hyenas or even iguanas to worry about. He closed his eyes, happy that Evelyn was there holding his hand.

THE END

ABOUT THE AUTHOR

Preston D. Gill Jr. is an award-winning reporter and newspaper editor who has pursued his passion for journalism for over two decades. In writing fiction, his goal is to have readers draw their own conclusions with the story's message and moral. Along with a love of reading and writing, he also enjoys outdoor activities, including camping, hiking through the mountains, whitewater kayaking, and fishing, and has spent summers volunteering in various national parks. He is seldom in front of a television—except during football season. When not volunteering or traveling, he lives with his wife, teenaged son, and English Mastiff near Baton Rouge, Louisiana.